Demon in My Veins

My Demon Lords #1

Sydney St James

INKED PRESS

Character List

<u>Shero</u>

Lioria

<u>Series Harem Members</u>

Alastor

Shax

Raum

Oriax

Valac

Belial

Eligos

Contents

Life always finds a way.

-Dr. Ian Malcolm, Jurassic Park.

LIORIA

T here might be a demon in my veins.

It is a truth I have held onto every time one of the uppity gentlemen at the tavern makes a comment about what a shame it is that I am not a lady of good pedigree.

For all they know, I might birth the next Demon Lord. Wouldn't they regret their words then?

I hold onto that as I stare up at the sneering face of the man wearing the Demon Lord's livery.

"Pretty bitch like you? That's a shame." He shakes his head as he scrawls something on the paper.

I'm already in hot water with Mistress Claridieu, so I don't dare say anything. He doesn't need to know that even if I was a respectable woman I wouldn't consider *him* for a husband.

My cheeks hurt from holding this smile. "Anything else?"

"No." His gaze travels over my body. "Lioria. Such a fucking waste."

My ears begin to burn and I imagine stabbing him with that crude pen. My name marks me. With that one word, one name, it communicates everything most people think they need to know about me.

I'm no one. I have no family. I have no lineage or pedigree. Nothing to offer a future spouse except myself.

The delivery man turns and lumbers away. I take a step down and swing the cellar doors shut harder than necessary.

"What an asshole," a voice says from the shadows below me.

I pause and tilt my head. There's only one woman who would be lingering in the dark. "Malka?"

"Yes. Sorry. Here."

I grab the lantern and skip down the sturdy stone stairs to the large cellar below the Silver Roo Inn. The scent of burning wax hangs heavy in the air. I'd arrived much earlier today to assist with the quarterly shipment of the Lord's Tonic. Normally, this is an event in and of itself. Our inn receives the shipment for the entire area around Suncrest. In a few weeks, during the Laborer's Festival, it will be passed out as a token of well-being from the High Demon Lords.

Malka stands at the foot of the stairs leading up into the inn. She's gripping the rail and biting her lower lip. Her nearly black hair is braided and pinned to her head like a crown. Just like the mistress likes us to style it. But unlike me, Malka wears a thick blindfold across her eyes.

"What are you doing here?" I set the lantern on a crate and grin at her. "Mistress have you coming in early, too?"

"Yes." Malka gestures at the crates. "Is that it?"

"What? The tonic?"

"Yes."

I tilt my head to the side. "It is. Have you...?" I lick my lips. I don't want to offend her. "Have you never had the Lord's Tonic?"

"No," she says.

That nearly makes my jaw drop.

I gape at her. "Are you serious?"

"I-I told you. We didn't have much in the way of school where I lived. And no one brought it out that far."

"We're going to fix that." I shove my sleeves up to my elbows, then grasp the top of the closest crate.

"Lioria, no," Malka hisses.

"Sh. It's fine. No one will know."

She glances up the stairs and shifts her weight from foot to foot. It's a fight every time I see her to not overstep and assist where I'm not wanted.

Most people take one look at her blindfold and steer clear.

"Damn it. This one's wedged on too tight," I mutter.

"Lioria, no," she whispers.

I whirl to stare at her. "You don't even know the stories."

"How could I? Just stop."

I squeeze between the crates and grin at her. "Will your friends keep an eye out?"

She goes completely still.

Most people don't acknowledge why she wears the blindfold. I think it's stupid to ignore her situation.

Malka can see spirits.

"I... Yes," she whispers.

"Great."

There was a crate in the last lot that had a top that wiggled.

I've never heard of someone who can see spirits making it this far into adulthood. Many are driven mad with the whispers of souls waiting to be reborn. From the little Malka has said, I have to wonder how she's managed this long. The way she talks, she can not only see and hear the spirits, they can touch her, too. Though she only said that once, after I convinced her to drink with me. All too often, girls like her are locked up by their families, ostracized, all because no one knows what can be done to help them.

I find the crate, grip it at opposite corners, and wiggle the lid.

"Everything clear?" I whisper over my shoulder.

Malka's head swings toward me. "There's a lot of movement, but so far so good."

"Who do you think is coming later?"

"I don't know. Someone important?"

Malka chooses to wear the blindfold. I can only imagine it is easier on her to not see the spirits she must walk through. If she were merely blind, there would be treatments available to her, or at the very least, seeing stones in place of eyes. The old fishmonger uses them. Says it's not the same, but better than being sightless since his accident nearly a decade ago. Unlike him, there isn't a thing that can be done for her.

As far as I am concerned, Malka is the strongest person I've ever met, and anyone who treats her as a pariah is shameful.

The lid lifts from the crate, at last.

"I've got it," I say over my shoulder.

"Mistress is pacing around, hurry," Malka says over her shoulder.

I pull out two tonics, drop them in my apron pocket, then shove the lid back down just as I hear a door creak open overhead.

So much for watchful spirit friends.

"Malka? What are you doing down there?" Mistress Claridieu calls out.

I shimmy and slither between the crates. I'm a sturdy woman and they stack these crates in tight.

Malka wrings her apron in her hands. "Oh, I was just…"

I rush over and shove my arm through the crook of her elbow. "She was helping me. I forgot to count the crates as they were loaded in and I didn't want to run the risk that we got shorted again."

Mistress Claridieu frowns at me. She's a tall, burly woman with strong features browned by the sun and time. I quite like her. Like me, she was an orphan, and look how far she's come. She owns the biggest inn in Suncrest.

"Why didn't you count as as they unloaded, girl? What's in that head of yours?"

"It wasn't her fault," Malka says. It's unlike her to stand up to someone for any reason. She continues twisting her apron in her hands. I don't even think she's aware. "The man, he… He kept bothering her."

I nod. "You know how they are. City men who think country girls will fall all over themselves for them."

Mistress Claridieu scowls. "What's his name? I'll not have someone wearing the lord's livery harassing honest girls."

The man was an ass. I hand her the delivery slip. "I believe it's the name in the top corner."

She pockets the paper. "Malka, the silver is waiting to be polished. I need it done by noon. Will that be a problem?"

"No. Not at all."

"Lioria, finish your count, and then find me." With that, she turns and lumbers back up into the tavern.

Malka and I stand there holding our breath until the door clangs shut. I double over, heart hammering. Today is not the day to get on Mistress Claridieu's bad side.

"Gods, I'm sorry," Malka whispers.

"Don't worry about it." I fish the two small, glass bottles out of my pocket and hand one to her. "Have one."

"But, the festival..."

"Suncrest is the largest town in this area. They deliver so much there's always a crate or two left, even a month after the festival. No one is going to miss these two."

Malka takes the bottle without hesitation. As if she knows exactly where my hand is, even with the blindfold on.

Makes me wonder about the spirits in her life and how well they guide her.

"Do you even know the story behind the tonic? Come sit."

"No."

"I know this is going to surprise you, but I actually read a lot of Eden's history."

Malka turns her head toward me. "You?"

I laugh. "Okay, more accurately I used to get in trouble, and as punishment, they'd send me to the library. I'll spare you the longer story."

"That's for the best."

"Before the High Demon Lords founded Eden, so, well over a thousand years ago, the continent was ravaged by war so bad it scarred the earth. The damage was so extensive that the earth began poisoning people. The sickness spread everywhere, affecting all manner of creatures. Human, Vodu, Yokai. The High Demon Lords searched high and low for a solution. They knew the earth needed to heal, war must come to an end, and we needed a remedy. A ceasefire was agreed on, and later, the High Demon Lords would negotiate the peace treaty that would lead to them crossing the ocean to Eden. The story goes that the High Lords Alastor and Oriax were able to work with powerful Vodu and Yokai to heal the earth, while the other High Lords created the Lord's Tonic. And now, four times a year, we drink a little of it to remember why we hold onto the peace we have here in Eden."

"I've never heard that story before," Malka says slowly.

"I've always wondered why the gods and goddesses didn't come back to stop it all," I wonder out loud.

Ages ago, so long that it's almost a myth now, the gods and goddesses all banded together to fight a great war for the safety of the people under their care.

They entrusted the earth to the Demon Lords back then, but other creatures pushed back. They didn't want to follow the gods' plan. The seven High Demon Lords set themselves apart. I've never been able to find out how that happened.

I twist the wax-covered stopper, breaking the seal. "Make sure to stop by the children's theater during the festival. They do all the old stories with puppets and masks. It's adorable. According to one of the books I read, the High Demon Lords' ingenuity scared all the other powerful beings into wanting the High Lords to abandon the continent. They already knew the seven of them were powerful adversaries in war, but the part they played in healing is what truly scared the other beings in power."

"Is that so? Hm." Malka tilts her head to the side, as if she's listening to someone, then twists the top of her bottle just like I did.

I want to ask so many questions, but I think she'd avoid me if I got too curious.

The stopper comes out of both our bottles with a little wiggling about. I tap my bottle to hers.

"To the High Demon Lords. May we have another season of peace."

Malka nods then lifts the bottle to her nose and sniffs. "It smells like flowers..."

"I wish it tasted like it smells." I chuckle before wrapping my lips around the end and tipping it back.

There's a decidedly medicinal flavor to the tonic that no flowery flavor can cover up. It's not unpleasant, but it sticks to the back of the mouth until you can taste it in your eyeballs.

"Gods," Malka croaks and shakes her head. "You weren't kidding."

"It's an acquired taste." I take the bottle, wax, and stopper from her.

"I'll say." She shakes her head. "Well, that was an experience. Best be getting on to that silver."

"Do you have any idea who we are expecting?" I ask as she heads up the stairs.

"None."

I sigh and dust off my skirts, waiting until I know Malka is safely in the tavern. Her guiding spirits haven't let her down yet; I've never seen her so much as stumble. Still, I worry about her.

Grabbing the lantern I head out the other way. The cellar doors let out onto the small courtyard behind the tavern where we tend to tasks away from patron eyes.

Today is going to be a good day. I feel it in my bones.

I step through the door into the dim interior of the kitchen and blink, waiting for my eyes to adjust. Almost immediately I hear the floor creak as someone steps on the squeaky board Mistress Clairdieu claims she will replace soon.

"Lioria?" Mistress Claridieu calls out.

I turn, giving her my best smile. I'm not her favorite serving girl by a long shot. She's a fair old woman, but she's never really liked me. Unlike the respectable girls I don't mind if a patron feels me up if it means I make a little extra at the end of the night, but I'm never late and I don't leave early. A girl like me, with no marriage prospects, has to be able to pay her own way in this world, and no one is lining up to marry an orphan girl with no history of her lineage. Everyone is so obsessed with increasing their chances of birthing a future Demon Lord to the point that happiness and love don't matter.

"Yes, mistress?"

Mistress Claridieu's brow furrows, and she stares at me for a moment.

Oh, dear.

What have I done now? Does she know about the tonic?

Does it have anything to do with our upcoming guests?

A horrid thought occurs to me.

Is she going to give me the rest of the day off? Does she only want to work respectable girls?

Mistress Claridieu has been in a fit the last few days, buzzing around, cleaning every nook and cranny. She claims gentlemen are coming to stay here. Real gentlemen from one of the cities. For what reason or purpose, she hasn't shared, and I am wasting away in curiosity. There's no possible reason for anyone of importance to come to Suncrest. But if she doesn't let me work...?

She thrusts a metal filigree ball into my hand. It's cool to the touch. Almost cold.

I drop the rag onto the stack of trays and lift the ball for a closer look.

"It's beautiful," I whisper.

My nose is almost pressed to it. I can see straight through the other side. It's empty, which I find curious until I spy the sigil etched on the inside.

Ah.

Now I understand.

Grinning, I turn the ball in my hands.

Old magic things like me. I don't know how else to describe it. She's probably tried using the thing for days now. All her favorite girls have probably tried as well. I don't have much affinity for magic, and I haven't the faintest idea why devices work for me.

"Can you make it work?" she asks.

"Maybe. What's it do?"

She presses her lips together in a tight line.

I can't help but grin at her. "Alright, I'll figure it out."

Some devices jump to life in my hands. Others take a little coaxing. Clearly, this one wants me to be a little sweet on it.

I turn the device in my hands, admiring the detail on all the swirls. I've never seen anything quite so fine. It's beautiful. I can't believe Mistress Claridieu doesn't display it. That's how pretty it is.

"Can you make it work or not?"

There's an edge to her voice that makes me hesitate. As if she's nervous or frightened.

I pause and look at her, waiting until our gazes meet. "It'll work. I promise. I just have to convince it to like me."

She frowns. "It's not alive."

"No, but magic isn't entirely without life, either. Object like this? It's like they're... Sleeping? Dormant?"

Mistress Claridieu's brows rise. "Hibernating?"

"I suppose." I lift my shoulders. "I'm not a scholar or a mage. Just a girl with enough curiosity to figure it out."

She rolls her eyes and waves a hand at me. "Tell me when you've figured it out."

I feel it then.

It's sort of like running your fingers over a smooth surface, searching for one crack, a seam, the tiniest of imperfections. Only with the device, it isn't physical. It's mental. Somehow.

"Wait," I say softly.

I curve my mental fingers into that seam. I don't push the pieces apart as much as I flatten, elongate my mental fingers so that I slip inside the device. Something on the device's side tugs at me, and I know I've got it. There's this rolling, dipping sensation, like riding rough waves, and then it's over.

"My word," Mistress Claridieu mutters.

My eyes pop open.

The ball glitters now with a spark of light from within. It's brilliant.

There's an almost imperceptible dome around us.

Mistress Claridieu turns toward Kirra, the cook, who is gaping at us, her spoon hovering above the pot she's been tending.

"Can you hear me?" Mistress Claridieu asks loudly.

Kirra cocks her head to the side.

"Can you hear me, Kirra?"

Kirra slowly shakes her head.

Mistress Claridieu turns toward me and lets her head fall back. "Oh, praise the gods. I thought the damn thing was broken."

I hold the ball up at eye level. "Is this some sort of sound barrier?"

"It is." She fixes me with a serious stare. "I can't believe I'm about to ask this of you, but I need you to attend the gentleman's meeting, operating this device, so they won't be overheard."

Oh, that sounds enticing.

She thrusts her finger under my nose. "You will shove wax in your ears, and you will not listen to what they have to say. Is that understood?"

"Yes, mistress," I say like a good little girl.

She eyes me.

We both know I'm going to listen a little.

She shakes her head. "One of these days you're going to get yourself in trouble, Lioria."

"I know."

"Figure out how to make the area larger. Go into the private dining hall. Now. You need to cover the whole thing."

I'm giddy as I ease my magic out of the device and deactivate it.

No more cleaning trays for me.

Mistress Claridieu turns her attention on two of the other girls in from the tavern with empty mugs.

Kirra catches my eye and I circle around to where she's minding the pot for lunch service. Her dark skin gleams with a sheen of sweat from tending the food. Unlike me, she is from a distinguished family that can trace its lineage back hundreds of years. Kirra is like me, though. We both chafe at the boundaries of what society wants for us. Which is how she came to be employed here; where she bucks tradition by cooking for us common folk, when she could easily be one of the most in-demand cooks at any of the wealthy houses in town.

I asked her once why she chose to cook for the tavern guests rather than for a family. She said it wouldn't be a challenge, and she isn't catering to any man, ever. The tavern folk are happy to eat her tasty food and ensure she knows her efforts are appreciated. Not for the first time I wish I was inclined to love women. Kirra and I would scandalize the whole region by not caring one bit about our prodgeny.

Sadly, neither of us are so inclined. We kissed once after a night of too much drinking, and have agreed to never speak of it again. She's more like a sister to me than a lover, and I wouldn't trade that for anything.

"I tried my hand at something earlier," she whispers.

"Oh?"

She nods at the little drawer next to the stove. "Over there. Should still be warm."

I glance over my shoulder before opening the small drawer.

Inside are four fan-shaped pastries.

"Hand-pies. I read about them," Kirra whispers. "Take them."

"All of them?"

"Yes."

"For me?"

She scowls at me. "Are you trying to get us caught?"

I giggle and quickly shove the small pastries into my apron pocket. "You're the best, Kirra."

She grins at me. "And you're the worst."

"I can't help it."

I pause only long enough to pour myself a mug of spiced tea before I duck out the back entrance.

The sun is doing its best to peer through the clouds. I hope the rain holds off. Not because of the gentlemen's meeting this afternoon, but because I heard talk from the sailors about over-burdened ships headed this way with refugees from the continent. Unfortunately, the peace the High Demon Lords negotiated didn't hold. Everything I hear from the continent is more war and death. It's no wonder people try to escape to Eden, the land of peace.

Last fall, one of those ships capsized during a storm. Bodies washed ashore for days. It was heartbreaking. Our fishermen did what they could, but it was too late by the time anyone knew they were in trouble.

It seems like the Yokai, Vodu, and Demon Lords of the continent are always at odds. Eden, by contrast, is a peaceful nation, but that is because the seven High Demon Lords wish it.

I think back to the story I'd told Malka. If things had gone differently, if the other powerful creatures had been willing to accept the High Demon Lord's terms, would the continent be embroiled in conflict as it is now?

How should I know? I'm a serving girl, but I do wonder.

I hold the device under my arm and fish out the first pastry. It's bite-sized, so I pop it in my mouth. The crust is flaky, but it's the insides that make me moan. The first flavor is sharp citrus I don't recognize for a moment. Lemons! I distinctly recall Kirra hoarding two lemons she bought off a merchant. The sharpness is soothed by a sweet jelly, creating a buttery, tangy, sweet aftertaste. I groan in ecstasy at this bit of perfection.

Kirra has out-done herself this time.

"What is that?"

My eyes pop open and the day suddenly seems less bright.

I blink a few times as I stare at a wall.

No.

I look up. And up at a man with peach-fair skin, more freckles than I've seen on anyone in the whole of my life, and hair that looks like copper. He is an amalgamation of features I've never seen before. His green eyes are locked on my mouth and for a moment I don't know where or when I am, but I'm happy to be here. Especially if my companion is half as interesting as he looks.

Are those freckles painted on? Or was he born like that? Is something wrong with him? Does he have a skin disease?

That thought makes my heart nearly stop. He's far too handsome to die so young.

I glance around, unsettled to find myself still in the yard behind the tavern.

Was he summoned by the device? Is he real? Or a figment from history?

I've heard about people with skin that fair, but I've never seen them. The elements here are too harsh for delicate bodies unable to withstand the sun, heat, and the battering of the ocean.

He leans toward me and inhales. "Are there more?"

My stomach does a little flip and I sway toward him, as if caught in a thrall.

"I'm sorry. Who are you?" I ask slowly.

He's staring at my cup now and it's the first time in my life I've been jealous of an inanimate object. "What's this? Is that chai? No, the smell's not right. Do you mind?"

I can barely string together a sentence before he's taken my mug out of my hands and drinking from it. I'm torn between outrage and fascination. A droplet runs down his cheek. I have the strangest urge to lick it off him. The mental picture alone is enough to make my thighs clench.

His clothes certainly aren't from these parts. He's wearing too many layers. A tunic, some sort of under coat, an overcoat, and a cloak? In spring? He'll be dead of heat exhaustion when the clouds part, if the sun doesn't fry his delicate skin to a crisp. I've always heard that southerners don't have what it takes to live any farther north, but that seems ridiculous.

The man drains my mug completely, then stares at the bottom, as if he's shocked it's all gone.

"What was that?" he asks.

"Where do you get off asking me what I was drinking when you just drank it all?" I'm honestly not irritated; I'm baffled and intrigued. A little turned on, if I'm honest. But I should be annoyed.

He glances at the mug, then back at me before smiling sheepishly. "Sorry, I smelled something amazing and followed my nose. Then I heard you moaning and..."

One side of his mouth hitches up and he lifts a shoulder.

Cheeky bastard.

He's somehow rugged and refined all at once. That hair is too long. I want to push it back out of his face, but I think that's part of his appeal.

"Thought you'd get a show?" I snag the mug from him. It'll be my hide if it disappears.

He shakes his head. "That was a food moan."

"Oh, there's a difference?"

His smile widens and heat blossoms low in my belly. "I can show you if you like?"

Be still my heart. I want to drag him into a closet and ride his face.

But I can't.

I'm not a prude by any means and I have no reservation about bedding a willing partner. I certainly don't do it while at work. But I haven't had a sweetheart in months. Not since my last two finally settled down with respectable girls, and I cut ties.

As charming as he is, I must sort out the magical device. If the mistress caught me fooling around with him, I doubt she'd give me another chance. I'm not willing to risk my perfect position here on the account of a handsome man who will be gone soon. No matter how much I want to see what he's hiding in his trousers. Besides, the moment he knows my name, he isn't likely to pay me any mind.

There's one thing I know is a fact: no one on this planet will look out for me better than myself.

"As delightful as that sounds, I think not," I say after a moment's pause. "I am otherwise occupied right now."

He dips his head lower. "What about later?"

"You aren't used to hearing no, are you?"

"Not usually, no."

"Well, then let me take this opportunity to acquaint you with the word. No."

He sighs and his shoulders drop a little.

There's one thing I know is a fact: no one on this planet will look out for me better than myself.

Why do I feel like I kicked a puppy? This man is big enough he could probably pick me up with one arm. I have no reason to feel guilty for turning him down, even if I'm already regretting it.

"Will you at least tell me what you were eating?" he asks.

"How did you smell it?" I glance about. He must have come round from the stables. Is he part of the gentlemen's party? Are they here already?

"I have a good nose." He shoves his hand into his trouser pocket. "I'll pay..."

Kirra will skin me later, but there were four pastries, and I can always use a little spending coin.

"Fine." I sigh, acting more put out than I am, and fish a single pastry out of my apron pocket. "But there aren't any more to share with you, so savor it."

He leans down and takes the pastry from my fingers with his lips. His tongue swipes against the pad of my finger and he winks at me.

Oh, this one is dangerous.

Why do I have to be working right now?

His eyes widen and he tips his head back, groaning loudly. The sound is seductive and I can't help but wonder what other sounds he might make. He presses his fingers to his lips, as if he's worried he might lose a single, flaky crumb. His chest heaves and I'm quite proud of my Kirra. I watch him chew, then swallow.

He shakes his head, face creased as if in pain. "And you said there aren't anymore? Did you make it?"

"No."

He takes my hand and presses a coin to my palm. "That was lovely. My journey has been well-worth it."

I snort and am half-tempted to part with one more simply because Kirra deserves to be appreciated for her little creations. Mistress doesn't mind her experimenting, but the ingredients can get pricey.

He backs away from me. "Should you change your mind about the other thing, come find me?"

And then he's gone.

I chuckle and roll the coin between my fingers, but it feels strange. I glance down and freeze in horror at the thick gold coin I have between my knuckles. I hold it up.

I've never seen a gold coin before.

This must be a mistake. He could not possibly have paid me a gold coin for my tea and a pastry that was barely a bite for a man of his size.

Mistress Claridieu's voice rises from inside, and I make a hasty retreat through the private dining hall's serving entrance.

The main tavern is typically big enough for even our busiest of nights, so most of the time, the hall is used to store things, but it's been cleaned out and polished from floor to ceiling. It smells like vinegar and citrus, so someone must have done a last pass this morning.

Tables are set up in a U formation. A sideboard is pushed up against the wall and will serve as a buffet. Now, I need to figure out how to work this new device before the lords show up. I pop the last pastry in my mouth and groan.

These were worth a gold coin.

 BELIAL

I stride along the waterfront, hands in my pockets. I can still taste the sweet and tangy pastry on my tongue, but it was the woman whose finger I'd licked it from that has captured my thoughts. My human body is elated. It feels as light as a cloud. There's a ball of warmth spinning so very fast in my chest, pushing back the constant worries of my kind.

But more than that? My demon is awake. And it wants.

These days it feels like my demon half is always asleep, leaving me with an itchy, sort of half-awareness that isn't pleasant. Like a sunburn that's almost healed, only it never goes away.

What was it about her that has roused me like this?

I hadn't lied when I told her I'd followed my nose, but it was her moan that had enticed me to investigate. I'm still not sure why. It's not like humans interest me a great deal, generally speaking. Their lives go by so fast and then they're gone. Before I ever truly know them. There are humans who have served me for three lifetimes now who I can't recall as well as I can her face, the shine of her hair, or the taste of her skin.

It's not as if she was a great beauty, either. Even now, I can catalogue her appearance. Five-foot-six to - eight, depending on her shoes. It was clear she spent a good deal of time in the sun. Her medium brown skin is bronzed to a lovely tan. Her bountiful, curvy figure is the type to occupy a man's mind with undressing her. She had a slight widow's peak, giving her a heart-shaped face. Her nose and mouth were broad and expressive. With her dark brown, wavy hair pulled back, it made her seem more graceful.

A woman like that was wasted on utilitarian cotton clothing. She should wear something clingy. Or nothing at all.

My demon growls, and my darker desire blooms.

I want to have her. I haven't wanted anything other than my next meal in so long; I revel in the sensation.

Eligos falls into step with me, and I have to wonder if he can sense this change. Of us, his demon is probably the strongest. Or was. Things could have changed in the years since we've met with the others. "What are you thinking about?"

By some minor miracle, we are the first to arrive. Seeing as this is Eligos' province, it's only right. Neither of us are suited for leadership, so it is a testament to our stewards and staff that our respective provinces are flourishing.

"I think I might bed a woman."

He turns his head and studies me. "You haven't in a while. Feeling the testosterone?"

"No. There was a girl at the tavern..."

Eligos eyes me with no small amount of curiosity.

In all our lifetimes, the seven of us have been close. But Eligos and I are bound on some deeper level. I don't think our creator understood. We were created out of the same spark, unlike the others. In some lifetimes, we've been brothers or sisters. Once we were twins. A few times we've even married. We're always friends. But this time is different, more intimate. We are inseparable. The love I feel for him has never been greater.

A perfect solution would be for us to take the same lover. But that will never happen. I spent our early twenties trying to figure out what kind of woman interests him past the orgasm, but none have. I'm not sorry. In all the millennia we've been alive, Eligos and I have never tired of each other. Ours is a bond that transcends time, body, and soul. I welcome this lifetime, where we might love each other more completely. I just wish we both enjoyed more physical pleasure from it all.

"My demon wants her, Eli..."

"Really?"

"Does that upset you?"

He snorts. "Not in the slightest. Though I do pity her pussy."

I deflect Eligos' wandering hand with a chuckle. There are too many eyes, and we are supposed to be attempting discretion.

"You'll destroy her with that thing if you don't go slow."

"She said no."

"She what?" He scowls at me as though he's offended. "I'm not awake enough to respond to that nonsense. What's wrong with her? You're delicious."

I chuckle. "I think she was working. I'll have to try later..."

He sighs and tips his face up toward the sky. "There won't be time later, or have you forgotten?"

"No..."

The meeting isn't the only thing we're here to do.

Alastor might chide us in public, and even in front of the others, but it's all part of our act. Everyone—even our brethren—expect a sloth and glutton demon to cut corners and leave our work to our staff. Which we do, but not for the reason people expect. With our leadership so fractured, it's much easier for Eligos and me to move about. Not as many people note our comings and goings because we are not tied to the capital. Our freedom allows us to take a more direct approach with those encroaching on our territory.

It's not just Yokai and Vodu. There are humans who would seek to destroy the peace we've so painstakingly built. And tonight, while the others are asleep, we must investigate another incursion under the cover of darkness.

"Try to fuck her before the meeting? Maybe one of us will pay attention," Eligos says.

I jab my elbow at him. "Not interested in the least?"

He snorts and glances at me. "All your women are loud and annoying. Enjoy yourself. Treat your demon. He doesn't come out very often. I'm a little jealous..."

I grin at Eligos and decide that tonight, after we finish with our errand, I am fucking his ass. But that thought doesn't stir my cock half as much as the memory of the woman's moan.

I want to hear that again.

"We already know what they'll discuss today." I grimace and glance over my shoulder, toward the inn.

It has been sixteen years since the seven of us were in one place. We've never gone this long without being together.

It's rather surprising that after thirty years, we still don't know who killed us. The whole event is still a bizarre episode of our history that doesn't make sense. It holds sway over how we move about and why the others have all been distant.

We haven't talked about it outright, but we are all weaker. Our demons have lost some of their power. Not one of us can assume demon form any longer. And that is a secret we must protect. If our enemies on the continent find out, they will come for us harder than they already are.

I wouldn't say that my brethren are frightened. I'm too proud for that. But why else would the others have tried so hard to separate Eligos and me if it wasn't out of fear that we'd make an easy target?

I refuse to let dread rule my life ever again.

Today, the others will arrive with their carefully prepared arguments for why this faction or that was responsible for our deaths.

My only contribution is a single question.

What the fuck does it matter?

We died.

We came back.

Our stewards and the councils managed Eden just fine in the fifteen years it took us to mature into these bodies. Another fifteen have passed, and we are still at peace. The system works. It's seamless. Of course, regrettable things happened. Things one of us could have dealt with swifter, but we cannot be all things to all people. We are demons, not gods. We were created for the bowels of hell, not the mortal earth. We are more than we were, but not entirely what we pretend to be.

There are more important things to concern ourselves with than a crime committed against those with the highest chances of rebirth. To me, that is a victimless crime. An inconvenience at best, and I'd much rather spend my time trying to get up a certain girl's skirt to appease my demon.

Besides, our power is waning. We can ignore it as much as we like, but those are the facts.

LIORIA

The damn device might just suck me dry of magic.

I figured out how to work the thing. It's all about visualizing the space you want to cover and maintaining that boundary.

And it's fucking exhausting.

Thank goodness Mistress Claridieu took one look at me after my success and demanded I lie down. Of course, she didn't mean anywhere comfortable, like a nice, plush bed upstairs. There's a wide bench in the actual storage closet of the private dining hall. I stole the pretty, long cushions off the bench no one will sit on and made myself a marginally more comfortable spot to recuperate where I won't be bothered.

I hope these gentlemen don't have much to discuss.

If Kirra made another of those delicious little pies, I just know I'd feel better.

"What are you doing hiding in here?"

I crack open one eye and peer up at the silhouette of an unfamiliar face.

"I don't reckon *you're* supposed to be in here." I push myself up and squint, but the light is behind him. He has locs almost to his shoulders, but that's about all I can tell. "What, or who, are you looking for?"

Mistress Claridieu doesn't know this, but her favorite serving girls use the private dining hall to meet with their lovers.

"You should run along," he says.

Annoyance flares. Usually, I'm more even-tempered, but that damn device has exhausted me in every way. "And what do you know about where I should be?"

I pick up the offensive little thing and toss it from hand to hand.

He lets go of the barn-like door, letting it swing open to admit more light. His skin is a fair, coppery brown. A man with a complexion that perfect had never labored one day under the sun. And what color are his locs? Are my eyes playing tricks on me?

Who is he?

He reaches for the device. "What's that?"

I snatch it back and frown at him. "You are over-stepping, sir. I am where I am supposed to be. The hall is closed to guests. I do not mind the company, but this conversation is taxing and I wish to rest."

He drops to a knee next to me. The light falls on his face and I realize that his hair is a deep, beautiful violet.

Shit.

He must be one of the lords. No one but a lord could maintain hair that hue.

Fuck my life, Mistress Claridieu will have my head if I offend him.

"You're a saucy little thing, aren't you?" His gaze is on the device. "Do you know how to work that?"

"Yes. It is because I know why that I'm here." As if that might explain and excuse my behavior. I can only hope. Most of the time, I try my best to be brave and tackle my failures head-on, but this time I don't dare. If I say nothing, will he let this slide?

He frowns, then turns those gold and brown eyes on me. "This should work with only a drop of magic."

I shrug. "I don't have much, but old devices like me."

He rises only to straddle the other end of the bench and lean back against the wall. For a few moments, we study each other openly. I'm too tired to be nervous or smart.

His square jaw frames a face with strong features. There's something about the angle of his cheekbones that is somehow delicate, which brings a balance to his face.

"Walk me through what it's like."

"Well, first I feel—not with my hands—around the object until I find the seam. I pour my magic into it, then visualize the area I need to cover." Belatedly, I also realize this could be a mistake. What if he isn't one of the gentlemen? What if he's here to sabotage things?

"Don't pour. Never pour yourself out for anyone. Next time, imagine it as a drop. That device shouldn't take much from you. It's designed so that anyone should be able to operate it." He leans his head back and folds his hands over his stomach as if he's said all he's going to and now it's time to nap.

At least he doesn't appear angry.

"Could you have closed the door, at least?" I say before I can stop myself.

His full, kissable lips quirk into a smile. "I thought it might be presumptuous if I locked us in a closet together."

"Oh, I'm sharing my bench now, am I?"

"Yes."

I reach over and pull the door mostly shut, blocking out the light. With the window cracked, there's a cool breeze stirring the air. This isn't half bad. It's pleasant, even.

"You're tired because you depleted all your mana," he says softly, as if he's about to drift asleep.

"That's what I assumed. Thank you for the tip."

"Do you always speak so impertinently to gentlemen?"

I sigh. So he isn't letting it slide. "No. I don't think a gentleman has ever spoken to me before. What reason would they? I've never heard of a gentleman sneaking naps in closets before. Tumbling girls, certainly."

He chuckles. "The local lords, they don't come here?"

"Oh, that's politics. I don't concern myself with that."

"Do they not treat you well?"

"The local lords are fair, I'd say. But that doesn't make us equal in their eyes."

"You see yourself as equal?"

"For all anyone knows, I might birth a Demon Lord. Who is anyone to tell me I'm less than anyone else?"

"You're an orphan?"

My meaning did not escape him.

"Yes."

"What's your name?"

"Lioria."

"My light." He chuckles. "That seems fitting."

"My what?"

"Lioria. It means, my light."

"Oh. I've never heard that before. That's rather lovely."

"What do you think of your Demon Lord?"

"Demon Lord Eligos? I don't think anything of him. I've never seen him. There's no reason for him to come to Suncrest, anyway. Probably better if he doesn't."

"Why's that?"

I bite my lip.

Shouldn't have said that...

"Who are you that you're so concerned with what a common serving girl thinks?" I counter.

"You're interesting. Not many people are. I'm no one of consequence, I promise."

"You're only being half-honest with me. Which is it? Am I interesting? Or are you no one?"

"Clever girl." His eyes are, but he's smiling now. "The views of normal people are important. When people forget to listen is when history repeats itself. Humor me, please?"

"No. I want to protect my friends more than I fear you."

"Cleaver and loyal."

"Don't forget impertinent."

"Lioria, I'm convinced you're wasted on this place. Run away with me?"

It's my turn to laugh. "You're a funny one."

No lord would take an orphan girl with no lineage or pedigree for a wife. Probably not even a mistress. It's one thing for a casual tumble in a closet, but we all know those liaisons are about the moment and nothing more. I might not be the smartest girl, but I understand the way of the world better than most.

"Do you mind it? The way others see you?" he asks.

"Do I mind if people hear my name and know I'm an orphan? No. Not at all. Or is it not a truth that even the poorest of orphans might give birth to a Demon Lord when one of you dies?"

He opens his golden eyes and I can't help but grin back at him. "You're exactly right."

"Is it really true that the moment after you die your soul goes into a new body?"

"Yes."

"Are you aware of it?"

He tilts his head. "Not in the way you mean. We aren't supposed to remember the time when we're dead. It's more a feeling or impression of descending into fog—and then nothing."

"If that's the case, then why should I be ashamed? What if you die and I have you as a baby?"

His eyes narrow. "I don't usually find myself attracted to my potential mothers."

I laugh and wave him off, pointedly ignoring his comment about my attractiveness. "Polite society dictates that you must marry certain people so their chances of having you for a baby increase. Your wife or another woman of pedigree. You get no say in that. Me, on the other hand? I'm free. No one cares who I fuck or what I do. The moment I aged out of the orphanage, the world became my oyster. I can do whatever I want and no one cares, because I'm an orphan. There's no pressure on me to make a smart match. I'd say most people are glad I don't want those things."

"You don't know your parents? Never did?"

I shake my head. "As best anyone knows, they passed during the plague. I was barely born when they died, and somewhere in the shuffle my parentage was forgotten."

"I'm sorry," he says softly.

"I'm not. I don't want your pity. Unlike you, I'm free to do as I wish."

"What will you do when your mistress says you're too old to wait tables?"

"I'll marry. But not before I'm thirty. I want to have some fun. I'll find some sweet farmer or fisherman whose wife died in childbirth or was taken by the seasonal sickness or who had an accident. There's always a widower in need of a wife to tend the family around these parts. I'll be happy to love them as if they were my own, and grateful to step into a comfortable life."

He shakes his head and folds his hands behind his head. "You have it all figured out."

"I can't decide if you're mocking me or serious."

"Both. I dare say you have us all figured out."

"Oh, I'm not just an impertinent light skirt, am I?"

"You'd be happy if that's what everyone saw you as, wouldn't you?"

I say nothing.

It is who I am, to a degree.

What purpose is there in spending an entire lifetime apologizing for my birth? I can't help that my parents died in a plague. Why should I suffer, all because someone else forgot to write down who they were?

I refuse to apologize for seeing the freedom of my circumstances. I have the chance to be selfish and live for myself. Why shouldn't I? How many lifetimes have I lived where I toiled away, doing exactly as was expected of me and finding no joy in it?

Suddenly he sits up. His eyes look as though they're shimmering gold, not just golden. "Do you want to get out of here?"

I don't chuckle. I don't doubt one bit that he's serious. Any other day I'd be tempted, but if I bailed on Mistress Claridieu now? I'd be out of a job for certain.

"If you asked me that any other day, I'd more than likely say yes." I roll the device between my hands. "Why did you have to pick today?"

My thoughts stray back to the coppery-haired gentleman from earlier. This loc'd lord is clearly one of the gentlemen attending the meeting, but what of the other one?

For the rest of today, I need to be on my very best behavior. I wouldn't say I've stepped out of line, but Mistress Claridieu would not like to find out I'd been so casual with two gentlemen.

He sighs and flops back to lean against the wall. "My timing is always off."

"You'll do better next time." I smile fondly. "That's what the nanny at the orphanage used to say."

His eyes are closed, but he's smiling. I have this urge to crawl across the bench and lay my head on his shoulder while we both nap. I remain where I am, though, content in the silence.

I sleep for a while, because the next thing I know, it's far too bright. I hear a man's groan and Mistress Claridieu's gasp.

I pick up the device from where it's sitting on the bench between us and rise, pausing only to curtsey to the gentleman.

"I'll see you later, Lioria," he says as I make my exit.

Mistress Claridieu must have spent another few moments trying to talk to my loc'd lord, or she'd be on my heels. I'm not sure where I should go or what I need to be doing, so I wait for her out in the yard.

The sounds from the tavern are lively. It's mid-afternoon. I'm rested and as ready as I can be for this event.

Mistress Claridieu lumbers out of the dining hall, her eyes wide as she shakes her head. "You are a lucky girl."

I'm inclined to agree, but I say nothing.

She paces away from me then back, fingers pressed to her lips.

It's just a bunch of lords and gentlemen. She's acting like the High Demon Lords themselves are coming to our humble tavern.

Mistress Claridieu stops in front of me and plants her hands on her hips. "We'll move a chair over for you, but you will need to sit facing the wall with your ears waxed. You don't want to hear a word the gentlemen say, Lioria. Do you understand me?"

"Yes, mistress." Oh, but I do want to know.

"This is very important. Do not listen in. No matter what. Don't listen. I wish I didn't have to put up one of my own girls, but no one has a way with old things like you do."

Her words are touching. I wouldn't have thought she viewed me like that. I might not be her favorite, but I do like and respect Mistress Claridieu. She was an orphan like me who went on to own the Silver Roo. If I had greater aspirations in me, I'd want to be like her.

"It'll be fine. The young Lord actually gave me a tip on how to use it."

Instead of comforting her, Mistress Claridieu's brow furrows deeper and her eyes are so wide. "Get yourself some tea and a snack, then... It'll be time. Go on."

What about this meeting is so damn special?

The kitchen is bustling. I manage to steal a roll off the tray fresh out of the oven and a mug of lukewarm spiced tea. I return to the yard and eat my meal in peace. The tea perks me up enough to chase away the mind-fog from having napped in the middle of the day. I no longer feel drained and weary, either.

A few girls are going in and out of the hall now in pairs. They scurry as though Mistress Claridieu is driving them. No doubt she's terrified everyone.

They're just men.

They might be self-important and pompous, but do they really inspire so much fear?

I slip into the hall after the last pair has retreated. There's one chair facing the corner. Like I'm the kid in class who can't stay out of trouble.

The closet is closed now, and the cushion is back where it belongs. It's just me.

I amble over to my seat. There's a small tin waiting there. I pry the top off and find a lump of wax and strips of cloth.

Lovely.

I take the strips, roll a ball of wax between my fingers, then wrap the cloth around it. I wonder if there's a way to exclude me from the device's bubble? Would the gentlemen know?

Footsteps thump on the floor while I ponder how I might pull off that trick.

"I do not wish to be disturbed. Leave," a man says behind me.

I turn and look at the tall man with long, wheat colored hair. His skin is like burnished bronze and his eyes are a brilliant green I can see from across the room. He is handsome, though that word seems too weak. Beautiful? There's a masculine edge to his beauty that makes it hard to describe him. He's tall, with a lithe body and finely tailored clothes that mold to his form. Any other time, and he would have turned my head. Today, I'm growing a little leery of attractive gentlemen.

I don't budge or cower under his gaze. "This room is reserved for a special event."

He arches a brow at me as if I'm the idiot here. "I know."

"I'll not be leaving, sir." I add in a curtsey because I must.

His gaze narrows, and he tilts his head to the side. "Who are you?"

"I am Lioria. I'm to attend the meeting today." I lift the device in my hand so he could see it. They had requested this service, after all.

"Ah." He nods and crosses the room. He stops so close my skirts brush his legs and I can smell brine on him. As if he just stepped off a boat. His fingers grip my chin. "You're one of mine, then."

I take a step back, out of his grip. "Sorry?"

"Never mind. Sorry. Are you prepared? Do you understand that you may not listen to what we discuss?"

"Would you happen to know if there's a way to..." I scrunch up my mouth. "Can I be on the outside? We both know wax isn't going to block out everything."

He tilts his head to the side and his brows are almost at his hairline. The way he's studying me now is not entirely pleasant. I feel like an ocean oddity trapped in a barrel. "No. Not at all possible, but a very good idea. Who taught you how to use this?"

"Well, no one. Sir. Mistress Claridieu handed it to me this morning, and I taught myself how to... Shape it. Oh, that's not entirely accurate. There was a gentleman a little while ago who gave me some instruction."

"What did he look like?"

"Dark skin, purple locs—"

"Eli. Well, at least he's here."

The large doors on the other side of the room are thrown open. Men are coming into the hall now, led by a tall, muscular man. The sides of his head are shaven and his brown hair bound into a tail at the nape of his neck. The rest falls to his waist with little braids mixed in. He's scowling over his shoulder at my coppery haired gentleman.

Shit.

The blonde man turns his attention back on me. There's a spark in his eyes now, and I fear I'm the cause.

"Listen to as little as you can. We'll talk later..."

Normally, I'm eager to talk to a gentleman as handsome as him. But more than that, he's powerful, and he's seen a use in me beyond what I'm willing to offer. Men like that make me nervous. Usually, finding out I'm an orphan is enough to divert them, but this one doesn't seem deterred.

I shove my one wax ball into my ear and press it in as deep as I can. Hearing more than I should no longer sounds like fun.

The coppery haired gentleman catches my eye and winks. I'm smiling before I can stop myself.

If only I'd been born with good sense.

I whirl to face the wall like a good little girl and sit. The chair has a very nice cushion, which must be by design. I smile at the wall. Maybe Mistress Claridieu likes me more than she lets on?

I roll another ball of wax into the cloth before sticking it in my other ear. The men's voices are muted and I can't make out words when they're all talking at once. Once my hands are free, I hold the ball between my palms and run invisible fingers over the device again. It's faster this time, as if my fingers remember they've been. Instead of pushing all of me into the device, I do as the loc'd lord suggested and envisioned a single drop slipping into the crevice.

The same dome as before pushes out, moving through objects and people. I picture the hall in my mind and nudge the dome to fit the shape. There's not much in the way of sensation for me. It feels kind of like stretching sore muscles, but in a good way. There's no resistance. Just fluidity. Despite what the blonde man said, I try to move the boundary so that it excludes me. And nothing happens. I slide my foot forward and the dome expands to keep me within it.

Well, fuck.

At least I tried.

I sip my tea and lean back, abandoning good posture in favor of comfort.

There's no telling how long this meeting will take, but I hope they don't drone on into the night.

All at once, they stop. It's quiet.

Did something happen?

I cock my head to the side.

"Alastor, really?"

With only one speaking, it isn't so difficult to make out their words.

But to name someone Alastor? After a Demon Lord? Clearly, nobility has different rules.

"Oriax—" The rest of whatever the man says is too soft for me to hear.

A knot of dread forms in my stomach.

Alastor and Oriax?

I've met three gentlemen today who have no place in Suncrest. All of whom seem to be around the same age. And now I've heard two names of Demon Lords.

My heart begins to race and I sit very still. This could be coincidence, but I do not want to find out. My life might be quiet and insignificant, but I like it. I'm not ready to be reborn. I want to live this life, but I won't get the chance if I anger a demon.

ELIGOS

We haven't been together more than ten minutes before Alastor and Oriax have exchanged heated words about nothing that matters. Shax doesn't help by wading in on some unrelated, nonsensical matter.

Fuck this whole disaster. I knew I shouldn't have come. This so-called meeting is pointless if the two of them start fighting.

We're supposed to open with a discussion about our last death.

Raum and Oriax are certain our assassination was orchestrated by either the Yokai or Vodu. Maybe a combined effort of the two, though that would be impressive. There's no love lost between the two groups since the continent court was over-thrown. At best, they tolerate one another, only uniting when it comes to attacking demons. Not that I can blame them. We've made this mess.

Shax and Valac have a new theory about our death all the time. I can only imagine how exhausting they are to be around this lifetime.

Belial and I are at least honest. We have no fucking idea who killed us and, to be frank; we don't care.

The only holdout is Alastor. He's never said what he thinks. And as the natural leader among us, I don't think he will ever weigh in. Not until he's ready to take action, which is no doubt driving Shax mad with rage.

Belial prods my thigh under the table and I pick my head up off my crossed arms to glare at him. I have to be here. I don't have to be in a good mood. I've been grumpy ever since that woman so rudely woke me up.

More curious is that my demon has also risen to the surface. Ever since I bantered with a witty little serving girl.

"What are we doing about the refugees?" Oriax asks.

Oh, bother.

I have to be careful. I cannot show my hand.

I sit up and clear my throat. "Extra resources have been allotted to this part of the region to offset the influx of people."

Oriax turns and looks down his nose at me. Most lifetimes we get on well enough, but not this one. He's more serious, more up-tight, and my lazy approach to every life is getting under his skin.

"I couldn't help but notice this town lacks a harbor master," he says.

I prop my chin on my hand and stare back at him. "Oriax, are you questioning my decisions?"

"How do you know who is coming ashore? How do we know if Yokai or Vodu are—"

"Oh, not this." I throw my head back and groan. "Had I known—"

"Oriax?" Alastor's cool voice silences us both. "Let's refrain from stepping on each other's toes, please?"

Alastor stepping in like this unsettles me. Is he concerned? Is there some news he hasn't shared with us?

It's tricky admitting refugees. There's a fine dance to it. Either people are admitted the formal way, or they aren't. What with how bad things are on the continent, I cannot in good conscience turn people away. The refugee settlements keep to themselves and I have spies among them. They're all just people wanting a chance at life.

Oriax's eyes blaze and he glares across the room.

That's one thing that never changes. Oriax chafes at his boundaries. If we let him, he'd run the whole country. I'd be happy to hand my region over to him, but the others would riot, and I'd get dragged right back in. I've tried. It's pointless.

I lift my hand and look at Alastor. "I have a question."

Youth never looks right on Alastor. It's the stiff way he carries himself. Like he has a stick shoved all the way up his ass and can taste it. He's still probably the best of us, which is why I trust his decisions to guide us.

"What is it?" Alastor asks without breaking the stare-off he has going on with Oriax.

"What, exactly, are we here to discuss?"

"Bringing us all back to court?" Shax interjects. Because, of course.

The room goes quiet.

Valac catches my eye from across the room and shakes his dainty little head.

Well, shit.

I stumbled right into this mess.

The seven of us have never been dead all at once. Even during times of conflict, there have always been two of us still breathing. Our deaths threw Eden into an economic decline. There were plagues. Famine. Our stewards handled it all as best they can, but they aren't us. While our magic is waning, we have the ability to change the course of nature to a degree. Ever since we woke from our post-freedom stupor to the horror we'd created, we've been slowly trying to pull the planet and people back from the brink of destruction.

It's exhausting.

"No," Alastor says and turns from his staring match with Oriax. "I don't think the time is right yet. Not until we know who our enemies are. They set their trap and waited. They could have another trap ready for us."

That was the problem with this cycle. Plots and schemes were no longer just this lifetime, but across many.

"This isn't right." Shax points across the room. "You're just trying to hog all the power for yourself. You've changed, Alastor."

"Do you seriously believe that?" Valac mutters.

I roll my eyes and glance at Belial, but he's already given up on this conversation. He's staring across the room at the woman from earlier. The one I shared the closet with. I've never been so delighted to share such a small space without getting my cock sucked.

The others drone on. Belial drags his attention back long enough to chime in once or twice. There's only so much interest either of us can feign in this whole plot.

Out of everyone, the current arrangement to keep our power spread out over the country suits us best. Shax and Oriax want to be at the center of it all, but those two have always seen themselves as opposed to Alastor on nearly all points. Raum and Valac go with the flow, more or less, though they have also voiced displeasure at their roaming being limited.

I lean back in my seat, dismissing the current conflict from mind. It doesn't matter to me what the consensus is. I have no intention of moving from the home Belial and myself have built for ourselves in this lifetime.

Which makes the woman across the room that much more fascinating.

My cock stirs and I steal a glance sideways at Belial.

It's been a while since we fucked. I love him more than I ever have, but our lives have become routine. And we're barely thirty. The desire cools a tiny bit, which makes me pause and look back at our little magic wielder.

There's something about her I can't explain, but she has her hooks in us both. I've only just realized all the little changes. A sense of greater awareness, along with a slight sheen, laid over the others. My demon isn't quite asleep, like Belial's. More like it's stretched out inside of me, caught between sleep and wakefulness. I never know when it might become aware.

Like now. I'd venture my demon has never been closer to the surface than right now.

My whole body is ready, and I'm only just aware of this.

My demon wants her.

I look back at Belial and the urgent need for her diminishes.

Belial glances at me and smiles. I reach over under the table and drag my finger down the side of his thigh. He catches my finger in his hand and squeezes. One little touch to let me know he's always there for me.

We love each other. And yet, something has been missing. I don't know if Belial notices it, but I have. I love him and his body. I love who we are together. And yet, I crave something else.

I curve my hand around his and squeeze him back. How long have I been aware of the emptiness?

As far as I can tell, it's always been there. This chunk that's just missing. Belial does his best to mold himself into the shape I need, but how is that fair to him?

Is this woman what we've been missing?

Time and time again, Belial has suggested one woman or another for us to share, and while I've humored him on occasion, we are never attracted to the same person.

Until now.

I study the back of the woman's head who has found herself at the center of our focus. There hadn't been much light to see her by in the closet. But that wasn't what had drawn me to her. It was her voice and the soft way she spoke about her freedom. I chafe at my bonds daily. She inspired me, to a degree. That's how it began. And somewhere between then and now, she enticed my demon.

Alastor and Raum are going back and forth about something, bent over a scroll.

I lean over to Belial and tug at our joined hands to get his attention.

"Is that her?" I whisper as softly as I can.

He inclines his head, but only a little. Neither of us wants to draw the attention of the others. "You should meet her—"

"I did."

Belial turns his head to stare at me, eyes wide. I can't decipher his thoughts, not that it's a skill any of us possess. But I don't have to. Hope shines on his beautiful face. He's always been the most innocent of us, and I love him for that.

"Would you share?" I ask, growing more fixated on this idea of having her between us, coming together in pleasure. My demon practically purrs.

"Yes," he says without hesitation. Belial leans in closer. "I want to take her with us. I *want* her."

I feel a trickle of the demonic in that strained word.

She's woken up not one demon, but two.

LIORIA

If I clench my jaw hard enough, I can make my ears rumble. It helps to drown out some of what the Demon Lords are saying.

I'm the poor little mouse thrown in with the predators.

A hand grips my shoulder.

I jump, letting out a squeak befit of a mouse, and look up at a man whose very presence makes me uneasy. He's dressed like Eden nobility, but his face looks like that of some of the eastern merchants. The ones who will barely speak to anyone.

We blink at each other, then he points at his ear.

I reach up and tug the fabric and wax out.

"We're taking a break in the hopes that clearer heads will prevail." He speaks lower, almost kindly. "Are you holding up, okay?"

"Y-yes, thank you."

I drop the barrier. Using only a drop at a time has worked well and I'm not the least bit tired.

"I imagine it will be an hour or so," he says. "Take this opportunity to eat, if you like."

"Yes, thank you, sir." I bob my head while still sitting, but he doesn't seem to mind.

This is like one of those children's pantomimes I saw growing up that detail the adventures and exploits of the High Demon Lords. Only I'm the foolish mortal caught up in their story now. I've seen enough to know that nothing goes well for mere humans close to a demon.

I use my apron to make a sling for the ball, then head outside, using the external door leading toward the lane behind the tavern.

The sun has mostly set and the sea breeze is cool on my heated skin. I hadn't realized how warm the room was.

I'm not used to fear. I find fear is a mostly useless emotion that only makes me act without reason. There's also not much to fear in my life. I live at the boarding house. The city watch protects us. Mistress Claridieu provides my employment. About the only concern are storms, and there isn't anything anyone can do about those. I have a happy, simple life. Or I did.

My legs are jelly as I lean up against the side of the private hall.

"Lioria," Mistress Claridieu barks from the kitchen entrance. She's just a dark silhouette, but I would know her voice anywhere.

"Here, ma'am," I say and step into the light.

She beckons me to follow her into the kitchen and the tiny room tucked under the stairs that is her office. And lounging in her seat is none other than the loc'd Demon Lord. The one with the coppery red hair has a hand braced on the back of what would otherwise be Mistress Claridieu's chair, if it weren't currently occupied. There's so little room that both Mistress Claridieu and I remain standing on the opposite side.

My throat seizes up and I cannot speak.

Mistress Claridieu closes the door behind me, but it does nothing to ease the buzzing in my mind.

"Lioria, these two gentlemen wish to buy out your contract."

That one sentence changes everything.

There's no way either Mistress Claridieu or I can refuse them. And what do they want with me?

"Lioria?" The gentleman with the violet locs leans forward. "Would you be a dear and provide some protection for this conversation?"

I nod and reach into the apron-sling. In moments, the now familiar dome pushes out, covering the four of us.

"That's better." He leans back and sighs.

"Lords, Lioria is a good girl, but she is headstrong and—"

"Madam?" The coppery haired lord leans forward. "We don't have much time—"

"Belial?"

The coppery haired lord glances down.

Belial. He is supposed to be the strongest of the seven. They call him a brawler. The stories say he once arm wrestled a thousand men and not one of them so much as bent his wrist.

Oh, gods. If this is Belial, then the demon with the violet hair and golden eyes must be Eligos. I don't know much about him, despite him being the one to provide for this province. And he asked me about himself?

Eligos looks at me for a moment. "Will you answer me one question?"

"Anything, my lord," Mistress Claridieu says quickly.

"This device, was it here before? Or did Alastor send it?"

Mistress Claridieu glances at the ball in my hands. "It belonged to the previous owner. I was never able to make it work. When Lord Alastor contacted me, he asked if we might be able to provide privacy…"

"I see." Eligos is frowning now. "You meant well. I know that. However, Oriax will want the device and her. Many fairy artifacts are useless now because no one can use them. He'll want to study you, piece by piece, until he understands how you do it."

My head is pounding now.

"Belial and I want to offer a counter. Right now, Oriax is focused on the meeting. It won't occur to him until later to secure Lioria's employment. At most, he's considering the possibilities she could open up for him." Eligos' golden eyes are on me and I can hardly breathe. "You're the woman with all the choices now."

But is there really a choice? It's not like I have a say. No one would deny a Demon Lord what they wish. This is merely lip service. An act. And we all know it.

"There's nothing special about me," I blurt out.

Mistress Claridieu glares at me out of the corner of her eye.

Eligos and Belial continue to study me. Their faces are uniformly blank, giving away nothing. There's none of the charm from earlier.

"My lords, I could part with the device," Mistress Claridieu offers.

Eligos shrugs. "I don't care about that. Do whatever you want with it. Actually, whatever Oriax offers you for it, add at least three zeros to that number as your counter. You'll still be underpaid for it."

Eligos gestures at the desk. "It is your contract."

I swallow, fear and anger warring within me.

It's only a matter of time until my mouth gets me into trouble.

"I'm not sure why you're asking me. It's not like anything I say matters."

I stare right back at him. "And you are a High Demon Lord, sir. What I want doesn't matter. I must return to my duties."

My rational brain knows I'm being reckless. These men are powerful. They could snuff my life out in a moment, but that doesn't stop me from deactivating the device and turning my back on them. My heart races and walking is difficult, but I manage to make it out into the courtyard again. The evening breeze is cool on my too-hot skin. What will become of me? Can I escape this? Do I want to? Should I?

I've always respected the High Demon Lords. I might not believe in the gods. Not really. But every day, I see what the High Demon Lords have done to create a peaceful, safe place. Without their oversight, I would have died as a babe. I feel loyalty to them I can't explain. But where does that end? When is it enough?

A figure stumbles against the gate leading to the road. Billowy skirts are the only indication of gender in the low light.

"Hello? Do you need help?" I call out.

The figure whips around, and though I can't tell who she is, I must know her.

"Who's there?" the woman whispers as she clutches the gate.

I take a step toward her. "Malka? It's Lioria."

Her whole body sags and for a moment, I think she might collapse to her knees. I rush over and open the gate. She grips my arm and staggers into the courtyard. She gasps and pulls back, but I don't let go.

"It's me. Just me," I assure her.

She sways into me and drops her forehead to my shoulder. Her whole body is trembling. In all the time I've known her, she's never initiated contact. Until now. It's enough to make me mentally shove aside my own problems.

"What is it, Malka? What's wrong?" I ask softly and grip her shoulders.

"My brother has found me," she whispers.

"What? You have a brother?"

She shudders and her knees finally give out as she collapses to the ground. "They're here to take me away and lock me up. They won't let me be. They just won't. They hate me. He's always despised me. Told me he couldn't wait to lock me up..."

I glance about, but the stone fence gives us some privacy.

Malka has a family. I'd always assumed she was like me. An orphan. She even has an orphan name...

Unless Malka isn't her real name.

She said she'd never had the Lord's Tonic before. She doesn't know the history or stories.

"You aren't from Eden," I whisper. It's so obvious now.

"No. No, I'm not. I'm so sorry. I don't want to drag you into this."

I pull her to me and hug my arms around her, all while I try to comprehend her fate. How is it the same thing is happening to the both of us tonight?

"They want to take me back. They want to control me. Lock me away. I'll slowly go mad. I'll try to hold on, but..."

We both know what happens to people gifted with the sight.

"Calm yourself, Malka," I whisper.

"My name isn't Malka..."

"Don't tell me what it is." She clings to me while my mind races. People like her are the only ones for whom the Demon Lords can do nothing. Besides, something tells me it's probably best if we don't involve the lords. "Your family? Do they know you're here at the inn?"

"I don't know. The spirits warned me they were in Suncrest, then some of the girls for the late shift arrived talking about a lord and his lady from the continent looking for a missing sister. He won't mention my... My gift unless he has to."

The bastard.

I grip Malka's shoulders tight all while my mind races. "What do you want to do?"

"I want to be free," she whispers. "I... I could walk into the wilderness..."

"Malka, this part of Eden is hostile and the land cruel. It won't be easy to survive here if you leave town. But I don't know how you can stay here, either."

She swallows. "The spirits will help me. They helped me stow away on the boat that brought me here."

I muster a smile, though she can't see me. "Well, I'm glad you found some kind ones. Thank them for me, yeah? You've been a good friend."

"I don't know what to do, Lioria... The watch will catch me out after curfew..."

"No. No, they won't. We are going to find a place for you to hide. It probably won't be comfortable, but we need to get you out of sight for now."

My mind is made up. I cannot save myself from the mess I'm in, but I can help her.

She shakes her head. "No, you shouldn't get involved. My brother, he's..."

"He's no one here. He is not an Eden lord. I have nothing to fear from him." Brave words I can't back up, but Malka needs to hear them. "I'll draw you a map. There's a boy I grew up with. He married a girl and they have a farm outside of town on the main road. You tell him I sent you, and you pay him. They'll keep your secret and help you get on a wagon or something heading west. Don't stop too long in the small port towns. It'll be too easy to find you. You want to get to a big city, somewhere you can get lost in the crowd. Or further inland, where it would be too much trouble to find you."

"I don't have any money..."

I pull the two gold coins from my apron and press them against her palm. "You do now. Well, you will. I'll get Mistress Claridieu to exchange them for smaller coins. I'll bring you an extra dress. Pick out the hem and hide half the money in the fabric."

"That's... That's genius!"

I chuckle. She must come from a lot of money to not know a trick as basic as that.

"If I can get back here with one of my dresses, there's a good chance the night watch could think you are me. They wouldn't bother saying anything to me if I were caught out late. You'd be able to slip out easily enough..." Though traveling at night had its own risks. It would be best if she could slip out with the farmers heading into town in the morning.

"Do you think so?" Malka whispers.

"Yes."

The fear on her face breaks my heart. Family is one of the most prized things in life. Everything in Eden revolves around who you are connected to by blood. And Malka's is persecuting her. The fear coming off her is palpable.

Getting her out of Suncrest safely will be my last act as a truly free woman. I don't know if we'll see each other again. I hope we will. In a better time than this.

BELIAL

The meeting lasted late into the night and did little good. We are still divided about how to proceed. As expected, Alastor wants us to all remain in our respective provinces. But not for the reason the others expect. I can't share that information, though. It is Alastor's plan.

It is hard to watch us be this fractured. Shax especially opposes Alastor ferociously. Oriax no doubt feels the same, but he's more restrained and willing to play the subtle game of politics to get his way. For the first time, I think the two of us and Alastor have the closest relationship. I just wish we were all unified.

Eligos pats my ass with a light touch. "Ready?"

I stare out over the sleepy town of Suncrest from my vantage point atop the pointed roof. "Only waiting on you."

"We have maybe four, five hours to do this."

"Then we'd better get moving."

I bound forward, wrapping shadows around me so that any mortal eyes won't be certain of what they're seeing. My demon is stirring, but not strong enough for me to use my wings. I could cover a lot more ground with them. But Eligos would be left on foot, and he does not like to be carried.

Our bodies stretch, becoming both physical and shadow as we streak across the land.

The blight is still strong in the wasteland south of the Suncrest coast, not that it was ever a lush, green land. But it was worse because of us. I'm glad to see green things encroaching on the dead earth and signs of nocturnal life.

If we can leave things alone, nature will heal itself. It will take hundreds, if not thousands, of more years, but this earth is slowly coming back to life.

Tonight isn't about observing new life.

Alastor didn't pick the location and time randomly, as the others want to believe. Unbeknown to our fellows, Eligos and I have been conducting an investigation. Shax is right that not all of the refugees are humans fleeing the conflict on the continent. The boundary stones on the coast repel any Yokai or Vodu, to a point. There is always a way through any barrier. Ours is no exception. Tonight's meeting was a cover for the three of us to speak face to face.

We have no proof, but the three of us believe our former spymaster was in on the plot to kill us. It's made it harder to trust the humans who support us and is, in part, why Eligos and I chose the residence we did. We're also the least likely to fill this role, which makes us perfect for the job.

Eligos darts ahead of me, then changes direction. I follow him as we turn more inland and away from the coast.

I don't know how many miles we've traversed, but the coast is a distant memory. The breeze is dry and there is no brine on the air. But the darkness is broken by many little fires lighting the meager homes that have been erected this far out.

The earth out here in the wasteland hasn't recovered. It won't support life, which is why there are no towns, farms, or settlements this far out. And that makes it perfect for refugees fleeing the continent. These settlements are, at best, twenty years old and survive on those who are able to travel to procure food. The refugees live in a communal setting, with each person contributing what they can peacefully. It's a system that makes it easy for our spies to pick out dissenters. Eventually, Eligos will need to take direct action, but his hand has not been forced yet.

We find a high vantage point and come to a stop.

"It's smaller than I expected."

"That's what worries me," Eligos says. "Come. This way."

We drop to the ground in a shadowed space between the ramshackle buildings. The people are working with substandard building materials. There isn't anything we can do about that given where they've chosen to settle. If things were different, if they'd come to one of us, we could settle them more comfortably. But most won't.

Unlike the people of Eden, who have existed on a steady diet of Oriax's version of history, many refugees know some version of the truth. Our brethren on the continent haven't been as successful in wiping away the past as we have been. What we've taken to calling the Vodu and Yokai are staunchly opposed to letting us wipe the slate clean.

Eligos leads us around the perimeter of the settlement to a normal looking door. He taps in an odd rhythm, then waits.

The door cracks open on silent hinges.

Eligos slips inside while I scan the area for any eyes. When I'm satisfied nothing out there is moving, I join them and close the door behind me.

The interior does not match the exterior.

Outside, this place appeared to be doing its best job to fall apart. But inside? It's cozy, well-lit, clean. Well, except for the sizeable, blue-gray fae staked to the floor. Its face is elongated and its teeth jut out of its mouth.

"Thought you'd be here earlier," a gravelly voice said from the doorway leading deeper into the house.

Eligos is quick to cross to the man and offer his arm. "Pan. Good to see you."

Pan grunts and clasps his hand around Eligos' forearm.

It's been a few lifetimes since I saw Pan, and each time his form is different. I've often wondered if he is the same Pan about which so many stories were woven, or simply carries the name out of respect. Whatever or whoever he might have been, this is who he is now. Older, gnarled, and living for revenge. His horns have been trimmed while his hair is long and knotted. In the privacy of his home, he's foregone clothing, but when your lower half is mountain goat, there's not much to see.

Pan doesn't serve Eligos out of love or loyalty. In this, we are merely united against a common enemy. The court of the continent might have been broken and its power dissolved, but it is still a nuisance trying to jab at us from afar.

"Who is this changeling?" Eligos asks.

"He called himself a forerunner." Pan holds out a silver fairy band. "This trinket is newly made, which means—"

"One of Oberon's brood?"

"Fuck," I mutter.

How long since his death? And he's still plaguing us?

We demons might have scarred the earth, but the fae cannot act as though their crimes are not worse. Just older and easier to forget thanks to their god's favor.

"Yes. One of them is a smelter," Pan says.

That's not good.

"What has he said?" I ask.

Pan shrugs. "Not much. My tricks don't work on him. He is the first one to approach me, not the other way around."

"I see," Eligos mutters. "Once we're done here, move. I don't want them sending anyone after you."

Pan snorts and we both know he will do as he pleases. It's a sign of just how unsettled Eligos is that he didn't pick his words with more care.

I push my sleeves up. "Let's see what secrets I can draw out of him..."

Everyone has a weakness, and my gift is exploiting that.

LIORIA

I stare at the altar in the foyer of the women's boarding house. The altar here is nothing fancy, just a pressed metal depiction of the host of gods, goddesses, and deities leaping into the clouds as they head off to face the menacing, nebulous threat.

I've grown up on this story.

Thousands of years ago, our world was under siege by something new. Something with ill intent. Back then, our gods and goddesses were locked in an eternal conflict between themselves, pitting their followers against each other. But when an outside force threatened the whole of humanity? The gods and goddesses put their difference aside, banded together, and went to go protect us. In their stead, the Demon Lords were charged with shepherding humanity.

I'd always imagined the Demon Lords as these powerful demigods, with auras that would make all knees weak. Listening to them bicker last night, they appeared so very human.

I heft the bundle of my belongings and turn toward the door without offering up my morning prayer for the first time since I got so sick I couldn't get out of bed last year. I've always been a poor devotee to our gods, and that guilt has made me question myself. After the last twelve hours, I don't know that I care about the war anymore. For all we know, the gods abandoned us and the High Demon Lords are the closest thing to deities we have now.

Today, the gods have abandoned me.

The boarding house is quiet. I barely slept at all last night. There were girls up and down the hall chattering about all the handsome gentlemen at the inn and the mysterious couple from the continent. A number of times I almost admitted my fate to the others, but in the end, I said nothing. I don't know how to tell any of them what's happening to me. I should be afraid, but I am clinging to my rage.

Overhead, the sky is overcast and gray. I trudge to the Silver Roo without haste. There's no one around the courtyard, which isn't surprising.

I set my bundle down on an empty keg, then circle around to where I last saw Malka. The canvas looks undisturbed, and I hold my breath as a draw the fabric back.

The space is empty save for the mug I brought her last night.

I blow my held breath, relieved that at least one of us is escaping.

Wherever Malka ends up, I hope she gets to decide her own fate.

I trudge back around to my things and into the kitchen.

Kirra whirls from the central island where she's kneading dough. The light is behind her, throwing her dark face into shadow so I can't discern her expression.

Does she know?

I stand there with a lump lodged in my throat while Kirra and I stare at each other. Then, with a choked sob, she throws herself at me. I drop the bundle with a grunt as she barrels into me and crushes me to her chest with strong arms. My body trembles and I lay my head on her shoulder.

We don't speak. We stand there for long moments, both our bodies shuddering with silent sobs.

"What will you do?" she whispers and steps back as suddenly as she embraced me.

I sway on my feet and brace a hand against the counter. "I guess I'll find out when I get there."

Kirra stares at me for a long moment. "You could go to the continent."

"Yes. I could." I grimace. "I'm too scared to go there. Too much talk of war. Too many people coming here to escape what's going on over there."

"Head inland." Kirra grabs my hand. "Find one of the refugee settlements…"

I stare at her. Does she know the gentlemen are not just lords, but High Demon Lords?

There is nowhere I may flee that they would not find me if they so desired. The gods supposedly gave them dominion over the earth and everything on it. That includes me.

"No. I won't bring this attention on them." I'm hiding behind an honorable argument, but the truth is I can't see a way to escape. Not if half the stories are true.

Our lords are benevolent, but they have also been violent. For all the peace and amenities we enjoy in Eden, I cannot forget that there is another history behind our lords that is not so kind. It will not be me who alerts them to the presence of refugee settlements.

Kirra clutches my hands. "Let me make you something, then. Something special for the road?"

"I'd like that."

"That red-headed one asked if I was interested in a job. I told him no before I heard..."

I chuckle. "You wouldn't want to cook for just one lord. You'd get bored."

She lifts her shoulders. "This place won't be the same without you."

"Mistress will do a lot less yelling..."

"Or just yell at me." Kirra rolls her eyes and turns back to her dough. "When do you leave?"

"I don't know. Last night is a blur..." I pause and look around the kitchen before chuckling bitterly. "I don't work here anymore."

"Well, I'll not kick you out of my kitchen. And I won't have you working, either. Pull up that stool and talk to me?"

At first, the conversation is stilted. Neither of us knows what to say. But after a little tea, our tongues loosen. We laugh until my sides hurt and I squeeze tears out of the corners of my eyes. She makes a whole dozen of those little pies, this time with jam, since she's out of the candied lemons.

I'm, enjoying the scents of the Silver Roo when the door leading to the tavern swings open. We both turn. I'm expecting Mistress Claridieu.

But it's not the mistress standing in the doorway.

It's Oriax.

He stares down his nose at me with cool disdain. Like I'm a bug that offends him. He's wearing a sapphire blue robe that glimmers when he moves. It isn't belted very tight, and as he breathes, the front gapes open, revealing a long strip of bronzed flesh. His long hair is loose, hanging down his back in a shimmery wave. Regardless that this is not his kitchen, he stalks across to me and plants his hand on the table, leaning down until our faces are inches from each other.

"Change your mind, and come with me," he says.

Stunned, I stare at him. His words and demeanor do not align.

He lifts a hand to tip my chin up. "Your gifts will be wasted on those two. They only want you to spite me."

"Excuse me, sir." Kirra plants her hands on her hips and glares at the interloper. "Guests are not permitted in my kitchen."

His voice lowers, taking on a sensual edge. "Come with me, and I will unlock your potential. You could do great, important work with me."

There is something seductive about him. He's gorgeous. And he is a Demon Lord with ulterior motives. If it weren't for his interest, I wouldn't have to pick up my life and move. He is right about one thing. Ultimately the choice of where I go is up to me.

I can lay the blame at his feet for now, and that makes it easier to twist my anger around myself like a shield.

"Sir?" Kirra stalks around the table. "Sir, I really must ask you to—ah!"

Oriax doesn't take his eyes off me. He holds up his hand and I see Kirra's arms waving frantically. It takes effort, but I tear my gaze from Oriax and gape at Kirra. She's standing with her back to the strip of exposed stone between the hearth and workspace. Her elbows are extended on either side of her, while her forearms flap about. Her eyes bulge and her jaw is forced open as if on a scream, but no sound is coming from her.

"Please, sir—don't," I squeak out.

This is all because of me. Because—

The tavern door bangs open and I'm blinded momentarily. I scramble back off the stool as something heavy drops to the ground. I hear a pained grunt right before a crash of pottery.

I blink away the brilliant splotches of light.

Oriax is on the ground, easily a dozen broken mugs lying on the floor, and poised over him is Belial. The light coming through the open windows glints off his red hair, making it blaze.

And he is not alone.

Eligos stands just inside the door, and I swear I see a faint purple and black aura around him as he glares at Oriax.

Kirra!

She's not against the wall. I glance about and spy her down on the ground, poking her head around the central island at the tableau taking place in the kitchen.

"Oriax, do you dare poach what is ours?" Eligos' voice is not human. It seems to vibrate with power.

I *belong* to them now, do I?

My temper flares, but I hold my tongue.

"Can't you do anything else?" Oriax sneers up at Belial. "Or are you only good with your fists now?"

Belial grabs the front of Oriax's robe and shakes him. "I didn't want to fuck up your pretty face beyond repair."

Eligos takes three steps and kneels next to Belial. They aim twin expressions of barely controlled rage at the other Demon Lord. "Back the fuck off."

They stay like that for several moments. Despite my own anger, my body trembles. I can hardly breathe. If they get angry, if they begin to fight, they could wipe this whole region off the face of the planet. We'd all be dead.

Kirra waves at me, beckoning me to the relative safety behind the island, but I don't budge. If anything happens, I don't want her to be a target. If I can throw myself at their mercy to stop this, I will. I don't understand why my trick with artifacts is so valuable.

"Fine." Oriax holds his hands up and turns his head to look at me. "But should you ever desire a change of pace, I am but a letter away."

Belial growls and lifts Oriax off the ground nearly a foot by his robe. "Shut up, you silver-tongued devil."

Oriax's head falls back and laughs. "So predictable, Belial. I haven't harmed your treat. Do you *really* want to fight me here and now? Do you think you're up to it?"

"Do you *really* want to take on two of us at once?" Eligos counters. His tone is haughty and cold.

It drives home to me that these men are not human. They are demons and they have dominion over all. They did not have to ask for my contract last night. These immortal, all-powerful creatures have lowered themselves to mundane labor negotiations.

Why?

None of this makes sense.

"Stop. Please? All of you," I say.

Three sets of eyes turn on me. Not a one of their eyes are rounded and human. Their pupils have become slits, the rest of their eyes a vibrant color.

Eligos' are a deep purple, so deep the slit of black is almost imperceptible.

Oriax's eyes are a brilliant green, with the black slit seeming to suck everything into it.

And Belial's are a coppery red, almost orange that threatens to overpower the blackness dividing them.

Belial leans in closer until he's almost nose to cheek with Oriax and says, "She is decided for us. Not you."

Oriax sighs. It's a long-suffering sound, as if he's accustomed to being put out by these two. "Yes, yes, I heard. Will you get off me?"

Eligos reaches out and grips Belial's shoulder. They don't do anything. At least nothing I can see, but they seem to shrink a slight degree. The tense atmosphere in the kitchen dissipates and I can breathe again.

Eligos waves at the broken mugs. "And clean this up. It's not fair to force others to fix your messes."

Oriax makes a disgusted sound in the back of his throat. He flicks his fingers and—is something under his robe glowing green?

The pieces of the shattered mugs rise from the ground.

The tavern door swings open and Mistress Claridieu stands there gaping.

We all watch as piece by piece, the dozen or so mugs are put back together, right down to the fine dust between the cracks. They float to a stretch of empty tabletop and I continue to stare as if they might break out in a jig.

"There. Happy?" Oriax asks.

Eligos or Belial grunt by way of an answer.

"Very well. I'll be leaving shortly." Oriax glances over his shoulder at me. "Expect my letter, treat."

Mistress Claridieu moves out of his way, and then it's the five of us.

"Shit," Kirra mutters and hustles over to the oven to rescue the pastries.

Belial is at her side in an instant, peering at the baking sheet with her while Mistress Claridieu takes it all in with wide eyes. I feel Eligos watching me. Unlike Oriax, who appears to have just risen, Eligos is dressed in boots, breeches, and a long coat, as if he's ready to leave. I am acutely aware of him as he crosses the kitchen to my side.

My future is no longer my own. Like it or not, I belong to them now.

"I'm sorry we scared you," he says in a voice for me alone.

"Better get used to it," I mumble.

This will happen again. Maybe not this same conflict, but I imagine I will see more behavior like this between the lords if I am to work for them. I can't imagine that I will be able to take up some out-of-the-way job. I draw in a steadying breath and steel myself to meet his gaze.

"I'm fine. Thank you for your concern, my lord." I add a little curtsey, though it seems silly to stand on such formality.

"Not for you!" Kirra snaps, followed by a loud thwack.

My eyes go wide and I whip my head around to stare at Belial, shaking his hand and recoiling from Kirra.

She shakes her finger under Belial's nose. "This is not your kitchen. You can't just take what you want. You're already stealing my best friend from me. I won't let you take anything else."

"Belial?" Eligos calls out.

Belial wisely retreats to join us on the other side of the island.

"I just wanted a taste," he mutters under his breath.

I'm still gaping at him. Just a few moments ago, he was about to throw down with another Demon Lord. Now he's pouting because a cook smacked his hand? What on earth am I getting involved with? And what was Kirra thinking?

Eligos trails his fingers down my arm and I shiver. They're both standing so close they tower over me. There's a tightness slowly knotting up my muscles, causing my panic to rise the longer they remain intent on me. And yet, despite their heavy-lidded gazes that speak of desire, I feel something else from them. It's more like...

I struggle to find the word.

Comfort.

Their nearness makes it feel as though everything will be okay. Which is not at all reflective of reality. I highly doubt I will come out of this unscathed.

"We intend to leave soon," Eligos says.

I sway slightly on my feet, and Belial places a steadying hand on my shoulder. Eligos' fingers are still on my wrist and I'm more aware of those two places of my body than anything in my whole life. It's as though something inside of me is reaching for them. Magic? Is this what makes me different? This ability inside of me?

It's hard to wrestle my brain into focus.

"I'm ready," I say in a husky tone, and it sounds as though we're having a much different conversation.

"Good." Eligos' fingers drift up then down. "After you've said your goodbyes, the carriage will be waiting."

The pair of them turn and exit back into the tavern.

The door swings on well-oiled hinges several times, giving us diminishing glances of the lord's backsides.

Kirra and I both let out a breath.

Mistress Claridieu rushes forward and grips my shoulders. I don't know if I can handle more today, but I look up at her worry-lined face.

"I'm sorry," she whispers. "I'm so sorry. I didn't know. I had no idea it would lead to this."

Kirra circles the island to stand with us, her quiet solidarity welcomed. I'll miss her. So much.

My anger is a weakly flickering candle, but I bear no ill-will to my mistress. I take her hands and squeeze them in mine.

"I know," I whisper. "None of this is your fault. With any luck, they'll bore of me quickly and I can simply come home. Though you won't need me by then."

"You'll always have a place here," Mistress Claridieu vows, and it stops my heart.

All this time I saw myself as apart from the others. She pulls me in for a tight squeeze.

I meet Kirra's gaze finally.

"This is it, yeah?" Kirra mutters. "Time to get going? With them? After that shit show?"

I wipe at my eyes. "Yes."

Kirra grabs a rag and mops up her face while she stares at the floor. Has she realized who they are yet?

"Better take some tea with you," Mistress Claridieu says.

Kirra's brow furrows. "What? You don't think they drink tea anywhere else?"

Mistress Claridieu shakes her head. "Not like our tea, they don't."

Kirra rushes to the large tin sitting on the counter. She doesn't open it, just turns and thrusts it at me. "There's more in the storage room and I've been saying for ages I need a container that opens easier. Damn thing is going to stick on you, so keep something around to wedge it open. You'll need at least two strong pots a day to deal with those two. This should be enough to get you through two months at least, maybe three, if you're careful."

"You know I'm not. I'm greedy."

"Course you are," Kirra mutters.

I glance between the two women.

"Thank you. Thank you both," I whisper. "I haven't told anyone. I don't know what to say."

"What can you say?" Mistress Claridieu whispers, earning a glare from Kirra. "Go. Go now."

I nod.

"Someday one of you will tell me what the hell is going on," Kirra muttered.

"Someday," I say softly and hug the huge tin to my chest.

"Let me bundle up your food, then get on the road."

I drag my feet every step of the way. Kirra has to march me through the tavern and out the front door.

Three carriages are in the process of being loaded. My two gentlemen are standing next to a honey-colored one with gold scrollwork along the exterior pulled by a team of four chestnut horses. There are footmen bustling about wearing honey-colored jackets with sweat pouring off them. A little distance away are mounted soldiers that match the footmen, no doubt the Demon Lord's guards.

Belial sees us first. Now that the drama in the kitchen has played out, he looks tired. Dark circles stand out on his creamy skin. A slow smile spreads across his face, banishing the weariness and for a moment the events of the last day are wiped away. I'm back in that first moment when I didn't know who he was. My body warms and my heart begins to beat faster.

He crosses the distance between us, that connection never breaking. My knees are weak as I look up at him with that hungry gaze aimed so blatantly at me. Even their men must think I'm a trophy being collected.

That thought brings me back to my senses.

I don't know what I've gotten myself into, but I can't imagine I will come out of this unscathed.

I hug the tin and my bundle of things to my chest. Not that they're much protection.

He takes the bundle and holds it out. A footman rushes over and grabs it like it's some precious cargo.

"Are you ready?" Belial asks, and holds out his hand for mine.

I glance from his hand to Kirra, but her face is stony.

She gives me the bundle of pastries, but glares at the Demon Lord. "Those are for her, not your bottomless stomach."

I've never loved her more than I do right now, and I will miss her.

With a nod, she turns and walks away without another glance.

Best friend.

I always liked Kirra. I'd have enjoyed spending more time with her had I known the fondness was mutual. I will miss her and all the rest.

Belial turns and presses his hand to my lower back. My body seems determined to betray me. The warmth stirring inside me is hard to ignore, but I cannot lose my wits. For once in my life, I need to think things through. This man is now my boss. That changes everything. I might be reckless and foolhardy, but I am not stupid. Bedding either Belial or Eligos spells nothing but disaster for me. I cannot give into these feelings. For my own safety and the benefit of the future I still want, I cannot fall into their beds.

Women bedded by Demon Lords have, in the past, been treated like a commodity, even being sold off. That practice has been outlawed, but that doesn't mean it has stopped happening. And that's only for a fuck that doesn't result in a bun in the oven. If that woman becomes pregnant? Her whole life changes. We're required to learn the basics in school. They indoctrinate us young to value lineage because that's what ties some to the Demon Lords. It's how they can track who might or might not have a Demon Lord for a baby. Were I to carry one of their children, I'd be taken care of for the rest of my life. But that's a cage of sorts, and I'm not interested in being locked up. I want my freedom.

"I'm sorry in advance," Belial says.

I frown. "Why?"

He leans in close. "Eligos' feet reek."

"I'm sorry...?"

He sighs and leans in closer. "He's going to insist on taking his boots off once we get on the road. Help me convince him not to?"

Oh, my word. Is this what my life is now?

Eligos opens the carriage door and holds out his hand to me. As if he—the High Demon Lord—intends to help me—the common serving girl—into the carriage. I stop, still staring at his hand.

"I'll hold the tin," Belial says, as if my concern is what I'm carrying and not the absurdity of it all.

He lifts the tea tin out of my hands while Eligos continues to stand there, hand out. He's pulled his locs up into a chaotic yet regal fan atop his head and the top few buttons of his shirt are already undone.

"I-I'll sit up top," I say, not terribly keen on being in such close quarters with them.

Eligos smiles. It's as if he knows what I'm thinking. "Nonsense. There's no room, anyway."

Belial's breath warms my neck, and he speaks almost directly into my ear. "We'll make far better company, my lady."

His lady? Is he mocking me?

My mind and body are not at all in unison. One is screaming at me to use my better sense, while the other wants to throw all caution to the wind. Instead, I allow my new employer to help me into the carriage. I sit with my back toward the driver. The carriage is not a large space and my heart begins to hammer in my chest as Eligos, followed by Belial, climb in and sit across from me.

"H-how far are we going?" I ask.

Eligos winks at me. "It's not a question of how far, but how fast."

The carriage lurches forward. Belial braces his hand against the window and scowls out, but the horses hit their stride. The thunder of hooves surrounds us as four guards join us, two on either side.

Suncrest is rapidly racing away from us and my eyes are glued to the window, watching all the familiar sights fly past.

"Have you ever left Suncrest?" Eligos asks softly.

"No," I whisper.

I've only ever been a few miles out of town to visit the home of friends. It feels as though a tether in me is stretching tight. We pass through the gates and the land opens up on either side of the carriage. Carefully tended plots of land are clustered close together. Community gardens. Families rent the space to grow what food they can. Soon enough, even that's gone.

Belial has his legs stretched out on one side of me, his feet braced against the bottom of the bench. His boots are beautifully tooled leather that lace all the way up. He's chosen dark colors for travel. Charcoal pants, a creamy shirt, some sort of black undercoat stitched with a russet red. His gray jacket is unbuttoned and already suffering from the travel. It'll be creased and wrinkled before long. I suppose it might be my job to sort that out later.

Come to think of it, I don't actually know what I am to do for them.

I glance at Eligos. His feet are on the cushion next to me—boots on—and reclined as if he is going to sleep at any moment. But I don't believe this act. I've seen him at rest, and this is not it. This is a carefully curated picture of ease that is supported by his mismatched and wrinkled clothing.

There are lines on both their faces that weren't there yesterday. Some new concern? A topic during the meeting I hadn't heard?

"Now that you have me, what is it I'm supposed to do?" I ask. I'm not brave enough to be any bolder. I'm not sure I want the truth.

Belial glances at Eligos, who lifts a shoulder.

"What do you want to do?" Belial counters.

I pause and consider how to respond, but there isn't anything to say save the truth. "What I want to do has ceased to matter."

"Not necessarily." Eligos cracks an eye open and looks at me. "You were wasted there. Think of the opportunities."

My temper flares. It's probably my grief and fear speaking, but at that moment I feel like an inferno has been lit inside of me. I shouldn't speak, but when has that stopped me?

"I was happy," I say. Who is to say I will thrive at our destination? "Is all of this really to save me from Oriax? Lord Oriax?"

Shit. Do I call him High Lord? High Demon Lord? I don't know the proper words.

Belial wrinkles his nose. "You can call him fuck face for all I care. We don't stand on ceremony in private."

Eligos chuckles while I stare at him.

The silence draws on, becoming tense, probably because I find no humor in this.

"It had nothing to do with Oriax in the beginning." Eligos tugs at the topmost button of his shirt and grimaces. "Most people try our patience. You did not."

I wait, but he does not continue. I look from Eligos to Belial and back.

They're serious.

These two have completely uprooted my life because I'm not annoying?

"Then I'm to simply exist in your orbit and not annoy you?" My frustration is leaking through. If they've acquired my services to fuck me, the least they could do is be honest about it.

Belial grins at me. It's such an open, honest expression that's so very difficult to merge with the knowledge that he is also a Demon Lord. "You could entertain us?"

"Oh, I'm an entertainer now? Should I dance a jig and make you laugh? Maybe shatter your eardrums trying to carry a tune?"

Eligos snorts and runs his fingers through Belial's hair. "I believe my love had a different kind of entertainment in mind..."

Belial leans into the touch. He makes me think of an over-eager puppy, only this one has jaws that could bite the world in half.

I might be a flirt and a light skirt at times, but I am not stupid. Were they mortal men, I'd say yes, enjoy myself, and be done. But they are not men. They are demons. Entangling myself with these two will do nothing but endanger myself. And speaking of danger...

"Do you think someone is still trying to kill the High Lords?"

"How much did you hear?" Belial asks.

"Not much. I did what I could to hear as little as possible, but some of you are very loud."

Eligos grimaces. "Shax."

The two gentlemen share a look. Eligos shrugs then Belial does this little head wiggle.

"Do you two not communicate like us mortals?" I ask.

Eligos chuckles and grins at me. His white teeth flash in the dim interior and for a moment, I stop breathing. He's beautiful in a way that seems to stop time.

"When you've known each other for as long as we have..." Belial drapes his arm around Eligos' shoulders. "You don't always need words."

He shifts to lean against Belial. They make a lovely study of opposites; Belial's strength to Eligos' grace. "You are aware that our last death was sudden?"

"You were all killed while attending a joint, closed meeting in the capital. No one knows who did it." Though everyone has a theory. I've heard them all over ale.

He nods. "There is division between the seven of us about how to act. We've spent the last fifteen years fixing what happened in the interim. Now, some want answers, while others are looking forward or nurturing their own interests."

Belial shifts about before drawing his arm back. "And then there's Shax, who wants us to all return to the city and sit in council. Such a fucking bore."

Eligos rolls his eyes. "That has more to do with his eternal conflict with Alastor."

Councils and city and personal interests are nebulous things that I don't grasp, even if they define my life under their rule. But as I listen, I come to one conclusion: the High Demon Lords bicker like children. Like brothers.

This morning's incident in the kitchen feels less dire when viewed in that light.

I unwrap the parcel of pastries as my stomach wakes up. As I pop one in my mouth I glance out the window to find the scenery racing past at a sickening pace.

"What is it? What's wrong?" Belial asks, leaning forward.

Eligos sighs. "She just noticed that we're traveling faster."

I hurriedly chew and swallow the pastry to peer out the window. Except my stomach lurches, and the world seems to spin.

"It's a spell that folds the ground under your feet," Eligos explains.

I watch the ground fly past under the guards' horses' hooves in a blur.

"I've never seen anything like this," I mutter.

I also think I'm going to be sick.

Looking straight ahead eases the discomfort.

Belial stretches his arms up, but the jacket stops him level with his shoulders. Frowning, he tugs at the buttons, popping one off, then shrugs out of the coat. When neither of them reach to retrieve the button, I bend forward and grab it.

"You'll see more like it, too," he says and tosses the jacket onto the bench next to me before folding his hands behind his head.

Honestly, they do act a bit like children. It's hard to be afraid of them now that I see them as bickering brothers.

"Tell us about yourself, Lioria."

"There isn't much to tell."

"Did you know your parents at all?"

"No. No, nothing is recorded about my birth. The only thing that was noted was that I was found with their bodies and no identification. The theory is that they came to town looking for medical care. But it's only a theory. There were three baby girls orphaned at the same time. This could be their story and I was simply abandoned. What about your parents? Or do you even consider them parents?"

Belial tilts his head.

"It's different for each of us," Eligos says. "This time around, I was born into a holding family. They knew the time of the birth closely coincided with our death, so chances were high I wouldn't be their child."

Holding families were the children of Demon Lords. Their lineage was carefully maintained, intermarrying with other families to increase the likelihood of producing another Demon Lord down the line.

"My family had no idea." Belial grimaces. "Came as quite a shock to them. In all fairness, they hadn't wanted another child either."

"Am I allowed to ask how that went? What happened?" My curiosity is getting the best of me, which no doubt will improve my mood. Besides, what else are we supposed to do to pass the time?

"For holding families, it's all very routine," Eligos explains. "Established holding families often practice communal living and pass babies around, sharing in the care until the fifth year when the first signs of demonic awareness happen. I presented on my fifth birthday and I was then put in the care of my staff."

I nod, understanding this better.

Each Demon Lord maintains a household that transcends lifetimes. What that entails or means in practice, I haven't the slightest idea.

My heart aches for a young Eligos, never allowed to be a child. "That... It sounds lonely..."

He smiles softly at me. "Not as much as you'd think. You cannot imagine us as children as you know them. We are—at best—foreign creatures amongst your kind when we are young. Our bodies know what we are before our minds do. Some mothers have claimed to know the babe in their womb was not human."

That's impossible, though an interesting story. Everyone knows, thanks to those like Malka, that a spirit does not inhabit a body until the first breathe.

Belial leans forward and grins. "I presented while I was trying to steal some apples."

I narrow my gaze. "What does presenting mean?"

They both shrug.

"When we present our demonic power. There's usually something that creates a heightened emotional response. Falling out of a tree, for example. It's different every time," Eligos says. "This time I was excited about...something. A purple aura enveloped me, and my hair changed color. It's never turned back."

"I tore a tree limb off. A whole limb. Clean off." Belial chuckles and shakes his head. "I didn't tell anyone until I was seven. I wasn't ready. And, it had been so long since I was born into anything but a holding family, I wanted to have a normal life for a moment, with all the chaos that family brings."

"Whereas I could not wait for peace and quiet."

They share a glance, something only they understand, and I suddenly feel like I'm getting a window into something special. I'd like to find someone who will be fond of me, maybe smile at me the way these two smile at each other.

I will never aspire to love. I covet it, but I've never dared hope for it.

"How were you two reunited?" I ask. "Let me guess? It depends?"

Belial nods. "In my case, my family fell on hard times. They needed the money badly, so I wrote a letter to my household. Had them come get me and deliver the Lords' Sum to my family. I told them over family dinner one night."

"Do you still speak to them?"

He shakes his head and his brow creases with sadness. "No, it was... messy."

Eligos runs his fingers along Belial's neck in comfort. I move my fingers under the cloth, as if it's me offering that comfort instead.

"It was business for mine," Eligos says. "I wasn't attached to anyone, and the way I was raised, no one was attached to me, either. Very neat process."

It all sounds so sad to me and I quietly mourn for the children they were. Even if they weren't children as I knew, they had a youth they never got to enjoy or experience.

Belial leans toward me now, eyes narrowed. "I see what you did there, my lady. You got us talking."

"She's a crafty one, isn't she?" Eligos mutters. "What was your education like in Suncrest?"

I shrug. "I can read and write. I know a little history and magic. That's about it."

Eligos perks up. "You can read and write?"

"Well, yes. Or did you think we were all ignorant country folk?"

He waves his hand. "No, no. That's not what I meant. We've seen an overall decrease in literacy since the plague. So many died. Children had to work to feed themselves. In most areas, the rules about attending school were relaxed. It was actually surprising to hear that wasn't the case in Suncrest."

How I wish that had been the case. I could have skipped so many boring lessons. "We weren't allowed. They used to scold us and say that the High Demon Lords would be so sad."

Eligos' gaze narrows. "Would we now? And what did you do?"

I grin at him. "I skipped when I could."

"Of course you did."

"It didn't do me much good. I got sent to the library to read."

Belial slaps Eligos' thigh suddenly. "That's it. She's our secretary now."

He stares at Belial, eyes gone wide and glinting gold. "That might be the most brilliant thing you've ever said..."

Both men turn to stare at me with wide smiles that leave my insides a little warm.

There's something wrong with me. Seriously wrong if I can be both furious and attracted to both of these men. Honestly, I have no shame.

"What do you say, Lioria?" Eligos' smile is teasing and I get the sense that there is a layered meaning I don't understand. "Think you can keep the two of us in line?"

"It sounds to me like no one can."

Belial throws his head back and laughs.

I can't look away from Eligos. One side of his mouth is hitched up, giving him a mischievous glint.

"You know us so well already," he says.

"I have a question." I clench my hands under the cover of the cloth. This is my life. "Do you intend to fuck me against my will?"

Belial's green eyes flutter wide while Eligos smirks.

"That all depends on you," he drawls.

Belial shifts in what I might call discomfort.

Time to draw my line in the sand and pray my contract will protect me. "Like I said yesterday, being an orphan allows me more freedom than others. I'm not looking to trade that freedom."

Eligos' relaxed posture hasn't changed, but apart from our little contract negotiation last night, this is the most interested he's sounded. "Even if you're taken care of in luxury for the rest of your life?"

"What good is a pretty cage? And that's not the point. I asked a direct question, and you're trying to divert me."

He spreads his hands. "I'm merely pointing out benefits. But, if you want a direct answer... No. I do not intend to fuck you against your will. Unless you ask me to. My demon likes the struggle. Bel?"

Belial clears his throat and darts a glance at me then Eligos. Unlike Eligos, Belial appears concerned.

He clears his throat then tugs at his shirt. "The key word is intend. We can intend all sorts of things, but when our demon side takes control..."

That gives me another question in a way. "Would you have fucked me at the inn without telling me who you were?"

"Yes," Eligos says without hesitation. "And afterward, I'd have given you a choice. Remain where you are, or come with us. You're only taught part of the process, my dear. There's always room to bend the rules, if we want something bad enough."

He's staring at me again like he can peel my clothes off. My body is intensely aware of his admiration, but my mind feels detached. Clear, somehow.

"What aren't you telling me? I'm nothing special. At best, I'm average looking. I'm difficult and stubborn. So why?"

Belial shrugs. "I don't think any of us can answer that. Sometimes our demons recognize something in someone our human part can't. It could be that your spirit was once someone we knew in another lifetime. Someone who was important to all of us. Could be nothing to do with you at all. There's not a nice, neat answer."

"You see past the rat race," Eligos says.

"Rat... Race?" I tilt my head to the side. "What...?"

He waves his hand. "Words from another lifetime. You've chosen to step outside our social structure and forge your own path. I admire that. I envy that, if I'm honest. Maybe I hope some of it will rub off on me if I rub on you?"

I huff a little at his cheeky question.

"You said no," Belial says softly. "People don't often have the ability to say no to me. And then you made me laugh."

Is he trying to say that he knew I was interested in sex? And still said no?

Now that we've begun, I don't know what to say. Neither of them have come out and said it, but it's clear their relationship is more than friends or brethren.

Eligos claims the rules may be bent, but I don't think I should trust them.

"She's going to say no again," Belial says softly.

"I know." Eligos' eyes are glittering gold. "It's catnip."

Belial nods slowly as his gaze rises to meet mine. "And that's the problem. My human mouth can promise one thing that my demon side has no intention of honoring. What I want and promise are, in the end, meaningless. The simple fact is that you are of interest to both aspects of our being. Human and demon."

I'm regretting this conversation.

Hiding behind ignorance was better.

Is he telling me it's simply a matter of time? That my decision means nothing?

No, it's better to know.

He leans forward and wraps his massive hand around my wrist.

"What are you—"

Belial plucks an object out of his pocket. It looks like a child's bracelet. "This is another fairy device. Vodu."

"Oh, good idea," Eligos says.

Belial slides the silver hoop onto my left ring finger. I'm frozen, my thoughts sluggish, which is why I don't object. He says a word, and the hoop begins to shrink. The band becomes thicker until it hugs my finger perfectly.

He leans back with a grin. "There."

"That ring?" Eligos flicks his fingers at the jewelry now wrapped around my finger. "That only works if you have very fine control, or are frightened."

"What does it do?"

"It creates a barrier, much like the one you did last night. Only this one is physical, and has been proven to work against demons."

I stare at the ring for several, long moments. What will my choice ultimately be?

BELIAL

Darkness covers the grounds. I should be exhausted after the last few days of travel, dealing with my brethren, and spending the entirety of last night interrogating the changeling. Instead, I can't seem to occupy one spot for longer than a few moments. Not since we departed the carriage.

"You're still up?"

I turn as Eligos stalks into my bedchamber.

"You ever think it's odd how our speaking and thought patterns mirror current times?" I ask.

"It's conditioning. The first years we spend around humans acclimates us." He flops down on an armchair and sighs. He's barefoot in just breeches and an untucked shirt that's being held together by two brave buttons. His hair is bound up with a strip of satin cloth, as if he'd thought about sleep, then stopped.

"Surprised you're still awake."

Eligos grimaces, then pushes to his feet and stalks across to stand beside me, as if it's the best spot to admire the darkness.

"I thought we'd get some answers," he mutters.

I grunt.

It is concerning that our wasteland search yielded nothing. The changeling only told us that the forerunners are here. That they're waiting to herald change.

In advance of what?

We've held off a conflict with the continent for hundreds of years. Will the Vodu and Yokai continue to press us?

There's no official harbormaster in Suncrest by design. We're still stretched too thin, simply fixing the last thirty years. With the war on the continent ramping up, we don't have the resources to streamline welcoming refugees to Eden. So we haven't bothered. Each week, we get a rough estimation of how many and from where, but they aren't concrete numbers.

The wards along the coast make it more difficult for Yokai and Vodu to come ashore undetected, but it happens. Not with any great regularity. And usually, the Yokai or Vodu in question are seeking refuge of their own. Over the years, the seven of us have taken in dozens of magical beings. Some remain, while others move on. They're free to live here, so long as they respect our rules and the history we've given the people here. There are people among the refugees who resent our take on history, but for the most part, they are willing to hold their tongues and keep the peace they risked their lives for. Eventually, we will have to do something more formal, but for now, this is enough.

Eden is this perfect little bubble. Or at least we try to make it so. Of course, merchants and travelers bring in their version of history, but it has never caught on. It bothers me sometimes that our people are so easily led by our deception.

If it makes their lives easier, is it okay?

It's the same question I ask myself each reincarnation cycle. I have never found an answer that settles me. With each passing lifetime, we are more human, and accepting our past wrongs becomes harder.

Which brings me to now, and what we've already done.

"Did we make the right decision?" I ask.

Eligos grunts.

The plan was simple and elegant. Entice Lioria to join our joint household and let things progress as naturally as possible. Of course, she had other ideas.

My demon side isn't thrilled with how today went. That part of me wants to gorge on her sex, willing or not. The human part of me is more optimistic. Lioria might be practical, but she has a hedonistic side that calls to me. I'm much more certain that in time she will come to us of her own free will.

Oriax complicated matters. I don't think the others are aware of this conflict between the three of us. The only reason Eligos or I realized what had been put into motion was because we, too, were stealing glances at the woman.

Eligos props his chin on my shoulder. "It's better if she hates us than if she were left up to Oriax's schemes."

"He's different..."

"He's scared. We all are."

"I'm not frightened."

He snorts. "Of course, you aren't. You're either too dumb or too brave for fear."

We're quiet for a moment.

Eligos doesn't come to me for physical contact often. He says I'm all muscle and a poor bedfellow, but I've needed this contact. His presence calms me, but at my core, I'm still unsettled.

"She hates us," I whisper.

"I don't think so. She's angry at times, that much is certain. We might be easy targets right now, but in the end, our motives were in her best interests. Besides, she does like us. Good thinking with that ring, by the way."

"You think so?"

"It serves a much greater purpose on her finger than in a safe somewhere."

"You really think Oriax would do something to her?"

Eligos shrugs and slides his arm around my waist. "I think we are at the end of an era that has lasted too long, but no demon wants to hear that. Earth was always intended for man."

He has a point there. We demons are refugees. Our world was taken from us, and this was the only place we had to go. And look how well we've fucked it up. The dissenters we're hunting might be the good guys in this conflict.

Millions of lifetimes could never fix what we've done.

"She did share her pastry with you," Eligos whispers.

I smile, but I don't hope. I can't.

"How much do we tell her?" he asks.

I glance at Eligos. "How much will we trust her?"

"If she's going to be our secretary, she'll eventually know everything. Well, almost everything..."

This plan was simpler when it was just about sex.

Eligos takes two steps before flinging himself down on the window seat. "Have you paused to wonder why are we both so fixated on her? Why our demons are waking up? Could we be playing into a scheme? What about her is so special? Or do we merely recognize her spirit?"

I hate him for voicing the question I've been wondering myself. It's all too coincidental.

"I don't know," I mutter.

He's leading me to an answer I already know. Or at least a solution. But I don't like it. If all of this is just the randomness of the universe, I can't see how this plan will make Lioria trust us.

Eligos is quiet. He's leaving me to come to the conclusion on my own.

Most people see Eligos as a lazy idiot. He's put a lot of work into crafting this image. Lifetimes. As a sloth demon, it's what is expected. But behind all of that is an intelligent, crafty man who stole my heart. Granted, I didn't put up much of a fight. This life we've built this time around has fallen together so perfectly that I have to wonder, could this be the universe rewarding us? Have we finally tipped the scales? Could Lioria be just what she seems? A lovely woman who could round out the end of our lives? Or is she something else?

I won't be the one to see it, and that frustrates me.

"We have to bond her," I say into the silence.

Eligos says nothing, because he's already accepted it as a matter of fact.

"What if she says no?"

He tips his head back and looks at me. "She won't."

"How are you so certain?"

He smiles and his eyes glint a stunning gold. "Because our little light skirt is a curious kitten. It's all in how we present it, Belial."

This lifetime is special. Eligos and I have been close in every life we've lived. We've loved before, but this is the first time we've come together so seamlessly. Which has made our mutual lack of sexual interest an ever-present problem. I want Eligos to be happy. I want to satisfy him. And yet I cannot.

Everything in me wants to give us this one chance at complete happiness. So many lifetimes have been spent locked in one conflict or another. This world might never know peace, but is it too much to ask that for one lifespan we can be happy?

I sit on the bench and draw his legs over my lap. "Tell me how we go about this in a way that will not scare her off..."

 LIORIA

I lie awake in the softest bed I've ever touched and stare up at the diamond pattern of light on the ceiling while spinning the ring on my finger. How is this my life?

The kind woman who led me to this room said this is where I'll be living. It's three times the size of my room back at the boarding house. I have my own hearth and bathroom. The bed is big enough I can barely touch either side with my arms extended. There's a bookshelf, as if these people expect me to own books. And the wardrobe! I could live in it, it's so big. I have windows with glass panes and a crystal clear mirror that reflects everything I'd rather not see.

There are rich people in Suncrest who don't live half this nice.

I push myself up and peer around me.

It's awfully light outside for there to be no bells. Unless there are no bells. Or could I have missed them?

That thought sends me flying from bed. I hop on one foot while untangling myself from the linens before diving for my clothes, still bundled together.

Last night when we arrived, I practically sleep-walked my way to the room. It never occurred to me to lay out my clothes. There's nothing to be done about the wrinkled state of things, unfortunately.

I dress as fast as possible and spare only a few moments on my hair. For once in my life, it's not a frizzy mess. My sturdy clothes are not grand or fine, but neither am I, and I will not pretend to be anything other than I am.

Upon exiting my room, I stand in a long hallway and stare at the brilliant glass globes that radiate light. Are these magic lights? I've heard about them, but no one in Suncrest has ever been able to afford them. And here they are in servant's quarters.

A door down the hall creaks open and I jump.

An older gentleman in a dignified butler's coat steps out. His gaze sweeps toward me. The moment our gazes lock, his bushy white brows climb toward his hairline.

"Hello? Excuse me." I hide my hands in the folds of my skirt to keep from twisting the material into knots.

He clasps his hands behind him and ambles toward me with no hurry in his step. "You must be the new girl."

"Yes, I'm afraid I overslept…"

He chuckles and waves at me to follow him. "There is no oversleeping in this house. Come with me. Let's get you fed."

I hurry to follow him. "But, um, should I be somewhere?"

He smiles back at me. "Do you know where you're supposed to be?"

"No," I answer slowly. I'm not sure the talk about me being a secretary counts. The very idea of making me a secretary seems ludicrous. Besides, don't they already have one?

"Well then, let's focus on what we know you need, which is a good meal in you."

I can't help but smile at him. Anyone who is house staff looks down on us serving girls in Suncrest. I'd just assumed that gentry staff would be the same.

"What shall I call you?" the elderly butler asks.

"Lioria."

He pauses and offers me his hand. "I am Edward."

I take it and grin at him. "Pleasure to meet you, sir. I hope I'm not putting you out."

He turns to a larger door at the end of the hall and pulls it open. "On the contrary, I'm very curious about you."

"Oh, there's nothing of interest with me," I say.

"Edward!" A dignified older woman with dark skin and a crown of fluffy braids hurries over while looking me up and down. She's taller than most men. I barely come up to her shoulder. "You! You must be the girl. Let me have a look at you."

"Mrs. Jurrah, this is Lioria. Mrs. Jurrah is the housekeeper here at Privale."

I remember to curtsey finally.

She keeps hold of my hand and squints at me, her mouth puckering up like she tastes something sour. "What are you good for?"

"Uh, sorry?"

"Can they not hold two thoughts together between them?" She sighs and releases my hand. "We'll see about some warmer clothes. I dare say you'll freeze in those light garments. The climate changes drastically away from the coast."

Edward gestures at me. "I was going to take her to the kitchens—"

Mrs. Jurrah shakes her head. "No time for that. The young lords have been up all night, restless as can be." She gives me a curiously pointed look. "I take it the meeting did not go well, and they want their new plaything."

I stare back at her, unsure what to say. She isn't unfriendly exactly, but I don't think I've made the best impression.

When I don't speak, Mrs. Jurrah continues. "They've asked for you twice already. Past time for you to do whatever it is you do."

Edward's eyes widen. "This early?"

Early? It's almost mid-morning.

Mrs. Jurrah shrugs. "They never left. I'm not going to complain."

Edward turns to me and inclines his head. "It was lovely to make your acquaintance, Lioria. I look forward to working with you."

"Yes." I grin at him and curtsey again.

Mrs. Jurrah waves for me to follow her. Her strides are so long I almost have to jog to keep up.

"It is my job to keep Privale running smoothly." She spares me a smile. "You'll do as your told when you're told, and I won't hold your hand and show you around."

"Yes, ma'am," I say and decide that the less I say the better.

"Lords Belial and Eligos might prefer a more relaxed home, but we do not forget for whom we work. You'll find that most staff have served one or the other, like their parents before them, for generations. It's work we're proud of. Keep that in mind. Everything we do reflects on them."

"They seem very in touch with what common people need," I venture, unable to help myself.

Mrs. Jurrah peers down her nose at me. "Exactly. And if that means our household is unconventional, then everyone benefits."

I want to respond, to make it clear that these are things I've come to understand, but I cannot speak and jog.

Suddenly she stops. I speed past her and don't stop for three more paces. I turn and look at her, but her face has gone serious. She takes two long steps, closing the distance between us.

"We do not speak of the lord's relationship," she says in an odd voice. Almost as if it pains her to speak of it.

I'd wondered about the touches and smiles, but neither of them had come out and admitted anything to me. "They're together?"

"We don't speak of it." Mrs. Jurrah begins walking again, every bit as fast as before.

That's as much of a confirmation as I need.

I'm surprised by the bite of jealousy and disappointment.

I have no right to feel this way. They are powerful beings. I am human. I have no rights to their affection and nothing I know about their history leads me to believe they keep romantic partners for more than sex. If I'm honest, part of me is jealous. I want them to want me, not each other. But that goes against the promise I've made myself that I will not be tempted by them. I will remain in control of my life.

Same-sex relationships aren't uncommon or even frowned on, though they're less frequent in the lower ranks of the working class I grew up in. There's a lot of money to be made in marrying and having babies if your bloodline is the right one. And most people can only afford one spouse in the household bearing children. It isn't as much of a concern in wealthier circles. They can marry one spouse for the money and lineage, another for love.

The only reason I can think of to hide Belial and Eligos' relationship is safety. They were all killed during a meeting together. Since their return, they've remained spread out. It stands to reason two of them together all the time would make an appealing target.

We climb up stairs, traverse yet another hall before passing into a servant's hall all without trading another word. It's a warren of twists and turns and it occurs to me that the house might be as large as the whole of Suncrest. At long last, Mrs. Jurrah pauses outside a set of double doors and draws a deep breath.

"Make yourself ready, girl," she says.

She doesn't give me another moment. She pushes the door open and breezes inside. I follow her into a room that could have fit almost the whole tavern. The room is bathed in sunlight from the large windows that take up most of the far wall. To my right are two large desks facing each other from across the room, both piled with things. Papers, scrolls, envelopes, boxes, and who knows what else. On the other side of the room is a large sitting area with two sofas and a daybed arranged around the fireplace.

Something on the daybed moves.

I freeze as a blanket is tossed back and Belial sits up. His hair is a mess, and he's shirtless. Thick, dark tattoos swirl over his shoulders. He bounds out of the bed to the sound of groaning. That's when I realize that, nestled into the cushions, is Eligos.

My cheeks heat. We just walked in on the two lords snuggling.

Belial grins as he comes around the sofa and grips my hand between his. "Loria! Finally. Did you sleep well?"

"Yes."

He pulls me around to the back of the daybed so we are standing over Eligos, who shows no such inclination to get up.

Eligos reaches up and straightens the cuff of my shirt, his fingers brushing over my knuckles. My skin tingles at the contact and I find myself being drawn back under their seductive spell. "Perhaps you can entertain him now and I can get some sleep?"

Belial smacks his hand away. "You can't sleep."

Eligos sighs. "Mrs. Jurrah?"

I glance over my shoulder to find the housekeeper gathering dishes onto a tray. "Yes, my lord?"

"See to it Belial and Lioria are fed, will you? Then know we'll want some privacy."

I swallow hard.

I've been somewhat alone with the both of them, but this is different. It's not the tavern or carriage. Here they hold all the power. I am no longer my own person. Part of me belongs to them, and I don't know what to make of that or my situation. But I have the ring for my protection and my wits for the rest.

Mrs. Jurrah leaves without a backward glance and I am alone with my two lords. Belial is holding onto one hand while Eligos draws circles on the back of the other. There's nothing sexual about the touches, and yet I feel a stirring low in my belly. An awareness that they are men as well as demons.

I clear my throat and withdraw my hands.

Neither seems to notice. They're too busy having another one of those silent moments of communication and I am forgotten. Then, as if pulled by the same thread, they look at me.

"Lioria?" Eligos pats the space next to him. "Come sit. We have things to discuss."

I fix him with a stare. "Are you asking me to join you in bed?"

A sensual smile spreads over his face and he slinks down lower. "If a bed is what you want..."

I hold up my hand as if I can stop him. "No."

Belial chuckles. "Eligos has a condition, you see. He can't sit up for more than a few hours a day, so he works from here."

I look from one to the other.

They can't be serious...

Can they?

Eligos laughs and reaches for my hand. "He's teasing, but I have an aversion to desks. My request is innocent, I promise. But if you so choose..."

"Fine," I huff, doing my best to act as though those little touches didn't stir desire in me.

It's not entirely comfortable to lounge about on a bed wearing a corset, so I sit opposite of Eligos. This way, I lean against the curved arm of the bed.

Belial grips the back of the daybed and leans forward. The sunlight bathes him in a golden glow and his hair glints like fire. His chest is ladders of muscle and sinew, the likes of which I've never seen. Not from the strongest deckhand, and I have the sudden desire to lick him. But, that is Eligos' right, not mine.

Did they mean to share me? Take turns?

No.

I will not ask.

"Now?" Belial asks.

Eligos rolls his eyes. "Yes. Now."

"Now what?" I ask, with no little amount of dread.

Eligos sits up and fixes me with a rare, serious expression. "There is one small thing to consider before making you our secretary..."

I hold up my hands. "I'll be happy scrubbing things."

"Nonsense." Belial slides down, so he looms over me with that goofy smile of his. "You'd be wasted cleaning."

One side of Eligos' mouth is hitched up, as though he has a mischievous secret, but it fades as he pushes the blanket down and folds his legs under him. "There is business that must be attended to that is of a sensitive nature. Material that cannot be spoken of to anyone outside our inner circle, and those we trust."

I nod slowly, not liking where this is going.

"Of course, with that knowledge comes a certain amount of risk to you and us. To that end, we create a magical bond that protects you and us."

"A bond?" I glance between them, unsure about this. "I'm afraid I don't understand..."

Eligos leans against the opposite arm, mirroring my pose. "It's a magical way to ensure you don't intentionally or unintentionally reveal our secrets."

I study him then Belial, both of whom are watching me.

There's another reason here. Something I am unaware of. It has to be my ability to use the device. What did they call them? Fairy artifacts? Isn't fairy a type of Vodu?

Focus.

I need to think through this very carefully. "How does it work?" I ask. "Does this bond mean I'm tied to you for the rest of my life?"

"No," Belial says quickly.

Eligos shakes his head. "Nothing like that. You simply won't be able to talk about anything you have seen or worked on that has a discretionary spell on it.

That spell links to the one you agree to. It also serves to protect you. Without the bond, anyone could kidnap you and torture information out of you.

That sounds like something I'd rather avoid.

"It also means we're better able to protect you." Belial is oddly serious. "We take the safety of all in Eden personally. But if I'm honest? Our people matter the most. You're who we trust when we can't be here. You're who really keeps this place going."

I find there's a lump in my throat.

"Okay," I mutter, because I'm still not entirely convinced. And yet, I was always going to say yes.

Edward was kind to me. I'm determined to find my place here.

Eligos turns so that he's facing the fire and scoots close to the middle of the daybed. He pats the space next to him. "Come closer. I'll only bite if you ask me to, kitten."

I freeze with my hands braced on the mattress.

Belial shoves Eligos' shoulder. "He's trying to be funny. Don't mind him."

"You never know, Bel. She might like my bite."

I'm not convinced, though part of me wishes I'd thought they were human for just a little longer. I've never been with two men before, but I'd be up to the challenge. Demon Lords are another matter. Besides, I know better than to fuck where I work. Nevertheless, I scoot over, so I am sitting next to Eligos.

With no warning, Belial vaults over the back of the daybed to sit on my other side.

"Give us both a hand," Eligos says.

I offer them both a hand, palm up.

Belial seizes my wrist and pulls my hand in front of him, cradling it to his chest. On my other side, Eligos runs his fingers over my palm with just enough pressure to not be ticklish. We both watch Belial stroke a finger down each digit, like he's tracing something I can't see.

His touch is gentle, and I find that I cannot look away. My heart beats a little faster and I hold my breath, as if I can delay what's to come and simply remain in this moment.

Belial holds up his right hand and Eligos leans past me. There's something wrapped around his finger with a sharp end. He presses it to Belial's index finger and a single drop of blood wells up.

My lungs are burning. I let out the breath only to suck it back in as Eligos pricks my finger next.

Belial turns to look at me. His gaze has gone dark green, and I find I'm completely enraptured by him. His lips begin to move and he presses our fingers together, allowing the blood to mingle.

There's no question about it now. There is a demon in my veins.

I don't know the words he's whispering, but it's like a door has opened and I am basking in warmth.

We sit like that for I don't know how long, staring at one another. I'm vaguely aware of Eligos stroking my hand. It feels as though he has me grounded so that I don't float away.

Belial blinks a few times and I have to wonder, is this what it's like with all their most trusted servants? Or is it different this time?

He lifts my hand to his mouth and licks the finger. I'm so surprised I sit there watching while my core grows molten.

It takes effort to remind myself that I am not special. I am merely held in their thrall. The candle does not think of the moth. I would do well to remember that and not get singed.

"My turn," Eligos says, and tugs on my hand.

I turn toward him, still in a bit of a daze. I'm acutely aware that Belial is closer now, peering over my shoulder in a way that his breath warms my skin.

This time I'm somewhat prepared.

Eligos pricks his finger, then mine. He peers sideways at me, those gold eyes of his glinting in an in-human way. The moment our fingers touch, I feel it again. A doorway opening to somewhere warm. Somewhere I want to be.

I blink and my breath stutters in my lungs.

What would it be like for them to want me? Not in a passing fancy, but genuine feeling?

My thoughts are giddy and childish, nothing to be acted upon or spoken about. But they're there.

I blink several times, trying to force the world back into focus.

Eligos' nose is almost touching mine. His gaze is on my mouth and I can smell...

Is that caramel?

Belial grips my shoulder, holding me back as whatever spell dissipates. "Lioria? Lioria. Eli, pull yourself together."

"Gods," I croak and begin to scoot off the bed, but Eligos still has my hand.

"Almost," he says, steady as can be.

Unlike me.

My insides are quaking. It feels as though every nerve ending was scrapped. Everything is overwhelming. Belial's breath on my neck. Eligos' grip on my hand. My breasts have grown heavy and my nipples are chafing. All over my skin is hot, to the point that it's hard to breathe.

Eligos lowers his head, no doubt to lick the remaining blood as Belial had.

"Is that necessary?" I whisper.

I'm so hyper-sensitive that I'm not sure what that touch will do to me. Gods, what did I almost do a moment ago?

He tilts his head to the side and says, "Yes."

Unlike Belial, Eligos holds my gaze as he wraps his lips around my finger. His tongue runs over my skin once, then flicks against it.

I jump, startled because that was not a human tongue any longer.

Eligos blinks a few times and his grip relaxes. I pull away from him, only to lean against Belial. He holds my shoulders and peers down at me.

Sexual energy practically crackles in the air and I have to wonder, would it be so bad to give in?

"Why don't you lie down while we attend to some business with Mrs. Jurrah, hm?"

I want to say no. I intend to say it, but instead, I nod.

My body is heavy and sluggish, my mind weighed down.

I'm about to fall asleep.

"Eli," Belial snaps. "In the hall, please?"

I hear a snarling sound before Eligos stands and walks off the side of the mattress. I stare at his backside.

Is that...

Does Eligos have a tail?

"Lie down, sweetness," Belial whispers and eases me down onto my side.

This is not an appropriate place for me to sleep, and yet there is no fighting the weight pulling at my eyes. Not even the lust pumping through my veins can keep me awake, and so I pass into a dreamless sleep.

ELIGOS

The world sparkles with layers of colors invisible to human eyes. I pace out into the hallway and stop, staring at a candle in wonder as amethyst shades dance within the heart of the flame.

What is happening to me?

The sensations are familiar and foreign. I can't grasp my thoughts. It's all so jumbled.

Belial closes the office door behind him. I think we're alone, but I can't tear my gaze from the fucking candle. He reaches over and snuffs out the light, freeing me from the spell.

"What the fuck is this?" I whisper, and hold out my hands.

My skin is still the same ebony shade it's been since my birth, but I can see the ridges of plates that make up my demon form rising to the top, pushing at the dermis level as if I'm about to shed my humanity.

None of us have been able to assume our demon forms in three to five lifetimes. And now mine is barely contained.

Belial takes my face in his hands and pulls me close until we are nose to nose.

"Breathe. Breathe with me, Eli," he whispers.

I want to crawl into his cool green eyes and find relief from the itching that's plaguing me.

"What's wrong?" My voice is wrong, more of a deep rumble.

"Breathe, Eli. You need to pull it back in."

"What?"

"Your tail."

Shocked, I turn. Which is stupid because I only catch a glimpse of the tuft tipping my jet black tail. I reach back to feel at my spine, and sure enough, it's there.

It's been a few lifetimes since I was able to do more than make my eyes go demonic. I haven't had the power to shift forms. And now I'm on the precipice of shedding my humanity.

"How?"

Belial shakes his head. "It has to be her blood. I don't know. Maybe she's part fae or something else and doesn't know it?"

There's always the chance that she's something new. It isn't unheard of. Wild magic, toxins, and the will of the universe have created quite a few new creatures we know nothing about.

That's highly unlikely. No fae blood has ever made one of us react like this on an almost feral level, and during our worst years, we tore through man, fae, and other alike. The answer is something unknown.

I shake my head. "No, maybe angel? Nephilim?"

It's been hundreds of years since I last heard rumor of a Nephilim, but it stands to reason that any alive now wouldn't know what they were. There's always the chance that she's something new. It isn't unheard of. Wild magic, toxins, and the will of the universe have created quite a few new creatures we know nothing about.

Belial smacks my shoulder. "She almost kissed you, you lucky bastard."

"Then why'd you stop her?" I snap.

I don't feel lucky. I feel on the brink of shedding my mortal body, and that is dangerous. Part of the reason why we adopted human forms is that it can be incredibly difficult to control ourselves otherwise.

Belial takes my face between his hands again and brushes his lips over mine in the sweetest kiss. "Breathe with me. In..."

Together we suck down deep breaths.

"And out," he whispers.

My mind goes numb the longer I stare at him and I'm able to grasp the threads of my humanity. If I pull hard enough on them...

There's a unique sensation to pulling one's tail back inside your body. It's strange, like needing to scratch an itch you can't reach. It's an unpleasant relief that makes me groan.

"There you go," Belial whispers.

I splay my hands against his chest. "Did you not feel this?"

He nods and holds up his left hand. It's tipped with long, black claws. "Oh, I did, but I stopped my wings from unfurling. Just barely." He waves at his shoulders.

I turn him in place, but his skin is smooth and perfect. Except for six purple crescents right about where each set of his wings would sprout.

And I'd just missed that?

"What the fuck, Bel?"

I turn to look at the door, but Belial grasps my face in his hand and forces my attention back to him.

"She's special," he says. "We knew it when we met her. Her ability to use fairy artifacts was a sign. Our demons warned us. We just didn't realize how much. There's a reason we were drawn to her. Maybe it's who she is, or what she is, or a combination of the two. We won't get answers right now. She's asleep. She doesn't see it yet. Remember the plan."

I nod, because of course he's right. "Should we ask Alastor? Mention to someone else? I know we can't ask the others. Oriax would begin a campaign to control her... Someone in that room had to have felt something besides us."

Belial's gaze turns sad. "Do you think Alastor wouldn't do the same? Valac? Even Raum? We're all alike. Our power is fading, Eli. If we dangle her in front of them, they'll devour her in a desperate attempt to regain a drop of our former strength. And that isn't fair to her."

The plan must be followed. She has to come to us, not the other way around. If we give in to our baser instincts, we will lose her and whatever it is growing between us that might be our salvation or the missing piece of our hearts. When we unlock this mystery we'll have to decide what to do. But that will be a combined discussion. With Lioria.

It's a strange day in hell when Belial is the one talking me down.

He wraps his arms around me and squeezes tight.

If the others find out how close we came to taking on our demonic forms, they're going to want Lioria. Oriax alone will want to poke, prod, and bleed her dry until he's bottled whatever she did to us.

"Bel?" I look up at my love. "We can never speak a word of this to the others."

He looks at me for a moment, then nods slowly. "Agreed."

I let out a shaky breath.

We've done our best to fix our mistakes and the damage we caused this earth. It's only natural that at some point, we would fade away like so many others before us. Without the gods, magic beings will wane and fade. Many already have. What magic is left is but a trickle.

I'm confident that without us, this world will continue.

All things have a season.

We have outlived ours.

It's time for humans to truly rule their lives. No outside forces. No gods pulling their strings. Just people. But that is a transition many years off.

Belial kisses my brow, then my cheek. "Come. Let's rest."

As if his words make me aware of myself, I realize how heavy my body feels and I'm acutely aware that neither of us slept last night. He wraps an arm around my waist and ushers me toward the stairs.

One thing I know with certainty, Lioria is ours now. Nothing will ever change that. We are bound in this lifetime.

LIORIA

I wake the next morning before the sun, which isn't surprising seeing as how I slept almost the entire day before wandering around until I found someone willing to show me back to my quarters. It should have been impossible, but I slept most of the night. Now, as I stare up at the ceiling, my mind is struggling to make sense of what happened.

What I want to know most is whether or not what we experienced is normal, but I have a sinking suspicion that my lords will not be honest with me. And why would they? I am a lowly servant.

There is one thing I cannot deny.

I almost kissed Eligos, and I wanted very much to crawl onto Belial's lap. There was sexual tension tying the three of us together. But neither of my demons made a move.

Gods above, I want them to kiss me and ravish me. I want to be held down and fucked. I want to watch their faces as I make them come undone. It's this carnal thing so strong it scares me into second-guessing myself.

Entangling myself with them further would be a mistake. An enjoyable one, if I had to guess, but a mistake nonetheless. Besides, their relationship transcends lifetimes. I might be a practical woman, but eventually, I want more than to share a man's bed when it suits me. I'd like to be loved one day. Or at least have someone grow to care about me.

My Demon Lords might find me interesting and appealing now, but I cannot allow myself to get swept away by some fanciful idea that they will love me. In all the stories told about the Demon Lords, not one is a love story. There are tales that include a passionate encounter, like the Seige of Tokyo when Valac infiltrated enemy lines and seduced the general's wife, or the Trials of the Triumphant, when Alastor negotiated peace while bedding his enemy.

These are not happy stories. And while I might be an orphan, even I deserve to be happy.

I must not become involved with the Demon Lords outside of my role as their secretary. I'll treat them like I've treated handsy patrons my whole life.

I can manage. At least I hope I can.

With any luck, they don't make a habit of working half-dressed.

Was it my imagination, or does Belial have freckles on his chest? Does he have them everywhere?

I throw back the blankets and shiver. It's chilly in the mornings, and I never lit a fire. Normally I wouldn't dream of being up this early, but I've slept so much I can't just lie about. The fire is the first thing I tend to, and after that, my bladder. The maid who helped me find my way to my room last night made sure to show me how the magic fueling the bathing chamber works, and I am delighted to discover it is warm first thing in the morning. And not just a simple spell to banish the chill in the air. The tiles themselves are warm.

After washing myself head to toe, I use a fair bit of magic to speed along doing my hair. I'm thrilled that it's less frizzy and more manageable in this climate. It's still wavy, but I have to do a lot less to make me look respectable. For the first time in a long time, I braid my hair and leave it down. I also skip over my worn, tired dresses for the one pair of trousers I own. They're a caramel color, with a matching vest that has long hems split to fall over the hips to the knees. I even got a little fancy and embroidered yellow flowers on the collar.

I'm delighted by the result. I've spied a few women wearing trousers working about the property and I'm envious. It also might be the smart choice. One complaint I've always heard is that trousers make a woman look more like a man. Maybe my appearance will repel the lords? Time will only tell.

By the time I'm done, I can hear the faint sounds of life around me. I'm starving, but the only place I know how to get to is the Demon Lord's office. I leave my room with a flimsy plan to head to the office and ask for directions to the kitchen from someone along the way.

Only, I don't run into anyone and make it safely to the doors of the office.

Fuck.

Now that I'm here, I'm not certain I should be. What if Eligos and Belial are sleeping in there again? Or what if they're doing something else?

The jealousy prickling my skin is childish, but I never claimed to be a woman of good sense.

Besides, I'm going to see affection between them. Might as well treat it like normal. Especially since I get the feeling they are both going out of their way to tempt me.

With a deep breath, I open the door and step inside.

Candles are already lit and the room is warm.

Neither of the lords are on the daybed, at their desk, or anywhere in the room.

"Well, shit," I mutter and take a few more steps into the space.

What am I supposed to do now?

I wander over to the desk facing the windows and run my fingers along the edge. The piles of things on top are actually organized quite neatly, and there isn't a speck of dust or anything to speak of. The desks are twins, with almost identical piles on top.

I trail my fingers along the beveled edge, circle around to the other side, and freeze.

I am not alone.

A, well, I think it's a woman. She's kneeling between the desk and chair, a rag in one hand, gaping up at me.

"What are you doing down there?" I ask.

She springs to her feet, glaring at me.

She's barely as tall as my shoulder. And her skin. It's this molted white and gray shade. And are those rocks? Does she have rocks stuck to her face? That's when I notice the slender, pointed ears jutting out from her silvery hair. I blink at her a few times while she dusts off her gray dress.

"What are *you* doing in *here*?" she counters.

I'm immediately dying of curiosity. She's not human, that much is obvious. Is she Vodu? Or Yokai? I've never met either.

"I'm the lord's new secretary. Who are you?" I ask, because that's more polite than, *what are you?*

Her gaze narrows, and she leans toward me, inhaling deeply.

"Are you smelling me?" I ask.

Her features relax and her eyes widen. "You're telling the truth. Well. That's surprising."

I chuckle. "That I'm telling the truth? Or that I'm a secretary?"

She nods once. "Yes."

Oh, I like her.

I grin and offer her my hand. "I'm Lioria."

She looks at my hand with narrowed eyes. "You recently bathed."

"This morning, yes."

"Teill." She puts her small, cool hand in mine.

"What were you doing on the floor, Teill?" And is she supposed to be in here?

"Cleaning." She whirls away from me and scowls at the ground. "Belial. If he wasn't so precious, I'd string him up by his toes and skin him alive. That man gets crumbs everywhere."

"He does seem motivated by food."

"Well, he is a glutton demon."

I perk up at that. "You mean there are different types?"

She glances at me like I've lost my mind. "Of course."

"I'm sorry. I don't mean to offend. Before a few days ago I'd never seen anyone but humans."

"No offense taken. Most people in Eden haven't seen fair folk or their like. I'm not sure the Demon Lords count, though." She's back on her hands and knees, plucking crumbs out of the carpet with her fingers at lightning fast speed. Suddenly, she sits up and looks at me. "You have no idea what I am, do you?"

"None at all."

"It's okay, most fair folk wouldn't know what to make of me, either." Her cheeks turn a slight gray. Is she blushing? "I was born a Brownie, but I got poisoned when I was little and it petrified me. I would have died if Belial hadn't found me. So, now I look like this. I owe him my life."

That is quite the story packed into just a few words. I want to know more. Everything. But I can't push. I'm already on rocky ground with her.

"Did he bring you here, then?" I ask.

"I followed him." She bends back to her task. "I was too little to do much back then, but he let me be, and now I can look after him and his lord."

"Brownie, is that a Vodu or a Yokai?"

She glances up at me again. Her charcoal brows are almost to her silvery hairline now. "Oh. Okay. Vodu, I guess."

"Is that not what you're called?"

Teill waves a hand. "I've got to clean."

Either I'm bothering her, or she doesn't want to talk about it. Regardless, I'm not about to make an enemy out of the first non-human I've met.

"Would you like some help?"

She frowns at me. "Why would I want your help?"

"Um, well, I don't know..."

Teill laughs. It's such an honest, gleeful sound. "Love, I gather magic from cleaning. The last thing I want is for you to clean something, because then I can't."

"Oh. Oh! Okay. I understand now." No, I don't.

My stomach growls loudly, and she eyes me warily. "Hungry?"

"Yes."

Teill pulls open one of the drawers, then glances over her shoulder. She lays a finger over her lips, then opens a silver box and pulls out something wrapped in wax paper.

"What is it?" I ask.

She tosses it at me. "Caramel."

I gasp. "I can't take this."

She winks at me. "You didn't."

Oh, I like her.

Before I can open the wrapper, the door opens. I shove the candy in my pocket and whirl to face Mrs. Jurrah. She sees me, and her nose tips up with a sniff.

"What are you doing here?" she asks in a haughty tone that lets me know she isn't happy to see me.

"I didn't know where else to go..."

"I see. I imagine you'll want to eat. Teill?"

"I already ate," Teill says over her shoulder. "But you know the lords will be in a mood if they find out Lioria hasn't eaten."

Mrs. Jurrah clasps her hands together and sighs. "Very well."

I watch the older woman glide out of the room.

"Teill?" I whisper.

"What?" She doesn't snap at me, but I fear I'm wearing on her patience.

"Have I done something wrong?"

She snorts. "You're breathing. Don't mind that old bat. She's miserable and dreadfully old-fashioned. To make it worse, you exist outside her accepted social structure. Like me. We aren't ever going to be on her good side. Better accept it now."

"That's unfortunate," I mutter.

I want to ask her more questions, but I don't dare. Instead, I wander over to the other desk and study the piles. They're organized, sort of. Letters are in a pile. Scrolls in another. Many of them are unopened.

Is all of this just from when they were away?

This might be a job for an army.

Something chimes. It's not a clock, it's different.

Teill's head pops up. "Will you be a dear and grab whatever that is?"

I turn. "From where?"

"Middle shelf, see that box? Open it and see who it's addressed to," she says. "Damn thing won't work if they let things pile up inside of it, which they will. Oh, it would be wonderful if you can take over sorting things. It's certainly not my job."

The wall on the other side of the desks is floor-to-ceiling bookshelves. A few items are tucked between the books here and there. A long, rectangular box sits in front of some small volumes and I flip it open.

Inside is a letter with a green wax seal. Belial and Eligos' names are written on the paper in a flourishing script.

"It's to both of them." I peer closer at the box. "Why's it in here?"

Teill laughs. "You are a country bumpkin, aren't you? Bless your soul. It's a letterbox. You put something in it and it sends it to another box. The High Demon Lords all have one that sends letters to the capital where they're rerouted. Used to be there was a whole room for boxes just to connect all the lord's residences. They streamlined it a bit, though there's still the mailroom for less important stuff. You know what a pain it is to clean all those boxes spitting out letters?"

"That's amazing," I whisper. "So, where does something addressed to the both of them go?"

"That's your job to figure out. Not my problem anymore!" Teill cackles, but she takes pity on me. "I put it on whoever's desk has the smaller piles."

I look from desk to desk. "When is all this from?"

"Oh, it always looks like this. Some of those things are probably decades old."

"Decades?"

The doors open and Mrs. Jurrah enters with another maid carrying a tray that has far more food than I can eat on it. She summons Teill and me to a table and chairs across the room. Teill complains about not being hungry, but accepts the food given to her.

I try the tea first, but it is bland. There's no zing, no spice to it. Pleasant, but not what I'm used to. I think longingly about the tin in my room and vow to remember to have some with me tomorrow.

"Mrs. Jurrah? Is there something I can do to be useful?" I ask slowly.

Her brows rise almost to her hairline. "That's none of my business. I merely manage the household."

With that, she turns and leaves the room.

"Miserable old hag," Teill mutters and wrinkles her nose at the door.

"Is she always like that?"

Teill barks a laugh. "She's being nice."

"Nice?"

Teill nods and rolls her eyes.

I chew on my lip for a moment. It would be nice to have friends, people I can ask questions and learn from, but it appears the human residents of the house are avoiding me. Except Edward. He's a nice man, but I don't think this question is appropriate to ask him.

"Do... Do we all have the bond...?" I'm not sure how to ask my question.

"Yes. Well, yes, most of us. Not all the staff does, but people like me, you, Mrs. Jurrah, anyone who regularly deals with the lords is bonded."

"What should I do in the meantime?" I glance at the desks. I'm so accustomed to doing something that the idea of being left idle makes my hands itch. "Maybe organize all that?"

Teill perks up. "Could you? *That* mess gives me hives."

"I just open all those papers and read them? What if I shouldn't see something?" I ask.

Teill waves a hand. "If it's for the lord's eyes alone, it will be spelled and you can't read it. If you can, it's understood that staff might be reading and handling matters."

"Oh." That's a relief. "Then it's about time to get down to work, I suppose."

After we eat, Teill spends time cleaning up every last crumb while I decide to begin by tackling what I believe is Belial's desk.

Since the scrolls take up the most space, I begin with those. Several are detailed lineages of families with glittering embellishments and the sweet, demure face of a woman drawn where there's space. I'm not certain what those are, but I can guess.

Holding families who can already prove their families have produced a Demon Lord are always trying to improve the odds of having another. Any Demon Lord, not just the high seven, will pay handsomely to compensate a family for such a child. I place those scrolls together and force them from my mind. I don't want to become a High Lord's concubine. Those scrolls have nothing to do with me. And yet, part of me wants to burn them out of spite.

The next one I can't read, so I move it next to the spelled letterbox. The fourth one requires quite a bit of reading before I grasp that it's commentary on proposed changes to market restrictions on bread, and it needs both Belial and Eligos' approval.

It's some time later that I pause to take stock of how I've organized things, make a list, and catalog everything with notes so I don't have to actually remember every document I've read.

There are so many urgent items I'm not sure how anything actually gets done if it must pass the bottleneck of Eligos and Belial.

Teill departs at some point while I'm busy and I'm alone until close to noon, when the door creaks open. I'm deep into a paper discussing why the bread topic is so dire. In some cities, bakeries are mixing their flour with things that shouldn't be in food to stretch out their ingredients. Others are using faulty scales to over-charge customers. I'm finally beginning to understand the issue at large.

"What juicy gossip are you reading?"

The sensual voice slides over me, and I stop breathing. Glancing up, I find a rumpled Eligos standing with his hands braced on the desk. He's wearing trousers, a loose shirt, and a robe over it without shoes. His locs are pulled back, and he has a strip of satin tied around his head.

He's so handsome with the light behind him, making it appear as though he's glowing.

"Sorry?"

He chuckles. "You're working too hard. It's making *me* tired."

It's my turn to laugh, only he's looking at me with a mix of sensual and serious curiosity.

"Did you just wake up?" I ask instead.

"Of course." He pushes off the desk and turns, swinging his head left then right before heading straight to the daybed, where he flops down.

I reach for my list. "There are some matters here that are time sensitive."

His voice is muffled, probably from the pillow he's face-planted on. "They always send things and say it's time sensitive."

"Well, why don't we attend to them and get it over with?" I suggest.

Eligos grunts.

"Is there something else you would have me do?" I ask.

"Come keep me warm?"

It's a strength of will that I say, "You have a fire and there are blankets."

"Yes, but neither are as enjoyable as you."

I ignore that statement as best I can, which is difficult considering that my face is on fire to the point I'm blinking back tears.

I'm nothing special. Why is it they want me?

He sighs and grows quiet.

And he's out.

I actually make it through the rest of the scrolls on Belial's desk, clearing a great swath of the surface. But that is only the beginning. I'm considering where to begin tackling the rest when the doors open.

Belial side-steps through the opening, balancing a jug of something and a plate. He pauses when he sees me, as if he's surprised.

"Want some help with that?" I ask and set aside the letter.

"No. No, carry on." He nudges the door shut with his foot and walks closer, eyes large. "What, um, what are you doing?"

"Organizing. Are you here to take a nap, too?"

He glances over his shoulder at Eligos and sighs. "That's where he went."

"Did you just wake up, too?"

"What? Me? No." He chuckles. "Just finished training, and I'm starving."

He sets the tray of what looks like eight sandwiches on the now empty space along with the pitcher.

"I met Teill this morning."

"Oh." He brightens. "How's she doing? I hardly ever see her. She's mostly a night owl."

I tilt my head to the side. "I can't decide if she likes me or hates me."

"Then she likes you. If she hates you, or even dislikes you, you'll never see her. Brownie magic. They're very good at invisibility."

He crosses to Eligos' desk, grabs the heavy chair with one hand, and lifts it as if it's nothing. I gape a little as he carries it over to sit across from me.

"I can move," I say hurriedly.

He waves at me. "No, no. Want to tell me what you've read?"

I pick up my list and offer it to him. "It's all right here."

He shifts in his seat and I'm reminded of a particularly guilty little boy trying to hide what he's done. "Yeah, but can you just tell me what it says?"

"Of course."

I begin with the discourse about bread while Belial eats and am surprised to find how much he has to offer about the situation. He paces, and I pen his counterargument before sending that response off through the letterbox. I might have opened and closed the box a few times just to see if it might magically reappear, but it didn't.

Belial insists I eat one of his sandwiches while we work through the other items I considered time-sensitive. He's so serious. It's like he's a completely different person as he explains things to me or gripes about how shortsighted someone else is being.

"That leaves us with these two piles." I gesture at the scrolls I can't read and the lineage.

Belial grabs the ones with the lineage listing and grimaces before shoving them off the side into a bin. "That's where those belong."

"But what are they?"

His lips curl. "Concubine offers. Throw them away from now on."

Demon Lords don't marry. The conflicts caused by the families who'd tied themselves in marriage to the demons were some of the worst. And as a result, demons do not marry any longer. But they must produce offspring. Strengthening the line and all that.

I want to burn those scrolls to ash and scatter them so it is as if those women never existed. It's such a powerful urge I make a conscious effort to refocus on the remaining scrolls I cannot read.

"That leaves these," I say.

Belial grimaces and glances at the daybed. "Eligos will have to handle those."

"We can't do them now?" I'm itching to have at least one thing accomplished today.

Belial's shoulders droop and he sighs. "Reading is difficult for me. The letters twist and turn. It's worse with spelled documents. The words just swim around the page. Because of the spell, I can't use other aids to make reading easier."

"Oh, I had no idea. I'm sorry. I didn't mean to be rude."

He waves at me. "It's not rude, I just... A dyslexic Demon Lord. It sounds like the setup for a joke."

I gesture at the stacks of paper. "Why not bring someone in to help you?"

He grimaces and pushes the plate away, then props his elbows on the desk. "We tried. It... Didn't go well."

Not for the first time, I have to wonder what he means. He and Eligos have mentioned not tolerating others very well. But they're so easygoing it's hard to see where they wouldn't get along with anyone.

"Well, how about tomorrow morning I sort through more things then we can tackle them after you train? Just like we did today."

Belial beams at me. "Perfect."

"Wonderful."

Belial stands suddenly. "Eligos?"

I watch him stalk across the room and rip the blanket off Eligos' sleeping form.

"Eli? Eligos? Wake the fuck up."

When he doesn't so much as budge, Belial crawls over the back of the daybed, braces his foot against Eligos' hip, and shoves his lover straight off the bed and onto the floor.

"Ow!" Eligos bounds to his feet, hands balled into fists, and glares at Belial. "What the hell, Bel?"

Belial just grins back at him. "Morning."

"Fuck you," Eligos mutters.

Belial sits on the back of the daybed and braces his elbows on his knees. "You have to do a few things, then you can nap again."

"Fine." Eligos flops down, but remains upright, leaning against the arm much like he did yesterday. "Lioria, what am I doing?"

They both look at me. It's an odd and curious moment.

How did these two get anything done before?

I get up and grab the scrolls. "I'm afraid I don't know. I can't read these, and this will be everything I've organized today."

Eligos' eyes track me as I cross the room. There's something about it that makes me feel naked. "You're a busy little beaver, aren't you?"

"A what?"

He sighs and pats the bed next to him. "Never mind."

I'm leery of getting too close after yesterday. The desire to kiss him is still in the back of my mind as I cross the room. I'm trying to figure out an elegant way of handing off the scrolls and keeping my distance when the doors open again and Mrs. Jurrah enters.

I want to put space between me and the lords, straighten my clothes, do literally anything else but be where I am. But it is too late. Her gaze has already landed on me and I hear her sniff of disproval.

"My lords." She bends her head, her tone reverent. "The girls are ready to take measurements."

Saved by domestic necessity. I hand the scrolls to Belial because if I touch Eligos, I might combust.

"Measurements?" Eligos sits up and frowns. "What for?"

Mrs. Jurrah's brows lift. "Clothes, my lord. Unless this young woman won't be needing them. Is she perhaps not staying?"

I try very hard to not dislike people, but this woman spares no insult. For now, I'll stay on my best behavior.

"What?" Belial frowns. "Of course, she's staying."

"Don't dress her up too much," Eligos insists. "We work from bed, not the desk."

Belial perks up. "Trousers are actually a good idea. Lioria—"

"I will handle it," Mrs. Jurrah says and gestures at me to hurry up.

In all my life, I'd have never seen this moment happening. It's utterly bizarre and I haven't the faintest idea what to make of this. So, I leave because I fear otherwise I'll be drawn in by them like yesterday. And as enjoyable as it was to imagine being caught between two handsome, strong men, there's a downside to power that I want to stay away from.

I follow Mrs. Jurrah's quick pace from the study, doing my best to keep up with her.

"I noticed you sent letters out today," Mrs. Jurrah says without glancing back at me. "I trust they were lord's business?"

She isn't looking at me so I indulge in rolling my eyes. Gods forbid I send a personal letter.

"Yes, Belial and I tackled some pressing matters," I say.

She makes a sound, as if she doesn't believe me.

I wonder as we walk why Mrs. Jurrah has judged me so harshly. Because I'm an orphan? An unknown? Hired without her input? What could it be? I doubt I'll find out, but part of me is resolved to either make her hate me or love me.

LIORIA

The industrious ladies of the house measure every inch of me. I've never been fitted for clothing before. I purchased the trousers and vest outfit and had them tailored to me. To date, that's the most money I've spent at once. That was a far different experience than standing in a room of women, completely naked, while the rest twist, turn, and bend me. They're efficient, and even complimentary, but I don't have a moment to ask even one of their names.

Seems today will not be my day to make any human friends. I'll have to find time to loiter wherever the others eat and see if I can't find companionship. It won't do if I begin to see myself as part of the lord's circle.

They are above me, and that isn't something I can forget.

After I select the styles I desire from a slim book, they're gone and I'm left feeling a little melancholy.

I'm lonely.

My life has been noise and activity from the day I was little. When I wasn't playing, I was doing chores. And when I was doing neither, I was helping someone else. Or getting punished. And it's stayed the same.

This is my chance to change my fate. To do something else. And I would do well to make the most of what opportunity has befallen me.

It's late afternoon. I could return to the study. But I'm not going to. I'd like to do a little exploring.

The servant's wing is quiet this time of day, but I walk through the whole of it so I familiarize myself with my new home. I discover another entrance to the main house, as well as a small herb and vegetable garden. I'm peering at the neat rows when I sense someone behind me.

I glance back to discover a familiar, age-lined face.

"Edward. Hello again."

He smiles and holds a pipe to his lips. "Nice to see you again, miss."

"Is this yours?" I ask and gesture to the garden.

"It's the work of a few, but I have the most time to tend it." He winks. "Not much use inside the house these days. My old bones just don't move fast enough."

"Would you be amenable to showing me around?" I ask.

His brows rise. "Amenable? Are you sure you're a simple country miss? You speak almost as good as a lady."

I blush because I know where my mouth has been. "Whenever I got in trouble at the orphanage, I was banished to a quiet room and told to read. I read the books in that room at least five times apiece before I started complaining about the lack of new books. So, they sent me to the small library at the church. I spent a lot of time there. Little of it was by choice."

Edward chuckles. "Do you enjoy it? Reading, I mean?"

"Yes. I think the purpose was to dissuade me from certain behaviors. Instead, I read things that changed how I viewed myself and my position in life." I read stories about brave people and fantastic tales of heroism. Who a person's parents were hardly mattered in those stories, and it's where I drew my own inspiration from.

Edward smiles at me and takes the pipe from between his teeth. "I find myself understanding why the lords took a liking to you. Come. I'll show you around."

He walks me through the garden, pointing out varieties of plants I haven't encountered before and what their uses are. Some are medicinal, others for food, and some are the makings of magic. It's fascinating and new, since I've never done more than dig a few holes for seasonal flowers in front of the church. We sample berries fresh off the bush and Edward pulls down bright green fruit he calls pears.

Kirra would love the variety here, and I wonder if she's reconsidered the offer to work here.

I'm licking the fruit juice off my fingers when a deep voice speaks right behind me.

"That's why I always carry something with me to wipe my hands on."

Edward and I both start. I glance over my shoulder at Belial, smiling down at me with a handkerchief in his hand.

Edward drops into a deep bow. "My lord."

"Oh, don't do that," Belial mutters.

Edward halts his bow and straightens with a wiry smile. "These old bones... I fear I need to go rest."

"Go." Belial waves his other hand. "Eligos will have my head if he thinks I kept you."

Edward smiles fondly, nods again, then backs away.

I belatedly take the handkerchief and wipe my fingers while considering Edward's behavior.

"Shouldn't I be more..."

"No," Belial says before I can find the words.

I frown at him. "We're too informal. What if—"

He waves his hand at me. "The answer is no. There are too many people who can't stop bobbing and bowing. Do you have any idea how frustrating it is to carry on conversations with the tops of people's heads?"

I snort a laugh. "And what do you think I see the most of when I'm serving ale?"

Belial throws up his hands. "You get it then."

I can see his point. To an extent. For now, I choose to revisit this later.

"Did you and Eligos finish those scrolls?" I ask.

He shrugs. "It was all stuff that's been handled already. Nothing that needed our attention."

I can't help rolling my eyes, but I don't ask.

"Walk with me?" Belial asks, his voice gone soft and seductive.

He's dressed in boots, trousers, and a shirt that's half untucked. It's a sloppy look. Not at all one, I'd have expected on a High Demon Lord. But I'm coming to find out that our lords are very different from what I've imagined them to be.

"Sure."

He turns and we stroll away from the small garden toward nothing at all. Or at least, that's what it seems like. We don't speak, but it isn't uncomfortable. There's something both whimsical and calming about Belial's presence. He sees the world through eyes reborn, and with all the wonder. At the same time, his lifetimes of experience make him a calm, steady rock.

I understand why Eligos is drawn to him.

"How are you?" Belial asks suddenly.

I glance up at him and wrestle my thoughts back to the present. "Good."

"Yesterday didn't scare you off?"

I chuckle. "I think it's too late to be scared off."

"Never know," he mutters.

We crest the small hill and I find that we've come to a pond. It's not a decorative pool with statues and ornamental plants like I've spied in the cultivated gardens. This one is a little wild, though the banks have been tended.

Belial looks down at me and my heart is racing. He doesn't have to touch me for my body to flare to life. All it takes is one look.

"If you ever feel that we are too much, tell me?" he says softly.

I nod because I'm not sure I trust myself to speak.

He reaches up and slides his thumb along my jaw.

"Bit of fruit," he whispers. "Another thing?"

"Y-yes?"

"Never run from us. It wakes the demon."

My skin tingles as he pulls away, and for a fraction of a moment, I see a glimpse of lust in his eyes.

Eligos isn't the only one I've come close to kissing.

ELIGOS

I swirl the wine in the cup as I stare out into the night. The breeze coming down off the mountain is frigid. It's the last attempt of winter to hold on, so I let it beat at me. I welcome the physical distraction, since I've been hyper-aware of my semi-erect cock since the bonding yesterday. The only time I got any relief was when Belial tried to take care of it, but once again, I deflated.

Have we ever loved the same spirit? Is this our bodies recognizing a past flame? Or something else?

Lioria's bond isn't settling nicely either. Most humans we bond we are aware of for a time, and then it fades. Sort of like a tiny pebble in your shoe. You just get used to it because taking it out is too much of a bother.

Her bond is more like scraping a burn. It's this constant, jarring awareness of her at all times.

Did we make a mistake?

"Hasn't shown up yet?"

I glance back at Belial. Unlike me, he has on a fur-lined coat. He parts the sides and wraps the garment around the both of us.

"No, but it's early, still."

"I was able to confirm the others have heard the word 'forerunners', but don't know what it's supposed to mean."

"Shit," I mutter.

Yokai and Vodu have always tried encroaching on our shores. Our boundary wards do the bulk of the work keeping them out, but there's always a few sneaky ones who can get past the boundary.

"Is it just me, or are we seeing more interlopers?" I ask.

Belial takes my cup and sips the wine. "You aren't wrong."

That's not what I want to hear.

"What are they planning?" I ask the wind.

With Lioria under our roof, that uncertainty seems somehow more dire. As if now we have more to risk. But what is the threat? What's being planned? And why haven't we heard anything about it?

Alastor has spies among the various courts. Shouldn't one of them know something? When was the last time we discussed rumors from the continent? We've been so focused on our own borders, I'm sorely lacking in knowledge of other countries.

"I don't like this," I mutter.

"Neither do I."

"Shax wants to talk again."

"About?"

I shrug.

Who knows these days?

"Probably something else about Alastor," Belial mutters.

Shax and Alastor have always had issues, but it seems like those conflicts are more frequent as of late. I can't worry myself over their personal conflict. Some lifetimes it's like this. For one reason or another, some of us don't get along and there's nothing to be done about it. But Shax's issues are not personal and that's what strikes me as strange.

Is he being a good lord? Or is he playing another game?

Only time will tell.

LIORIA

When I wake up the next morning, I can't help but feel as though something is off. I sit up and glance about my too-decadent room, but nothing is amiss. Its pristine beauty merely underscores how much I feel out-of-place still. But I am not without hope.

Dealing with the lords can be a little trying, but the work was interesting. I grew up thinking of the Demon Lords as great, distant beings who managed important things. But watching how seriously Belial focused on the simple matter of bread has shifted everything.

I might not be important, but the lords I serve touch the lives of every person in Eden. And I'm going to help. I'm not just serving drinks and food to weary fisher folk, I'm part of the entity that means a family scraping by will get the bread they paid for. Literally.

Tossing back the blankets, I don't shiver quite so much.

There's a fire in the hearth, but I didn't light one.

I blink at the door, but it's still locked. Then, how was the fire started? By who? And when?

That's when my gaze comes to rest on the neatly folded pile of my clothes from yesterday on the desk. They are on the other side.

I cross to look at the pristine fabric and notice the grease stain on the cuffs is gone. I hold up the vest, but that little blot of blood from when I scraped my knuckles playing with children is gone.

Someone cleaned my clothes. Someone who came into my room and started a fire.

I turn in a circle, noticing slight changes now.

And not a speck of dust.

What was it Belial had said? If Teill doesn't want to be seen, she won't.

I get ready as fast as possible and decide to skip my plan of passing time where the other servants eat in the hopes of making a few friends around here. It's become dreadfully clear to me that the rest of the staff are avoiding me. It makes me miss home and my friends. There is no Kirra here to eat my feelings with. No Malka to exchange stories while we stare off into the ocean. I'm alone, save for the lords and Teill. It's lonely.

The study is just as I found it yesterday. Pristine, thanks to the industrious woman currently pulling books off the shelves to dust between them.

"Do you do that every day?" I ask.

"Of course."

She's so incredibly quick and it is all done without stirring other objects.

"Teill?" I clasp my hands behind my back and walk toward her.

She doesn't pause in her task to glance at me. "What?"

"Did you clean my room while I was sleeping?"

She glances briefly over her shoulder, a wrinkle of annoyance making the stone on her brow seem larger. "What of it?"

"Thank you." I grin up at her and hold my arms out. "And you got the stains out of my favorite outfit."

"Don't speak of it," she snaps.

"I really appreciate it."

Teill whirls toward me, her face a darker gray now.

"Don't speak of it," she squeaks out.

I've offended her.

"Never again," I say.

She jerks her head once and spins back toward the books.

Shit.

"A letter recently arrived," she announces. "I haven't looked at it."

"Thanks," I say before I can stop myself.

"You're welcome," she says in a lighter tone.

There seem to be rules I know nothing about, so I say nothing at all as I retrieve a letter with the name Shax on it in bold, block like letters.

"Any idea what I should do with a letter not addressed to either of the lords?" I ask.

"Is it Shax?" Teill asks.

"Yes."

She sighs. "He never puts who the letter is to, only his own name."

"Oh."

I open the letter and skim the contents. The block letters are neat and tidy, but the words are passionate. In one sentence, Shax blames the influx of refugees on Eligos, then Belial, before aiming fingers at players on the continent before asking advice.

Refugees aren't a problem on this part of the island.

While I'm on my second read-through, the study doors open and Mrs. Jurrah enters with a maid I think was with her yesterday.

"Breakfast, come eat," Mrs. Jurrah says sternly. As if we're children.

I don't need to be told twice.

"Lioria, I have a matter that needs the lord's attention," Mrs. Jurrah says as I take the first bite of my breakfast.

I perk up at that. A chance to get on her good side, perhaps? "Oh? What is it?"

"The annual Laborer's Day festivities." She shakes her head. "The lords have not announced where they'll be spending it, and both households are getting... Anxious."

In all the years I've been an adult, I've never been able to enjoy the festival. Serving girls are one of the exceptions to the general ban on no required work. Can't have a self-served festival, after all.

"What exactly do they need to decide?" I ask.

"She knows nothing," Teill says between bites.

Mrs. Jurrah stands up a little straighter, as if she can't believe she must converse on my level. "In past lifetimes, all the lords would to go their region's main city and preside over events. Belial and Eligos... Well, they have not. So the households need to know how to disguise their absence."

My eyes go wide. "They'd do that?"

Mrs. Jurrah shrugs. "It's a simple thing, really. Happens quite a lot. People merely want to see their lord. It's comforting. And sometimes if what they're seeing is someone wearing a glamour...?"She shrugs.

My initial reaction is shock. But as I mull it over, why shouldn't Belial and Eligos spend the holiday together? Isn't that right, too?

"I'll do my best to drag an answer out of them."

Mrs. Jurrah nods and leaves hastily, as if this is the last place she wants to be. Teill loses no time rushing back to her cleaning, muttering annoyed words. Which leaves me to figure out my own tasks.

Today I start on Eligos' desk and work through the scrolls there. Most of them are the same sort of courting scrolls.

The letters are much quicker to work through. The dispatches are often short and to the point, though some of them have a more personal tone. There are requests from what seem to be old friends, business inquiries, and so much more. It's harder to classify the documents, but I do the best I can.

Mid-morning, I glance up to realize I'm alone again, and on the heels of that realization, the doors open and Eligos enters.

He's wearing what might be the same trousers from yesterday, but they're rolled up to his knees. The shirt must have lost its battle at some point because it's gone, and he has one arm through his robe, hanging off his shoulder. With so much skin bare, I can see faint, almost invisible black lines that swirl against his dark skin. I want to trace them, but an intimate touch like that is a very bad idea.

"Morning," I say brightly.

He groans by way of a greeting and heads straight for the daybed.

Chances are high he'll go to sleep again.

I grab Shax's letter.

"Before you settle in for your nap, can we handle this one thing?" I hold up the letter. "I won't bug you until later if you do."

He cracks one golden eye and glares up at me, but there's no heat behind it. I fully expect him to say no. It doesn't appear as though he's actually awake. Instead, he pats the bed next to his head.

"Sit," he says.

He had said they work from bed. It appears to be a literal statement.

What does he do that tires him out so much?

I perch on the edge of the bed and hold out the letter to him.

Eligos pats the same spot next to his head again.

All too easily, the memories of the other day when I came so close to kissing him rise to the front of my mind.

That will not happen, I promise myself, and scoot closer. Not all the way to where he wants me, but close enough I'd have gotten the side-eye from my boarding house mistress.

Eligos sighs, then turns and lays his head on my lap. He holds one hand up. I put the letter between his fingers and he tilts the page to better read it, leaving me with the warm weight of his head and the odd feel of his locs pressing into my thighs. Were I wearing skirts, I wouldn't feel his hair quite so clearly. But in pants? There's just a thin layer between us, and I am acutely aware of the scent that clings to him. His warmth is pleasant, and I think I'd rather like learning how to slow down from him.

My whole life I've had to push myself. I've had to work hard, never be late, toe the line, do exactly as is expected of me. But my Demon Lords seem to have a different outlook. One I don't want to emulate exactly, but I don't have to work myself to death anymore.

Eligos hands the paper back to me and closes his eyes. "You answer it."

"Me? But it's to you."

"You'll know the answers better than I will."

"But..."

Eligos already has his hands folded over his chest, his robe covering most of him, and his eyes are closed.

"Are you seriously going back to sleep now?" I ask.

"Sh."

"This is not happening," I mutter.

"I work late hours."

Eligos rolls to his side so that he's looking up at me with his face inches from my pussy. He draws tantalizing little circles on my thigh. What would that feel like on my clit?

I swallow and muster a bright smile. "Oh, then I can prepare a list of things for you to do later."

His gaze narrows, and I can tell he isn't amused.

But he doesn't refuse.

"May I ask one more thing of you before I leave you to your nap? Well, two, if you don't mind?"

He sighs. "If you must."

"Your household needs to know where you're spending the festival."

Eligos grunts. "Wherever you and Belial go, I go as well."

His answer is strange, but I don't know how to interpret it. Me and Belial? I'm bound to serve both of them. It makes more sense that I would go where they go, but I don't ask for clarification. I'm not sure I want to. Things are too charged, too new, and I don't dare complicate things.

"I will pass along your message," I say and set the letter aside. "Um, the other is a little more delicate. I think I offended Teill this morning."

"That's not difficult to do. What happened?"

"I, um, I think she cleaned my room and clothes last night..."

He lifts his head and blinks at me. "She did?"

"Yes, and I thanked her... Why are you cringing? What's wrong with thanking someone?"

Eligos presses his hand on my thigh. "Brownies are... Well, they're particular. Teill is different, but some things are just born in you."

"What did I do?"

"You thanked her. To her face." He settles back down, shifting a bit until he's more comfortable. "She might not let you see her for a few days. Teill is still young and she can overreact. Best thing to do is leave a snack on your mantle. If it's gone in the morning, then you know she's accepted your gratitude. If not, well, keep leaving one and we'll just hope she comes around. That's all you can do."

"Okay," I say slowly.

I brace my hands on the mattress so I can extract myself from the bed.

Eligos presses his hand on my thigh. "You stole precious moments from me. Your penance is to sit here and do nothing for an equal amount of time."

His words are ridiculous and yet the threads of desire wind tight inside of me.

I haven't been with a man in months. Not since my last two on-again-off-again partners finally settled down early this spring with good little girls. I knew it was coming and I wish them both the best. I hope that right now, their wives are growing round with child as they experience a bountiful harvest or haul.

During the journey, I had thought to find someone among the staff with whom I could have an arrangement. I'm a woman. I have needs. But that feels gross and oily now. I don't want any man right now.

But two specific demons?

Clearly, my soul is more depraved than I ever realized. The ladies at the orphanage were right about me, after all. Should I write them a letter? Tell them they were right?

Eligos draws my thoughts back to the present and I'm acutely aware of a throbbing at the apex of my thighs. He's continued these little touches, swipes, and circles.

Maybe foregoing dresses was a terrible idea.

BELIAL

I stare down at the crispy form of a body reduced to nothing but its carbon elements. There's no indication of what race or species the creature once was.

That's the thing about fire elementals. They operate well with simple instructions, but once things get a little complicated...

"What can you tell us?" Eligos asks in a far more patient tone than mine.

The humans around Privale have no idea how many magical creatures call these forests home. It's why Eligos and I relocated here. If our lives were truly under threat, this is the safest place for us. Fuck the capital. We've already proven it's easy to kill us there.

The manor is just over that hill.

"Was it violent?" I ask.

The little elemental bobs in the air. As a consideration for us, it has banked its flame, which causes its molten body to cool and harden to a thick, black skin that is more like stone. Embers burn in its eyes, nose, and mouth, the only places it remains vulnerable.

"It attacked usss," the little thing insists.

Eligos and I share a look.

The elementals here are young. Too young to have much ability to communicate. They are creatures born of magic and the elements. We rescued this clutch of them a few years back, when they didn't possess the ability to speak. But they'd been smart enough to understand our gift of freedom in exchange for patrolling the swamp area that bordered the Privale lands to the south.

This was maybe the third time they'd encountered anything aggressive, and the first time they'd had to kill.

"Is everyone alright?" I ask the little creature. I can't tell them apart, but they feel a little different. Like Eligos and myself, they were all created out of the same spark.

It bobs higher in the air. "Yesssss. Thank you."

"That's what's really important. I'm sorry it came to this."

"Thisssss issss what we train for."

I incline my head. "We are grateful."

"Asssss are we."

"We'll take it from here." Eligos offers a heavy sack to the little elemental.

The elemental squeaks with joy, and for a moment, its skin fractures, flashing red before it gets itself under control. Eligos and I politely find somewhere else to look. It's only polite to pretend we didn't see that. Our little clutch of elementals is trying very hard to appear dignified, but they're still so darn cute.

Lioria would convince them all to become her friends, no doubt.

The elemental takes the bag and is gone.

"What did you give them this time?" I ask.

"Marshmallows."

I sputter a laugh and try to picture the elementals enjoying marshmallows. Do they eat them? Sit on them? Or burn them to a crisp?

One look at the charred body, and my good humor evaporates.

There is a conflict on our doorstep and I fear we are not prepared for whatever the Yokai and Vodu have planned.

"What is it, do you think?" Eligos asks.

I kneel and press my hand against the burned-out husk of a body, collapsing it into dust.

From the ashes, I lift an amulet carved with runes. I recognize some but not all of them.

"Oriax would know what it is," Eligos says.

"If we take it to Oriax, then he knows, and if he knows he's going to get involved. You know Alastor wants to keep whatever this is quiet."

"Yeah, well, what's your solution then, hm? Who else are you going to ask?"

"Alastor." It's the most obvious answer.

Of course, giving the medallion to Alastor means we will never see or hear about it again. It's not my favorite solution, but it's the best we have right now.

LIORIA

Teill is not in the study the next morning, but the offering of a pear on my mantle was gone. I try not to obsess about this.

I stand just inside the study, but it feels empty, which is a first. It's spotless, which is expected. What I wasn't expecting was for the twin desks to be gone. Even the little marks in the carpet have been buffed and fluffed out, no doubt thanks to Teill.

A large desk has been set up facing the room almost directly in front of where the letterbox sat. Two smaller writing desks sit flush to the front. Most impressive is that the mound of letters and other things is smaller.

What on earth have they done now?

I inspect one desk, pulling open the drawers to peer inside. When I find the silver box with the candies inside, it clicks.

This arrangement is for my benefit. It's thoughtful and surprising, I suppose.

I circle around to the shelves and check the box.

There's a letter waiting from Shax. I open it to sate my curiosity and end up grimacing. While I didn't sign my name to the correspondence Eligos instructed me to send, Shax clearly knows he isn't speaking with one of his brethren. His words are gruff and a little condescending. I don't know what he looks like, but I'm fairly certain I'd know his voice anywhere. What bothers me are the last few lines about leaving lord's business to lords.

If I left Belial and Eligos to their own means, I don't think anything that wasn't supremely urgent would be seen to.

I decide to leave that for Eligos. While my two lords are mild-mannered and pleasant, I don't think they're all similar in nature. I'm trying to decide where to start when I hear a chime.

Another letter.

I open the box and find a folded piece of paper.

Frowning, I open it and read the single sentence.

A little bird told me you're writing letters, treat.

Oriax.

He doesn't sign his name, but he's the only one who has called me treat.

I should leave it and let Eligos or Belial deal with him, but I'm curious.

The pen is in my hand before I can stop myself.

Are you calling your brethren animals now? I think some of them will take offense to that.

I blow on the paper until I'm satisfied it's dry enough, then slide it back into the box.

Settling in to work, I begin leafing through the documents. Most of them are dry and dull. I wade through them and make my own notes. Much of what's said goes over my head, but wasn't that expected?

There are a few that make little sense to me. It's as if the words I understand have another meaning.

That one goes onto the pile for later.

The letterbox chimes before I've made it through five documents.

Grinning, I pull the same paper out, this time with a new line.

I'd like to think we're a little more restrained than animals.

They're just words on paper, and yet I hear the words in his voice. It's low and a little rough. I hear a slight emphasis on the word restrained, as if we're having an entirely different conversation.

Are you trying to seduce me? Do you think I'll want to come to you? What are you after?

I can't be direct with Eligos and Belial. They'd take words of that nature as an invitation for more. Things are different with them. I have no such desire to appease Oriax. He does not hold my contract and I know better than to trust him.

This time I don't pretend to work.

I wait.

The clock ticks down the minutes and I fidget with my cuff in the hope he'll respond sooner. Still, at least five minutes pass before the chime sounds again.

You can come wherever you like, treat. I'll bet you taste beautiful.

My face flames at the words. I read them over and over again, but their meaning is quite plain.

I glance at the clock.

If Mrs. Jurrah follows her routine, she'll be here any moment.

I scamper across the room and toss the paper into the fire. It goes up in a puff of green smoke. I recoil and press my hand to my heart.

"Teill, I really wish you were here right now," I mutter in the hopes that she might appear.

She does not.

My anxiety knots my stomach up, so when Mrs. Jurrah does come with breakfast, I can hardly eat. I'm waiting for Oriax to send another note, but time passes without a chime from the box.

Eligos ambles in a little earlier than usual, fully dressed for once and wearing shoes. I pause to take him in and he smiles at me.

"Do you approve?" he asks.

I freeze, unsure of what to say about his choice of clothing. It's relaxed. Trousers, a shirt, and vest, with a robe-like coat over it. His hair looks brighter, more vibrant purple.

His smile dims a bit. "You don't like the desks."

Oh, gods.

I glance down at the new furniture.

"Yes. Yes! This is a very nice arrangement," I say in a rush.

"Good." He smiles and braces his hands on the back of one of the two chairs facing mine. "Do you need me? I'm not ready to be awake yet."

"Then why are you wearing more clothes than usual?"

He grins at me. "Belial and I have business to attend to later. What are you doing?"

"I'm just sorting through things..." My gaze lands on Shax's letter. "We did receive a reply from Shax. I don't think he appreciated my response."

That makes Eligos pause, and he frowned. "What do you mean?"

There's something about the way he asks the question that makes me pause. Why is it my first reaction is to cover up Shax's words? I shake that off and hand the letter to him. He unfolds it and his scowl lines around his mouth deepen until the word I'd use to describe his expression is thunderous.

"That arrogant bastard," Eligos mutters and crumples the letter in his fist. "I'll deal with him."

He drops into the chair, opens a few drawers, and mutters to himself. I pull out some blank pages, set them in front of him, then offer him a pen. Eligos takes both and bends over the desk. He mutters something and the words seem to float and shimmer on the page. What I expected might be a short, stern warning becomes at least half a page before Eligos sits up, folds the paper, then scrawls *Shax* on the outside.

Eligos hands the page to me and I dutifully take it and put it into the letterbox.

He blows out a breath and props his chin on his hand. "Well, fuck. Now I'm awake."

I wince. "Sorry..."

He glances up and frowns. "This isn't your fault. Shax has a bit of an ego on him."

"It could have waited."

"No." Eligos stands and stretches his arms up over his head. "Shax needs to learn that the world does not cater to his wild whims. How much do you know about us?"

I shrug. "What they teach in school. I mean... Not much."

He nods, then beckons me. "Come. We're going to talk about what they don't teach you in school."

I don't hesitate.

Eligos waves for me to join him once more on the daybed. I at least wiggle off my shoes before climbing up on the opposite side from him and lean against the armrest. But I'm surprised when Eligos begins to pace in front of the daybed.

"It's probably easiest if we start with Valac." He pauses and holds his hand up about shoulder height. "Did you see him? Short, very petite?"

"No," I say slowly. "I saw very little."

Though I do remember a boy with a kind smile vaguely. Was that this man? Demon Lord Valac?

Eligos nods, then fixes me with a serious stare. "Well, you should always stay away from Valac. He'll be pleasant in letters, but the moment he meets you, he will try to fuck you."

I'm not sure how I should respond. I freeze under Eligos' sharp gaze, feeling a little in danger right now. Only my lord's brow is furrowed.

"Actually," he mutters. "Scratch that. I think I'm confusing lifetimes... Is it this lifetime or...?"

How strange it must be to manage what you know about people over lifetimes?

Eligos fixes me with a stare. "Valac is vain and likes beautiful things. You can appeal to his vanity to get what you want. He is a lust demon, so sex is always on his mind. But every few lifetimes he gets a bit... Fluid."

"What? Like water?"

"No." Eligos' mouth twists up. "You'll understand when you meet him."

"I-I see. No sex with the lust demon. Got it."

Eligos' lips quirk up into a smile. "Good. Valac is often on our side when it comes to matters of state. He's our ally in most things. Liberal socially, conservative when it comes to the rule of law. He can be relied on if you get him to commit, but he is lazy, stubborn, and possessive of what he considers his."

"Should I be taking notes?" I ask.

He waves his hand. "No, this is just general knowledge. Obviously, Belial might think differently on some points, but he and I are generally aligned."

"What would the others say about you?" I ask.

Eligos snorts. "Probably that we are simple-minded, selfish, and lazy. All of which would be true."

I don't argue that point, but my observations tell a different story.

"Oriax." Eligos resumes his pacing. "You've met him, more or less. Oraix is a driving force behind many of our laws. He also spends a great deal of time nurturing the mage's academy. He wrote most of the texts. He's a lot like a cat, if I'm honest. Aloof, unreliable at times, charmed with his own wit. He is quick to anger, though, and that can be a problem."

I think back at those flashing green eyes. Oriax cut an intimidating figure, but he was also incredibly handsome. "What kind of demon is he?"

"He's a wrath demon."

"I never knew there were different types."

"Hm, probably because Oriax thought it would be too confusing for humans. Not all are as clever as you."

"How many kinds of demon are there? What's the purpose of different types?"

"Many. Some of us are the only one of our kind, but that's rare. The type of demon we are is what we specialize in."

"What is a wrath demon good at? I assume it's not just being angry."

"No." He chuckles. "It's more like... You sense that person's inclination. Oriax knows what buttons to push to make someone act out of anger, or what topics to avoid to keep negotiations peaceful."

"Oh..."

"The seven of us are generally considered to be the strongest of our kind, respectively." Eligos studies me for a moment longer. "Do I tell you things that will distress you? Or do I protect you?"

"Honesty is the best policy." And my curiosity needs to be satisfied.

Eligos sits next to me suddenly, so close his shoulder presses to mine. I swallow and inhale his soothing scent.

"We're losing our power," he says so softly I have to replay his words to really hear them. "Out of all of us, Oriax fears that the most. He's obsessed with halting our decline, which is why I fear he wanted you. He will do anything, go to any lengths, to restore us."

I barely dare breathe.

The High Demon Lords are weaker than they once were. Is this widely known? What about other demons?

Eligos turns to look at me. "Never allow yourself to be alone with him, understood? I don't know if that ring will protect you from his magic. It's untested."

I nod because I don't trust my voice.

"Are you scared?" he asks in a gentle tone.

"It's unsettling to hear you say you are losing your power." What about the conflict on the continent? What happens if the lords are weakened and we're attacked?

He shifts so that he's leaning on the armrest facing me. His eyes are heavy lidded now. "We aren't too weak to protect what's ours. Just not powerful enough to, say, destroy a continent."

"Did that happen?"

His gaze drifts away from me. "We just about did a very long time ago, when the world was a different place. Belial and I agree that there's only so much power we should be given. It's not a bad thing that we are weaker than we once were."

"But Oriax disagrees?"

"Hm. Oriax... He and Alastor have always been locked on opposing sides. Oriax will make decisions, at times, based on what will irritate Alastor the most. It's really fucking annoying, but it makes Oriax predictable. In a way. The same way Belial and I are predictable."

I nod slowly.

They're sounding more and more like quarrelsome brothers and less like majestic, powerful creatures out of time and space.

"Next there's Raum. He's the least troublesome of us all. And probably the best. He won't ever trouble you. If anything, he's too tender."

That makes me pause. "The Great Raum? The greatest tactician?"

Eligos snorts. "That's how Oriax describes him?"

"It's in the books."

"Gods." Eligos laughs. "Oh, he must hate that."

"It's not true?"

"It is, but those tactics were a combined effort between Raum, Oriax, and Belial." Eligos' lips are still twitching as if this is some great joke.

"Oriax seems to like to tweak history."

"Much of history depends on the lens through which you view it." Eligos shrugs, then goes still. "There is much you do not know."

That sentence is burdened with meaning I don't understand. What else is there? I want to crawl into his mind and better understand all of this, but part of me is afraid of the truth.

Instead, I ask, "What kind of demon is Raum?"

"Envy." Eligos grins. "You'd probably get on with him, but that would make me jealous."

"I don't know if that's a compliment or if I should be offended."

He picks up my hand and I stop breathing. Once again, it's as though my body is pulled toward him. Is this me? Or is he seducing me? Do I care?

Eligos presses his lips to one knuckle, then another, and another. He lingers on the last one, staring into my eyes. My lungs are burning, but I don't dare breathe. I don't want to break this moment.

The study doors burst open, but Eligos doesn't seem to notice. He lowers our now clasped hands to rest on his thigh.

"Alastor is an ass," Belial announces as he stalks past the daybed and circles around to stand in front of the fire.

I'm frozen to the spot, keenly aware of Eligos' hand twined around mine and that I should not allow this. So why haven't I moved?

Belial turns and though his eyes bounce casually from Eligos' face to mine.

"What has Alastor done now?" Eligos asks.

Belial waves a hand. "You know. The same stuff. What are you two doing? I'm surprised you're awake, Eli."

"I had to handle a matter with Shax."

Belial's brows rise. "Oh?"

Eligos peers at me, then his lover. "You know how Shax is."

Belial looks at me. "Was he an ass? Do you want me to punch him for you?"

I pull out of Eligos' grip and hold my hands up. "No. No, please."

"I was giving Lioria a run-down of our motley crew."

"Oh?" Belial crosses to perch on the opposite arm of the daybed. I cringe a little at his boots on the cushions, but I doubt there's any stopping him.

"We've discussed Valac, Oriax, and were just talking about Raum."

Belial nods. "If you ever want to know history, don't go to Oriax. You want Raum."

"I thought Oriax ran the academy?"

Belial waves his hand. "Oriax picks and chooses how he wants people to learn about history. But if you want the real version, Raum. He probably has some artifact or junk piece from the time."

"Is he a collector? Like of the fairy objects?"

Eligos chuckles. "Nothing of the kind. More... Old human things."

"He's a sloth demon, too. Did you tell her that?"

"I mentioned it."

Belial slides down and extends his legs alongside mine, trapping me between them in a way. It's as if they are both determined to see just how far they can push me. "Then, Shax? He's an asshole. Never forget that."

Eligos twines a piece of my hair that's escaped my braid around his finger. "He is."

Belial sighs. "He's not all bad. He's fiercely loyal. Reliable—most of the time. And he's sometimes the only one who can strike a balance between Alastor and Oriax. Shax would hate hearing this, but he balances them out."

"Shax is a greed demon." Eligos tugs on the hair, and I resist the implied command to look at him. "He's also the creature responsible for coming up with the idea of your contracts."

Now that's interesting. "Oh? Really?"

"And unions," Belial adds.

"Doesn't that go against his nature?" I ask.

"It depends which way you look at it." Eligos releases my hair with a sigh. "Greed can take on many forms. Used to be, Shax was quite greedy with money or things of perceived value. He hoarded them until those very objects passed out of value. For something to be considered valuable, people have to want it."

Belial nods and chuckles. "He was so greedy he killed his greed. It's made him a more balanced person. He can be a complete ass, but he's not all bad."

"That brings us to Alastor," Eligos says.

Belial catches my eye. "Pride demon."

"Is it true he's the most powerful?" I ask.

Eligos tips his head to the side. "It has been centuries since we last tested ourselves against each other. Hard to say."

"I wouldn't want to go up against him," Belial says in perhaps the most serious tone I've heard from him. "There's no one cleverer than Alastor. He adapts faster than the rest of us. Even Raum. The way Alastor sees things..."

Eligos drags a finger down my shoulder. "He was a favorite, you see. In... The time before."

A favorite of the gods?

Both my gentlemen are quiet now, and I don't know what I should say or if I should speak.

The chime of the letterbox is far too loud in the quiet space.

Neither of the lords seem to notice.

"I'm going to check that," I mutter just loud enough so my intentions are clear.

Eligos eyes me as I get to my feet and step over him, but he doesn't stop me. I retreat across the room under the false hope that a little distance would ease the mood. But it follows me, and I am acutely aware of Belial watching me.

There are two letters in the box. Both from Shax.

Given how our exchanges today have gone, I take both to the daybed and hand them to Eligos. He sighs heavily and takes them.

"What now?" He tosses one at Belial. "If I have to read these, so do you."

Eligos carefully opens the letter and frowns.

Belial laughs. "This must be a reply to you. What did you say to him?"

"I just told him what I thought of him," Eligos mutters, then glanced at Belial. "We have a problem."

"Oh?" He held out his letter.

The two exchanged pages, similar expressions of concern marring their handsome features.

"I see," Belial says slowly and glances up to meet Eligos' gaze. "We can't today. We..."

"I know." Eligos folds Shax's reply and tucks it in his pocket.

The two lords communicate with nothing more than the most subtle facial expressions. A twitch of one eye, the slight curving of a mouth, a wrinkled nose.

"It can't be Mrs. Jurrah," Eligos says in a soft tone.

Belial's gaze rises to me. "No. But—"

"No," Eligos says in a hard tone.

Belial draws up a knee and props his elbow on it. "Do you think it's danger-ous?"

Eligos grimaces, appearing to wrestle with this question, but finally answers with a terse, "No."

They continue staring at each other, and I remain a voyeur.

At long last, Eligos shakes his head and sighs. "I don't like it."

"I don't expect you to."

"Who is going with her?"

"Teill."

Eligos snorts. "Teill is currently upset with Lioria."

Belial waves a hand. "She just needs a push. She's fine."

Eligos looks up at me and shrugs. "Don't ever forget, if I had my way, you'd be right here."

"What is it I'm doing?" I ask slowly.

"Shax needs to deliver a sensitive message that cannot pass through the letter-boxes. He needs it hand-delivered, but both of us are tied up with things here." Belial gestures to Eligos. "I take it that's why you're dressed?"

"Naturally," Eligos drawls.

I blink a few times. "Then I am to travel to Demon Lord Shax?"

"No. Not that far. Just my estate," Belial says.

"His main estate," Eligos clarifies.

"I see..." I say slowly. "Is that now? Or..."

"The sooner you go, the sooner you can come back." Belial rises from the bed and comes around to stand next to me. He takes a large signet ring off his finger, then lifts my hand and speaks words I don't understand.

I can't help but feel like a blushing bride as he slides the heavy ring onto my middle finger. It's far too large. It would probably fall off my thumb, it's so large. But then the warm metal begins to shrink, right down to the proper size for my finger.

"There." Belial strokes my fingers with his. "Everything I have and all that I am now answers to you."

It is just a ring, but it feels like more just happened that I don't fully understand.

BELIAL

We watch the magical carriage leave out the servant's entrance together. There's an awareness of her that is new. I'd thought it was simply an obsession. A fancy that would pass once the luster had worn off.

Now I fear that isn't the case at all.

"Do you feel that?" Eligos whispers.

"I could point directly at her," I mutter.

We still don't have a clue what she is or why Lioria draws us the way she does. I had Teill gather a few of her hairs while cleaning her room after Eligos told me about their budding friendship.

I'm glad that Teill has taken to Lioria. She's always been a bit of a loner, and I worry about her like a father might. Besides, if Lioria is in danger, a boggarting Brownie is quite fearsome.

"What is she?" Eligos asks.

I wish I knew.

I turn from the windows and stalk back to the hall with Eligos in my wake.

"This plan isn't working," I say.

Eligos chuckles. "It's only been a few days. She's settling in."

"That's easy for you to say." I bite back the rest of my thoughts.

"Why? Because I ignore her insistent way of ignoring us? You think she came over and sat with me of her own accord? Do you realize the mental hoops I'm jumping through to orchestrate this? It's exhausting."

"I just want to..."

I curl my hands into fists and imagine shoving my fingers into her hair.

I want to touch her.

I want to kiss that pert little mouth of hers.

I want to fuck her until I'm imprinted on every cell in her body.

And then I want to watch Eligos do it all to her again.

Maybe take turns.

My cock is hard, which comes as no surprise. It happens whenever I catch the scent of her tea or hear her laugh.

Eligos runs his fingers up my outer thigh. "Oh, hello there..."

I freeze in no little panic as my erection seems to deflate.

Eligos takes my hand and squeezes it gently. "I understand."

"I don't. Why is this happening? Have we been cursed? Is she a witch?"

"Not an old blood witch, no. You know that's impossible."

"Is it?"

Eligos shrugs. "Raum would say no. Oriax yes. What answer do you want?"

"I want her, Eli."

He inclines his head and pulls me into our study where we are the safest from prying ears. Not that anyone is around this area to listen. Our staff is discrete.

I tip my head back. "This was a mistake. This whole damned plan."

"It was a short-sighted plan," Eligos agrees, which I didn't expect. "You're doing such a good job restraining yourself. I'm proud of you."

He's doting on me, doing his best to meet my needs as he can. But it's no use. If I were a better man, I'd do the same for him. But I am a selfish creature being denied what he wants.

We've tried three times now to be intimate since returning with Lioria. Neither of us can maintain an erection. In all my lives, only old age has had this effect on me. It's maddening to have the woman right there and not be able to touch her.

Eligos pulls me to him and wraps his arms around me. "As her employers, we have constant access to her. But, that damn contract means we cannot make the first move... It seems our little light skirt isn't as tempt-able as we'd hoped."

I squeeze my eyes shut and try to ignore the almost constant growl of my demon. "I'm not good at denying myself, Eli..."

"I know." He leans in and kisses me. "I know. It goes against your nature. You're doing such a good job. The angels would be proud of you."

"Fuck those cowards," he huffs before his face lines with concern. "I've wanted pussy before, but never like this..."

"The festival is in a few days," Eli says.

I pause to think about what that might mean, but fail to make any connection. "What are you thinking?"

"Do you want to know? Or would you rather I plot and scheme alone?"

"Will it bring her into our bed?" I ask.

He shrugs. "One of us, at least. I think. It's all up to her."

"Don't tell me," I whisper.

There was a day when I wouldn't have waited. I'd have taken what I want. But I was a different creature then. We've all evolved and changed. I might want Lioria more than my next breath, but my desire to remain as I am is stronger. For now.

Eligos' plan might damn us, but that's a price I'm willing to pay.

"Let's get on with this," I mutter.

Alastor knew what he was doing, asking us when we were young and inclined to say yes to things we wouldn't with a few more years on us. To be fair, playing spy has been entertaining. But lately, it's been more work and less interesting. The more questions we uncover the more frustrating this job becomes. I'm not even sure what it is we're after.

"You want to do the honors?" I ask Eligos.

He grunts and pulls out the key.

We cross to the double doors and he slides it into the lock.

This key will fit any door, but open none of them. Instead, the very fabric of the doors themselves ripple, becoming a portal into what looks to be nothing.

Looking at it unsettles my stomach every time.

I step through into yawning darkness regardless, but don't venture far. Eligos keeps pace with me and we stand there, nearly swallowed whole.

This was a sad place before, when everything was as it should be. It's worse now.

Time ticks on and I resist grinding my teeth in frustration.

Eligos must hear something because he tilts his head and listens.

Eventually, I hear it, too. The quiet thump of feet in the nothing. And then a figure emerges. He's tall with a lithe body. His dark hair is swept back, off his stoic face that has always, in every lifetime, been some variant of the same. Strong, pointed jaw. Bow-like lips that never smile. Ruby red eyes. He's dressed in somber colors.

Right.

There's a funeral in the capital today.

"Fancy seeing you around here, Alastor," Eligos says.

"The boundary stones?" Alastor says, skipping the greeting altogether.

"What of them?" I shrug. "We don't have any new information. Our spies in the refugee camps don't know much of anything. A few of them have heard more rumors about forerunners, but..."

"What of the informant who told you of the first one?" Alastor asks.

Eligos smiles. "He's in the wind, sadly. You know how it goes."

If Alastor knew we'd allowed Puck past our borders, he'd skin us alive, then do it again.

"Damn it," he mutters. "The refugees, they're peaceful? No sign of unrest?"

"No reason to," Eligos says. "They're left alone and have full bellies for the first time in their lives. They aren't going to hurt a fly."

Alastor hums and I can practically hear his doubts.

What happened to the man who believed peace was possible if we all just tried to move past our history? We've all changed over the years, but Alastor's shift is more pronounced. That, or I'm simply noticing it more.

He pulls out a thick bundle of pages. "These are copies of all the communications from the palace spymaster. See if you find any worth in them."

Fuck me.

He intends us to do it now. In front of him.

"If you're going to assign activities, could you at least pick a more comfortable place?" Eligos says and takes a little more than half the stack.

Alastor merely crosses his arms over his chest.

What is with him?

I pick up the first page and begin reading.

This is going to take forever.

LIORIA

I t's completely silent inside the carriage. Teill sits across from me, slightly slumped over. I fear she was woken up for this trip. She had said she was a night owl. Maybe I should say nothing? It's nice to see her.

One thing I'm only beginning to realize is that I'm accustomed to people. Being in a tavern, I'd see dozens of people throughout my day. I know little details about their lives, hopes, and dreams. I'm used to talking about that and hearing the latest gossip.

Teill is the only friend I've made since coming here, and this fracture between us hurts.

The carriage begins to move with dizzying speed, so I find a spot to stare at off to the side.

I should have brought a book, but everything happened so fast I didn't get the chance.

Suddenly Teill sits up straight, her eyes squished shut. "I'm sorry I got angry. It's not like you understood. I just thought you did, so it surprised me and I overreacted."

I want nothing more than to squeeze Teill like my closest friend.

"I don't want to upset you. Can I make this right? Can we start over?"

She still isn't looking at me. "I just... You left the candy the first night, so I thought... And then..."

The candy?

I don't understand, which seems to be the common factor here.

"I promise to do better." And I can ask Eligos or Belial for clarification later.

Teill peeks at me. "Do you even know what you did?"

"Not really, but I upset you, and I'm sorry."

Her brow furrows, making the rock on the left side jut upward. "You've only been around humans. It's not your fault."

I grin at her. "I'm trying to fix that."

Teill ducks her head. "It's maybe wrong of me to have Brownie sensibilities when most of my kind wouldn't claim me."

"Fuck them. What matters is if you're happy."

He finally meets my gaze and smiles sheepishly. "Can we still be friends?"

"I was hoping we could."

Teill blows out a breath and stares over my shoulder. "Belial says I can't accept compliments. That it's a flaw all Brownies have. We can't bear to be thanked when our motives are so selfish. That... That's why I can't, I mean..."

Her words startle a laugh out of me. "I can so relate to that."

My words must surprise Teill because her gaze snaps to mine.

"I've always been a working girl. Gentlemen come in and thank me for doing my job, which I do so I can pay for my room and food. It's so awkward. Their thanks always felt...wrong."

Teill nods vigorously. "Yes! I just—I can't stand it. I want the ground to open up and swallow me whole."

"Would it be rude to ask what Belial and Eligos gift you? If it's rude, just ignore me."

Her cheeks tinge a light gray. "T-the candy..."

Candy.

What candy?

The silver box.

She stole a candy out of the box and gave it to me. What did I do with it? Where is it?

Wait.

What had Teill said earlier? She thought I understood?

"I emptied my pockets and put the candy on the mantle, so you thought it was an offering..."

Teill's gaze drops to the ground.

"That's why Belial doesn't touch the candy. It's not for him."

I've left the lords in the study each day. Belial probably sets out his nightly offering before retiring, so there's no way I'd have known.

"Sorry," I mumble from behind my hand then wince. "And then I went and left you a lousy pear."

"I like fruit."

"But not as much as candy."

Teill surprises me by laughing. "It's kind of funny in hindsight."

I snicker because her laughter is contagious. "It really is."

For several moments we are a mess of giggles and tears. It's a relief to understand the situation. Now that I know my Brownie friend has a sweet tooth, I can better offer her gifts.

Our laughter subsides and we both sit flopped back against the cushioned benches. I'm holding my stomach from laughing so hard.

"Alright, we will never have that conversation again, I promise you." I sit up, my cheeks hurting from grinning so hard.

Teill frowns, which is an adorable expression on her darling face. "I didn't like avoiding you."

"Did Belial wake you for this little trip?" I ask.

She rolls her eyes. "Yes. But I'm glad he did."

"Well, I'm not sorry because I'm glad you're here."

Teill studies me for a moment before speaking slowly, as if she's still choosing her words, "You seem like a very self-aware person..."

I shrug. "I try to be. There are fewer rules and guidelines for someone like me."

One side of her mouth hitches up and her gaze narrows. "You are aware the lords want to fuck you, right?"

I freeze.

"Sorry," Teill yelps. "Was that rude?"

"No. No, I don't think that was rude. I, um..." I close my eyes, which somehow makes it easier to speak. "I've been pretending to be oblivious... How's it working?"

"Well, you had me fooled. I thought you might be a little stupid. Are they not attractive as far as humans go?" She wrinkles her nose. "They're practically hairless. I know I don't have much hair, but I can't help it. I was petrified. My hair's never come back."

"Do Brownies generally have more hair?"

She nods. "I'd say most humans can't tell male and female Brownies apart. You used to think we only came in one form."

"Oh, that would be quite a lot of hair..."

Teill cocks her head to the side. "Is there something wrong with Belial or Eligos? Or both of them? Or do you not like men who also like men?"

I have no one to talk to about this to work out my twisted thoughts. "Is this something we should be talking about? Isn't Belial your lord, or something?"

Teill waves her hand. "Yes, but I don't intend to tell him anything. Not unless he asks and I feel it's in his best interest. I rather enjoy being a silent observer."

While I am incredibly curious about Teill's admission to watching, I desperately want to talk.

"They're Demon Lords. High Demon Lords. And... I'm just a serving girl who knows how to read and write." I lift my shoulders. "Involving myself with them seems... Dangerous. For the first time in my life, I'm being completely reasonable, and I hate it."

"Belial and Eligos would never hurt you. Well... Not intentionally, I don't think."

"Maybe not." I ease back onto the cushions. "I didn't know who they were when I met them separately. I would have made very different decisions had I remained ignorant. But now...?"

"What do you think would happen?"

"I've grown up on stories about the High Demon Lords. Not one of them is a love story. They don't marry. Right now, as an orphan, I have freedom. There are no expectations of me. But if I took one of them as a lover—"

"Or both? Is both not an option for you?"

My cheeks flush. "I'm not opposed to that, I've just never..."

"Oh." Teill waves her hand. "Continue."

"From my limited understanding, the women the lords take as concubines end up in pretty cages, their lives devoted to continuing the lord's line. I'm not sure that's a future I want for myself."

"What do you want?"

I shrug. "It used to be easy. I thought I'd work another five or so years until I got tired of the tavern or too old for the fishermen to flirt with, then find myself a widower with children to raise. Hopefully, someone kind who I'd grow to love over time and complete my life."

Teill nods slowly. "You aren't entirely wrong, but you aren't right either."

"How long have you been with Belial?"

"Oh... Almost a hundred years, I'd say. This is his third lifetime." She shifts, curling a leg under her. "You must always keep in mind that the lords control what is said about them. What you were taught and what people are allowed to know is intentional. Belial had a life partner when I met him. You've probably never heard of her, and I wouldn't quite call them lovers. But they were close. She went everywhere with him. Her death caused his heartbreak, and he declined from there."

I'm immediately jealous of this woman, and grateful. The stories we've heard are about the battles won and great heroics. But it's also the small things. Keeping elderly staff on. Rescuing a poisoned Vodu girl. Small kindnesses in the grand scope of their existence that can change the course of people's lives.

"You are right about your life being controlled, though. Belial and Eligos would go to great lengths to protect your identity from getting out, but eventually, you would be a target. You would probably be in their care for the rest of your life. That's not a decision to make lightly. You're smarter than I gave you credit for."

I laugh and cherish the compliment. "They are sweet, and they seem happy together."

Teill smiles fondly. "You know, I always wondered if Eligos had a thing for Belial. When Belial's partner died two lifetimes ago, Eligos was very young. He came to stay with Belial until the end."

"What did you do? Between his death and when he came back?"

"I lived with Eligos for a while. It wasn't the same, but I was very young. I'm still quite young, but I know things now."

"I would worry about coming between them," I say slowly. "They seem so content together. Why mess that up?"

"Why do you think you'd ruin it? What if you bring balance to their chaos?"

"What if they aren't missing anything? What if I'm just a passing fancy they get bored with? Is that enough to stake my whole life on?"

"If you truly feel that way, maybe they could change the rules for you? They are the ones who make them."

"That's an awful lot of trust to give someone. I don't know if I can, Teill. I like them, but is my interest enough to stake the rest of my life on?" My peace and confidence were hard won. I'm not entirely sure I want to give that power to someone else. Even my demon lords.

"Well, you are in a tough spot, I'm afraid. Belial is a glutton demon..."

"What's that supposed to mean?"

Teill's brows arch. "He's not used to denying himself anything..."

Is it possible I will need to leave my new life sooner than anticipated? What of Oriax? Would I trade one cage for another? And why me? I'm nothing special.

"If it seems like Belial might give in to his demon, I'll tell you," Teill says. "At least you'd have a head start then. Though, you are playing a dangerous game tempting demons like this."

I lift my shoulders. "I didn't know we were playing a game."

"That is the human way."

We both sigh and study one another. Unlike before, this silence is comfortable. I feel as though I can say anything, except thank you.

"Do you have plans for the festival?" Teill asks.

"No. I've never actually gotten to enjoy one."

"You'll love it. There's so much to eat and do. So many merchants will be there. And there's the Lord's Tonic business, of course."

"Do you go?"

"Yes! I glamour myself to look human, obviously." She pauses for a moment, her gaze taking me in from head to toe. "It wouldn't be a terrible idea to glamour yourself."

"I don't have that kind of magic. I have very little, actually."

Teill lifts a shoulder. "Doesn't matter. The lords have items. I bet they'd loan you one seeing as you're their favorite right now."

"Are there many non-humans around?"

"Oh, lots." She grins at me. "But you'll never know. The ones who live here obey the High Demon Lord's rules, and almost all of them are discrete about what they really are."

"Why?"

"Many of them give up everything. Family. Alliances. Wealth. All for peace. Or they're escaping something." Her gaze slides over me again. "We'll have to put some thought into your glamour." Teill leans forward. "I think we're almost there."

"What?" I look out the window and my stomach begins to churn.

She grips my wrist and tugs. "Deep breaths. Look at me."

"That's awful."

"You get motion sickness. Never travel by boat."

"It feels like the carriage is spinning."

She chuckles at me while the whirling sensation subsides.

"I know the carriage is magic, but isn't Belial's main estate a long ways away?"

"If the route is an often traveled one, the magic can fold greater distances."

"Oh."

Magic might be a way of life for many people, but there were few people growing up who could do more than light a candle or ripple water with their ability.

"Belial said you were meeting with Shax?"

"Yes."

"Have you met him?"

"Not really. I know he likes to hear himself talk. A lot. And he has a low opinion of me."

Teill wrinkles her nose. "Watch yourself around him. I doubt he'd hurt you, but he can be...odd. I've only met him a few times myself. Well, now that I think of it he might never have seen me..."

"Is he... Do you think he's dangerous?"

"Generally speaking, they're all dangerous. They broke the world."

"What?"

Teill sits ramrod straight. "Nothing. Never mind me. Vodu talk. I really should know better."

I'm not convinced.

The carriage slows until the scenery looks normal. We're passing down a tree-lined lane. The carriage turns, following the curve of the land around a pond and the official palace of the High Demon Lord comes into view. It's like nothing I've ever seen.

There are tall spires piercing the sky and windows taller than ten people. Even at this distance, I see gardens and a sprawling city. It's too grand for words.

Teill chuckles. "Oh, you are a country mouse, aren't you?"

"I thought... I mean..." I sit there and blink at her, unsure what I could possibly say.

"The town around Privale used to be nothing at all. Wherever the Demon Lords live, life follows."

We pass through a gate and an extensive nature park behind the palace before reaching the outlying buildings that serve to support the main house. Only this is a palace, and there's a small village within the walls. Even the servant's entrance is grand.

A footman opens the door and I look at Teill the moment before she winks out of existence.

"That's cheating," I mutter.

She nudges me and I exit the carriage, feeling too frumpy and small to be here.

The carriage and footmen move off the moment the door shuts.

"What do I do now?" I whisper.

I hear a slight sigh from the direction I think Teill is standing.

The doors open and a tanned woman wearing a sensible dress strides out as though she needs to be somewhere already. Her eyes lock on me, and I want to make myself scarce. Instead, I remain where I am as she strides up to me and thrusts out her hand.

"You must be the lord's new secretary. I manage the house here." She's maybe ten years older than me. Much younger than I'd expect the steward or housekeeper or whatever her title is.

"Ah, y-yes." I take her hand in a firm shake.

"Lord Shax is waiting for you, I'm afraid. Will you have time afterward to deal with business?"

"Business? I don't know what business you're talking about."

Her mouth screws up and her serene masks cracks with a barely contained chuckle. "That's not surprising. I have to take any opportunity that comes to get the lord's attention."

"At least he's consistent," I mutter.

That nearly breaks the rest of her mask, and for a moment she struggles to remain composed. I do my part by not laughing and giving her a moment.

"Thank you," she says primly. "This way?"

The woman leads me through the doors and past the guards.

Inside, the floors are gleaming marble. There are tapestries and paintings on the walls. I even see one of those rare, seamless images I've only heard stories about. But I'm too anxious to stop and admire the oddities. The interior is comfortably cool and yet more magical lanterns maintain a steady glow.

"I would show you the lord's study, but he will more than likely want you to return quickly."

"Is it possible to communicate that business to me? Forward letters, perhaps?"

She glances at me, a slight furrow marring her otherwise elegant brow. "Aren't you busy enough?"

"To be honest, I'm merely doing my best to get up to speed."

Her lips quirk up into a fleeting smile. "We do the best we can. If you don't mind, I will reach out about a few things?"

"Please, anything I can help with, I will."

She stops suddenly. We're in the middle of a grand hall with windows that look out onto a beautifully cultivated terrace.

All this time I'd thought Privale was a grand palace. By comparison, it's homely and cozy. This place is opulence, and it isn't even the central palace.

"I'll remain out here if you need anything," she says and nods at the door to my right.

"Oh. Oh!" I drop my voice to a whisper. "Lord Shax, he's in there?"

"Yes."

"Did he seem…. What was his mood, if I might ask?"

"He didn't complain any more or less than usual."

I nod, but that doesn't tell me much. I still don't know what's so sensitive that I need to handle it in person.

Right.

It's time to face the High Demon Lord who has a reason to not like me.

Lovely.

I draw in another breath before tugging the door open and stepping into the room. I'm not sure if Teill joins me.

The room is spacious with comfortable sofas and books lining the wall. Most of the colors are in autumn hues, which somehow makes such a large space rather cozy.

And there, standing in the middle of it all is a tall, well-built man staring out the windows. His hair is so pale it looks white. It could also be the medium brown and bronzed tone of his skin that offsets the light color so well. Even in profile, he is beautiful to look at.

"If it's going to be much longer, bring me something to eat," he says.

Ah, that voice.

"No need to wait, my lord." I smile broadly at him and curtsey, though maybe not as deeply as I should.

He turns toward me and frowns. His gaze skitters over me and his frown deepens. I regret my clothing immediately, though it's not as if I have anything nicer. There's just something about the way his gaze assesses me that makes me feel as though I'm lacking somehow.

"You? You're the new secretary?" he demands.

"Yes, my lord."

He crosses to stand in front of me in three, long strides and takes my jaw in his hand, turning my face this way then that.

"What's so special about you?" he practically growls.

Normally I'd shove him right off me, but my better sense is showing. I remain perfectly still, my eyes on his throat, and say nothing.

"I heard Belial attacked Oriax over you. Is your pussy really that good?" He leans in, pressing his nose to my cheek, and inhales. "Interesting..."

I can't think past the fact that this man—this demon—holds my life in his hands. Literally right now. If he wanted he could snap my neck.

"Sir, I'm just here to act as a courier." It's difficult to speak with him holding my face like this, but my words come out clear enough.

He turns my face so that I'm forced to look at him. His eyes are not human at all. The pupils are slits in his amber eyes. It's his demon side smirking back at me.

"That's not all you are. I heard that Belial almost broke Oriax's jaw for you. I would have paid money to see that." He smiles, and though I wouldn't call it a pleasant expression, I don't get the sense I'm in danger.

Shax lifts his other hand to stroke my cheek while he continues to stare at me. And my lords said that Oraix would treat me like a thing to be studied.

His fingers slide over my cheek in a gentle caress and the grip on my jaw relaxes. "You aren't fucking them, so why are you important? Hm?"

I flinch back. "How dare..."

Too late I remember myself.

This earns a laugh from Shax. He's mercurial, angry to amused so quickly I don't know what to make of this.

His eyes morph from slits to rounded centers, and his face relaxes, the harsh lines smoothing out until he is fully human again. "What would it take for you to pick me rather than them? Hm?"

I gape at him, not sure what to say.

Shax cups my face with his hands now. "What do you say?"

"Sir, I'm just here to ensure your message is delivered. That's it."

His gaze narrows, and he sighs.

"You're no fun, little barmaid. Still, I can't believe my brethren would send you."

"I'm just their secretary." I reach up and take hold of his wrists firmly. "That is my only goal, my lord."

"Too bad..."

His words pinch the pit of my stomach.

Shax leans in and presses his lips to mine. I'm so surprised by the move I freeze, while his tongue strokes across my lips. He steps in closer, so that the hard planes of his body press against me, creating an answering warmth low in my abdomen. He doesn't force the kiss deeper, merely flirts with my lips until I can't quite remember why resisting him is a good idea.

Something pinches my bottom. I jump with a squeak and push the Demon Lord away.

Shax grins at me like a mischievous boy.

"It was a pleasure, little barmaid. Give my regards to my brethren." He nods at a nearby table, but I don't take my eyes off him. "The package is over there."

I step back, running into something warm and solid that isn't visibly there.

Teill.

She didn't leave me, and Shax doesn't seem to know she's present.

Shax bows low to me, and yet it feels like an insult. Then he turns and is gone, out the door and on his way.

I let out a shaking breath and Teill winks into view.

"Oh, my word," she mutters and clutches me to her. "What an animal. No manners. None at all. Are you okay?"

My knees are weak.

The ring!

Why didn't I think to use it? Wasn't it supposed to protect me?

An undercurrent of lust I don't want to admit to curls through me.

"I... I want to go home now." I press my hand to my stomach and lock eyes with Teill. "You cannot tell Belial what happened."

Teill's brows arch. "Not sure that's possible..."

"Why? What do you mean?"

She gestures at my face. "There's demonic energy on you. We can maybe scrub your face with salt, but I think his lordship is going to know what Shax did."

LIORIA

The meeting with Shax left me shaken. It wasn't the first time a man got too handsy with me. It wasn't even my first unwilling kiss. But it was the first time I felt that vulnerable. I was me, and yet... I feel as though something inside of me were pulling me toward Shax.

Worst of all?

If I were really and truly honest with myself, I liked that thread of fear. Shax was handsome, and there was something about his inhumanness that appealed to me. Dark desires rolling around in the back of my mind whispered seductive words about being taken by him.

But then what of Belial and Eligos? What would they do?

"Here." Teill thrust the little container she'd been mixing at me.

I peered at the contents in the low light of the carriage. "What is it?"

"A mixture of salt, some sage, and oil. Scrub it anywhere Shax touched."

"It will work?"

Teill lifted her shoulders. "I don't know. You'd maybe be able to wipe away traces of a less powerful demon, but he *wanted* to mark you. You're practically glowing with it."

I scooped out some of the mixture and rolled it between my fingers. The oil coats my skin while the coarse grains abraded me. "They're going to blame me for this."

Thanks to the shadows I can't see Teill's face very well. "I don't know if they'll be human enough to be reasonable..."

"I have to run away," I whisper.

"Don't jump to silly conclusions." Yet Teill's tone is still hesitant.

Breaking a contract is bad enough, but if I break a contract I signed with a High Demon Lord? I'll probably be thrown in prison. If I'm caught.

An employment contract is a method of protecting employees, but also facilitates a way to grade employers. It's an agreement that locks in how much I work, what a fair wage is, how I am to be given time off, or compensated for additional work. It also outlines rights and protections for employees. But it also clearly states the punishments for breaking the agreement.

I signed my contract stating that I agreed to work for my lords for the span of one year. It's the same agreement I signed every year to work at the Silver Roo. I'm well acquainted with the consequences of breaking my contract. There is, of course, a clause for dissolution of the contract.

But I don't think my lords would be willing to let me go.

I've allowed myself to believe this polite façade, that our Demon Lords aren't much different from humans. But we have so many stories about the lords using their rage in defense of humanity. How their strength and power elevate them above the common man. And all this time I've been treating them like simple tavern patrons, because that is what I know. But they aren't. To them I'm a toy to be fought over. I'm a simple girl who only knows the fanciful things I've read in books. I am not equipped to deal with whatever this is.

Teill moves to sit next to me. "Don't get worked up. I'll deliver Shax's letter to the study. You go draw a bath. We'll load it with salt. By the morning, they probably won't be able to tell."

"You're a bad liar," I whisper and link my arm with hers.

She squeezes my arm to her side. "Tell yourself to believe me and I'll be better."

I can't muster a chuckle. "What's the worst that happens?"

"I... I'm not sure."

I settle back against the bench and stare at the ceiling of the carriage.

The lords brought me here for my safety, but it's clear that's not all they want. These incredibly powerful beings could take anything they want from me and there isn't a person alive who would dream of stopping them. They've been playing human when there's nothing mortal about them, even if their power is waning. It strikes me then how lucky I've been that I, a common serving girl, have been allowed the power to say no.

"What are my chances of reaching the continent without being caught?" I ask.

Teill snorts. "You wouldn't make it off the property."

"You think?"

"It's the bond. They have an awareness of us, which is awfully annoying. Normally demons wouldn't be able to see me when I'm invisible but this damn bond lets Belial know exactly where I am."

That nearly stops my heart.

"I didn't know that..."

Teill shrugs and pats my hand. "They probably didn't think to tell you."

I've never felt trapped before. Even when I was little and the orphanage was my whole world, I still had choices. Now, it feels like there are none.

My lords have been nothing but kind, but how long will that last? How long until their demons sway the men? Then there's no choice at all.

I've drawn both Oriax and Shax's attention. But all I am to Belial and Eligos is a plaything. A passing amusement. Their love for each other is a beautiful thing, and I know I'll never feel that from them.

Running away will only be possible if I can put great distance between us, and even then I don't know the full scope of their power. They could catch me in an instant.

I've fallen into a trap and I don't see a way out.

Teill and I don't talk much on the return journey. It's dark by the time we arrive at Privale. I'm happy to see more familiar surroundings and the relatively cozier atmosphere.

Mrs. Jurrah meets us, still dressed for work. Or more accurately, she meets *me*, as Teill vanishes before we exit the carriage.

The housekeeper's gaze sweeps up and down my person while wringing her hands. Did she fear the worst for me? Has she warmed up? "Well, you made it. I trust the trip went well?"

"Well enough. Is something wrong?"

She fixes me with an expression that makes the pinch in the pit of my stomach worse.

Mrs. Jurrah presses a hand to her stomach, as if she only just realized she was wringing her hands. "The lords left and said they don't know when they'll return."

Belial and Eligos are not here.

They might not find out about Shax's liberties with me.

"Did the lords leave any orders? When will they be back?"

"They didn't say."

I draw in my first easy breath in hours. Maybe the gods are out there and listening?

Or maybe I'm just lucky.

LIORIA

My lords have been gone for four days. There has been no word from them. I received no instruction about what my duties should be, and Mrs. Jurrah refuses to assign me any tasks or speak with me more than is strictly necessary. I think I've seen her hems fleeing from me a few times around corners. Most of the staff are old enough to be my parents if not my grandparents. Some are polite when I speak to them, while most simply don't respond. It's clear to me they have come to a consensus about me, probably based on something the delightful Mrs. Jurrah has said, and have decided to freeze me out. The only person on staff that has treated me with any kindness is Edward.

That old man is a delight. He's even taken to carrying around a few hard candy pieces that he gives me before telling me to run along and enjoy the fine day.

If it wasn't for Teill, I might have taken this opportunity to run away. Honestly, it still might be the smartest move. The staff wouldn't miss me and it could be days before the lord's return and know of my absence.

"Well, how does it look now?" I anxiously watch Teill's face in the mirror over my shoulder.

My hair is soaking wet and I've barely dried the rest of me off enough to not track puddles across the floor, which will send Teill into a cleaning fit.

She screws up one side of her mouth and sighs. "It's faint, but still there."

I groan and tip my head back.

Seeing as I had so much free time I've been taking hour-long salt soaks twice a day in an effort to get rid of whatever demonic energy Shax left on me. We've tried a few other things, but salt soaks have worked best.

I sit on the wooden bench next to the sunken tub and scowl at my reflection.

Why didn't I use the ring? This whole situation could have been prevented had I protected myself as intended.

I bite down on my lip.

Four days ago it was easy to tell myself it was shock. That I hadn't reacted because I was surprised and unprepared.

With a little time and cooling of my emotions, it's harder to believe the lie.

Part of me had liked Shax's harsh touch and demanding kiss.

Did I subconsciously choose not to push Shax back because I wanted him?

It's the question I've been trying to distract myself from asking.

Teill sighs and glances at the frosted window. "I've got to get moving. You coming?"

"Yes." I pick myself up off the bench.

"Festival is tomorrow..."

I grimace and wrinkle my nose. I'm not as excited about it as I was.

"Oh, stop your moping," Teill snaps. Her figure blurs and she's next to me, her hands in my hair. "It'll be faster if I do it."

I stand perfectly still as her magic swirls around my head. I don't know what or how she does it, but as my hair passes through her fingers, it dries and becomes silky smooth. The result is breathtaking. It's still my face and figure, but the way she is able to coax my hair into this cascade of dark brown silk is astounding.

"There," she snaps. "You can do whatever you want with it now. Get dressed."

The day after the incident with Shax, my new clothes arrived, and I learned that my lords have poor boundaries. Instead of my new clothes being made by the staff, which would help me look like one of them, Belial and Eligos had my clothes made by a tailor out of rich fabrics I can't even identify. It's not just the few outfits I'd requested. It's dresses I will never have an occasion to wear. Articles I don't even know what they do. Pieces that might be wearable? Or are maybe intended for other purposes?

I haven't worn them. The boxes are currently stacked up as tall as the wardrobe. I'm not even sure there's enough room in my quarters for what's been delivered.

I need these demons to come back soon so I can knock some sense into them.

Teill taps her foot while I put on one of my worn tavern dresses. I'm still doing the buttons when she grabs my arm and steers me out through the bedroom and into the hall. She remains visible for my sake, though it's late enough most staff has already turned in for the night.

I tried asking Teill why she cleans rooms no one has been in since the lords are away, but she just looked at me like I'd grown another head. Now I simply accompany her.

Since the lords' departure, I've indulged my curiosity. They said I could go wherever I want and I've put that to the test. There are rooms in this manor I'm fairly sure no one has used in a decade. But I've also discovered wonders. Like the glass dome observatory. The library.

Tonight Teill starts in the strangest room I've seen yet.

The chapel.

I thought it strange at first there was a chapel in the house. Growing up, we all went to church. The church didn't come to us, but Teill explained that most great houses have one.

We cross the threshold into the narrow, windowless room and Teill's form blurs as she begins her routine. I tried helping two days ago. Yesterday she lost her patience and told me to just keep her company.

Tonight I wander the length of the room, peering at icons and candles that have no significance to me. It's wholly unlike any other church I've been to. Which is really only one, so it's not like I have a large frame of reference.

"Teill, why is this chapel so strange?" I peer around me. "Why don't I recognize anything in here?"

She laughs at me. "Because the lords were created by a specific god, so that is the god they worship."

"But I thought all of the gods appointed them stewards...?"

She hums a tune I don't recognize.

"Do you know something you don't want to tell me?" I ask.

Her shoulders draw up, but her back is to me now. "I don't know anything, love. I don't *want* to know anything."

"Aren't you curious? We're always told to offer up our prayers to strengthen the gods so they can continue to protect us. But what if the battle's over? What if no one won? What if they just left?"

She wheels on me, eyes wide. "Don't say things like that. Do you want people to hear you?"

I sigh and roll my eyes. "Alright. Fine. I'm heading to the study. See you there?"

Teill grunts a reply then winks out of sight.

Vodu and Yokai are supposed to be longer living creatures. Some of them were alive when the gods were still among us. What I wouldn't give for an hour to ask questions.

The study is cold and dark. The lights activate upon my entry and I spend a few moments lighting a fire.

It's not the same without Belial and Eligos here. That alone is strange. I don't know them well enough to have a routine. And yet, here I am. Missing two creatures who have effectively clipped my wings.

Most of the documents have been sorted and catalogued. I've even traded messages with someone in the capital to assist me with identifying which matters are ongoing, and what's been handled. What irritates me is that I keep being told I'm doing such a wonderful job when I haven't done anything.

I open the letterbox and find the folded paper has returned to me. Writing is scrawled on either side.

After our first exchange, I ignored his subsequent attempts to lure me into conversation.

Then he sent me a book.

An encyclopedia of fairy-made devices, with a note.

There are over twelve hundred devices listed in this book. Want to help me collect them all?

It's hard to read these lines and hear Oriax's voice. He was so commanding and cold in person, while his messages are often teasing. I haven't told Teill about this exchange. I already feel guilty enough about Shax kissing me. If Belial and Eligos knew about my communications with Oriax, they would be furious. And yet I can't stop myself.

School was never that interesting to me, but every day Oriax lets drop some crumb of knowledge that fascinates me. He hasn't mentioned the devices or me exchanging loyalties again. I just don't know what to make of this predicament I find myself in with these four men.

Demons.

They aren't mortal men, and thinking of them that way will only set me up for failure.

Truth be told, the incident with Shax has left me wondering what it is I truly want. Because deep down I have to be honest with myself. The idea of being caught between Belial and Eligos appeals to me.

What happens when the passion is gone? Are women really carted off and held against their will? Or is there a chance that I might carry on with my life? But do I think I will be the same person after?

The study door bursts open and I whirl to face Teill. She's grinning at me and holding a tray of small, velvet boxes.

"What are you doing?" I ask.

She sets the tray down on the only bit of cleared desk space. "We're going to the festival tomorrow, and you need a glamour."

My brows rise toward my hairline as she opens the first box and banishes all my fears. They'll be there when the festival is over.

ELIGOS

Our enemies are at our back door.

It's surprising that after all these years, neither Yokai nor Vodu have attempted to break through the boundary stone barrier on our southern coast. The climate is hostile, to say the least. It is a barren wasteland that spends most of the year in the clutches of winter. Even now, snow and ice hold sway while spring is about to turn into summer.

The true tragedy of this is the lives lost.

There are few pockets of humanity that we demons have left mostly untouched. One of the largest settlements was a group of people on our southern shore. They were the descendants of Aboriginal tribes, fiercely independent and resistant to the changes in the world. I don't know their history or how they survived in such an inhospitable land for all these hundreds and thousands of years.

The vision of the wreckage is burned into my mind.

The oceans are finally beginning to recede somewhat. We've moved boundary stones here and there when necessary. But we never did for our southern shore. The city that the people established there was mostly beyond the barrier.

They never stood a chance.

Nothing we did is enough. This fuck up is on us. We should have been more careful.

My demon is has only focused on one thing: our enemies are testing our borders.

Alastor must be keeping this information to the three of us, because I haven't heard from the others.

Belial comes out of the bathroom gloriously naked, water dripping off the hard planes of his body. His thick cock catches my interest, but he's still scowling and irritable.

Our plans are so completely fucked. We're both wound up, dealing with barely contained rage that I don't trust us around humans. And least of all Lioria.

I can feel her presence at the manor. I don't even have to look out the window to point at what wing she's in. And if I had to guess? She's in the office right now.

It would be incredibly easy to bound over the rooves, vault over the fence, and scale the walls to the study. I could be there in five minutes, maybe less.

But what then?

No, it's better if we stay here, in this secret apartment for tonight.

Tomorrow is the festival. It won't wipe away the problem, but it will lift our mood for a moment and remind us why we shoulder these burdens.

Belial crosses to wrap his arms around me, pressing his still damp chest to my back.

"What about tomorrow?" he whispers.

I look over my shoulder at him. "What about it?"

His fingers press into me and I let my body relax.

"I want to... Hunt," he says in a low, rough voice.

"Hm. Shall I propose a contest then?"

Belial kisses my shoulder then up my neck. I smile and let my eyes drift shut, enjoying his touch.

"What kind of contest?" he asks.

"Just a friendly contest to see who can get Lioria's attention."

He lifts his head and grins at me. The demon retreats in his bright gaze, allowing the human side to surface more.

"Prepare to get your ass kicked," he says.

"I'd settle for getting fucked."

Belial grabs my jaw and crushes his lips to mine.

LIORIA

The festival is all colors and smells and sounds. It's overwhelming. I keep trying to get a look while Teill drags me down another street to something she's intent on getting to.

It's early still. Technically the festival just began half an hour ago, but we've been in the town around Privale since shortly after breakfast.

I wasn't sure what to expect. Maybe something a little more extravagant than we had in Suncrest? At most, a handful of traveling merchants make an appearance. Maybe a few performing acts. The most likely source of entertainment is usually a boat from the continent bringing strange things. The big merchant ships are more likely to go to one of the bigger port towns to the southwest. But with the influx of refugees, we've been seeing a few more merchant ships a year.

The festival in Privale is like nothing I've ever seen.

The streets in the heart of town are closed off to wagons and carriages not long after dawn. Merchant stalls have been set up along the center of each street. Every plaza, square, and open space boasts some sort of entertainment. Many of the stall owners must attend year after year because there are lines forming in front of some by the time we traverse town.

I'd resisted delving into the clothes my lords ordered out of spite, but broke down for today.

The glamour ring Teill said fit me best is a beautiful piece that makes me look like a buxom, fair haired woman with a more angular face and stronger brows. My preferred clothes would have looked out of place on someone with such a refined appearance, and there just happened to be a dress I was dying to try on. It was pale purple with layered skirts and a neckline that was both respectable and revealing.

There were little embellishments of ribbons and beads sewn onto it that served no purpose.

In all my life I'd never owned something simply because it was beautiful. Even my special outfit that I'd embroidered myself was to serve as my feast day clothing.

The dress didn't suit my lackluster appearance, but with this glamour on?

I felt beautiful.

I almost wished my demons would see me like this. At least then their attraction would make more sense.

Where were they? Was everything okay?

The days of silence are beginning to get to me. I know I'd barely met them and been drawn into their orbit, but I felt their absence acutely.

"Lioria!" Teill grabbed my hand. Her glamour kept her features while giving her a more human skin tone and hair while also hiding the petrification. "Look!"

We're in a line that's quickly formed behind us. If I stand on tip-toe, I can look through the people to the stall ahead of me.

"What are we waiting for?" I ask her.

Teill closes her eyes and tips her head back before groaning the word, "Honey candy."

I chuckle. "Honey candy? Really?"

Her fingers dig into mine and she leans in close. "You don't understand. This is Ammit honey candy. There isn't anything in the world quite like it and I need you to buy some for me."

"Me?"

She shoves a little coin purse at me. "They always limit the amount a person can buy every year. I need you to buy some for me. Whatever they'll give you."

The line begins to move, inching forward a tiny bit. Other vendors are beginning to open up and I have a nice chat with a local woman selling a variety of seasoned nuts that have been grown on this land for generations. Next to her was finely tooled leather items. A leather book cover caught my eye, but I didn't dare touch it. My mind was not yet made up about whether or not I would be trying to escape my fate or remain here.

If I run, I will need every coin I have.

Finally, we reach the edge of the stall with the word Ammit painted on a banner behind the woman flanked by bees that seemed to be made of candy. There was little to display, other than a plate of hexagonal hard candies. Off to one side was a pointed stick with pearlescent phases of the moon.

Teill is deep into negotiations for her purchase, so I pick up the stick to better look at the design.

The wizened woman sitting in the corner of the booth leaned forward. "What do you see?"

I blink at her. "Excuse me?"

Her dark gaze fixed on me in such a way that I had to wonder if this person was human. "What does it show you?"

I gingerly set the object down. "It's a beautiful piece, but I'm afraid I don't know what it is. The moons are lovely, though."

The woman's brows shoot up. "Moons, you say?"

Teill snatches my wrist and pulls me sideways. "She'll buy the same."

I offer the money to the second person, acutely aware of the older woman staring at me as I acquire Teill's coveted honey candy.

"What was that all about?" I ask Teill as she pulls me away from the stall.

She glances over her shoulder.

I pitch my voice lower. "They weren't human, were they?"

"No, but they come here legally every year. Just stick close to me," she says and pulls me through the now crowded streets.

She has a destination in mind and I'm happy to take in the sights for now. It's so many new sounds, colors, and smells. If I weren't so excited I might be overwhelmed.

We draw closer to the open green where larger tents have been erected.

I grip Teill's arm. "What are those for?"

"Performing troops. Come on."

"Don't you want to check them out?"

"No, and neither should you. It's not even entertaining. It's all just a scam."

To say I'm disappointed would be an understatement, but maybe she's right?

On the fringes of the wide-open green space are more booths, stalls, and tents. I know exactly which one Teill is headed to because it has a line. Only this time, she pauses as she takes up her spot to wait and looks at me.

"They only allow one person in at a time. If you want to wander, I'll come find you."

That makes me perk up. "Really?"

She waves her hand. "Sure."

"Shouldn't we set a meeting spot?"

She smirks. "I promise you, I can find you anywhere. Go see the pitiful performers if you want."

I hug her, which makes her whole body stiffen. "Thank you!"

Then I'm gone.

I head back toward the large tents, but pause to admire all the things being sold. Most of it I don't understand or know what its use would be, but it is clear that these people take pride in their work. And that's something I can appreciate. I wind my way through the rows and stalls. My salary here at Privale is generous, but I can't bring myself to spend a coin.

Ahead, the crowd parts and I pause.

The old woman with the stick is standing a couple dozen yards away staring at me. It's as if there's some power that has parted the people, making a clear path between us.

The hair on the back of my neck stands up and I do not want to get closer.

I dart between two stalls and rush away from her.

Can she tell I'm wearing a glamor? Does she sense Shax's touch?

I wander haphazardly, covering as much distance as I can.

A man steps out in front of me with a charming smile and bows a little. His actions are so direct I automatically curtsy.

"Would a lovely lady like yourself like to hear tales from the continent?" he asks.

That does spark my interest. "Oh, yes."

He turns and gestures at canvas walls that have been erected around a small space tucked back against hedges that border where the wide open green begins to turn back into the town.

"Thank you," I say over my shoulder as I follow a young man and woman headed past the canvas walls.

I try to pay the man at the entrance, but he waves his hand and tells me to keep my money.

There isn't a stage, just a few rows of benches and maybe eight other people who aren't attached to the production. There are several men wearing some sort of foreign-looking robe that is held together by wide belts tied in an ornate fashion. It's their shoes that I find the most curious. There are straps that leave most of their feet bare save for the solid sole they walk on.

Has Eligos ever seen these?

I take a seat in the middle. I think I'm the only person here alone, which is fine.

Despite the refugees coming through Suncrest, I've never heard much about the continent except the eternal conflict between Vodu, Yokai, Demon Lords, and humans. It seems so pointless from this side of the ocean, but maybe I don't understand enough?

Regardless, I don't think that old woman will find me here.

A few more patrons are brought in. I'm twirling a ribbon around my finger when I hear a crashing sound that resounds with a metallic timbre. A man strides across the open ground in front of the benches holding what looks to be a dinner plate suspended on a wooden frame and some sort of mallet. He taps the plate again, creating a softer crash of sound.

What a curious object.

"Welcome to tales from the Continent!" the man says and spreads his arms wide.

I scoot to the edge of the bench.

The man is attractive in the classical sense. Medium brown skin, jet black hair, and expressive hazel eyes. His strong, square jaw frames a mouth that seems prone to smiling. There are well-worn lines around his mouth and eyes, as if he is accustomed to smiling or laughing often.

"Sit back and let me regale you with a true account of our past the demons don't want you to know." He holds his arms out, gaze sweeping the crowd.

Two men step forward and take the dinner plate and mallet from him.

"Many years ago, so long that not even our friend with ten arms can keep track on his one hundred fingers," he pauses for dramatic effect and winks at the audience while wiggling his fingers.

Does he know how math works? Ten arms, five fingers each, does not equal a hundred. Unless they have more fingers on the continent?

"This land was being ravaged. Not by Vodu. Not even by Yokai. It was the demons who scarred the earth first, laying waste to our ancestors."

My stomach clenches and I sit up straighter while an urgent voice in the back of my head screams at me. I shouldn't be here. I shouldn't listen to blasphemy like this. But I'm frozen in place. Is this my curiosity holding me captive? Or something else?

The other patrons are muttering to their friends, but our storyteller pushes on.

"I know what you're thinking. Our Demon Lords are kind and benevolent—in this lifetime. But what were they like before they were worshiped and celebrated?" The storyteller's smile is gone and I don't like the look in his eyes. "What if I told you all that you know is a lie?"

A woman to my left stands up, dragging the man at her side with her.

The storyteller swings his head toward them. "Don't run from the truth. Your lords have fed you a steady diet of lies, because demons are the father of lies. They destroyed this world and now seek to subjugate us. Don't be a calf, fattened for the slaughter. Open your ears."

This is too far, even for me.

It isn't the first time I've heard people speaking ill of our lords, but it's always been hushed whispers about something someone overheard somewhere else. I've never heard rhetoric like this spoken so plainly.

The storyteller's gaze sweeps the audience before landing on me.

"Don't let them seduce you with sweet words. The Demon Lords are killing us. They're selectively breeding humanity to serve them. Don't grow complacent. Don't listen to them."

A man darts past the canvas wall, sweat pouring off his brow, and announces, "We have to go. Now!"

The storyteller whirls and sprints for the narrow space between the hedges and the canvas, all while I'm still in shock over his words.

Father of lies?

What nonsense.

The other men with the storyteller all bolt, leaving a handful of us frozen by their damning rhetoric.

I stand up, fueled by anger, hands clenched into fists. "The Demon Lords ensure anyone who wants an education receives one. If everything is a lie, wouldn't someone have written something about it? Wouldn't there be evidence somewhere? I'm a poor girl from a small town, but I can read and write."

One by one, people turn toward me.

"Am I right? Or am I wrong?" I ask them. "I grew up in a fishing town. Every few years some poor soul gets an arm or leg caught in the nets. It's terrible. They get medical care at little to no cost. And if they lose a limb? They're fitted for their choice of magical prosthetic that means they don't have to find another form of work to support themselves. The only reason I'm alive is because of the kindness and consideration our lords have for the poorest of us. Where is the lie in what I've said?"

Several of them meet my gaze, nodding or muttering in agreement.

Four guards rip quite literally through the canvas walls using knives. They pause, studying the scene.

I point in the direction the storyteller went. "They went that way."

An older gentleman pushes to his feet. He's practically scowling. "Five young men. They all ran that way. Catch them!"

"There you are!"

I turn to find Teill scowling at me with her human face.

I'm shaking now, the whole exchange leaving me unsettled.

She stalks across to me while looking me up and down. But she doesn't scold me. She gently takes my hand and says, "Come with me."

There are more guards milling around now.

"What happened?" I whisper to her as we weave our way away from the green.

Teill peers at me. "You were there, not me."

"They said the lords were lying, that demons are the father of lies."

She snorts. "What else?"

"They didn't have time to say much, just that everything is a lie."

Teill doesn't appear surprised by this.

I squeeze her hand and stop. We're in a narrow path between booths and out of the way. "What was he talking about, Teill? You know something, don't you?"

She sighs and glances around before fixing me with a steady stare. "History is complicated and long. Believe what you want to."

"What are you saying?"

She steps in close enough a casual bystander might think we're lovers.

"Lioria, the demons, and my kind, have been around for millions of years. Many things have happened in that time. Enough that there is probably some truth in any accusation that could be laid at the lord's feet. And at the same time, how much good have they done? Who are we to judge them? I don't. I'm not interested in concerning myself with anything beyond my life. My own kind poisoned me and left me for dead. If Belial hadn't found me, I wouldn't have survived. When I hear the nasty things people want to say about the lords, I hold on to the fact that without Belial, there would be no me."

I am by no means a devout person of faith, but without government-run orphanages and schooling, I'd have died as a baby. In a way, my lords saved me, too. And that is a debt that cannot be repaid. So what if many lifetimes ago something horrible happened? It's not like I'm blameless. We should not have our lives judged by one action.

BELIAL

My prey is crafty and aware it is being stalked. I allow the figure to retreat to the very fringes of town where traveling vendors have set up tents and carts. Little does she know I've herded her here so that there might be fewer to observe this exchange.

I don't know where Eligos is or if he's even left the apartment yet. I hope he is watching Lioria.

It seems we are not the only ones interested in her.

The old crone vanishes between the flaps of a tent. I remain where I am and watch for anyone to join her, but the creature remains alone as far as I can tell.

Merchants from the continent, especially those who are not human, are always watched closely. Most have come and gone from Eden for hundreds of years in peace. But every now and then, someone sneaks past who does not wish anyone well. After what we saw on the southern coast, I am not lenient. I do not intend to be kind.

I want answers.

It feels good to fly again. I'd forgotten what it was like. We need Lioria. This time away from her has left me with an increasing hunger that no food can satisfy.

I drop to the ground, still holding the invisibility spell around myself, and step into the tent where the crone vanished.

The space expands around me. The tent walls become red and the ground is covered in plush carpets and pillows. A brazier burns some sort of incense, creating a haze in the confined space.

And directly across from me is a creature I haven't seen in at least a thousand years.

What was the crone stares at me with milky eyes so round I might fall into them. She's a serpopard, a creature that is both snake and leopard from the ancient days. Our respective deities were never friendly, so her fear doesn't surprise me.

She springs up onto her paws, only to drop down to her belly. Her body is covered in a fine, golden fur with black leopard spots, save where the fur gives way to scales. Her neck and tail are impossibly long with similar golden brown and black coloring.

"M-my lord!" She bows her head, ears, and tail twitching.

"You followed one of mine. Why?" Does she know something I do not?

"I don't know what you're talking about."

I reach down and grab her at the base of her skull. The skin is cool and scaled to the touch as I force her to look up at me. Her eyes roll in her head as she searches for a way to escape.

"Do you really want to try me today?" I growl at her.

"No. No! No, please, my lord?"

I wait while she shifts and her eyes slowly stop searching for something else to look at. She stares at a spot in the middle of my brow and sighs.

"I know not what I saw, only that I felt... Compelled. I had to follow. I don't know why," she says.

Damn it.

I wouldn't say that Eligos and I felt compelled to be near Lioria, but it isn't far off.

"What is she?" the crone asks.

Even in this form, I can see fine white hairs around her muzzle. She must be positively ancient. I release her then lower to the ground. I will not give her answers, but maybe I can garner a little information myself.

"She's human."

The serpopard settles in, milky eyes somehow bright as though she's seeing something not here. "Human, you say? Or wearing the guise of human, hm?"

It's a question I would like answered myself, but I will not give anything away. We've tested Lioria's hair. We've tasted her blood. Both are human. If she is something other than what she appears, it isn't a magic we can crack.

"Enough about that." I wave my hand. "Merchants always know more about the ripples in the world than anyone else. Ammit's honey is universally welcomed into all countries."

She takes the abrupt change of topic in stride. "Yes, we take great pride in our work."

"Is war coming to Eden?" I ask her. "You would know. War hurts your trade."

She regards me for several silent moments. "There are those who wish to strike at the heart of Eden, but they have failed for hundreds of years. Thousands. And we do not wish them success. Their goals are not ours."

"I wasn't aware."

The serpopard chuckles and her head bobs toward me. "Have faith in what you've built and cherish your peace, little lord of demons. Do not trouble yourselves with the childishness of others."

If she knows anything, she isn't going to tell me.

Lioria

Food is exactly what I needed, and Teill knows all the best places. The only difference is that the tavern she takes me to is here year-round. It's an adorable establishment built partially into a hill, which allows it to have one of the coldest cellars for miles and miles around. The chilled cider is so cold it makes my teeth ache.

Teill was right about her assessment.

History is long and complicated. Whatever the lord's sins might have been in the past, their present is different. Yes, Eligos and Belial might be lazy but they both take their roles seriously. I see it in the attention they give when I write their letters or when I leave and they attend to sensitive business I'm not permitted to know about.

At the end of the day, I'm only alive because of their efforts to make Eden a better place. They give not just one lifetime, but many to the people of this country. So what if they like to relax a little every now and then?

I watch as Teill spins around the paved courtyard in front of the little tavern. A trio of musicians is playing a lively country dance, and where there is music there must be dancing. I'm not quite ready to dance. My spirit still feels burdened, but I enjoy watching others be happy.

A burly young man with twinkling eyes and a full beard catches Teill around the waist. He swings her in time to the music. She's a little unsteady on her feet, but his gentle, guiding hands move her about with him as they go through the steps. She clearly doesn't know what she's doing, but her ox of a man guides her with a deft hand.

I draw in a deep breath, relishing the scents of food and all the mysterious creations beyond.

The storytellers' words still haunt me, but it's the old woman with the stick that makes me check over my shoulder every now and then.

Teill stumbles toward me. Her cheeks are rosy red and her eyes bright. I've never seen her look this free. She cups my face with both hands and taps the end of her nose to mine.

"Oh, okay." I chuckle and place a steadying hand on her shoulder.

"I really want to fuck him," she says, plainly, with no attempt to be quiet.

Someone at the other end of the table gasps. I grin at her then peer over her shoulder at the burly, hairy gentleman currently eyeing her hips. At least until he catches sight of me and whips his head around and his ears turn bright red.

That is adorable.

"Does he know that?" I ask her.

She shakes her head.

"I think he's interested." I lean in a little closer and whisper, "Is he human?"

"Yes." Then she frowns. "But what about you?"

I pull her hands away from my face. "I will toast to your accomplishments and wish you many orgasms."

Teill gasps.

"Go." I wave her off. "You'll find me when you're done. Or you won't. I'm a grown woman. I can handle myself."

She continues to frown at me. "I don't like the idea of you alone."

"I wouldn't be a real friend if I didn't tell you to enjoy yourself."

She purses her lips and clenches her skirts with both hands. "Are you certain?"

"Yes."

She thrusts a finger under my nose. "Don't get into trouble and stay away from performers. They're all just scamming you out of money, anyway."

I tug one side of her skirt, turning her in place, then give her a gentle push.

Teill needs no further encouragement. I watch her cross the open space where other couples are still dancing and take a big handful of the man's shirt before tugging him down. I do my best to hide my grin behind my mug as the man's face flushes and his eyes bulge. Teill looks up at him expectantly, but he's studying her hand clenching his shirt. He gently pulls her hand away, folding it between both of his before pressing sweet kisses to her knuckles.

The gentle giant of a man leads Teill out of view and I hope that I don't see her again today.

I wander away from the tavern, toward the city center where there are larger shops. But it's too noisy, so I follow the sound of music through narrow streets until I find myself in some sort of cultivated garden overflowing with delicate flowers. A small band of musicians are playing to an audience sitting on the thick grass. I join them for a while, letting the music soothe away the rest of my anxiety. The purple beverage I bought from a wandering vendor helps and I find that even my strong constitution falls victim to the sweet spirits.

More and more people are beginning to don masks. This isn't a tradition we followed in Suncrest, but I've heard about it.

Some laborers can't truly relax, especially if they see someone they know from their job while at the festival. I don't know where the trend began, but around mid-afternoon, adults begin donning masks to hide their identity so that they might enjoy the festivities freely.

I follow my nose, tracking a particularly tempting aroma several streets over where a vendor is selling spiced meat on a stick. It smells divine and I happily part with some coins to taste it.

The first flavors hit my tongue and I tip my head back, groaning in delight. My mouth is on fire while something that's almost candy-like hits the back of my throat before warming and mellowing out the different elements. I devour a whole skewer and lick my fingers.

The last time I tasted something this good was when I met Belial.

My heart thumps painfully against my ribs.

I miss my two lords and I hope they are safe wherever they are.

I tidy myself up a little and follow the crowd. There's cheering and noise up ahead that draws me toward it until I'm standing on tip-toe to peer over the shoulders of taller people.

I catch a glimpse of coppery red hair.

The need to get closer drives me. I shoulder my way through. When I can't push through, I resort to pinching until I'm right up front.

It's Belial.

The black and gold harlequin mask covering his eyes isn't enough to disguise him from me.

What's he doing here? How long since he returned? Is Eligos with him?

Belial clasps hands with a man almost twice his size over the top of a keg. They're grinning at each other for a moment. A young man steps up and places his hand over theirs.

"Ready?" he asks Belial and the man. "On your mark, set, go!"

I bounce on the balls of my feet as the two strain. Belial grins and I hear his laugh through the cheers right before his shoulders bunch and he slams the man's hand down.

He bounds to his feet and thrusts both fists in the air while people cheer wildly. I'm so caught up in it I clap right along with them.

A serving girl swoops in with a tankard. There's something about the way she's smiling up at him that makes me want to gouge her eyes out. But Belial merely lifts his cup to his opponent, then drains it before handing the cup back to the woman. He turns in place, grinning at the crowd. Another man moves to take the vacated spot on the other side of the keg, but Belial shakes his head and backs away.

There's too much space between us.

The crowd begins to disperse, and I'm once more pushing between bodies, trying to keep that red hair in view. I'm almost certain I've lost him when I stumble between two people and manage to steady myself with a hand on a firm arm.

And I look up at a harlequin mask and a grinning face I've missed so much more than I want to admit.

"That was incredible," I say instead of *hi, hello,* or *where have you been?*

He takes my hand from his arm and presses a kiss to my knuckles while his gaze travels down my body. "Not nearly as incredible as you look, my lady."

Only he isn't seeing *me,* is he?

The face he's appreciating isn't mine.

"You're too kind." I straighten and back away.

Belial takes a step toward me.

He's dressed in threadbare clothing I've never seen before. If I didn't *know*, with a certainty I can't explain, that this masked man is my Belial, I might wonder if he's another fair man.

I shouldn't be here right now.

"I'm not kind at all." He swipes his thumb over my knuckles and tugs me closer. "Dance with me?"

"W-what?"

He tips his head toward where another cluster of musicians is setting up, right in the spot he'd arm wrestled moments ago.

"Dance with me." This time it isn't as much of a request as it is an order, and I feel myself being pulled under his spell.

He doesn't recognize me as Lioria. Right now, I'm a random woman, nothing more. It's almost like our initial meeting, but without everything that came after. I want so badly to do it all over again and indulge in ignorance. Would it be wrong of me to let him? Would he know?

The song starts up. It's a lively jig and people cheer.

Belial grasps me around the waist and spins me. I squeal and grip his forearms as my decision is stripped from me. I don't know the steps, but Belial does. When I move wrong, he simply picks me up and moves me in the right direction. We spin and twirl with others as the music swells.

Belial grips me by the hips and lifts me. I brace my hands on his shoulders, acutely aware that even with the glamour, I am a big woman. But he isn't breathing hard, and he's grinning up at me as though this is the most fun he's ever had. And I feel myself pulled deeper into this spell.

He slowly lowers me, my body sliding along his in a way that should be indecent. Before I can catch my breath, we're spinning again. Around and around the impromptu dancefloor we go. He's holding me so tight now and I am torn.

Does he see me as this random woman? How far will this go? Has my indecision about my lord's interest caused their feelings to wane? Is that why they stayed away this long?

The dance comes to an abrupt stop. While the other dancers are bowing and curtsying to their partners, Belial holds me close.

"You're stunning when you smile." He reaches up and smooths his thumb between my brows. "Don't take this the wrong way, but.... Stop over-thinking whatever you're worrying about."

I take a small step away from him. It's all I can do when everything in me wants to get closer. "What would you know about my worries?"

"I only know that a woman as beautiful as you shouldn't worry about anything."

His words are sweet, but they aren't for me. This face is not mine.

The music starts up again, and he pulls me into another dance and then another. We drink and we dance, all while I silence my concerns so that I can have this one moment. If he doesn't know who I am, if he hasn't realized it, then I'm safe to enjoy what I cannot otherwise.

His body is every bit as firm and solid as it looks, and unlike the onlookers, I know about the thick, black tattoos he's hiding. He always keeps a hand on me, and if not a hand his eyes. We split and rejoin while dancing, and I'm constantly aware of his interest.

Suddenly Belial spins us away from the people and past the ring of tables. He presses my back against the side of a shop and cages me with his body. On one side, his knee blocks my escape, and on the other his hand at my waist.

He bends toward me and I freeze, caught between this beautiful moment and reality.

Belial stops short of kissing me. Barely.

"You remind me of someone," he whispers.

"O-oh?" My brain isn't working well enough to craft a better response.

He pushes my hair back off my face. "Yes. Would it upset you if she has my heart?"

I'm upset right now.

Who is he talking about? Me right now? Me at all? Someone else?

"Sorry," he mutters and swipes his thumb over my lips.

I'm reminded of the pastry he took from my fingers. Clearly, I'm not thinking straight because I part my lips and flick my tongue against his thumb. His eyes are harder to see because of the mask and shadows, but I see them glint a brilliant emerald.

Would it be such a bad thing to have the fantasy?

He leans down until all I can see is him. Belial is my whole world. I curl my hands into the fabric of his tunic. Everything in me feels stretched toward him.

His lips crash into mine.

This isn't the sweet man. This is the hungry demon.

He lifts me a bit and presses his thigh between my legs so that I'm quite literally riding him, all while people walk past. I twine my arms around his neck and pull him closer. He moans into the kiss and shifts.

Is that his cock?

Someone shouts, words my lust-addled brain can't understand. Belial lifts his face from mine and I bury my nose against his neck, the better to smell him.

"Mind your own business," Belial snarls.

I stroke a hand over his shoulder, as if I can soothe him with a touch. He presses his hand over mine then eases me to my feet. I'm grateful for the wall while the world spins a little around me.

Did I drink more than I realized? Or am I drunk on him?

My body is too warm, too needy, but I can't ask him for what I want. Not with this face.

He brings both hands to his lips, kissing one knuckle then the other while peering at me with interest.

"Come with me?" he asks in a low, seductive voice.

This is my chance. All I have to do is say yes, and the choice is made. But what comes after? What if he's upset to learn my identity? What if I don't tell him and he sees demonic energy on me tomorrow? Would he know?

There are too many unknowns to proceed. I need to pull away.

"No." The word feels dragged out of me. My throat burns and my body sways toward him, as if it can betray my mind.

"We can stay here," he says with that lop-sided smile I've come to cherish.

I never thought it would hurt to want someone like this. I've always kept my heart walled off. Every man I've been with has been meant for another, and somewhere along the line, I forgot that my lords aren't for me.

The emotion bubbling up within me threatens to overwhelm my senses. I push at Belial's chest and at first, he doesn't move. But then he takes a step back, giving me just enough room to dart away.

"Wait!" I hear him call out, but I don't stop.

I barrel past other revelers now wearing masks. I don't know where I'm going, only that the turmoil inside of me is threatening to pull me down into a swirling mess, not even Teill could tidy up. I run despite the ache in my side and the firm squeeze of my corset. I wind through streets and away from the revelry while the sun dips below the horizon.

My limbs are shaking and I am unsteady as I slow my headlong pace. The one saving grace is that the climate here is cooler. Were this Suncrest I'd have passed out from heat and exertion by now.

No less confused, I plod forward like a lost lamb without any idea what I should be doing.

I'd kissed Belial, and I wanted to do it again. But I cannot make that commitment.

The streets grow darker as I walk. I'm tired, hungry, and the alcohol is wearing off. But I don't want to return to the festival. At least not in the city center.

The best thing for me is to just retire for the night. It's been an eventful day. I've seen, smelled, tasted, heard, and felt so many new things today. I will spend days processing and reliving these moments.

I turn toward the manor that rises above the town, feeling sorry for myself and hating the emotion at the same time.

Has Teill gone home? Or is she still enjoying herself? She said she'd come find me when she was done, so I hope at least one of us is having a good time.

What right do I have to pity myself? Belial made no promise to me. I was clear to both my lords that I was not willing to part with my freedom. Shouldn't they seek pleasure with another woman if I reject them? It should be the perfect arrangement. I get their company without the trappings of being their woman. But now that I've glimpsed what that might be like, I'm jealous. I'm jealous of Belial and Eligos together. I'm jealous of who they might be attracted to. And I have no right. None at all.

They are the High Lords.

From the way the rest of the house staff has spoken, the lords barely acknowledge most humans. But they know my name. They know my plans for my future. I'm something in-between for them, but it's not enough.

Would my prospects be better under Oriax?

I know Belial and Eligos have said I cannot trust him. But can I trust them to put my best interests above their desires?

Oriax promises me knowledge. My magic might be too weak to do much with, but I can learn.

The sweet scent of cinnamon and sugar tempts my stomach into growling. I've nibbled on food all day, but I haven't had a proper meal. Maybe I should remedy that before returning to Privale? An empty stomach does tend to make me more melancholy.

As luck would have it, I find myself on the same street where Teill bought the honey candies. Ammit's stall has been packed up, but the adorable family is still selling a variety of candied nuts. I buy three little bundles—because that makes the little boy squeal in delight—before wandering deeper into the festival in search of something more substantial.

It's quiet in this part of town. At this hour most people will no doubt be in the central area where dancing and carousing will be more popular. Normally that's exactly where I'd be, but my insides feel bruised.

Am I expecting too much of myself? Should I choose to be happy over my change in circumstance?

Most women in my position would be thrilled. They would have a comfortable life, so long as they played their expected part.

I find myself in front of a temporary kitchen in a small square between stone houses. It's lit with hanging paper lanterns, and the food has a gentle, tantalizing aroma that makes me think of the soups Kirra would make during the cold season to settle stomachs. I order based on little illusions of the dishes. They're so lifelike I swear I can smell them.

At the first bite, I know I've made a wise decision. The flavor isn't too strong, and it sits well in my stomach, which is tied into too many knots to count. I feel my anxiety and stress decreasing. I might have tasted many different things today, but

I haven't had a proper meal. By the time I'm through, I've sobered up completely, and I am rethinking my return to Privale.

The only thing I'll accomplish sitting by the fire is thinking myself to death.

I leave the shop and continue meandering toward the manor when I become acutely aware of a male figure walking a dozen paces behind me. I'm still on the outskirts of the festival. That old woman's eyes come to mind and the skin between my shoulders begins to itch.

"I promise I'm not following you," a deep, male voice says. It's a kind voice, one with an undercurrent of humor.

I glance back at him with an arched brow. "That's exactly what you would say if you were following me."

His skin is so dark I can't make out his features well in the low light, but he grins.

Some people have the kind of smile that invites you to laugh with them. They are almost always kind souls who do no harm. And just like that, he puts me at ease. I find myself slowing my pace until he falls into step beside me.

We pass under a lantern and I am treated to a strong face with a nose that's been broken a few times and warm, dark eyes that draw me in. He's tall but not very broad. Judging by his clothes, he isn't a laborer. Maybe a shop owner? Some sort of educated tradesman? His clothes are nice, but worn. He's someone I'd have struck up a conversation with in Suncrest.

He squints up at the sky. "I'll have to rethink my strategy for talking to pretty ladies."

I chuckle until I remember it isn't my face he's complimenting. "Have you enjoyed yourself today?"

"Yes, very much. And you?"

I think over all the new things and can't help but say, "Yes."

"What party are you heading to now?"

"Oh, I'm not. I'm having a last look around before going home."

"So early?"

"I enjoyed myself too much. I'm afraid what I need now is sleep."

"You can sleep when you're dead."

I groan. "My feet can't do anymore."

He holds out his hand to me. "There's more than dancing tonight. Let me change your mind?"

He's charming, and not very long ago, I'd have taken his hand enthusiastically. But my heart is torn between two demons. Is that my problem, though? Do I need to redirect my interest? Is this the gods' way of changing my path?

I've never been a spiritual person. The gods seem so distant, so removed from our lives that I don't share the same level of faith with most people. And maybe that's wrong. What if this is an opportunity?

"Alright," I say slowly and put my hand in his. A pleasant warmth spreads through me and this just feels... Right? "Convince me."

My new companion tucks my hand in the crook of his arm and winks at me. "You won't regret this. Unless you do, and then..."

Now he has my interest. "What shall I call you?"

He lays his finger across his lips. "No names... Anonymity can be freeing."

Given that I'm wearing a glamour, I can agree.

"Where are you taking me?" I ask as he turns me down another street.

"To a house of pleasure."

"To see your mistress?"

He chuckles. "Not that kind of house."

We wind our way to the outskirts of the festival.

My gentleman escorts me to a theater with a dimly lit marquee. I wouldn't have expected it was open had I been walking by. He pays our fee and we're handed two masks, much like what Belial wore earlier. Only these are solid black.

Is that a muted moan I hear?

Curious, I stick close to my gentleman's heels as he leads me through a dimly lit foyer and through thick curtains before an attendant will only crack open the theater doors to admit us. My gentleman pulls me around to stand in front of him, and my breath catches in my throat.

I've never been in a theater this nice.

The walls are paneled wood with swirling designs in gold. Globes of magical light illuminate the space, just enough that I have the impression of limbs and bodies twining together. There are a handful of private boxes above us and a balcony. But my attention is focused on the stage. The thick, crimson curtains have been drawn back. Four beds of varying size are spread out on the space while people copulate and tease for all to see.

His hands grip my shoulders gently and he leans forward to whisper, "Do you see what I mean now?"

Somewhere, musicians play a soft tune that melds with the moans.

It's difficult to tell, but it appears as though the benches have been moved to clear the floor. There are couches and cushions everywhere, and plenty of bodies twining together in various stages of dress. I inhale the scent of citrus mingled with a sweeter incense and sex.

His fingers trail up the side of my neck while he whispers into the opposite ear. "Is this too much?"

"No," I whisper back.

"Would you like to watch?" His voice lowers. "Or perhaps play?"

My body is suddenly too warm. It's like I'm back in Belial's arms, when he kissed me without knowing who I was. I want so badly to feel his hands on me, but my mind cannot wipe away the identity of the man at my back.

He is neither of my demons. But if they are seeking the company of other women, is it wrong if I do the same?

"I want to watch. For now," I say.

I feel more than hear him chuckle at my back. He takes my hand and leads me along the path through the bodies to a large chair facing the stage. I'm not sure if the cushion in front of it is many mattresses pushed together or something else, but there are two groups on either side engaging in a variety of enticing activities.

A sharp crack sounds, so loud I jump. It's followed by an equally loud moan.

My gaze sweeps the room, searching for the source of the noise when I'm pulled off balance. With a squeak I find myself sitting across my mystery gentleman's lap.

"S-sir!" I'm all at once highly conscious of my size compared to him and the way my corset digs into me.

He presses his hand to my stomach, pushing me back against the padded wings that arch around the sides of the chair while his arm comes up to cradle my lower back. While I'm still sitting across his lap, this position is quite comfortable.

He lifts my left arm and drapes it around his neck before leaning in and whispering, "Watch, little one. And enjoy."

My will is weak, and I fall under his spell. He turns my chin toward the group on our left. There are two naked women writhing next to each other. One is fondling the other's breast while the men around them use their mouths on every inch of their bodies. None of my lovers have ever been that thorough with me and I wonder what it would feel like to be licked from head to toe.

"On the stage," my gentleman whispers, in a voice gone rougher with lust.

A trio has taken command of the bed on the far right. The two men are wearing trousers only while the woman has on a chemise so thin I can see the dark brown of her nipples even at this distance. One of the men roughly fists the material and jerks her toward him. I gasp, but the woman seems to lose all rigidity, relaxing completely against him until the other man has to come prop her up between them as she sucks the rough one's neck.

The two men don't allow her to tease them long before they each take one of her arms and turn her to face the bed. The two men seem to glare at one another for a moment. The rough one pulls his partner toward him and kisses the man briefly before shoving him away and pointing at something.

"Do you like the company of multiple partners?"

The voice at my ear startles me. I'd been so drawn into the tableau that I'd almost forgotten my very mortal chair.

I chuckle and glance at him. "It seems like a decadent idea, but I wouldn't know."

He trails his fingers across my shoulder. "That's a shame. A woman as lovely as you should be worshiped."

The lust cools a bit, because once again, this isn't my face. I'm not sad that I'm plain looking, but I can't take joy in the compliment either.

I look back at the stage to find that the ring leader of the trio has lifted the woman's hem to expose her to the audience from the hips down. Her skin is rosy under the lights and though I can't see much from this distance, the way she rocks up on the balls of her feet is familiar. Delicious anticipation.

The other man is kneeling on the bed in front of her now. At this angle, I can see his pants are down and the firm curve of his ass. The woman leans forward and greedily licks his cock at the same time the rougher man slaps the back of her thighs. She rocks forward onto the cock as a moan rips out of her.

I've never seen anything like this.

The scene is not unique. All around us, people are touching and fucking in full view of everyone else.

To think, all this time I'd playfully called myself a light skirt. I don't think I'm brave like these people. I couldn't do this, but I hunger to watch.

"Easy, love," my gentleman mutters and tugs at my left hand.

I glance at him to find I've fisted the collar of his shirt and am slowly strangling him.

"Sorry," I say and shift, though I don't know where I'd go.

He pulls me back and undoes a few buttons. "Never apologize."

"Never?"

His gaze is on my mouth. I can practically feel his lips on mine, but I hold myself back.

This man isn't who I want, and I don't know if I can use him to satisfy my need for another. Well, two others. That's a bit much to ask of a man.

I look to the stage where the men are kissing over the woman's back while it appears as though they're sharing her body. My breath catches while desire winds around me. I'm dimly aware of my fingers sliding against my gentleman's neck and shoulder, kneading his skin. It's the strange necklace he's wearing under his shirt that's most distracting for some reason. As if I've felt this before.

"Do you like watching those two men with their woman?" he asks.

"Yes."

Multiple partners is a luxury of the wealthy. In Suncrest, the most I ever saw were a few families with two women, but I've never seen a woman with her men before.

My gentleman takes my chin and turns my face to look at him. He's pushed his mask up, baring his face.

"You should be well cherished," he says.

I can't meet his gaze. I glance down at the thin strip of skin I can see below his neck and freeze.

The necklace he's wearing is distinct. I can only see a small portion of it, but I know it well. It's formed by rectangular plates linked together to form a regal band that lies on the collarbones. The metal isn't silver, but something else. Turquoise inlay frames what at first glance appears to be some sort of floral pattern, but is really complex sigils and runes that create the magical glamor.

I know this because I spent most of yesterday trying to rationalize how I might be able to wear it before accepting the fact that it was too precious for the likes of me.

He's still talking, and I only catch the end of what he's saying. "You should have everything you want."

I smile, doing my best to feign a demure innocence while finding somewhere else to look.

This man is no stranger.

Eligos.

For several long moments, I stare at the writhing bodies while barely daring to breathe. My mind is both empty and full of chaos while I work through each emotion coursing through me. Excitement. Shock. Outrage. Lust. Hope.

Am I certain this is my lord?

His body is the same size, though his coloring is a little lighter and warm toned, where this glamor plays up the cool tint to his dark skin. Is he trying to disguise the markings on his body? How would I know without removing his glamor?

If it is him, does he know who I am? Can he recognize me?

Belial didn't. Or he gave no indication he was aware of who I was.

Not once did he ask my name or offer his own. He also never looked at another woman, not even the serving girl who kept tugging her neckline lower.

What if Belial knew it was me the whole time?

That idea makes my heart race. I know I should find the idea a violation of my trust, but I don't. I knew it was him and I teased him into kissing me. Because that was what I wanted.

Teill knew Shax had kissed me at a glance. She'd insisted the lords would know as well. Does Eligos see the evidence of Belial's kisses on me? Or does the glamor disguise that?

His hand remains at my waist and the other on my knee. He isn't doing anything to me, and yet I've never wanted to be thoroughly fucked more in my entire life. Is it because of the scenes playing out around me? The man under me? Or my own pleasure-wired brain?

My gaze drifts back to the trio on the stage to find that a third man has joined them and the things they're doing to her are things I haven't dreamed of.

I'm reminded of Shax's fingers digging into my jaw and the way my knees went weak.

I want to be filled by both my demons. I want more hands on my body. I want to exist on a diet of pleasure and desire, gorging myself like my glutton demon.

"Careful," Eligos purrs into my ear. "Squirming like that..."

I turn to look at him, and his words die on his lips.

The glamor is so good I can't see a hint of gold in the dark depths of his brown eyes.

My request is lodged in my throat. I want to see him, my demon. But if I do that, there's no going back. I'll be committed to this path.

"Would you share me with someone?" My skin flames so hot I briefly consider sliding off his lap and praying for the ground to swallow me up.

The man I am almost certain is Eligos studies me for a moment. His brows are slightly lifted and his lips still parted.

Belial's kisses were demanding and hard. He'd taken what I'd offered, then wanted more.

What would kissing Eligos be like?

I'm leaning in before I can stop myself.

"Are you sure you want to do that, little—"

I press my finger across his lips, not wanting to lose the illusion that we are just two normal people who don't know each other. Whose lives won't drastically change just because we fucked.

"Right now, what I want is to be between two men whose only focus is me. Who make me feel desired. But it can't be just any men..."

Gold flickers in the depths of his dark eyes and I think I see his glamor shimmer for a moment, as if it can't entirely conceal him.

He stands abruptly and I gasp, grasping his shoulders.

"El—uh, sir? Put me down," I whisper.

"I finally have you exactly where I want you. The last thing I'm doing is letting you run away from me," he says in a very familiar voice.

He strides through the people to a well-lit stair leading up, twisting around and around. I gasp when we emerge into a room that my eyes struggle to take in.

The floors are like crystal, and below us is the theater with the erotic display of bodies spread out like a visual feast. The walls on the left and right slant downward, until they meet what must be the flat roof of the theater. I can see the same sort of shimmery material forming the roof to this sensual den, while the side that faces the street has double doors leading out onto a balcony. There's a bed larger than any I've seen before decked out in deep crimson and purple. There are other pieces of furniture, a lounge, armchairs, but my attention keeps going back to the people below.

Eligos finally sets me down, but he keeps my back pressed to his front. I lean against him and feel his cock. How much control was he exerting earlier?

"This is your only chance to change course, my dream," he whispers into my ear while his hand encircles the base of my throat, pulling me back against him. "I don't promise to let you escape, but I could try..."

Why is one of the most powerful creatures on this planet yielding for me? I'm no one, and yet I'm in control.

This is what I want.

I lean my head back against his shoulder, admiring the face he's wearing. There are aspects of Eligos layered into this disguise, but it isn't the same. I miss his face, yet the illusion of what we're doing has me enthralled.

I draw his arm around my waist and lift his hand to my breast. I might not be as debauched as I'd once thought myself, but I know the basics of what men like. Eligos knows the rest. His fingers press against me, causing the boning of my corset to press against my nipple.

"You would deny me what I want?" I mean the question to be playful, but it comes out heavy with desire.

He turns me in place, our noses bumping. "Never."

It's as though I'm poised on a cliff, one wobble away from falling over. His lips meet mine and it feels as though I'm falling or floating. I'm not sure which. His lips slide against mine while his fingers tunnel through my hair. His teeth sink into my lower lip and I whimper. Where Belial was hard and demanding, Eligos is sensual and teasing. I clutch his shoulders and pull him closer, wishing we could dispense of our clothes already.

A loud bang makes me jump and we both turn toward the double doors now open onto the balcony. A large, dark figure crouches on the railing, and for half a moment fear courses through me. The figure steps down off the rail, his form becoming familiar.

Belial.

"How...?" I stop myself from asking because that might end the game.

"You said you wanted to be shared by two men, didn't you?" Eligos whispers into my ear with that unfamiliar voice of his.

Belial steps into the light. He's still wearing that harlequin mask that does nothing to disguise him. Anyone who has ever seen him in this lifetime would know it was him. But the way he stares at me, as though he intends to devour me, is new.

"You took your time," Eligos says over my head.

Belial stalks across the room. Belatedly I realize he might actually be unhappy with me. I did run away from him. There's no flicker of surprise as he comes closer. It's as though this face is exactly the one he expected, which means I was the only one not in on the secret.

The sting of realization is brief and passing.

I'm far happier to learn that their interest has not waned.

Belial almost walks straight into me, but instead grabs me by the hips and lifts. I squeak and grab his shoulders, which frees up his hands to hike my knees up around his hips. Eligos becomes a hard wall at my back, and now I am well and truly trapped.

There is no going back, even if I wanted to.

Belial leans in and I hold my breath, but he stops just short of my mouth.

Eligos reaches up and grasps Belial's chin between his fingers, redirecting Belial's attention over my shoulder. I feel the press of Eligos' shoulders as he leans over me. Belial's grasp on my knees tighten as he meets Eligos' mouth in a sweet, gentle kiss that is the complete opposite of the tense atmosphere currently holding me in its thrall.

"Later. We'll talk about it later," Eligos whispers.

What will we talk about later?

They both look at me, trapped between them now, with similar crooked smiles and heavy-lidded gazes. How is it they're so alike and completely different?

Belial leans in, running his nose along my cheek until our lips are almost touching. "Do you like the way he tastes?"

"Yes."

He presses a light kiss to the corner of my mouth. "Do you want him to fuck you?"

LIORIA

"**I** want both of you," I manage to say though my voice wavers.

Belial snorts and leans back. "Then why'd you run from me?"

"I'm sorry," I say and curl my arms over his shoulders.

His expression isn't cold, exactly, but he's holding himself back. "If it's him you want, just say it."

"That's not—no."

Eligos' hands slide up from where they're splayed against my stomach. I hate the corset that makes it difficult to feel his touch.

"Tell him the truth," Eligos whispers.

I lick my lips while my insides tremble.

"I ran because I wanted you too much," I say though my voice is strained. "Part of me wanted you to fuck me there on the street, and... You wouldn't have known it was me. It felt wrong. And at the same time, it's all I could think about. I didn't want to lie. I wanted you to know it was me, and—"

Belial's mouth crushes mine. It's the same hard, demanding kiss as before.

Eligos' fingers reach my neckline. The fabric has little to no give, but his talented fingers dip past the material to caress the tops of my breasts.

Belial takes my jaw in his hands, fingers pressing firmly to my skin. It's not the same near-painful way Shax gripped me, but it's similar enough that my body relaxes. Belial stares down at me and his pupils narrow, as if they're about to go demon. "Use me as you desire, that's all I ask."

Oh, gods...

Belial looks over my shoulder at Eligos. "I need a taste, but..."

"Too high?" Eligos asks.

Belial nods and Eligos reaches up to cup the back of Belials' head. They touch foreheads and everything in me aches to be part of whatever this moment is between them, even if it isn't my place.

"What's wrong?" I muster the nerve to ask.

Eligos smirks, which is an odd expression on the earnest, open face he's wearing. "My lover here wants you so bad he's afraid he might lose control and hurt you."

I stare at Belial.

Eligos takes my wrist and guides my hand down to Belial's impressive cock.

"Gods," I mutter.

I've always scoffed at men bragging about the size of their dick. An inch in either direction is only good if you know how to use it. But this? Belial might just split me in two. I want to try, though. I need to.

"See?" Eligos mutters.

"Enough," Belial growls out.

Eligos chuckles, releases my wrist, and cups my mound. "He's impatient to taste you here. I can't wait until he tastes you."

"She's wearing too many clothes," Belial says.

Eligos clutches me to him and steps back. "Then how about we fix that? But first... My lady, do you need...?"

I tilt my head to the side. What else could I possibly need?

"You mean, is my contraceptive charm current?" I glance over my shoulder at Eligos.

"Yes," he says with a wry smile.

"It is," I whisper. Which means I will not bear them a potential demon heir.

Gods. I want to move or do something, but I'm frozen in anticipation.

Belial kneels and eases my feet to the ground, but only so that he can pick at the laces of my shoes then slide them off. Eligos makes no such move. He pulls me back against him, hands splayed on my sides.

"He's going to fuck your pussy with his tongue," he says in a lower voice and I clench my thighs together. "Has anyone ever done that to you?"

I shake my head.

"Then you're in for a treat," he whispers and I feel the first tug at the laces.

Normally, the first time I tumble a man, there's nervousness about my body or what he might say. The anxiety that's seized my tongue is different. I'm afraid of the pleasure and how much I might want this. How it will change me. But most of all I want to please them.

"Careful," Eligos warns. "I like this one."

Belial rises up on his knees, grabs the neckline of the dress, and yanks. I gasp as the fabric rips at the shoulders while he snarls, "Then buy another one."

The dress falls to my feet, leaving me in still far too many layers.

"Look at her," Eligos says in a tone I might call reverent. "Look at how this corset—"

"Take it off," Belial growls.

Eligos leans in and lets his lips caress the shell of my ear as he whispers, "So impatient. Goddess, tell him to worship you. Go on. Do it."

My tongue sticks to the roof of my mouth and I can't say anything.

Belial grins up at me, but it's feral and a little scary given how angular his face has become. "I will worship my goddess..."

He reaches up, only his hands aren't entirely human any longer. His fingers are inky dark with long talons instead of nails. I press back against Eligos as Belial grabs handfuls of my chemise and the underskirt. His nails slice into the fabric, rending the underskirt in two. He curls his hands into fists and pulls, cutting the material to ribbons.

"He is going to eat you up," Eligos says with glee, then whispers softly. "Don't be frightened."

"I'm not," I say while staring into Belial's green gaze. That part of him is still human.

"I can feel you trembling."

"I'm not frightened in the way you mean."

"Oh?" Eligos purrs.

The corset loosens, and he guides my arms up while the underskirt pools at my feet. My skin is so warm and flushed that my head begins to throb. If one of them doesn't touch me soon, I might pass out.

Eligos slides his hand through the rips to splay his hand over my lower ribs, but that's not where I want him to touch me.

Belial stretches up and runs one claw down my sternum from my collarbone to the low neckline. I hold my breath as he crooks his finger. The fabric gives with no resistance.

Just how sharp are those talons?

With a few more slices, the chemise flutters to the ground in tatters.

I stand there caught between shock at how fast it happened and anxiety about whether or not they will find me desirable with the layers gone. Belial sits back on his heels, hands at his sides, while his gaze roves over me. It's so intense it feels like a caress.

"Look at how much he wants you," Eligos whispers. "But I'm the one who gets to touch first."

He pulls me back against his chest and lifts his hands to cover my breasts. I whimper and tip my head back.

"You are such a dream," he mutters against my neck.

"My turn," Belial growls.

I feel his hands at the waistband of my drawers right before he shreds the pretty, lace-trimmed garment. The move is savage and should alarm me, but instead, I find myself aroused by this display.

Belial presses his lips to my now exposed thigh, just above my stocking. He kisses across one leg to the other as he slides the stockings to the floor, leaving me completely naked between them. Eligos' fingers slide over my nipples and I moan as sensation zips through my body.

An inhuman growl makes me freeze.

"I think he's impatient," Eligos whispers. "Never run, understand?"

I nod, because I don't trust my voice right now.

He takes a step back, tugging me to follow while Belial remains kneeling on the floor. His hands are completely inhuman now. They're larger and the talons are almost twice as long. Whatever his skin has become, it gleams like starlight.

"Pull it in," Eligos says, sounding more like himself. "Look at me."

Belial's gaze drifts over my shoulder.

Eligos repeats himself, firmer this time. "Pull it in."

Belial closes his eyes and inhales sharply. His forehead wrinkles, as if he's in pain maybe, and I watch as his creamy, fair skin creeps down his wrist to the backs of his inhuman hands, all the way to his fingers.

"That's it. Isn't he a good boy?" Eligos croons.

Belial's shoulders sag and he opens his eyes to give me a lopsided grin.

"Tell him he's a good boy and he can have his reward now." Eligos pinches a nipple suddenly, causing me to gasp. "Do it. Tell him."

I cringe at the words, but at this point, I'll do whatever they ask of me. I'll say anything. But I don't want to merely parrot Eligos' words. Their open adoration gives me confidence. I lean my head back against Eligos' shoulder and lift my hand to trail my fingers along his jaw. In my head, he isn't wearing the glamor.

Belial tracks the movement. His eye are human again and the deepest green. His lips are curved in an almost smile that delights me.

"Does my good boy want his reward now?" I ask.

Eligos chuckles and squeezes my breast, causing me to squirm.

Belial grins and leans forward. "Oh, yes."

"Where?" Eligos asks.

"Over there."

Eligos lifts me into his arms again and I only panic a little as he carries me to the lounge. He sits with his legs on either side of the cushion and leans back, becoming part of the furniture.

I'm not entirely certain what they have planned. They're both still completely dressed while I am not. I draw my knees up, ankles crossed, feeling exposed.

I catch sight of the theater below us and gasp.

"Forgot about the show?" Eligos asks.

"C-can they see...?"

"No," he says quickly. "While neither of us are opposed to putting on a show, tonight is for us."

Belial sets one knee on the lounge and grabs my ankle. "I want my reward..."

The muscles across my abdomen tighten as he pulls and I resist him. I don't want to, but I can't help it.

"She needs to be coaxed," Belial says. "What are we going to do about that?"

"Coaxed, hm?" Eligos cups both my breasts, lifting them high on my chest.

Belial leans in, his gaze locked with mine and licks across both nipples. The sensation sends warmth pooling low in my belly and now I'm clenching my thighs together for a different reason.

"I think she liked that," Eligos purrs.

Belial braces his hands on my knees while he flicks his tongue across my nipple. I groan and turn my head toward Eligos' neck, as if I can hide my face. Firm fingers slide around my other nipple. I peer down at Belial's coppery hair. The sight of him worshiping my body makes me want something I don't have words for. But I *want*.

He looks up at me and smiles sinfully. "Do I get my reward now?"

I let my thighs relax as he pushes on my knees, parting them.

"Like this," Eligos mutters and grabs the underside of my knee.

I tense as he draws my leg aside so that it drapes over his.

Belial's face lights up and his gaze lowers to the apex of my thighs. "That's more like it."

The open desire on his face gives me the foolhardy courage to allow Eligos to do the same with my other leg.

I'm completely open to him now, naked, and vulnerable.

Belial lowers himself to his elbows then buries his face between my legs. I arch my back and shift my hips, but there's no escaping him now. I hear his deep inhale and panic swirls in my chest as I begin to worry about every little thing. How do I smell? What if he doesn't like how I taste? Does my stomach jiggle too much?

He tips his head back and groans in what I can only call delight.

"This is harder to watch than I thought," Eligos says in a strange voice that is both familiar and not.

Belial smirks up at Eligos. "First taste is mine."

And then Belial dips his head, and I feel the flat of his tongue against my folds as he licks me. My breath stutters to a halt and I stare up through the crystalline ceiling at the stars overhead. He spears me, delving deeper while another groan rumbles through him.

Eligos rubs his fingers over my nipples, overloading me with sensation. I grasp the edge of the cushions, but my fingers slip off the smooth material.

Belial grabs my hips and pulls me down a little bit, which forces my legs open wider.

"Hear how much she likes it?" Eligos says.

My brain has completely stopped working. I am not in control of my body any longer. All I can do is feel as Belial thrusts something thick into me.

"How many fingers is that?" Eligos asks.

"Three."

"Gentle."

"No," I moan before he stops.

Belial thrusts his fingers into me and I toss my head back against Eligos' chest. Belial's mouth blazes a hot trail over my mound while Eligos tugs my hair to the side and seals his lips over mine. He thrusts his tongue into my mouth while Belial gently strokes his tongue over my clit. My thighs are trembling now and I want so badly to be fucked in earnest.

As if he hears my thoughts, Belial pushes deeper, twisting and curling his fingers.

I need to touch them.

I press my hand to Eligos' leg and the other to Belial's shoulder. I hate the layers of clothing that separate us and vow that before long they will both be naked.

Then Belial's tongue flicks over my clit. It's the rawest sensation I've ever experienced. My whole body tightens, my spine bows, I draw my knees up, and I whimper around Eligos' tongue in my mouth. Belial is ruthless now, his fingers pumping into me as I soar to new heights.

He removes his fingers and licks my folds, causing little zaps of sensation to zip through me.

Eligos' hand is in my hair now and he's turning my face.

It's overwhelming with both their hands on me, and we've barely begun.

"What do you think of our glutton?" he asks me.

I whimper, unable to form words.

Belial's mouth kisses a trail up my stomach and ribs.

"Did you like watching those two men use their woman?" Eligos asks.

I nod.

"What about when they kissed, and she had to watch?"

My toes curl against his calves and my skin heats. I'm not sure why this question makes me shy, but I nod again.

Belial gently bites the side of my breast. I glance down, my gaze snagging on his as he looks past me to Eligos. My heart beats a little harder at the blatant desire on his face. Eligos reaches forward, fisting Belial's hair, and drags him up. I gasp as his bigger body pins me back to Eligos' chest, and then they're kissing over my shoulder, me caught between them.

I grin and slide my arms around Belial, relishing the chance to hold him as Eligos holds me.

They aren't gentle with each other like they are with me. Their kisses are demanding bordering on violent and I'm fairly certain Belial might be missing a handful of hair by the end of this. It is that passion that I envy. I bask in their love, soaking up what I can, while I can. I'm not the least bit bothered that I'm only an accessory.

My body relaxes and I pull Belial's shirt from where it's barely tucked into his trousers so that I can slide my hands along his smooth flesh. He's warm and deceptively human-like.

Belial turns his face toward me and I smile as I push my hands up his chest.

"I think she wants more," he says.

"Good." Eligos grasps my hips, pulling me back against his groin. "Because I want my turn, my dream."

Belial's gaze drifts down to my breasts. "How do you want her?"

"Do you have something in mind?"

Eligos' hands slide to my inner thighs and he trails his index fingers over my sex. I shiver, still sensitive from Belial's attentions while hungry for more.

Belial is focused on his lover's hands and me. "I'd like to watch her ride you."

Will he look at me with that kind of longing?

"I like the sound of that," Eligos says.

Belial's chin comes up and his eyes meet mine. "What do you say?"

Eligos strokes through my folds. I'm not sure if he's teasing me toward arousal, or trying to distract me from speaking. Regardless, I lean back against him content to let him stroke my desire.

"Do I get to make a request? Or do I only get one?" I ask Belial.

He narrows his gaze. "Are you getting greedy?"

"Yes."

He pushes my hair off my face. "What is it you wish? If you're a good girl maybe I'll grant you whatever it is you desire."

"I want you both naked. I want to see you," I say.

His eyes light up and he grins. "Is that all? Fuck. You could have said that sooner."

I bite my lip and watch Belial reach back behind his neck and drag his tunic off. But the mask remains. I almost want to ask him to dispense with it, but that would mean acknowledging this on all fronts.

Thick, black swirls curl over his shoulders and arms to his chest. He has pale, coppery hair across his chest and down to his trousers, that's almost invisible except when the light hits it just right.

He leans forward and kisses me with light, suckling kisses that make my body throb with renewed need. I can taste myself on him and I want more of what we're doing. I fear that tonight won't be enough.

Belial rests his forehead against mine. The mask makes it difficult to see his eyes. "I'm keeping my pants on. It's for your own good. Sorry..."

"You really think you'd hurt me?" I ask.

His lips twist up and his nose wrinkles. "Yes."

That lack of faith hurts me, as if his assessment of himself is somehow a personal attack on me. I don't understand these feelings but I decide to leave it. I run my palms over his chest and kiss him back.

Eligos spears a finger into my pussy and I gasp.

"It's my turn," he practically snarls against my shoulder.

I moan and shift my hips, but one finger isn't hardly enough.

Belial stares over my shoulder. "Our lady made a request. Take your clothes off. Now."

"I was going to."

Eligos withdraws his finger from my pussy then pinches my bottom. I yelp and pitch forward into Belial's arms. He chuckles and gathers me to him, burying his face in the crook of my neck.

"I'm sorry about earlier," I whisper.

He's quick to kiss me. "Sh. Now is all that matters. Watch."

I peer over my shoulder at Eligos standing next to the lounge. He's shed his coat and is working at the buttons of his vest.

"Doesn't he look pretty?" Belial whispers and turns me so that I'm sitting with my back to his chest and my legs folded under me.

I turn my head, the better to whisper into his ear. "He's always pretty to look at."

Eligos is watching us with heavily hooded eyes and an amused smile.

Belial is all masculine energy and strength with a hidden sweet side. Eligos is similar, but his masculine energy is more stalwart and persistent. It's his unexpected softness that I cherish, because I don't think he shows that to many.

I miss his purple locs. His glamor has disguised him with braids that he's tied back, but it's not the same.

He parts the shirt slowly, revealing the necklace that gave him away.

Did he pick it intentionally?

The shirt falls to the ground and I sigh.

"Now the pants, come on," Belial says.

Eligos smirks and his pants drop to the floor. I'm not sure when his shoes and socks came off, and now he's completely naked. He's gloriously made and I have to wonder if he expends a little magic to keep himself in such perfect form when all he wants to do is sleep the days away.

He wraps a hand around his cock, stroking it lazily from base to tip.

"What do you think? Am I worthy?" he asks with a mischievous smile.

"Oh, yes," I say, eager to get my hands on him.

He throws a leg over the lounge, lowers himself back to where he'd been, and crooks a finger at me.

"It's my turn, now," he says.

Belial pushes my hair behind my ear. "Ride his cock for me."

I crawl forward, only a little surprised when Belial grabs my hips and kisses the curve of my ass.

Eligos reaches out and grabs me by the shoulders, hauling me up against his chest.

"Don't make me wait," he says in a voice gone dangerously low while he stares over my shoulder.

"Mm, do you have some bite to go with your growl?" Belial taunts.

I reach over and take his chin much the way he's done to me and turn his face to me. "Eyes on me."

His lips quirk as if he's suppressing a laugh while his hands smooth down to my hips.

"I daresay you like being the center of our attention," he says.

"When you treat me so well, how could I not?"

I glance down at his cock only to look again.

Eligos' erection is impressive. He's certainly the most well-endowed man I've put my hands on, but that's not what alarms me. No, I'm not alarmed. Curious.

Belial chuckles and presses to my back. "I was wondering when you'd see that."

There's a curved bar piercing the flesh at the base of his cock, right where my clit would grind against him.

Belial cups my breasts, teasing my nipples and I shiver. "You ever seen anything like that?"

"N-no. Does it hurt?"

"You'll be fine," Eligos says.

I frown. "No, does it hurt you?"

That startles a laugh out of him and a slow grin spreads across his face. "No, my dream. That is for *your* pleasure."

"Really?" I'm curious now and lift my hand, only to stop.

Eligos grasps my palm and brings my hand to his cock. I greedily wrap my hand around it, sliding it up then down and allowing my fingers to caress the pierced flesh.

It's not a small, curved bar. It's sizeable to the point I can feel it under his skin.

"It won't hurt you?" I ask again.

"That's just it. Sometimes I like a little pain," he says.

Again I think about Shax's hard hold on my face and my weak knees, though those memories threaten to sour this moment with guilt. I still haven't told them about the kiss. I'm curious and I think I understand.

"Go on," Belial whispers. "Ride him."

I lean forward and kiss Eligos, banishing the darker memories in favor of new ones. He pulls me forward, guiding my knees and legs until I'm straddling him with his cock nestled between my legs.

"How long has it been for you?" Eligos asks.

I squint at him. "What? Like five minutes?"

He shakes his head and pulls me closer, which allows his cock to slide against my folds.

"Fuck," Belial mutters as he kisses across my shoulders.

"How wet is she?"

The next thing I feel are thick fingers twisting inside of me. I gasp and pitch forward against Eligos' chest while Belial finger fucks me.

"Very," he replies and pulls out. "See?"

Eligos tips his head back and I feel Belial's hand moving between us. I peer down and can just see his hand wrapped around Eligos' cock, spreading my arousal over his skin to his balls.

"Up," Belial mutters.

I clench Eligos' shoulders and rise up onto my knees. He leans in and I gasp as his lips wrap around a nipple. Every inch of me is alive and hyper-sensitive.

The blunt head of his cock presses against me. It's rather nice having an extra pair of hands around. I bite my lip and relax, letting gravity guide me down. At first, my muscles flutter and tense. Belial's fingers slide along either side of my folds and I relax, letting Eligos slide in deeper. It's a decadent sensation to have both men so focused on me right now. It makes it easier to let go.

I tip my head back and rise up just a little before pressing back down on him.

"Fuck," I mutter as he begins to stretch me further.

Eligos grips my hips. "Go easy."

"What if she likes it?" Belial counters.

"Do something more useful with your mouth than talk."

I grin at their banter. Words are beyond my capability right now.

Lips kiss up my neck as Belial gathers my hair to one side. Gentle fingers that must belong to Eligos trail down my abdomen to my mound, just over my clit. I bite my lip as he draws circles around the bundle of nerves.

I press down on him and groan as I feel his pubis.

Eligos' mouth meets mine in a hungry kiss as he rocks up into me. That precious little bar seems to roll back and forth. I clench around him as my inner muscles draw tight.

"Fuck," he groans. "That feels so goddamn good."

Belial's hand slides down my ass to where my body is joined with Eligos'.

"Her muscles are fluttering," Belial says.

"I know," Eligos grits out.

"Gods, I never knew…" I rock my hips back and forth. "It feels so good."

Belial grips my hair, pulling me back a little. "But what about him? Don't you want him to feel good, too?"

I nod, desperate for more.

Eligos ignores us and grabs my hips. He lifts me with inhuman strength then pulls me back down, moving my body in a circle.

"Oh, yes," I groan and do my best to move with him.

Belial reaches around to pluck at my nipples. It's so much pleasure, and this is only the beginning. Because I know now that I cannot simply walk away from them. I know their love is eternal and what we have is just lust, but I've never felt anything this all-encompassing before. I want to be selfish. I want to be part of this for as long as they'll have me.

Eligos thrusts up as he brings me down onto his cock and I rock forward. My vision blurs and I cry out as pleasure shatters me.

"Yes, that's it," Eligos growls, repeating the motion.

I'm not in control of my body. They move me, touch me, all while it feels like I'm rippling out of control and breaking apart only to come back to do it all over again.

"Fuck," Eligos groans and clutches me to him.

I'm boneless and spent, draped over him with Belial's hands on my breasts now. Eligos' breath fans across my cheek and neck, just as labored as my own.

There's something different about this joining, and I don't know what it is. But I want more of it.

"God, you two are… Fuck, that was amazing," Belial mutters against my shoulder.

Eligos reaches past me and drags Belial in for a kiss. I watch, content to bask in the moment, and then they turn their gazes on me. I smile as Eligos pulls me closer so that it is now the three of us, brows and noses touching. It's as if they're admitting me, for now.

I relax and press back against Belial's chest. His hand drops to my waist, hugging me.

What about him?

I bite my lip and peer over my shoulder at him.

"What is it?" he asks.

It does look as though he's more relaxed than I'd seen him as of late. Well, before their days-long absence, which I still need to ask about.

I lift my hand and stroke his cheek. "Are... I mean, are you sure I can't do something for you?"

Eligos grips my hips and shifts, causing that naughty bar to press against my clit. I gasp and my eyes cross for a moment. When I come back to my senses, Belial is kissing my palm.

"No, my lady." He withdraws, not physically, but he might as well. "That's... It's not a good idea..."

"Oh..." I glance at Eligos, but I can't look at him. Not with him still so deep inside me. Just like that, the warmth and contentment is gone. "Then, should I go?"

"No." The single word comes out of Belial's mouth, but in two voices. One human, and one not.

Eligos hugs me and rubs his nose across my cheek. "Fuck no. Pay him no mind."

"I mean, is it me? Am I a...?"

Belial slides to one side so that he's half standing, half kneeling, all the better to look me in the face. "I want you too badly and I don't want to hurt you."

My cheeks heat, but it needs to be said. "But what if I don't mind?"

He shakes his head, eyes closed. "No."

Eligos leans in. "Are you game for a little forced seduction?"

I blink at him. "Me? Or...?"

Belial's gaze turns thunderous. "Eli—"

"No." Eligos thrusts his finger under Belial's nose. "For that slip up you must be punished."

"This isn't a fucking joke. I could hurt her," Belial snarls.

"You could, but you won't." Eligos smiles back and slides his hands around to grope my ass. "And you need to have a little faith in our dream girl."

Belial's face creases as if he's in a panic.

"What if I hold him down?" Eligos is looking at Belial, but talking to me. "He's physically stronger than me when things are even, but I think I can take him. Would you suck his cock? That might be the best compromise."

"I fear I won't be very good. I don't have much practice." My skin heats with the admission.

"What you lack in skill I have faith you'll make up for with enthusiasm." Eligos winks at me. "If I think it's too much for you, I can take care of him."

I bite my lip.

His gaze narrows. "What's that look for? What are you thinking?"

"Nothing."

Belial leans in. "You know, demons always know when you're lying."

Father of lies.

Those words come back to me, but I banish them.

I grin sheepishly. "I was just... I want to watch you two."

He blinks at me, as if my words are surprising.

"Really? Now isn't that interesting," Eligos purrs. "What do you say?"

BELIAL

I drag my hand over my face, disturbing the mask a bit, so I have to adjust the damn thing. "I think I'm cursed and can't say no."

Eligos has the balls to laugh at me. Bastard is going to have his day soon. It wasn't that long ago *I* was having to pull *him* back. There's this energy between the three of us. It's unlike anything I've ever experienced before. We need to understand what's happening, but more than that, we need each other.

It's as though I've been waiting for this lifetime since my creation.

"Handcuffs or the old-fashioned way?"

I dare to glance at Eligos, though I know I shouldn't.

They're beautiful together, even wearing the glamor. Lioria is formed like one of the old goddesses, with a bountiful body that was made to be worshiped and enjoyed.

"Handcuffs."

I'd prefer if Eligos held me down. There's a sensuality in that option, but I don't trust his assessment. I've always been the strongest of us when it came to brute strength. Eligos' demon is more awake than mine, which changes things. But not enough for me to want to risk Lioria. So, as much as I despise the restraints, I believe they are necessary.

He whispers something at Lioria while looking at me with wicked intent. I know he's enjoying my torment, and I love him enough to allow it.

Lioria braces her hands on his shoulders and rises. They groan as their bodies separate and I briefly wonder if I might overpower them both and have my fill. But that won't rectify the situation. My demon wants to possess her body, and I've already proven that tongue fucking her only dulls the desire.

Eligos meets my gaze. "Go lie on the bed."

I don't look at her. I can't, or my tenuous hold on my control may very well snap. I cross to the big bed and push aside the pillows to sit with my back to the headboard.

Lioria is curled up on the lounge alone for the moment while Eligos purses the trunk of toys we left here.

I can't recall how long it's been since we locked up this room and made it invisible to all others. Years.

We've never brought anyone else here. This used to be our escape when Privale began to flourish. It was the one place no one knew about where we could be left alone. And now Lioria knows of it.

That only seems right to me.

She belongs with us.

Eligos jingles metal and I glance up, only to grimace.

Fucking hell.

He grins and strolls toward the bed, his still-damp cock bobbing with his movements.

I groan, knowing very well that's what he wants. "I hate those. Why not use the Enochian ones?"

"If you think you're that much of a risk, aren't these the most obvious choice?" He rattles the chains in his hands.

It's hard to argue with his logic.

The Enochian restraints are crafted from layering angel feathers dipped in gold. Once the metal parts were formed, the sigls and runes were etched into the cuffs. They're beautiful, and they fucking hurt. They were made to torment our kind.

The cuffs Eligos hold up are no less cruel, but of a different nature. The so-called leather is the hide of a dragon and unbreakable, even for someone of my strength. The chains are normal and inconsequential, because the real evilness is the spikes pointed inward. The spikes are manticore quills. The only name I know for them is Devil's Delight.

Struggle against those and knock yourself out.

I've learned that the hard way.

The Enochian restraints promise sweet agony. Devil's Delight forces the wearer to maintain perfect control or lose consciousness.

Neither are a wonderful option.

Eligos is right, though. If I genuinely fear for their safety, nothing is more effective than manticore venom. Not even Enochian magic. At least not anymore.

I hold out my arms and he climbs onto the bed. This close, he drops the playful act and looks at me seriously.

"Will you be okay?" he asks in a low voice.

It was always said demons couldn't break Enochian shackles, but I've done it. It's been a handful of centuries, maybe longer. That sort of thing is hard to forget. It was fucking painful.

"Yes," I say honestly.

I can't imagine hurting Lioria, but I dare not risk it.

Eligos grins at me. He's livelier than he's been in ages. I'd missed this mischievous part of him.

He fastens the restraints around my wrists, careful to leave them loose enough I can move a little without pricking myself. I know from experience the venom can knock me out for a solid week, and it does not degrade. The chains are fastened to links in the headboard before he returns to Lioria's side.

The only real way for me to sit here without risking myself is to grip the headboard above me with both hands. Any other way and the weight of my hand would be enough to envenomate me.

This is a terrible idea, but I'm not going to stop it. I'm a glutton in all the worst ways.

She doesn't see it because to her we've always been this way, but I can tell the difference she's made in us. Eligos is waking up, and I feel alive again.

He helps Lioria to her feet and steadies her. The biggest difference is his smile. He's grown so cynical in the last decade. It was like he was in the process of giving up. And then she walked into our lives and changed us. We aren't simply going through the motions anymore. There's something worth waking up for now.

The only thing that would make today better is if they'd get rid of the damn glamor and I could take this annoying mask off. But she needs the freedom this illusion provides, and I can't say no to her.

They both climb onto the bed and my skin prickles with awareness.

I don't like the glamor. The hair is too fair, her skin paler, and her face has lost the roundness. The worst offense is that the widdow's peak is gone. Whenever I look at her heart-shaped face, I want to smile. It's like the universe made sure to remind me in every way that she has my heart.

Eligos kneels behind her and strokes his hands down her sides while watching me. The bastard knows I'm jealous.

"How do you intend to play with him?" he whispers into her ear.

She grins and looks at me with that little chin-tuck that makes me think she's nervous. But my lady is brave enough to not let that hold her back.

When she doesn't make a move, Eligos makes another suggestion. "Why don't you say hello first?"

Lioria leans forward, walking her hands toward me. I tip my head forward and our gazes lock. She crawls to my side, but keeps her lips just out of reach.

"You want to tease me?" My voice is low, betraying the need inside of me.

"I still don't quite believe this is real," she whispers.

"It's very real, my lady."

"I don't think I've ever been acused of being a lady before."

I chuckle. She has no idea what I want to do to her. All in good time.

Lioria leans in, feathering gentle kisses to my mouth. I can't shift closer. The power is all hers and I chafe against invisible bonds holding me still.

If I lose control, I lose this chance. I do not intend to lose.

She reaches up, bracing a hand against my shoulder and running her fingers up the side of my neck.

I'm going to begin every day after today kissing that mouth. She just doesn't know it yet. This is our beginning.

"Feel him," Eligos says.

Lioria glances back at him, lounging against the footboard. The shadows fall across him, making the disguise less offensive to my eyes. My Eligos is far more attractive than the guise he's wearing. I hate this game they're playing, but in the end I'll get what I want.

"Feel him, like this?"

She wraps her hand around my cock without hesitation. Her eyes are bright and smile wide. She's enjoying herself. I knew the moment we met and bandied words that she wasn't someone we would need to coax. Much.

I close my eyes and let my head drop back as her strong little hands run over my erection.

What kind of men has she been with that she fears she won't be good enough at something?

Humans can be so dense sometimes.

Eligos grins at me, but I ignore him. "Belial, tell her what you like. Don't make her guess."

Lioria darts a glance up at me, and I know I'm fucked. She has me wrapped around her finger and she doesn't know it yet.

"Lick the crown. Tell me if you like the taste," I say.

There's no point if she doesn't enjoy this.

She regards my cock with interest for a moment, then leans forward. I'd imagined a quick, tentative swipe. Instead, she presses the flat of her tongue to the head of my cock and drags it across slowly. I stop breathing and my entire focus narrows to her and me.

"That growl means he liked it," Eligos says.

When did I growl?

He's next to her now, head propped on one hand as he watches. "This area right here? It's called the frenulum."

"Shut your mouth," I say. Or growl is more like it because what comes out of my mouth hardly constitutes as words.

Lioria glances up at me, but Eligos quickly refocuses her attention.

"Give him an open-mouthed kiss here and suck just a little."

She looks up at me and, God, I want to rip these damn cuffs off. There's no guile in her as she bends her head while eye-fucking me and presses her pouty lips to the underside of my cock. I suck in a breath, tip my head back, and close my eyes in an effort to maintain control. Her lips glide across my skin, constricting to suck lightly in just one spot.

"Oh, very good," Eligos purs.

I press my very human fingers into the metal of the headboard.

Fucking hell.

"Why don't you reward him a little? He's being so good."

Damn Eligos and his *helpful* suggestions.

Her tongue swipes the sensitive area once, twice. The third time she presses her tongue to me and licks back up and over the head, causing my eyes to cross. But that's not all. She's gotten a little brave.

Instead of pulling back, she presses down. I hold my breath as she explores me with her tongue while her lips constrict around my shaft.

"Eager, aren't we?"

Eligos glances up at me and I can't decide if I want to punch him or fuck him.

He leans in, pushing her hair over her shoulder. "He's too long to fit, so I like to make use of my hands."

"Shut up," I mutter.

Lioria sits up and my dick pops from her lips. The skin is glossy and flushed from her attention. Her breasts sway with the motion and I really hate these fucking handcuffs.

She reaches out and double fists my cock. "Like this?"

Eligos reaches over and grabs the slender bottle of lube from the nightstand. "Hands."

She presents her palsm hands up and he lets a few drops fall, one then the other.

"A little of this goes a long way."

She presses her hands together, spreading the lube, and looks at me. "Is this okay?"

"Whatever you want to do is okay."

She tilts her head to the side. "Still think you'll hurt me?"

"Yes. More now than before."

"You want me that badly?"

"Yes."

She reaches out and grasps my cock. The oil allows her to slick her hands over my flesh in a smooth glide.

"Oh, that does make a difference," she says with wonder.

"It doesn't taste half bad either. A little like vanilla."

I'm going to kill Eligos with my bare hands.

She bends forward and presses teasing lips to my cock while her hands tighten around my shaft. She leaves little kisses as she explores me, all while my balls ache and Eligos does his best to not laugh at my sensual torment.

I shift, needing to move and wanting more, but I can't guide her without my hands.

I need more.

"Don't tease the glutton too much. You don't want him getting creative."

I won't kill him. I'll tie him to a bed, keep him hard for a week, and never let him come.

She tips her head back, freeing my cock while her hands twist around my cock and up. Her eyes are still the same despite the glamor, and for that I'm glad as I stare back at her. "I think I like your creativity so far."

I lean forward. She tilts her chin up and there's just enough give in the chains for me to brush my lips to hers. Sure enough, there's a hint of vanilla on my lips now.

Her grin is brilliant and resolves me to my role.

Lioria bends her head and this time there's no teasing. She grips the base of my cock while her mouth slides down my length. My eyes cross and I shift my hips, desperate to move. I need more than these light touches.

She bobs a few times.

This is torture. Fuck this idea. It was a terrible lapse in judgement.

I move my legs restlessly, but the only direction I can go is to the side.

There's a brilliant moment of clarity and I grin. I see Eligos start out of the corner of my eye, but I move first, curling my legs to the side and my feet under me. Now I'm kneeling instead of sitting. Lioria glances up at me, but she's currently busy teasing the underside of my cock with her tongue.

"Careful," Eligos says.

I press my hips forward. Her eyes flutter wide as I bump the back of her throat. I don't linger. My need is too great for that and I withdraw. Her hands clutch me almost too tight as I slide through her grasp until I'm out of her mouth. But she doesn't sit up or comment. She remains where she is, eyes on me.

This is a moment I'm going to remember for the rest of my existence.

She's down on her elbows, round ass up, hair pooling around her to the point I can only glimpse her breasts, and her greatest desire is my pleasure. It's a humbling place to be when we've done our best to tease out her greed.

I pause only for a moment. It's all I can give her. And then I trust. It's not gentle, because I am no longer capable of it. But I am controlled. The feel of her vise like grip is extraordinary until I get to her mouth. And then it's heavenly. I groan and hold myself pressed to her throat. She swallows around me and I curse.

"Does that feel good? Is she pleasing you?" Eligos asks in a voice gone low with lust.

"Yes," I groan out and move my hips in a circle while her tongue lavishes me.

"He can get a little forceful..."

Lioria doesn't budge, and I am not as restrained as I'd like to believe.

I pull back and thrust again in quick succession. It's rougher than I want, but fuck. She feels so good wrapped around me like this. Knowing her, she's cataloguing my reactions and discecting it all. She's nothing if not a quick study.

Suddenly, she squeaks around me. I glance up at Eligos to find he's moved up next to her, and I can't see where his right hand is. I still my motions and watch, but it's what I hear that makes my balls tighten. That slick sound of a pussy being fucked. I inhale the scent of sex and her.

My hands flex on the headboard and before I can stop myself, I'm moving again. It's not gentle and a part of my mind is screaming to stop, but Lioria doesn't move. I have no idea if Eligos will allow her to.

The touch of her, the way she sucks when I trust it's too fucking good. And I want more. But my body aches for release. I try redirecting my thoughts, but she's becoming a master.

Her teeth scrape my skin. Not hard and maybe not intentionally, but I fucking love it. My eyes roll back and I thrust deep on a groan as pleasure rolls up through me. I've been celibate long enough that the prickling of my skin is euphoric. And then I'm coming, and she's wrapped around me so tight it seems as though we're knit together for all eternity.

Eligos pulls her off me and I snarl. Given the opportunity, I'd keep her to myself, our bodies locked together, until dawn.

He turns Lioria, pressing her down on the bed. My vision hazes, but I maintain tenuous control and lower myself to sit and watch Eligos kiss up her bare body. She moans and looks up at me, as if asking permission to pursue her own pleasure. I strain toward her, but can only get so far.

She falls back, her head pillowed on my thigh as Eligos sucks her nipple into his mouth.

I want that to be me, but between us I'm more likely to fall under the spell of rut.

Eligos pushes up and I watch him take his cock in hand and guide himself to her entrance. She moans and her lids flutter closed. There's just enough room between them for me to see Eligos' cock disappear inch by inch. She lifts her hips and runs her hands over him.

My lady is so very greedy, and I want her to have everything her heart desires.

Eligos hooks an arm under her knee, wedging her open, and pushes up. This is as much a display for me as it is an experience for her. I fucking love watching them. They're beautiful and uninhibited. Every sweet sigh and sharp gasp is part of the symphony.

Listen to me.

I sound like a fucking sap, and I don't care. I don't care about anything that isn't in this bed right now.

He teases her, varying the pace. Slower, then faster. Hard, then soft. She's babbling after a while, begging, threatening, and Eligos is no doubt loving this.

She tosses her head back on a scream, her spine bowing, and Eligos shouts.

It's so achingly beautiful. I want to gather them in my arms, but I can't, seeing as I'm still secured to this damn bed.

I close my eyes while their labored pants and sighs continue to build a sweet melody.

"Is it safe to let him go now?"

Lioria's question snaps my eyes open.

Her head is still on my thigh, but she's turned toward me and Eligos lays stretched out behind her.

He eyes me. "Hm..."

I stare at him.

If he leaves me in these things a moment longer, I'll envenomate myself out of spite and then he can handle everything for a week while I get to sleep in for a change.

He chuckles as if he can hear my thoughts. "I think so. What to do the honors?"

Her eyes are heavy lidded and I think we've exhausted her, but she slowly gets to her knees. I love that she has lost her shyness. She doesn't try to cover herself or present her body at just the right angle.

She's exactly as she should be.

"Come here," I say.

Lioria straddles my legs and I lean forward. She trails her fingers over my face, then presses her lips to mine. I suck down air.

"Get these fucking cuffs off me," I say.

She giggles.

The damn nerve.

"Do I just unbuckle them?" She stretches to my left. "Are they safe?"

Eligos winks at me. "Safe for you, maybe not him."

I flip him the bird with both hands while he moves to my other side and frees my right wrist. It takes Lioria a moment longer because she's so careful, but the moment my hands are safely free, I scoop her onto my lap and turn away from Eligos. I throw one leg over her to keep her pinned, tunnel my fingers through her hair, then kiss her. I kiss her the way I always want to, with my whole body focused on this one point of contact. As if I can make her feel this deep hunger that resides in me, all focused on her.

Eligos chuckles and I feel the bed dip, but I ignore him in favor of running my hands over her body. She gasps and squirms, all of her nerves so hyper-sensitive that she mewls.

I can't get enough of her.

"Move," Eligos barks and smacks the back of my knee.

I glare at him, but he holds up a damp towel. So it's time then. I reach out and he tosses one of the two towels to me.

Lioria is boneless in my arms. I glance at her, taking in the glassy-eyed, sated expression of bliss.

There's not much left in her today. She's exhausted.

I move back and Eligos begins swiping the cloth between her legs. I take a slower path over her chest and sides, down her hips, before wiping down her arms.

"What are you two doing?" she asks in a voice thick with sleep.

I lean over her and kiss the tip of her nose. "Getting ready for bed."

"Sleep? Already?" Her question turns into a hiss and she shifts away from Eligos.

I pull her toward me and kiss the side of her neck. "Yes."

She's content to let us care for her. Though I don't think her body gives her much choice in the matter. Before we can begin to broach any sort of awkward after talk, her eyes close and she begins to breathe evenly. Eligos chuckles and smoothes her hair. There's so much care in his eyes that it gives me hope. Hope that he isn't so far gone, that we can still find something in this world to be happy about.

I stare down at the woman gently snoring between us. This glamor of hers annoys me. I want to see my Lioria, even if I understand the reason she resists. I can't fault her for wanting the same freedom I craved for a millennia.

"I blinked, and she passed out," Eligos whispers.

I gently stroke my fingers over her hair.

"Do you feel it? Something different?" I ask.

"Yes."

We're quiet for a moment.

This little human has us wrapped around her finger, and she doesn't know it yet. If I've picked up on her hesitation and occasional withdrawl, then Eligos certainly has. I assume his reason for not assuring her more is because, like me, he's wrestling to identify what this is.

We've loved and lusted for humans before. But this goes deeper.

No human has called to our demons like this.

This act of maintaining our disguises is a farce. Neither of us are willing to allow her to simply walk away. She just doesn't know it yet, and I pray that when she comes to that realization, she doesn't hate us.

LIORIA

The cold wakes me. I'm huddled under a plush, thick blanket, but it does nothing to chase the chill away. I've become spoiled to Teill, popping in to tend the fire before I wake so that my room is toasty warm. My body aches, like I've done a month's work in a day. Only...

That's not right.

I roll to my back with a groan and wince at the ice-cold linens against my bare backside.

What happened that I went to bed naked?

I crack open an eye and peer around the dark room that is not my cozy suite at Privale, nor my cramped quarters at the boarding house.

Those are the only two places I've lived as an adult, and this bed is certainly not mine.

I rub my face, then blink around the decadent space.

The theater.

Gods.

I smack my cheeks in an effort to wake myself up.

It all feels like a dream. A decadent, sensual dream. My heart is racing as I peer around, but my lords have already departed. That sends a pang of disappointment through me. I'm not part of their relationship. I'm an addition. An amusement. I'd do well to remember that, even if it stings.

Seeing as they've gone, it's time for me to leave as well. No doubt someone will come tidy the place up and I do not want to be caught still here.

Gods, what if it's Teill? Where is she?

A little panic shoots through me as I recall her promising to find me when she was finished.

I do my best to find my clothes, but it's difficult in the dark. I'm lucky to locate my corset and the dress. The chemise is destroyed and I have no idea where the rest of the undergarments are, so I dress myself the best I can.

Thankfully, a peek out the window shows that it's still quite early. I pad down the stairs to the landing. The theater is full of people still, though they're asleep now.

There are blessedly few people around as I hustle my way toward the manor and through the gardens to the servant's quarters. Only a few curious people see me and none will know me with this face. They might guess, but they'll never know.

I creep into my room and close the door with a heavy sigh as I lean against it. The whirlwind of emotions is bubbling to the top. I can't hold out much longer.

Finally, I can think, and after a little spiced tea—

Teill winks into view on the other side of the room.

"Gods!" I scream and clutch my chest.

She points at me. "Where have you been?"

I gape at her disheveled appearance. I've never known Teill to look anything other than tidy. Her shoulder-length hair is standing up, in knots, and looks like there have been hands in it. She has red and purple marks on her neck and cheek. Her lower lip is swollen. And...

"Who bit you?" I demand.

She jumps and tugs the ripped sleeve of her dress up. "It was consensual biting. You! Where have you been? I've been looking for you all morning."

I sputter a laugh. "It's *barely* morning."

She huffs and crosses her arms over her chest. "Fine. I've been looking for you since dawn. I'm sorry. I..."

"It's fine." I plod toward the bed. I let my arms fall away from me, which makes my unsupported gown gape and strain.

Teill gasps. "Where are your undergarments?"

I glance down. I can feel their absence, but mostly because the seams of the dress and the inside of the corset aren't entirely comfortable against naked skin, not to mention how delicate and sticky the skin between my thighs feels.

"That's a long story. I want tea and a bath."

"You draw the water and I'll be back with a pot. We're using your tea, right?"
She pauses. "Was that an invitation, or did I read that wrong?"

I do my best to smother a laugh. "If you thought it was an invitation, then it
was. And I would rather use my tea."

She blinks a few times, then shrugs. "Lovely. I'm really developing a taste for it.
I'll be back."

Teill vanishes and I frown, peering about the room.

"How do you do that?" I mutter, but there's no response.

I take my wonderfully sore body into the bathroom. The sunken tub is plenty
big enough for both of us. I start the water, throw in some of the salts, then set
about extracting myself from my mostly ruined dress. By the time Teill literally
appears at the edge of the tub, I've removed my glamor and sit in chest-deep water.

"Whole place is still asleep," she mutters and dumps the tea leaves I'd set aside
into the pot.

"That's what I was hoping for."

She sheds her clothes faster than I did and quickly submerges herself, sitting
opposite me in the circular tub.

I draw my knees up and lean forward. The scalding water has done wonders for
my body. "You enjoyed yourself?"

Her unnaturally pale skin turns a slight gray with hints of pink. "Yes."

"Yes? That's it?"

She huffs a little, but her eyes are round.

My stomach drops. "Did he hurt you?"

"What?" Her gaze snaps back to mine. "No! No, they were lovely."

"They?" Now she has my interest. "I only saw one man..."

She shifts a little, then lowers into the water. "Yes, well, he's part of a nest and
asked if I wanted to meet the others..."

"Were they all great, big hairy men?"

Her gaze slides sideways. "Yes..."

I gasp in delight. "Are you going to see them again?"

"What? No. I couldn't possibly..."

"Why not?"

She gestures to her face. "They don't know I look like this."

"Well... What are they?"

"I don't entirely know. It's not like we discussed it, and given what I'm hiding..." She gestures to herself. "I didn't exactly ask. There's the human you saw and a basajauns. I'd never heard of them before, but he was quite large and almost human-like in their true form. They're shapeshifters to boot."

"And hairy?"

She flushes a darker pink and gray, but nods. "Head to toe..."

"The two of them?"

She shakes her head and covers her eyes with a hand, then holds up four fingers.

I squeal in delight. After my night with two gentlemen, I'm jealous. Only a little. "What's the problem? Wouldn't they understand?"

"I doubt it." Her gaze narrows. "What about you?"

I hold up my hands. "You can't tell? I thought you could see demonic energy."

When she doesn't say anything, I glance at her to find she's staring at me with eyes so wide I'm worried about them rolling out of her skull.

"What's wrong?" I pat my face.

"Y-you what?" she whispers.

I hold out my arms, still oblivious to what she and the lords can see, that I cannot. "I thought you could see demonic energy."

"They don't just leave it on everything they touch. That's intentional. Like, marking their territory."

And I was not marked.

That stings.

I suck in a breath and let my body slide down so the water closes over my head. I hold my breath while this new piece of information lodges itself in my head.

Shax chose to mark me out of spite.

Eligos and Belial had no desire to.

I'd thought we might have an enjoyable season together before their interest waned. I guess that is not to be.

Teill's hand grabs me by the hair and hauls me up, gasping.

"Ow!" I push her hand away.

She waves her finger in my face. "Stop stalling. What happened?"

I groan and cradle my head. "I need tea for this."

She pours us both a large cup of tea, adding a little sugar and a splash of milk to mellow out the bite, just the way I like it. I inhale the familiar scents of home before drinking greedily, despite the scalding temperature.

Then, I begin.

At the end, I can't look at her, so I stare at my reflection in the tea.

Teill is quiet for a while, as if she knows my turmoil. "You should take today off and figure out your feelings. What you want. You've done such a good job doing the lord's work. It's their turn to do their half. Rest and see how you feel about it after that."

We don't speak about it again. Instead, we share stories about what we ate and what we wished we'd eaten. I might not have earned a place in my lord's hearts, but I've gained the most wonderful friend. Men come and go. That's been the truth of my life. But my true friends have always treated me well. I hope to know Teill until my very last day.

Eventually, we drink the last of our tea and the water cools. We're both moving slowly as we get out. Well, I get out. Teill spends a few moments cleaning the tub and afterward has the audacity to look perkier and more refreshed. If I didn't like her, I might just hate her.

She tells me again and again to rest today and ignore the call of work, but I don't promise anything. I'm tired, but doubt I could sleep. I can't stand these walls right now, so I put on one of my old dresses, make myself another cup of tea with what's left in the pot, and head to the kitchens. There's only two people on hand. They've set up a small buffet of things, so I make myself a little meal in my pockets before heading outside.

It's warmed up considerably and I stroll about, nibbling on my food while I work the soreness out of my limbs. My mind wanders, never lingering on any one topic for long. While I hadn't settled on a course of action for myself, I'd started to feel as though this might be where I belonged.

After last night, I can't see myself staying here and not wanting more. It's silly to think that after two weeks I'm attached to my lords, but I am.

"Morning."

The voice makes my heart skip a beat and a few particularly tender places on my thighs twinge.

I'm not ready for this, but when was I ever?

I turn to look over my shoulder at Belial striding toward me, hands in his pockets. He's wearing a new suit of clothes and a pleasant enough smile. There's no harlequin mask this time, and for that I'm grateful. It is marginally easier to maintain my dignity given our silly pretense of being other people.

"Good morning," I say to him, though it's close to noon now. "Have you been to train?"

He grins. "Hard to train when I'm the only one who shows up. Is Eligos in the study?"

"I wouldn't know." My emotions are a riot, so I muster a little bravery. "I didn't intend to work today since I got through the backlog of communications. There's a summary in the office and a list of things that need your attention. Mrs. Jurrah also has some things she needs from you."

He brightens. "Oh, good idea taking the day. I bet I can convince Eligos to leave off work."

Something chatters in my chest and I do my best to power on. "Yes, I bet you can."

Belial says something else, but his words are drowned out by my thoughts.

"I'm sorry, my lord, I... I need to go." I manage to get all but the last two words out before my voice betrays me.

I whirl toward the servant's wing, grab my skirts, and run. But no one can race tears and win.

My heart will break and I will mourn, but I can heal. And most of all? I'm still free.

ELIGOS

I know she's here somewhere. The bond tells me as much, but I want to see her. She isn't in the study nor in her room. Is she trying to vanish on us?

Damn Belial for dragging me out of bed this morning. I know it was necessary, but for once I wish we could ignore our duties and focus on ourselves.

When we returned, the room was empty.

This wasn't at all how this was supposed to go.

I can't eat or sleep or find a shred of peace. As good as it was last night, I know we have to strike while Lioria is still under the thrall of lust or she might very well decide against us.

The study doors open and Belial stalks in looking as shitty as I feel.

"Well?"

He glances at me, startled as though he hadn't known I was there.

I sigh and swallow my biting remark. It won't do to needle each other.

"I saw her in the garden," he said.

"Why didn't you bring her with you?"

He shakes his head and stalks past me.

"What is it?" I demand.

"I never got around to telling you about Ammit's people, did I?"

"What about them?" I don't give two shits, but Belial can be single-minded sometimes. It's best not to try to out-stubborn him.

"One of them was very interested in Lioria. Didn't have much to say about it and I couldn't press the matter much."

That makes me pause.

There's no love lost between those who still pine for the Egyptian gods and us. At best we tolerate each other. But the dedicated group who vow to keep Ammit's name alive have always been a peaceful group, content to sell their honey and tend their bees.

Belial whirls, pacing the length of the study. He's more agitated than I realized at first glance.

"We haven't mentioned Shax," he says with a biting edge in his voice.

"What do you make of it?"

"He's trying to bait us," Belial snarls.

I would have thought last night would have taken the edge off. It seems he's even closer to a breaking point now than before.

"That sounds like Shax, which is why it isn't worth getting upset about, so long as he did not harm Lioria. And she isn't likely to tell us if she does not trust us."

"He'll never see her again, or I'll tear his throat out."

That is not a passing threat. Unfortunately, I doubt it's one Belial can make good on. Oh, he'd tear Shax's throat out. That is a given. But if we want Lioria in our lives, we'll have to come to an understanding with Shax.

I eye Belial's fingers, but his talons are sheathed.

There was a time when most of us had been enemies. He's killed us before, but it was a different time and we were mindless creatures back then. Still, a berserk Belial would be horrible news.

"What aren't you telling me?" I ask.

He wheels around, eyes gone a dark green and his pupils narrowed into slits. There's rage coming off him so strong it makes me take a step back.

"She was crying. Crying, Eli."

"Why?"

"I have a good guess."

"But you didn't ask why?"

Belial stalks up to me and jabs his finger against my chest. "I told you the glamor was a bad idea. I told you she would feel betrayed when she learned it was you. And now look!"

"What are you basing this off of? What exactly did she say? Or did you decide with that great intellect of yours that you already knew the answers? Because I think she made a clear choice in our favor last night only to wake up alone today.

And what for? Why was it absolutely necessary to drag me out of bed before dawn? Hm?"

"Oh, so it's my fault now?"

I sigh. "It's no one's fault."

Belial growls and grabs me by the robe. His nails slice through the fabric and he shoves me back against the wall with enough force I can feel the wood paneling crack.

My demon slips its leash and I snarl back at him while my claws lengthen.

A shriek cuts off both our snarling and I jerk my head up to see Mrs. Jurrah standing in the doorway, eyes wide.

Belial drops me suddenly and I land on my ass while he stalks away with nearly transparent wings twitching and fluttering in his wake. I haven't seen his wings in so long I almost forgot what they look like.

Shit.

FLORIA

The next morning, I feel physically better. The soreness is gone and thanks to a wonderful concoction Teill shared with me, most of the other marks have stopped bothering me.

If only it was as easy to mend my insides.

Which is why I woke up before dawn to get to the study absurdly early. It's not that difficult. I'd already come in earlier while the lords were away, and Teill doesn't comment on it when I enter. She is paying an exorbitant amount of attention to the far wall, but she will find a speck of dust anywhere.

It doesn't appear the lords touched the mountain of work yesterday, which is disappointing. What is the purpose of having me here if I'm not useful?

"Oh, the box chimed earlier," Teill says instead of, *good morning*.

"Thanks. You sleep alright?"

"Like the dead. You?"

"Well enough."

I want to be interested in Teill, whether or not she intends to see her hairy gentlemen, but my heartache has a firm grip on me.

Since there's not much else to do, I turn toward the letterbox. Part of me doesn't want to get close to it, while another part of me wants to find a folded sheet of paper inside that might comfort me. I know what my lords have said. Oriax is not to be trusted. And yet, he's been a steady presence for me when everything else is tumultuous. I know I can't necessarily trust his intentions. But what harm is there in asking how my day went? This easy correspondence with Oriax is a reprieve from the uncertain, choppy waters I've been living in.

My fingers lift the lid and I peek inside at a single sheet of folded paper. I groan and lift it out.

"What now?" Teill asks.

"More problems I can't solve."

I haven't told her about Oriax. No one knows about the pages we trade. There isn't anything worthwhile on them. It's simply a steady exchange.

Questions about my day.

How am I adjusting to the climate change between the regions? How much of the book have I read? Am I making use of the library here? Have I considered studying further? Do I know what tea was served at the inn? Are my lords being kind to me?

I've asked him as many questions. Especially in my lord's absence. Oriax is the only one of the Demon Lords I can converse without needing an introduction. He's been immensely helpful when he didn't have to be.

It's hard to remember that he's dangerous. That he wants something from me. Today's note is especially hard.

Did you enjoy the festival?

I don't know how to respond. It's all so jumbled still. I can't talk to him about the other lords.

But the festival was eventful. It occurs to me Oriax presents an excellent opportunity to better understand some of what I saw.

I did. It was pleasant to not have to work for once. Did you get to enjoy much of it? Or did official duties get in the way?

I send that while I mull over how to phrase my next question and busy myself moving things around on the desk. Thankfully, Oriax does not keep me waiting.

It was a busy day, to say the least. I don't just have my province. I have two universities with their own celebrations. But this holiday isn't about me, is it?

His words are artful and I think I can hear his voice when I read them. It is not lost on me that Oriax is important. He isn't just a High Demon Lord, he is the founder of the two most important institutions for higher learning in the world. And he is always at the other end of a letterbox for me.

There was an incident during the festival I would like your perspective on. I stumbled into what I thought was a performance, but instead, this man spoke ill of Eden and the High Demon Lords. The town watch ran them off before they could say much, but it was disturbing. Do people on the continent hate us so much because we have peace and they do not? Or is there something I don't understand?

This time I wait much longer. So long that I go and get Teill and myself a pot of water to make spiced tea and a bit of breakfast. When I come back, she's still glued to that wall.

"What happened over here that's got you...?" My voice trails off as I peer at what appears to be an indentation in the wood. "What happened?"

Teill clucks and shakes her head. "I don't know, but it looks like the lords might have had a fight."

"A fight? With who?"

She shrugs. "Each other, I guess."

Why?

The letterbox dings, but I stand there a moment longer.

What's going on? What don't I see?

I turn and retrieve the letter, only to find Oriax's reply is lengthy.

This is a topic better covered in person. Or over the course of a few years study, should you be so inclined? Your curious nature would make you a fine historian and your penmanship is lovely.

History is never straightforward. Context is king. Unfortunately, understanding is harder to come by. Demons have done the best we can to document the passing of time, but we are not perfect creatures. We are flawed and prone to our particular vices. Every one of us has had at least a few unfortunate lifetimes we'd rather the world forgot. But we are not the only ones with long memories. There are other creatures in this world who are staunchly opposed to us because of what those attached to us have done in the far distant past. I cannot blame them. When it comes to humans, they often hate what they do not understand. And we are rarely transparent about our motives or goals.

There are many who feel that we abandoned the continent and left the mortals there to death. It was the regrettable price of freedom. We did the best we could to establish other Demon Lords, but they do not answer to us. They rule as they see fit, or they have been overthrown. This is all out of our control, and yet the blame is also ours.

Maybe you should make a trip and we can discuss what else you heard? I'd be interested in hearing your thoughts on the matter.

Lovely words indeed.

His compliments soothe the inner ache that's kept me up, but at the same time, I know Oriax has his motives. At least I understand him to some extent.

Teill pauses next to the desk and peers at the page. "The lords can be jealous…"

I fold the page and tuck it into my pocket. "There's nothing to be jealous of, Teill. Besides, they already had me. That's done with now."

She hums and moves on to dusting the shelves behind me.

Did I perhaps make the wrong choice? Is Oriax not the master manipulator the others make him out to be? Would it be so bad if I explored my other options?

My heart wants what it can't have, so in this, I have to use my head. Only, I don't know what to choose save for one thing. I'm not ready to see my lords again.

BELIAL

The study is empty. No Lioria. And no Eligos. And I cut training short this morning. I can't do that again. I've quietly increased the number of men in the barracks until they're full. Alastor is doing the same at the capital, but it won't be long before others are aware of the move. But we don't know what to tell them. The raids on the southern shore are technically not our problem, so long as it doesn't cross our boundary line. Alastor has made it clear he doesn't intend to investigate further, but I can't turn a blind eye.

The others won't see the threat for what it is. Oriax is certain the boundary stones are all we need. Raum would rather war was part of his history only. Shax is too focused on political gain and glory. Valac, well, war bores him. And there isn't enough evidence that the handful of spies we've found amount to anything other than a fishing expedition. We don't have any idea what forerunners are or if we should be concerned about them. But something isn't right.

Unfortunately, I can't fucking focus on that.

I pick up the pages lying on the desk in Lioria's neat, swirling script and just stare at them.

I sense Teill before I see her. She's sitting on the window seat, hands folded on her lap, waiting.

"What did you do to the wall?" she asks.

"Sorry about that," I mutter.

Her gaze snaps to my face and I have to smother the urge to chuckle. She's so small and yet so fierce. When I first found her, she was so tiny and shrunken, I could hold her in one hand. I still remember my headlong race down the coast, searching for someone to save the little babe. Well, child.

"I didn't ask for your apology. I want to know what happened," she demands.

I turn to face her and lean on the desks while gathering my thoughts. "I was angry."

She crosses her arms over her chest and glares. "And what good came of that?"

"Nothing good," I mutter.

The dark cloud that is Eligos drifts closer. I peer over my shoulder and wait until he ambles through the doors. He's late today, which probably means he'd intended to give Lioria some space. Neither of us knows quite what to say. This has somehow become complicated when it was perfect.

"You're here early," he sneers.

"Oh, you two," Teill mutters.

"What? Do you have something to add?" he snaps.

I whirl to face him, only to find Eligos glaring at me, fists clenched at his sides.

This is what we know how to do. We spent so long fighting that it's still second nature for us.

Teill stands and shakes out her skirts. "So, let me see if I have this, right? You two finally get what you want without any consideration for the consequences, then you choose to fight and damage a wall I can't fix, and now you're ready to come to blows again? Over what? What's wrong with you two?"

Eligos turns his demonic gaze on her. "No one asked you."

"She's only recounting the truth," I say.

He's quick to glare at me.

I hold up my hand. "Regardless of our personal drama, we have work we must attend to. Together."

"That's my cue then." Teill winks out of sight. I feel her move lightning fast through the building before fading from my awareness.

Eligos sighs dramatically before flopping onto the daybed. He's just as miserable as I am.

"I think it's time we leveraged our network. We've missed something, Eli, and I have a bad feeling."

"Or are you trying to distract yourself from the mess you've made?"

I shake my head. We can both be petty. We have tried to change ourselves, but our nature is somewhat fixed thanks to our creator. But in this, today, I can choose a different path.

"I'll write to Alastor," Eligos says. "What about the town's borders?"

"I checked them this morning."

"And?"

"I found two broken stones."

Eligos sits up. "What?"

"Somethings happening, Eli. I don't like it."

 LIORIA

I found the history books in the library that are used at university and read the first volume yesterday night. I didn't understand all of it, and there was quite a lot of information about various noble families I don't care about. Eden as a country is a few thousand years old. There's a great deal of history I don't know.

The sky is still dark as I make my way from the library after returning the book toward the study.

I never responded to Oriax's longer letter, and I'm not sure how to continue that conversation. He was so haughty and arrogant when I met him in Suncrest, but he's been nothing but patient in his letters. Honestly, I'm not keen on adding another High Demon Lord to my social circle. It's probably best if I do some independent study on my own.

"Lioria?"

I pause and glance over my shoulder. Mrs. Jurrah stands in a doorway, candle in hand. The flickering light makes her look so much older.

"Morning," I say, trying my best to sound cheerful.

"It's early."

"Yes, I've been keeping Teill company."

Her face creases. "I see. I need a word."

I wait for Mrs. Jurrah to snuff the candle out and set it down before shutting the door and joining me. I blink away the bright spot in my vision. The magic lights that illuminate the manor are turned down to the faintest, so the candle isn't necessary. She falls into step with me and we begin a slow stroll toward the study on the opposite side of the manor.

"Is there something I can do for you?" I ask.

"Do you know why the lords are fighting?"

That's news to me and I stare at her with wide eyes. "No. No, I haven't the faintest idea. I haven't seen them much since they returned…"

I can't come out and tell her I spent the festival with them in disguise. That's way too much information.

"I've served Belial my whole life. My family is quite proud of that." She twists her hands together. It must vex her to have to come to me for help with something. "In all this time, I've never seen them fight like this. Never."

The dent in the wall.

"Teill mentioned something happened, but she didn't give me any details…"

Mrs. Jurrah stops facing me. "Will you speak to them? I have staff that doesn't want to come in because they are afraid…"

Shit.

"Anything to lower the tension."

"I'll see what I can do."

The words feel dragged out of me.

She hurries off without another word.

It feels as though my shoes are full of rocks now, so heavy that I make my way slowly into the study. Teill is bustling about, but she isn't humming and her mood seems subdued.

I ignore the desk. How much work would either have, anyway? Chance are, they haven't touched the lists I've left for them, which only serves to irritate me. What's the point of doing this job if they won't do theirs? What are they doing anyway?

Instead, I head to the daybed and lie down, staring at the fire. The flickering flames help calm my jumbled mind.

"What's with you?" Teill asks.

"Mrs. Jurrah wants me to convince the lords to stop fighting."

She snorts. "Why is it women must always fix what men break?"

"I didn't know they were fighting."

"That doesn't surprise me. You're avoiding the very thought of them."

"Do you know what they're fighting about?"

She's quiet long enough, I lift my head and peer at her methodically wiping down the decorative candlesticks on the mantle.

"You know what they're fighting about, don't you?"

She sighs, lets her arms drop to her sides, and rolls her eyes. "Of course I do. But... *They* need to fix this. Not you. Not me. *Them*."

"Mrs. Jurrah said staff is threatening to not show up to work. That's how frightened they are. Is it that serious?"

"It's always serious when demons fight. People who work for them are smart enough to know that."

Shit.

Things were fine during the festival. Teill is aware of the reason, but not me. I have to wonder if I'm part of the problem. If I somehow broke them. The clear solution is to remove me. I don't want to. I've grown attached to the lords and Teill, but if my affection isn't returned, the best thing is probably for me to leave. I'm not sure I'm suited to be an addition to a relationship. I'm jealous and my behavior the last few days has been petty. I'm not proud of myself.

Oriax's invitation is becoming more appealing. Even if he wants to poke and prod me, it could be worth it to pursue an education. There are a number of benefits to my position if I look at them from the right angle.

I can't see myself returning to Suncrest. I was content when all I saw was my simple life, but one glimpse outside those walls, and I can't simply go back.

This isn't the end for me, even if it feels like I might shatter. I don't love Eligos or Belial, but I care about them. If I stay here, I can see myself falling for the both of them. Which makes this more difficult.

Teill retreats and continues her cleaning while I lie there staring at the fire. The room gradually becomes lighter while dawn breaks. At some point, Teill brings me a cup of spiced tea, which means she's popped down to my room and helped herself to the tin. I don't mind. I'm grateful, because I will need tea and strength to get through this.

She sits next to me and for a while we are quiet, staring at the fire, sipping our tea.

"Do you want to get it over?" she asks.

I push up and cross my legs. I wore one of the new outfits today. It's gray, befitting of my mood. The pants mold to my body while the jacket has a full skirt that falls to my knees, almost meeting the tall, supple boots. It's more comfortable than I'd expected, which is about the only positive today thus far.

"I suppose that would be for the best," I say slowly.

She places her cup on the side table where Belial's current snack usually sits. "I'll bring them to you."

"What? Wait—"

But she's gone. Just vanishes right out of sight.

Damn, what I wouldn't give to be able to do that.

Eligos is probably sleeping and Belial should be training with the men, whatever that means. I've read their official communications, but I have no idea what it is they actually do. From my perspective, they lounge about a lot, doing nothing. So how does anything get done? Or does this country run on the backs of subordinates and stewards?

Something bangs in the hall and I glance up in time to see the double doors thrown open. Belial and Eligos each grip a door. They're nose to nose glaring at each other, and I think I hear the low rumble of growls. There's a menacing aura coming off them that's so powerful I'm filled with fear and want to slink onto the ground to cower.

This is what Mrs. Jurrah was talking about.

What could have caused this? Or was this always below the surface?

The reality is that I know so little about them. The history texts I read detailed things thousands and hundreds of years before. And all of that is their personal history. They've existed for so long I can't possibly comprehend the full nature of their relationship and old wounds.

One particular passage comes to mind.

The Attack of Hallowed Hill.

Belial, Eligos, Oriax, and Valac had been left to defend the forces flank amassed around an old holy site. They'd been treating the wounded and tending to women and children. But they were betrayed, and enemy forces captured the four of them. The dryads among the enemies grew trees up through the four demons' bodies, killing them slowly.

There was no doubt in my mind that Oriax wrote this particular passage. It was recorded with crystal clarity down to Belial's last words.

"I forgive you."

Supposedly, the twenty trees used to kill them are still there. The trunks are a deep red, as if stained for all time by their blood.

How can I possibly be anything to them?

It's arrogant to think that in the scope of time and so many lives that I matter at all.

Except I do. Maybe not for them, but the people who serve them believe I can fix this. They've put their faith in me to return us to the normal order of things.

I force myself to unbend my legs and reach out. I use handfuls of the blankets thrown over the daybed to pull myself toward the edge. It's hard to breathe through this menacing aura, but I manage to stand. Bracing a hand on the armrest helps while I waver with this unseen energy pressing in on all sides.

A spark of anger ignites within me.

Don't they know what their presence can do? Aren't they aware what their moods can do to us mere mortals around them?

"My lords."

I don't speak the words. It's as though they roll up from my belly, through my chest and throat, out of my mouth with a rapidly increasing force.

Belial and Eligos jump, then slowly turn their heads to stare at me with wide eyes.

And just like that, the suffocating force vanishes. I sway on my feet and glare at the two of them.

Eligos presses a hand to his chest. "What did you just do?"

Belial glances at Eligos in what I might have called a glare before what just happened.

"I think I'm the one who gets to ask that question. What are you two thinking? You have everyone scared to work. Mrs. Jurrah even begged me to talk some sense into you two."

Belial jabs a finger at Eligos' chest. "He upset you."

Eligos' eyes flash so bright I can see them from across the room going molten gold. "Me?"

They're so petty sometimes, arguing like children. This is that moment in the kitchens all over again.

"Enough of this," I snap before they can wind themselves up again. "Come in. Close the door. And let me know when you two decide to stop this childishness. You're lords. The earth quakes when you fight. Figure out another way."

What I want to do is knock their heads together, then put their noses in the damn corner. I'm angry enough I think I'd try it.

They keep one glaring eye on the other and close the doors like civil people. My knees tremble the closer they come, and I want to cower again.

"Turn it off. Whatever this is, turn it off." I lift a hand and swipe it across my cheek, only to find that I'm crying.

Belial snatches Eligos and hauls him closer. "What did you do?"

"Nothing! You made her cry."

"This is your fault."

Their growls rumble out like growing thunder creeping closer to disaster. My heart races, my skin tingles, and I want to run. This fear is trying to keep me alive, but it's still useless. I'm being smothered by it. I take a step back as my body wrestles control from that one small part of my mind that is observing this madness.

Eligos yells something, jabbing a finger at Belial, when suddenly a serpentine *thing* shoots out of his shadow. It curls around his feet, the tufted end of it flicking this way and that.

No, not a serpent.

A tail.

I'm gaping at him when the sound of ripping fabric makes me start. Three sets of wings unfold from Belial's back. They look like stained glass. They're a smoky black at the base, transitioning into a purple in the mid-sections, and ending in his signature coppery red hue. There are tatters along the edges, as if his wings have seen a hundred battles, and they jerk back and forth, stabbing the air. His shirt hangs in tatters from his shoulders.

When I glance back at the men, I start. Both men have black horns protruding from their brows. Six slightly curved spikes arc up and back from Belial's brow like a cruel crown while Eligos has two sets of regally curving rams horns.

What was it they'd told me?

The High Demon Lords can no longer shift forms.

I don't know or understand what I'm seeing, but they aren't fully human any longer.

If I stay here, I'm going to die. They're going to tear this place down around us and...

The ring.

I hold up my hand to look at the ring. I drop my meager magic into the device while choking back a sob. A dome envelops me, not that dissimilar from the one made with the ball. Only this dome is solid.

The relief is instantaneous. I expected physical protection from their fight, but I can't feel their bloodlust auras anymore. My thoughts clear while I suck down air. My whole body is still trembling, but the fear is morphing into anger.

What are they thinking? Where are my lazy, thoughtful, kind lords? What happened?

"Don't you two see what you're doing?" I shout.

Twin, demonic eyes turn to look at me and I take a step back. The dome might protect me, but my human brain still senses danger.

"W-what's wrong?" Belial asks with two voices. One is familiar, while the other is lower and discordant.

"She's afraid of you," Eligos taunts. His human and demonic voice have more harmony, but I don't think that's a good thing.

I back away two more steps, though there's nowhere for me to escape. "I'm afraid of both of you. Everyone is. What's gotten into you? Where did this come from?"

"Both..." Belial mutters.

"...of us?" Eligos finishes the question.

"Look at yourselves!"

They turn and seem to take in the other's changed appearance for the first time.

"What happened?" I whisper.

"Belial made you cry," Eligos says.

"You pushed her." Belial takes a step closer, jabbing his talon at Eligos' chest. "She wasn't ready."

"She's standing right here!" I shout. "Was the other night so bad that you two are going to come to blows over it? Gods, what happened to you two? How did you get here?"

Belial and Eligos stare at me. I know I've broken the unspoken agreement, but what else was I to do? This has gotten completely out of hand and if I'm to blame, I'm going to resolve it. I will not allow other people to be terrorized because of me and my weakness for these men.

"Lioria?" Eligos lifts his hand, as if he can touch the dome from halfway across the study. "That's the opposite of what happened."

"I don't need to know." I hold up my hands, as if I have any hope of warding them off. "I just want this resolved so we can put this behind us."

Belial places a hand on Eligos' shoulder. There's no hostility emanating off either now. It's almost like before, only with horns, a tail, and a set of wings.

Wings!

The silence stretches on and shame flushes my skin, but I remain where I am.

The pair of them look at each other, and I know they're communicating with nothing more than subtle glances again.

Good.

That, at least, can be repaired.

Eligos clears his throat, then looks at me. "Lioria, will you humor me by answering a question?"

"Okay," I say slowly.

"The other morning, why did you leave without saying something to one of us?"

"You were both gone!"

Belial shoves his hands up, only to grab his horns with both hands. His arms bulge, as if he's pulling on them while his wings flutter behind him. Eligos reaches out and plants his palm in the middle of Belial's chest, but it's not to push him back. It's like they're comforting each other.

Eligos's eyes bore into mine from across the room. "Someone cracked a boundary stone on the edges of town sometime during the night. Three have been destroyed now. We were notified of the first one early in the morning by…"

"Non-humans," Belial provides.

Eligos nods and continues. "We left you asleep to check on that and get break-fast. When we came back, you were gone, and the next time Belial saw you, you were crying."

"Lioria?" Belial calls out.

I take a few steps and grip the armrest of the sofa, that sits perpendicular to the daybed. I let the dome vanish and sit.

"T-the boundary stones?" My voice cracks, but is otherwise steady. That's a blessing. "Is everything okay?"

"Yes," Belial says.

I'm aware of both demons coming around the daybed on opposite sides to stand in front of the fire and me. They don't sit and they don't get too close.

Eligos lowers to the carpet in front of the fire, drawing one knee up to his chest while his tail curves around him. My gaze is drawn to the tufted end that flicks back and forth, much like a cat's tail might when it's agitated.

"I think there's been some miscommunication," he says in a voice that's totally human now. "I had every intention of keeping you in bed as long as you'd allow. But the stones..."

"I told you I should have gone by myself," Belial mutters.

"Gods. Oh, gods." I'm going to be sick. This is too much, and I've opened a door I can't shut.

Belial takes my face in both his hands. He's kneeling in front of me. The crown of horns isn't a bad look on him.

"What's upsetting you?" he whispers.

"Everything," I wail. "You're telling me this is all my fault..."

"I never said that."

I squeeze my eyes shut. "But that's the truth of it. You're saying the reason you two are fighting is because I left the theater?"

Eligos plops onto the sofa next to me. "I think we each jumped to a wrong conclusion."

I jump as something wraps around my ankle.

Eligos reaches down and tugs his tail from around my ankle, muttering, "Sorry, has a mind of its own."

"He's not sorry," Belial whispers.

"Gods," I mutter again, because what can I say? "Oh, gods."

Belial leans in closer. One side of his mouth hitches up in a mischievous smile that warms my heart. "They are busy right now, but we can hear you."

"That is not funny."

Eligos snickers. "It kind of is."

My anger isn't done.

I stare at one, then the other. "You let that come between you and scare everyone to the point they are refusing to work."

Belial swipes his thumbs across my cheeks. "It's time we discussed many things."

"W-what things?"

Instead of answering, Belial scoops me up, then sits with me cradled between his folded legs. I squeak and tense. There's some arranging of wings and something crashes to the floor, but we all ignore it. I'm too frozen to say or think anything. I don't dare hope, though I don't actually know what I should be hoping for.

"Let me make sure I understand what's going on?" Eligos turns to face us and I watch his tail slide toward me again. "When you woke up, and we weren't there, you assumed—what?"

"T-that was it. Which I understand. I did get emotional, which isn't anyone's fault. It just happened. A lot happened."

The tuft of his tail flicks across my knee. I can't feel the brush of hair through my pants, but I watch in fascination. It's easier to watch than look at these two.

Belial shifts, so I have to look at him or be more ridiculous than I already am.

"I'm not good with words. I trusted Eligos and did what he thought best, but I think what we need is a more direct approach."

Gods. My throat is so tight I can hardly breathe. I've wanted to vanish from embarrassment before, but nothing like this. "I'm trying very hard to remember that you are a person with free will and the ability to choose for yourself, because all I want to do is take you to my bed—"

"Our bed," Eligos practically growls.

"—and never let you leave." Belial's nose bumps mine. "You see, we already know that one night isn't enough."

"Lioria?" The tail in my hands wraps around my palm, squeezing gently. "We are picky bastards. We are not gods. We are imperfect creations with a vice we were made with."

Belial nods, along with Eligos' words.

"Both of us were drawn to you. I don't know why, and I don't care. Your presence fills a void in our lives that I don't know how to describe." Eligos presses a hand to his chest, brow furrowed in confusion. "It's like you belong here."

"We've gone about this the wrong way," Belial says. "We need to start at the beginning."

I look from one to the other. "W-what are you saying? What beginning?"

"I think what Belial means is that instead of proceeding forward under the guise that you're only here to work, we should be clear about our intentions." A sensual smile spreads across Eligos' face. It warms me, while also filling me with panic. This is all happening so fast. The tail tightens around my hand, as if he can sense my panic. "I know you have reservations and concerns, but we are motivated to move mountains if need be. You have all the power here, Lioria, and that's not something we are used to anymore. With us wrapped around your finger, you could be the most powerful woman in all of Eden. Maybe the world."

The very idea fills me with dread and I shake my head.

Belial chuckles and then I feel the press of his lips on my cheek. My whole being yearns for his touch, and that kiss immediately soothes me.

"I don't want anything so grand," I manage to say.

Eligos leans forward, and his tail tugs on my hands. I watch him get closer, filling my vision, until there's just the three of us. Nothing else. He presses his lips to mine in a lingering, gentle kiss. The anxiety choking me eases. A calloused hand on my jaw turns my face from Eligos. Belial's kiss is more demanding, but shorter.

"This is a lot to take in," I say softly. "It's overwhelming. Why? Why me? There isn't anything special about me."

Belial and Eligos share a look.

What do they know?

I'm surprised when Belial speaks. "With no record of your birth, it's impossible to say, but I'd guess that you aren't entirely human. Some traits can resurface generations down the line. I don't think you did anything, just like the flower does not summon the bees. We were simply drawn to you and chose not to resist because you appeal to us. I like your curiosity and sense of adventure. I want to show you things. Share things with you."

I bite my lip. Their assumed rejection stung so deeply. I was surprised to find how much it upset me when we'd made no promise. I'm similarly surprised now by the surge in hope. Hope that maybe my path has taken an unexpected turn, that I'm where I belong. For now, at least. They are still immortal beings.

Eligos' hand joins his tail around my palms. "You've made it clear this is not the path you'd have chosen for yourself. All we'd like is a chance to see how this works. A trial basis, if you will?"

"A trial for what?" I've barely come around to the idea that all of this isn't a big mistake.

Belial's hand strokes up my back. "To see how the three of us mesh."

"I—I don't know..."

And yet the time without them was agonizing.

Belial kisses across my cheek and whispers, "Then figure it out with us."

"And?" Eligos leans in a little closer. "If you are ultimately unhappy, we vow to let you go. We'll even write you a new contract if that's what you want."

It's everything I want without any of the risks.

This is too good to be true.

I'm no one, and two of the most powerful beings on the planet are fixated on me. I can't think of a logical reason why my life would take such a charmed turn or what could possibly be special about me for this to happen.

They're looking at me with twin gazes, hanging on my next words. I owe them some shred of honesty, even if I can't bring myself to confess about my entanglements with Oriax and Shax yet. "I don't understand why any of this is happening to me. I'm not special. I'm no one, even if there's something inhuman in my blood."

Belial chuckles and continues to nuzzle my cheek. "Sometimes that's just how the universe works. Happy little accidents."

Eligos twines our fingers together while his tail wraps around our hands and my wrist. "You're special to us."

My skin goes hot. "I wasn't—"

Belial turns my face and crushes his mouth to mine. Someone's hand digs into my hair and turns me. Eligos licks across my lips, then presses a peck to Belial's lips. I'm still jealous of the attention they shower on each other, but I love these little moments. There's something about seeing the enduring affection between them that gives me hope for myself. That maybe I'll feel that someday.

They both turn to look at me. These two handsome creatures want plain, ordinary me.

Eligos moves in. He bumps my cheek with his nose before kissing the corner of my mouth. Belial isn't as content to sit back and watch. He bends to tug the collar of my shirt aside and trail kisses down to my shoulder, while Eligos finally seals his lips over mine.

It's nearly overwhelming with both their attention focused on me.

A hand closes over my breast and I moan. I feel more than hear a low rumble as Belial steals my lips from Eligos.

"You're so greedy," he whispers, his words broken up by the smacking sound of kisses as he lavishes Belial's face.

I can feel Belial's cock against my hip and I want so badly to feel him inside of me. But in this state? As feral as they both are?

Fingers dip past the neckline of the short chemise to tease my nipple and I moan while Eligos tongue-fucks my mouth.

"Fuck, that's a beautiful sound," Belial whispers.

Eligos pulls back. I'm half-reclined across Belial's lap now with Eligos over me. Almost all the buttons on my pretty outfit have been ripped off, and Belial's hand is halfway down the front of my half-corset. Eligos strokes over my soft stomach and I suck in a breath. I've never been self-conscious about my size, but I am distinctly aware of the class differences and that their standards of beauty are different from us common folk. Except every time they look at me, it's like they're peeling off my clothes. They've never given me a single reason to hesitate. It's all in my head. I suppose this is part of what it's like to be human rather than demon.

Eligos' tail is wrapped around my left wrist with the tuft flicking back and forth against my palm. As if he's tempting me to pet the silky soft hair.

"A-are we going to talk about the wings, horns, and tail?" I ask.

Belial bends forward and buries his nose in my hair while his finger swipes back and forth over my nipple. "Our demons like you."

I shift my hips a little. "I can tell."

He sucks in a breath and I hear just the hint of a growl.

"Careful," Eligos mutters before dropping a kiss to my stomach. "You don't want to tempt the glutton..."

"Too late," Belial says in a voice gone low. "I need to taste you again."

My body heats at that statement and yet somehow embarrassment locks me in place.

Eligos smirks at me. Can he read my mind? "Do you want Belial to make you come?"

"Does it make me a glutton if I say yes?"

Eligos' eyes light up and he grasps my hands, then pulls me up onto my knees. Belial clutches the abused shirt and vest still clinging to my shoulders. Before I can tell him to be careful, the fabric is torn into pieces. Eligos' tail winds around my waist then pulls me forward. I gasp, marveling at the strength of his new appendage as he drags me forward over him.

"Perfect," Belial purrs.

"Wait!"

My belated attempt to salvage what had been a favorite set of new clothing is drowned out by more ripping. I feel the slight press of claws on my hips and thighs. It's just enough to make me gasp and hold perfectly still. But I needn't have worried. Belial kisses each and every line.

Eligos' finger swipes over my lower lip. "You're so beautiful like this. There isn't an ounce of fear in you."

I want to look over my shoulder. Belial continues to kiss my hips and thighs, all while the rest of me is so very vulnerable. I can't tear my gaze from Eligos'. "W-why would I be afraid? Should I be?"

His features become sharper, as if his demon is rising to the surface so that both parts of him reply with a single word. "Never."

He reaches up, pulling my face down to his. There isn't anywhere to brace my hands and I fear I might pitch forward onto him, but his tail has me.

I grin at him as our noses bump in that way I've come to cherish.

Suddenly something thrusts into me. I gasp, only for Eligos to seal his lips over mine. My vision blurs as I'm invaded and touched so deeply. My toes curl and I whimper while my mind struggles to process what's going on. Belial's hands grip my thighs. He doesn't have a tail, so what is that?

The mystery appendage flicks in and out, but unlike a cock it undulates, rubbing hidden depths that make me moan. I grasp Eligos' face, pressing closer to him because between the two of them my lower half is at their mercy. My fingers brush against the base of his horns and he shudders, a slight moan spilling out.

I run my fingers around the base of his smaller set of horns, delving through the locs that have been perfectly rearranged around his halo of horns.

"Does that feel good?" I ask.

He tips his head back. "Yes."

"Oh! Gods. W-what...?"

Everything in me coils low and tight in my abdomen. This thing inside me, it's vibrating back and forth.

Eligos chuckles and his hand slides down my body to my mound. "Oh, I see... You lucky girl you."

"Oh, my—*Belial*..."

My head is too heavy. It falls forward to rest against Eligos' brow.

"Want to know what *that* is?" he whispers.

The appendage slowly pulls out of me, only to press up, through my folds to my ass. It's a foreign sensation that both alarms me and makes me ache for more.

"Yes," I groan.

"That's Belial's other tongue."

"O-other tongue?"

Eligos grins at me. "His demon tongue. He's quite talented with it. I'm so jealous."

"Oh my—my... Oh! He's—"

Eligos' tail pulses and shifts around me, then I feel the tufted tip pressing against my mound while Belial continues to tease my anus. It's so much sensation. I can barely breathe.

"Someday we're both going to fuck you so full of our cocks we'll ruin you for any other man," Eligos says.

I can't imagine what that would be like. This is already too much, and no cocks are involved.

Belial growls something and slides his hand over my mound, between myself and Eligos' greedy tail.

"Mine," Belial snarls.

I sputter a laugh, but it turns into a moan as I feel his lips on my pussy and the thick intrusion of a more familiar tongue. His fingers are stroking me, making all that tension coil tighter still until I'm a whimpering mess. Eligos kisses me while I hold tight to his horns. And then I'm soaring as pleasure cascades through me. It feels like it's too much. Like I'll break apart at the seams or shatter.

Only, my demons are there to catch me.

My body is still throbbing from release as the room slowly rotates around me. Eligos is laying me back against Belial's lap using nothing but his tail. It's a little like what I think flying or floating might feel like. The thought makes me chuckle.

Belial bends over me and brushes his lips to mine. I'm greedy and reach up, intending to grasp his hair but get one of the curved horns instead. I pull him down, deepening the kiss while stroking along the base of his horns. The answering moan from him is just as needy as the one Eligos made, and I love knowing there are ways I can drive them just as crazy as they do to me.

"This needs to go," Eligos mutters.

The thin chemise tearing is my warning right before he slices the short corset from my body, leaving me in just boots and stockings. My head rests on Belial's knee while Eligos is poised between my spread thighs. He bends, licking over a breast. I shudder, my body still sensitive from orgasm and I look up at my demons.

I'm a fool if I think I can walk away from them. They've pulled me into their orbit, and have branded my soul. I belong to them in a way I can't describe.

"Eligos." I arch my back and reach for him. "I need you…"

ELIGOS

The sight of Lioria lounging back against Belial, her pretty tits thrust up and begging for attention, threatens to shatter my control. Everything about this is different and deeper on levels I can't begin to understand. Something is happening between us, and though I should pull back, I want it to hurry up. I want these two to be so interwoven with my soul that we do not exist apart from each other.

Belial smirks at me, but I see a different light in the depths of his eyes, too.

It's fear.

We could still scare her off. She's human and maybe a little other. But our true nature hasn't sent her running away from us. At least not yet.

Belial reaches down and strokes his fingers over her mound. Lioria's eyes roll back and she lifts her hips, hungry for more already.

"Are you going to give her what she needs?" Belial taunts.

As tempting as it would be to thrust into her tight pussy, I want to temper my need. Tease her. Show her that we can be more than mindless demons. I ease my control of my tail, allowing it a bit of free rein. The tufted tip slides up over her stomach to tease the underside of her breast. She's responded to our otherness with enthusiasm thus far. I only hope that if our true nature is revealed, she embraces all of us.

I lean forward over her. Belial takes this opportunity to run the back of his hand along my cock. The rush of blood to my erection is a relief after the last frustrating week. I let my eyes close, enjoying the drawn out anticipation as it simmers just under my skin.

Belial lifts his head from Lioria's lips, staring at me with a hunger that takes away my breath. "She's waiting for you to fuck her."

I glance at her, watching us. Her chest is rising and falling rapidly and her gaze zips back and forth.

Does she like watching us as much as we enjoy watching her?

I don't think I could give either of them up. I need the three of us to be together in every way possible.

Maybe it's the demon rising to the surface, but I can't proceed cautiously. I reach over and drag Belial in for a kiss, licking the taste of her off his tongue and lips. He's all too eager to comply, offering up no resistance. I know he needs release and I can't begin to imagine how he must ache. I vow to take care of him later, but the rest of this is for her.

We break apart, sucking down air, only for Lioria to reach up and boldly grasp me by the horn. In all my life, no other being has been so brazen. She has no idea what this does to me, how my demon surges to the forefront, only to be met with her kiss and soft body. All that energy turns into frustration the longer I'm not in her tight pussy.

"Fuck her, Eli. Do it," Belial says.

"Yes," she mutters against my lips.

I shove my trousers down enough to free my erection. Her legs are locked around me. Belial fists my cock and I groan, eyes rolling back into my head. He tugs me forward until I feel her slick heat. Lioria arches up, pressing herself against me.

My head screams at me to go slow. She's human and fragile by comparison. But now she has both hands locked on my horns. It's been so long since I felt them and the skin ringing the protrusions is almost as sensitive as my cock. I moan and thrust, losing the fight for control.

She pulls me down as she drives her boot heel into my ass. I swallow her whimper, hungry for more of those sounds.

I feel Belial's hand stroking her ribs and breasts between us. How he can maintain control is a mystery to me. I lift my head to peer at him and find him watching me with a ferocious grin splitting his face.

I love them both to my very core. It's not surprising, the nature of my feelings for him. We've known each other since our creation, but to feel that deeply about her? In such a short time? How?

Belial reaches out, his big hand wrapping around my jaw. He pulls me forward and I slide all the way into Lioria's pussy as Belial's mouth takes mine. I feel her hands against my chest, sliding down my abs. She grips my hips and grinds on me as Belial thrusts his tongue into me.

There's so much in my lifetimes to regret. I shouldn't have this. In all the good we've done, I can't have atoned for the wrong. And yet I'm not giving this up.

Belial releases me and sits back, which has the added benefit of propping LIoria up higher. She moans at the shift in positions and I gather her into my arms, using my tail to support her lower back, and lift her into my arms. Her body is mine now, and I work my cock into her. She tosses her head back, groaning and writhing. Belial's wings are gone. He slides down, kissing her shoulders and neck while he toys with her magnificent breasts.

All of this is perfect. So fucking perfect, and I don't want it to end.

A hand cups my balls, giving them a slight tug as I bury myself in her body. I shout as pleasure wraps around me and I know that our lives are changed forever, all because of this little human. My dream.

Belial's hands stroke over our bodies. He kisses Lioria's cheek, then my shoulder.

I don't want to move, and yet I know I shouldn't linger.

I sit up the rest of the way, Liora straddling me awkwardly. Belial scoots closer and takes her from me so that I can ease our bodies apart. She hisses and curls her legs to cover herself. For now, we both allow it.

Belial cradles her to his chest and carries her to the daybed, leaving me to clean myself off using the tattered remains of her clothing.

Large, purple marks mar the creamy flesh of Belial's back between the swirling, dark tattoos.

How long has it been since I had my tail?

I peer at it, twitching across my thigh. All this time, and it feels natural. Good even. But I can't walk around with the evidence of my true form for all to see. The others don't have this strength, and a week ago, neither did we.

What has she done to us? How has she changed us? Will this continue to happen?

I take a breath, close my eyes, and concentrate. My whole body itches as I pull in both my horns and tail. By the time that is complete, Lioria and Belial are cuddling on the daybed with a blanket thrown over them.

I rise and pull my trousers up the best I can. We're all a bit of a mess, what with our shredded clothing.

Belial pulls the blanket back and crooks his finger at me. "Get in here. It's too early to be awake."

I don't have to be told twice.

I slide in behind Lioria, who keeps glancing from me to Belial. Her eyes are both bright and sleepy while her lips are curved into a smile I might call content if I were brave.

"You really mean to sleep now?" she mutters.

Belial kisses her brow, then my hand, before placing it on her waist.

"Yes," he says.

"But..." She glances at me before turning to look at Belial. "But what about you?"

He smiles that loveable grin of his and bumps her nose with his. "All in due time."

"But..."

He presses his finger across her lips. "I'm different from Eligos. I have refined my control so that I don't lose it. But it's a balance. Right now, I don't trust myself not to hurt you. That's not a line I'm willing to cross until we're both ready, my lady."

"So, you didn't, I mean... My mouth wasn't enough?"

He tips his head back and groans. "God, I'm trying not to think about that. You were very good, but that's not what I want. And right now, I'm not willing to settle. I'd rather waste away from anticipation."

I'm proud of Belial. The others often think of him as simple-minded, that he's the least cunning of us all. But what they don't see is that his measure of control over his demon is the greatest out of all of us, because it has to be. Yes, some of the others might have greater magic, but Belial could ruin the earth between his strength and his sway over human desire.

How did I get so damn lucky with these two?

I know we promised Lioria this was a trial, but Belial and I are decided. We've said pretty words, we've promised her freedom, but neither of us has any intention of giving her up. Ever.

Lioria belongs with us.

BELIAL

Darkness swathes the landscape outside the windows. I glance over my shoulder at Eligos, still staring at Lioria like she might vanish at any moment. It feels that way. Like she isn't quite real and none of this is happening.

Today was...

I don't have words to describe it.

It was the wonder of my first breath all over again, only better.

Some memories are locked away, and difficult to bring up. As if our minds can only handle so much. Our creation moment is like that. I know it happened, and that Eligos was there. But the rest is normally out of grasp.

Right now, I feel as though I can smell heaven. I distinctly remember my first thoughts, the wonder at seeing followed by the heavy sensation of my body. When I saw Eligos next to me, I was filled with delight so profound, and I don't think I've ever been happier.

What we're building with Lioria might eclipse all of that, which makes me wonder, what is she?

She's our future, that much I know, and she needs to be protected.

Eligos joins me at the window. He wraps his arms around me and rests his chin on my shoulder. We sigh in unison, which just goes to show how in sync we are.

"Your demon still aware?" he asks.

I tilt my head to the side. "Yes."

"Mine, too."

That's not as much of a surprise. Eligos has been more in tune with his other half. Me, on the other hand, I've barely felt other than human. If it weren't for my abilities and memories, I'd question if there was any demon left in me.

But not anymore.

Eligos kisses my bare shoulder and chuckles. "You want to fly, don't you?"

Everything in me tenses, as if I'm poised to launch myself into the sky. "Yes..."

"Well, you should go stretch your wings. Got to work those muscles if you want to show them off."

I glance back at him and resist asking him to come with me. Eligos doesn't have wings anymore. But that's never stopped him from keeping up. The way he uses his tail is uncanny and beautiful.

I turn, looking across the room at Lioria's sleeping form. "What are we going to do about her? What do we tell her?"

"Nothing for now."

"Is that really best? Not being honest with her almost lost us our chance. If we don't come clean about everything, we run the risk of losing her trust."

"I'm not saying we never tell her, just that the real history is a lot to take in. We tell her when she's ready, not all at once."

His answer leaves me unsettled. I don't quite agree. I also don't know why I feel this way. But this is all so new and different. Until we figure out Lioria's connection with us, it's best if we proceed cautiously. She wouldn't be the first mortal to learn she has supernatural heritage. Normally we'd sense something about a being, but she's just human, as far as I can tell.

"Have you heard from Alastor?" I ask to change the subject. Something's been bothering me as of late, and it's time to talk about it. Especially with Lioria to consider.

"No. You know how he is."

I turn to look at Eligos. "What do you mean?"

He stretches his arms up over his head. "You know. He buries himself in work to the exclusion of everything else."

That is how Alastor has been as of late, but that is not the Alastor I remember through the lifetimes.

Eligos tilts his head. "What are you thinking?"

"Do you remember when Alastor was dividing up Eden? How it was back then?"

He snorts and covers his mouth to muffle the sound. "He showed up one morning and dragged me out of bed. He..."

I watch Eligos tilt his head and squint at me. He grows dangerously still, and my demon responds by rising to the forefront of my mind. I doubt Eligos will attack me, but I need to be prepared.

"What's going on?" he asks in a low voice.

"I don't know, but something's wrong."

Eligos looks back at Lioria and I know he's thinking the same thing.

"We should talk to Shax," I say, though it's the last thing I want. Especially since Lioria has not told us why Shax's energy has lingered on her face.

Eligos shakes his head. "No. That's too obvious. Let's... We should talk to Raum."

I grimace because Raum is, in many ways, Alastor's right hand. The kind of magic it would take to alter all our memories is strong stuff. And for it to last fifteen years?

"I want to comb through every exchange we can with Alastor. And I want somewhere safe for Lioria. If the worst happens."

Eligos nods and scrubs a hand over his jaw.

"Sorry," I mutter. "I didn't know how to bring this all up..."

He waves me off. "Go. Patrol the boundary. I'll make sure Lioria sleeps peacefully and handle our nighttime callers."

I reach out and squeeze his shoulder. "Have Teill on hand to sit with her, just in case she wakes up."

Eligos nods and turns toward the daybed.

I've felt for a while now that something was wrong. The obvious answer was us. That our era was coming to a close. But now I wonder if we didn't have blinders on the whole time. Have the scales fallen off our eyes because of Lioria? Because she is a brilliant light?

I can feel the impending threat coming. I just don't know where we'll be struck from.

LIORIA

Belial's tongue is down my throat as Eligos thrusts deep and my orgasm shudders out of me. I'm so hyper sensitive tears leak out the corners of my eyes while my body soars.

Eligos slumps over me and he lays his head on my shoulder. The spacious daybed doesn't feel quite so large with three bodies piled onto it, but we haven't moved for a full day. I'm completely boneless as my two demons shift my limbs and lavish my body with attention. I can't allow myself to consider what Teill must think about all of this, or I'm never going to be able to look at her. She never made an appearance last night and I'm anxious to talk to her. This is, after all, mostly her fault.

At the same time, I don't know that I've ever felt this content. I don't know how long this will last, but I know I can't leave them. Maybe it's selfish, but I want this for as long as they'll have me.

Eligos gathers me closer and stares at Belial. "Are you really going to train now?"

"Not now, no." Belial kisses my shoulder as he scoots in to trap me between their bodies. "But soon."

There's tension in Belial that wasn't there yesterday. I peer back at him, trying to understand this shift in his mood. "The stones?"

He nods and his face creases with worry.

"Is there more than just the stones?"

He smooths my hair. "Nothing you need to worry about."

I don't like that answer, but I also can't push for more information. There are things too sensitive for me to know about, and I need to be content with my role. Somehow. Which is an ever shifting, nebulous thing.

Eligos trails his fingers down the side of my face. "Stop thinking so hard, unless..."

I shake my head, knowing full well what he might say. "I'm too sore."

He chuckles and kisses me. I have to marvel at these seemingly innocent moments. Never in my wildest dreams would I have pictured these powerful creatures to be so kind and caring, even playful. It makes me uneasy to know I'm keeping things from them. But I don't want to hurt them, and it isn't like I've actually done anything. It's all in my mind.

The kiss with Shax was not supposed to be arousing. He did it to provoke these two, and that serves no purpose. And yet, my pulse races any time Belial or Eligos forget to be gentle.

Oriax's letters are a different matter. They've told me to stay away from him, and I have physically. But I don't want to lose that connection. I'm greedy for more. Always more.

Is it possible I'm corrupt?

Eligos pinches my nipple and I gasp. "If you don't stop that, I'll give you something else to think about."

"Ow!" I push his hand away and turn toward Belial, who chuckles and welcomes me with open arms.

His cock presses against my stomach, but we both ignore it. I don't understand his reticence, but I can respect his wishes.

Belial strokes his fingers over my face and stares at me with a look I can't explain. It makes me feel both small and powerful. Eligos nuzzles the back of my neck and wraps himself around me. I'm always between them, though they don't shy away from showing affection to each other.

As if they hear my thoughts, Belial reaches over and twines his fingers with Eligos' at my waist.

"Is this alright?" Belial whispers.

"Hm?"

He jostles their joined hands and I glance down to shield myself from his gaze. I'm too sensitive in every version of the word. "It's a little late to be asking that, don't you think?"

There's a slight tensing in Eligos' body behind me, and I wonder if I've said the wrong thing.

"I don't think there's anything to mind. You two have a beautiful connection. If anything, I'm envious of your closeness. You always have each other."

"And now we have you," Belial says simply.

I smile, because I know he means well, but deep down, it hurts. They will always have each other. I get them right now. "Yes."

He frowns at me, as though he can read me. "What's wrong?"

I pause at that. "Nothing..."

The lines around his mouth deepen.

Eligos gathers my left hand with theirs so our fingers are interlocked. "The bond we formed has changed. I—we—can sense you, in a way. I could point to you from across the country or a crowded room. And every now and then I get this... Feeling? It's not mine. It feels like you. Sometimes you're happy or aroused or... Sad."

"What? But I don't sense either of you..."

"Not surprising." Belial squeezes his fingers around ours. "It might come in time."

Eligos' words sink in. They have some sense of how I feel.

That changes things to some extent.

I sigh and settle on the truth I can give them. "I like basking in your affection for each other, but sometimes I feel like... I'm an addition to what you already have. A bonus, for now, and I'm jealous. Sad even because your love is enviable. I think it's natural to want that for myself."

Belial grips my jaw so tight my stomach flutters and he stares at me with eyes gone a deep green. "You aren't a bonus."

Eligos props himself up. I can see him out of the corner of my eye, scowling.

Belial's gaze searches mine for a moment. "You aren't an addition or a bonus. You're a core component, and I don't think either of us has any intention of allowing you to simply walk away. I'm sorry if we gave you the impression that we're merely having fun with you."

"He's right. It's like..." Eligos kisses my shoulder, then leans his head against mine. He presses his hand between my breasts. "You've settled here. Next to Belial. It's hard to describe... It's affection and awareness, like you're part of me now."

I struggle to swallow around the emotion lodged in my throat. It sounds a lot like how I'd explain love, but he can't mean that. We've barely just met. I care about them. I lust after them. But love?

This can't be real.

I sit up and my head spins.

"Look what you did. You upset her," Eligos whispers, as if I can't hear him.

Belial wraps his arm around my waist and pulls me back down between them. I push at his heavy, muscular arm, but he's not budging.

"We just met. You don't even know me."

That statement draws both their stares.

Eligos chuckles and kisses my brow. "We are not human..."

"I know that, but—"

Belial silences my words with his fingers over my lips. "We don't have answers, Lioria. This is all new for us, too. What matters is that you aren't a bonus fuck. You are not a passing amusement. You are a fixture for us."

"He's right." Eligos presses his lips just below my ear. "So don't go getting ideas about settling down with some human, because I wouldn't let you go."

Belial squeezes me a little closer, as if to say Eligos speaks for both of them. The way Belial holds me makes the growing panic subside.

I care about them, but love? I don't think I feel that for them. Not yet, at least.

The clock across the room chimes and Belial groans while squeezing me tighter. "I must go."

"The stones?" I've asked a few times, but they won't say anything else except some were destroyed.

"We'll keep you safe," he promises.

From what?

Is there some danger lurking out beyond the manor walls I don't know about? I thought Eden was safe, but is there a threat?

Eligos tightens his grip around me. "But for now, I'll keep you warm..."

I chuckle and trail my fingers down his arm. "Or, you could work."

He groans and buries his face against my neck.

I have to cut off communication with Oriax.

It already feels like I'm cheating on them, though I've done nothing wrong. I'll miss those conversations, but ultimately if Eligos and Belial need me, what greater purpose could I serve in this lifetime? I'll figure out how to be content.

I watch Belial vault over the back of the daybed to stretch his arms over his head. He's gloriously nude, the morning sun glinting off the coppery hair lightly covering his chest. It glints a fiery gold, making him glisten.

"He's handsome to look at, isn't he?" Eligos says into my ear.

Belial grins at us, in no hurry at all to leave.

Do I dare believe that these two want me? That it's as simple as that?

He glances at me, as if he senses my questions. There's something so pure and good about Belial. He's everything right in the world.

"We're very lucky," I say while our gazes are still locked.

"Yes." Eligos' hand trails down my stomach. "Yes, we are."

I groan and shift his hand up to my ribs. "I can't believe I'm saying this, but no more."

That makes Eligos laugh and hug me close.

Belial shoves what's left of his shirt into the waistband of his abused trousers. "Behave, you two. And listen to Lioria."

"Yes, daddy," Eligos mutters.

Belial smirks over his shoulder. "Your ass will be mine if you don't."

"Oh, promises, promises," Eligos calls after Belial's retreating backside.

I smile at the upholstery, not quite believing any of this.

Eligos' grip on me tightens. "Don't tell me you seriously expect me to work this early?"

"How does anything around here get done?" I shift around so I can look at him. "I don't understand it, Eligos. There's so many things piling up and I have to hound you to do the smallest thing."

He taps my nose with the tip of his finger. "That's because you only see part of what we do. I promise you, we work plenty hard."

"When?"

"Have you ever wondered what we do after we send you off for the night?"

My cheeks heat, because I've thought about it. But I don't exactly what to confess what my imagination supplied me with.

A smile spreads across his face. "Oh, what do you think we do?"

"I don't know. It's clear you didn't fuck on your desks."

That makes him laugh, and he strokes his fingers through my messy hair. "That's something that hasn't been done in a very long time... The truth is much more mundane. The bulk of what we do is usually during nighttime hours, and that's all I'll say."

I prop myself up, curious and frustrated.

He smooths his fingers over the wrinkles between my brows. "I've already told you too much."

"Fine," I mutter. "And the work that piles up?"

"We have an arrangement with Alastor. He picks up the slack for us. No doubt he appreciates your efforts to wrangle us to do more."

"Do the others not know? Why do you have to have an arrangement?"

He pinches my bottom and I squeal. "No more questions."

Eligos is no less serious as he studies me. His face is smooth, betraying no thought, and yet he seems... Worried?

Am I seeing this? Or feeling it the way they said they feel me?

"Why are you worried?" I ask.

"Something Belial said. Have you ever learned how to defend yourself?"

It's such a fast change of conversation, I blink at him for a few moments. "Not really, no."

"I think it's worth spending some time with Belial. Your proximity to us means you could be a target."

I hold up my hand and wiggle the ring at him. "Isn't that why you gave me this?"

"Yes, but what if you don't get the chance to use it? What then, hm?" He pats my leg. "It's better to be prepared than not at all."

"Am I allowed to bathe and get clothes from my room?" I am not used to sitting around idle.

He sighs and releases me to throw an arm over his face. "Fine. Go, if you must."

There's a dressing gown the one of the lords brought down for me at some point. I wrap myself up in it then pause, staring at the door.

Others will see me.

I hesitate with my hand out.

It's one thing to accept what's happening between us. It's another to be so open about it.

Before I can talk myself out of it, I push the doors open and leave the study, doing my best to keep my head high. Usually, there aren't many people about. Privale operates with a very small staff since neither of my lords maintain their own court, whatever that means.

There's so much I don't know or understand, and I'm not sure I can take much more. But I want to try.

I round the corner and a pair of maids freeze. They're old enough to be my aunties. My skin flushes scarlet, but I continue past as if it's perfectly normal to strut around nude save for a man's dressing gown. Thankfully, they're the only ones I run into.

The moment I'm through the door in my room, I close it and lean against the wall.

Before noon, the entire staff will know exactly what I am.

Belial and Eligos can say—and mean—that I'm equal in this. But I, and the rest of the world, know I am not. They can do whatever they like. I'm still human and bound to social rules they don't understand.

"Teill?"

I wait for a few moments, but she doesn't appear. I hope that maybe she's rethought her resolve to not see her festival gentlemen.

Belial and Eligos are hiding something from me. What or why, I'm not certain. It's a knowing that seems to sit just below my neck and irritate me physically and mentally.

Is this what they mean that we are connected?

I strip out of the dressing robe and head into the bath, mulling over everything that's happened since I left my room yesterday morning.

One thing is certain. Today I need to write to Oriax. I've mostly ignored the letterbox except to empty it a few times. Each morning is another note from

Oriax, and that needs to stop. While our correspondence is innocent and even instructional, I know that the words are anything but. Oriax's goal from the beginning was to sway me in his favor. I can't betray Belial and Eligos like that. Not now.

How does one break it off with a High Demon Lord when the relationship was never acknowledged?

I sink into the water and mull that question over until the water grows tepid.

The only thing to do is be frank.

I leave the bath and pace my room. When a knock sounds at the door, I let out a little shriek of surprise. The door opens and Mrs. Jurrah stares at me, eyes wide, while I clutch my robe around me.

"Gods." I cover my face with my hand. "Sorry. I'm so sorry."

"What's wrong with you, girl?" She peers around the room, then closes the door behind her when there's no apparent threat.

I'm not in the mood to talk to another person right now, but I can't exactly kick her out.

"I, um, hope you are well," she says in the most polite voice possible.

"Yes. Thank you." I mentally strangle my irritation and toss it aside. The situation with Oriax is of my own making. I can't take it out on someone else.

She asked me yesterday to intervene with the lords. How do I respond to that? Do I explain?

I hug my arms around myself. "It's handled."

Her shoulders relax and she closes her eyes. "Good."

Part of me wants to confess that the problem was my fault, but her judgment weighs heavily on me already so I say nothing.

I stand there as she bustles out, off to manage something else.

Maybe she already knows what's going on?

I turn to the mirror and dry my hair. In a few minutes, it's braided back out of my face and I dress in one of the outfits I would never have picked. If my demons are going to shred everything I have to wear, we're going to start with the ones I don't like.

The halls are empty as I return to the study. It's mid-morning and I anticipate Belial returning earlier than normal. Teill still hasn't appeared, so I settle at my desk with a sheet of paper and begin to formulate my letter.

Lord Oriax,

This has been weighing heavily on my mind. I hope you'll forgive me speaking my mind.

I've enjoyed our conversations. I appreciate your knowledge and willingness to share. I'm humbled that you would take time to personally write me. Please know you have my thanks always. That said, my situation here at Privale is changing. I would ask that our communications be limited to topics of business. I wouldn't want to give anyone the wrong impression.

I hope you understand the situation I am in.

Lioria

It's not enough. It's too short and ambiguous. There's room to read around my words and see meaning I don't intend. But I also don't think I can come right out and tell Oriax to stop flirting. I already fear he'll take this as a challenge, but I have to try.

The moment I put the paper in the box, I want to snatch it back and just ignore Oriax altogether.

How is it I always find myself mired in a mess?

It wasn't like I had an active role in any of this. I was simply doing my job and living my life when these demons swept me up in whatever this is. The only thing I know for sure is that my life is different. It will never include a widower with children and a farm.

I stare blankly at the floor, but no sense of sadness envelops me at the loss of that happy, quiet life.

If all the opportunity in the world were before me, I know that's not the life I would pick for myself. So why have I clung to that future? Is it fear?

What do I want for myself?

When I'm between Belial and Eligos, I have a sense of contentment. But it's gone now.

This would all be easier to accept if I didn't strain at the confines of the expected roles in life. I've never fit any mold well, and that's made my life difficult. I'm not unaware of this, even when I can't stop it. I'm simply this curious creature who will always want something else.

And that worries me.

What happens when I want someone else? Am I capable of settling down with my lords? Or am I flawed in some fundamental way? Perhaps all I need is more time to settle into my life here?

But things aren't certain here, either. The broken boundary stones, the strange performance at the festival, that woman who I'm still fairly certain followed me, and the fact that no one as of yet knows how the High Demon Lords were killed. It feels like someone's left the kettle on and we're all ignoring the whistle.

I'm agitated enough that I get up and pace.

By all rights, I should be floating around, fueled by lust and basking in the attention of my demons.

My demons.

That makes me pause and smile, because they really have intertwined us. I wasn't looking for anything permanent. When I met them, all I wanted was a little fun, but it's grown beyond that now. I want to be content with my two demons. I genuinely do. So why am I drawn to Oriax and Shax? What's wrong with me that I can't be happy with what I have?

The doors to the study open, and I turn to find Belial striding toward me. The sight of him takes my breath away. It's too early for him to be back from training, but here he is. He's freshly bathed and wearing the most ornately embroidered caftan coat I've ever seen. Nearly every inch of the rich, brown fabric is covered in russet red or gold stitching. By the time my gaze meets his, he's almost on top of me. I take a step back and my heart beats a little quicker at the intensity in his eyes.

But he's not looking at me with lust.

"What's wrong?" I ask.

The doors close and I glance over to find Eligos is also dressed. His violet locs are pulled back to display the regal angles of his face. His coat is of a similar cut, but he's left it, and the snowy white shirt, open to display several inches of dark skin.

The vest under his coat is in a brilliant blue with purple thread and tiny pearls sewn all over it.

They're both wearing uniform, grim expressions. Given the formality of how they're dreassed, it all seems so much more dire.

"What happened?" I glance between them. "Say something."

"We need to pay a visit today, and we need you to go with us." Belial speaks as though we're marching into battle.

"Okay. Are we leaving now, or...?"

Eligos sighs. "Best to just get it over with."

I glance down at my dress. It's nicer than anything I wore before, but there are so many frills and little tucks of material, I feel a bit like a holiday cake.

I gesture at myself. "Will this do?"

"You're perfect," Belial says without hesitation.

Eligos waves his hand. "Yes. Yes, perfect."

Their solemn, serious demeanor has me more nervous than before. "What kind of a visit is this?"

They glance at each other and grimace.

Eligos gestures to the door. "All you need to do is accompany us. We'll take care of the rest."

LIORIA

I've never seen either of my demons at a lack for words. They've been completely silent for the nearly two hours we've been traveling toward the coastal city of Rosenberg. I didn't have time to grab a book and looking out of the carriage makes my stomach want to revolt. I've tried a few times to tease my demons into conversation, but they won't speak.

Part of me wants to strangle them. What am I part of here?

I can smell the sea.

I lean back and inhale the familiar fragrance of the ocean. I wish I could get a look at the city, but we only slow once we're almost at the gates. Then we're rolling down cobblestone streets.

Rosenberg is a true city, where Privale is a sleepy country manor with a bustling town. Flowers adorn open windows almost everywhere. It's charming to see so much color against the backdrop of all these buildings.

Since neither of my demons are speaking, I lean against the window and take it all in.

How do people live this close together? They're literally on top of one another. It was bad enough in the boarding house where I'd known most of those women my whole life. Here though? I'd probably never meet the same person twice.

People's gazes seem to slide right off the carriage. As if they can't look at it. One woman nearly walks straight into the door when we pause to allow traffic to cross ahead of us. The woman starts, blinks at the carriage, then walks around it.

I get an itchy feeling between my shoulder blades.

What is it they won't tell me about?

"We'll be passing into the fae quarter soon," Eligos says at last.

I whip my head around him and stare. "Fae quarter? Here?"

He nods once, eyes closed, then says nothing more.

"You're both terrible," I mutter.

Belial stares out the window. I'm not used to this stony expression.

Just who are we going to see? And why bring me if they won't say anything?

We pass into what a sign says is the warehouse district. It's ringed by walls, no doubt to protect whatever merchandise is inside. The going is slower, as we have to give way to carts and other laborers, which gives me more time to look about.

A man grips a crate with two sets of hands.

I freeze, battling with the seemingly natural desire to glance at someone—anything—else. But I keep my eyes fixated on that man and his extra limbs. He turns, and I can see a second pair of arms attached to his torso a little below and behind.

Something flutters and I can't resist the urge to look away, only to watch a man flutter what seems to be fin-like things on his cheeks.

"We're in the fae quarter, aren't we?"

Eligos chuckles. "Clever girl."

"Is everyone here...?" I search for the word to describe all non-humans, but come up lacking. I just don't know much about them.

"Other?" Eligos offers.

I nod.

"Not all of them, no."

"Fae are Vodu, correct?"

"Yes." Eligos wrinkles his nose. "I wouldn't call them Vodu to their face."

"Oh..."

If I think about it, Teill hadn't called herself Vodu. She'd only adopted that word around me after I called her one.

Whatever we're doing, it's probably best if I say nothing at all.

We go past large warehouses and I take my time picking people out of the crowd my gaze wants to shy away from.

How is no one else seeing this? Or are they all accustomed to their non-human companions?

"Are there quarters like this in every big city?"

"No, there are only three in Eden like this. Most are merchants and the rest are usually fugitives of some sort."

I glance at Eligos. "Fugitives?"

"There are a great many countries on the continent, each with their own laws. In one area, giving birth to a demonic child is grounds for execution. Other laws include things like owning items made of iron, procreating outside your species... So long as their crimes are not violent and they keep the peace, we allow them to live here."

I've always been curious about the continent, but the reality is I know nothing.

We pass more warehouses and turn down what appears to be a city lane. There are no cobblestones here. The road is covered with moss and shaded by massive trees growing between the tall, narrow homes. Flowers aren't just growing in pots under the windows, they're even growing off some of the houses themselves.

The carriage stops and I almost stick my head out of the window to peer up at the leafy dome.

Belial finally speaks. "You can see better outside the carriage."

He leans over and opens the door, getting out first before offering me his hand. I don't quite scramble out, but I'm certainly not graceful. I turn in a circle.

At first glance, the buildings are similar enough to what I've seen in the city. The houses are narrow and tall, most four stories or more. Unlike the rest of the city, the stones aren't a silvery gray. Here they're pale orange or a light green. Dirt and moss line the cracks between bricks and little flowers dot the surface. It's enchanting.

My gaze meets that of a woman with a thin, angular face and large eyes. She's staring at me like I'm the oddity. I smile and curtsy, wondering who she is and why she's here. Is she fae? Or some other Vodu?

"Come on." Eligos takes my hand and places it in the crook of his arm.

Belial is on my other side with a hand on my lower back.

It's downright cruel to make me simply walk into a building when all this wonder is out here.

Unlike in the rest of the city, people pause to watch us. Whatever magic that shielded the carriage doesn't protect us here, and we have drawn the eye of every person and creature in sight.

The house my demons lead me to is one of the taller structures. I can't count the floors because they go above the canopy. The windows are larger and decorated with stained glass, while the stonework is a pale yellow. There's a stone banner carved above the door and words I can't read.

"What language is that?" I ask.

"A very dead one," Eligos replies.

More non-answers.

These men are infuriating.

The emerald green double doors open ahead of us and my demons proceed inside as if this is perfectly normal.

I'm eager to rush forward and see what's inside, while also wanting to linger and savor the wonder.

I cross the threshold and step onto a plush, springy moss. Golden flowers with black centers rise up from the ground to show us the path. Overhead, dozens of butterflies flit between long, decadent blooms dripping from the ceiling.

"Is this real?" I whisper.

Eligos sighs, sounding bored as usual. "Very."

"What is wrong with you? This place is amazing."

He makes a noise low in his throat as we stop in the middle of the foyer.

Everything around us is growing. The walls are covered in thick vines in alternating light and dark brown. Flowers and waxy-looking green things form sun motifs on the walls. There's a pleasing, earthy scent that compliments the sweeter fragrance of all the flowers.

The doors in front of us open as a gentle breeze blows through the house.

"Oh, God," Belial mutters.

Thin, nearly transparent curtains separate the entry from the rest of the house. A figure dressed in a loose golden gown steps through the curtains with her arms up. She's wearing a golden fan-like thing on her head with many dangling charms and chains. It's the same color as her hair, so it's hard to tell when one ends and the other begins. It's beautiful, but I have to wonder how heavy that is?

"Welcome, sun dwellers," the woman says.

Her voice conjures up the sensation of spring and warmth, lying out under the sun on a sleepy afternoon. I blink a few times, focusing on the finer points of her appearance.

She's tall, easily matching Belial for height, but otherwise, she's built like a gangly girl. All limbs, not a pinch of excess weight on her. She makes me think about the old sea-wives' tale about sea-dwelling women.

"Greetings to you," Belial says in a booming voice.

Eligos speaks without missing a beat, as if he's completing a sentence, "Daughter of the sun."

"Is this her?" The beautiful creature claps her hands and hops while staring straight at me.

Belial's hand shifts to my side and he tugs me a little closer. "Naexi—"

She squeals and rushes forward, seizing my free hand in hers. "I am dying to know everything about you."

Belial moves almost as fast, grasping her by the wrist. Eligos is facing me and his left hand is balled into a fist.

Naexi grins, looking from one to the other, as if their violent reaction is somehow a delight. Her gaze meets mine and I swallow. Her eyes are larger than a human's and turned up at the outer corner. Instead of a dark center to her green eyes, she has a sort of golden sunburst. Her lips are thin and wide. She's smiling broadly, which displays her second set of pointed canines.

Her gaze returns to mine. "Oh, they like you. The rumors are true."

Belial's growl only serves to strengthen whatever she thinks she knows.

It's Eligos who speaks. "Naexi Romys, daughter of the sun, shard of the Seelie, and Merchant Master of the Romys family dynasty, this is Lioria."

Naexi glances at Belial, still clutching her wrist, and wiggles her fingers. His gaze doesn't shift, but he releases his grip on her. It doesn't escape my notice that there are now red marks on her skin. My first instinct is to scold him, but what if she's dangerous?

She takes my hand in hers and pulls me forward. I'm surprised when Eligos releases me, so I let her pull me forward a few steps.

"Lioria? Lioria, what a beautiful name, so full of light." She lifts my hand and I awkwardly twirl in a circle, only to glance back at the demons with a fearsome scowl. "This dress is dreadful. Why didn't you come to me sooner?"

I eye her dress.

It appears to be a few triangles of material sewn together and tied around her neck. Her entire back is bare, and I can see enough to know she isn't wearing anything underneath it. Everything about her is so free. It's as if she's a butterfly made flesh.

Eligos inclines his head. "We'd hoped you might work your magic."

"This is going to be such great fun." Naexi squeals and pulls me close to her side, wrapping an arm around my waist. She pushes my hair away from my ear, then whispers, "We're going to make them salivate at the sight of you."

My eyes go round and I look from her to my demons.

"What? Is all of this a shopping trip?" I feel like the ground has tilted.

If we're shopping, why not tell me? Why all this secrecy? Why the stony faces and over-protective demeanor? And what's wrong with the wardrobe they've already bought? This seems like such an unnecessary waste.

Neither Belial nor Eligos say a word. Belial has his arms crossed over his chest while Eligos looks like he's searching for a spot to nap.

I want to strangle the both of them.

"Come with me," Naexi says in a sing-song voice.

Neither of my demons stops her, and I can't help but feel as though I'm the lamb being led to the slaughter here.

ELIGOS

I watch Belial pace. Showing up like we have, with no advanced notice, it shouldn't surprise Belial that she's making us wait. Honestly, we're lucky she'll even speak to us. Belial has not been kind to her over the years.

"I could get some sleep if you'd stop pacing," I mutter and eye the wine decanter across the room.

Fairy wine is a vice of mine. I can't touch the stuff. Normally, Naexi is polite enough to put it away. Either we truly did surprise her, or she's being spiteful. Judging by the complete lack of finger foods, I'm guessing this is spite. Her staff is large enough they'd have whipped something up without direct orders not to.

I'd take Naexi's spite for the rest of my lifetimes over any other fae.

She is sworn to the broken Seelie Court and those ties are strong with her. I'd still call her an ally, though I don't particularly like her.

"She won't say anything to Lioria," Belial mutters.

"Are you asking? Or trying to convince yourself? You knew when we came that we were taking risks."

Belial whirls, practically pacing a trail into the moss. "Yes, I know."

Our relationship with Naexi has always been a tenuous thing. She likes us. Belial hates her. I tolerate her. But when we need her? Oh, then she revels in her power. The one thing I can respect about Naexi is that she takes boundaries very seriously and understands why Belial will never forgive her.

I glance at him—did he spread a rumor?

It's not like him to be so cunning. The more likely option is that there is a rumor concerning Lioria. It shouldn't be surprising. We have many enemies who will want to know our weakness. Still, it's alarming that Naexi guessed or learned of the truth so fast when we're still settling into this relationship ourselves.

How many others know? How did it start? And with whom?

A knot develops in the pit of my stomach when I think about Alastor. He's not going to be happy with this development. Personal entanglements have always drawn his ire. They complicate matters and throughout the millenia, they've caused so much war and bloodshed. I understand why he is so closed off, but I also think that's wrong.

Our humanity makes us better. It's what changed us, to begin with. Without it, we're nothing more than the demons we were created to be.

I smell the breeze from under the door a moment before they open. Butterflies flit toward us and I'm fairly certain I can hear birds somewhere. Naexi emerges, flower petals sliding down her arms.

"Laying it on a bit thick, aren't we?" Belial drawls.

His cold tone doesn't deter her. She grins at him and strokes fingers down her sternum between her breasts.

"If I'd known that's what you're into, I could have delivered..."

Her form glimmers and then it's Lioria, standing there in a scrap of a dress with a golden crown. The sight takes my breath away, but only for a moment. Under the guise, it's still Naexi. She can manipulate her appearance all she wants, but she'll never capture that spark that is uniquely Lioria. It's not her physical body that has enraptured us. It's her. And Naexi, as beautiful as she is, can only be a pale imitation.

Belial grasps her jaw and growls, "Stop."

She sighs sweetly, then morphs into the familiar face we know from her.

"You didn't really come here for dresses for that delectable creature." She kisses the air and Belial recoils. "Whatever could you need little old me for?"

Belial practically bares his teeth and growls.

I don't blame him, but one of us has to remain civil. What's in the past is past. I don't like it, but we are timeless beings. Eventually, we're all going to piss each other off. The only way we'll get anywhere is if we reach a point of acceptance. And that's my role in this. I don't like what's happened, but I accept it.

"You're a lot more demony than you were." She glances at me. "What's happened to you two? Is this her doing?"

I reach into my pocket and pull out a single coin.

She pouts at me and closes the distance between us. The Romys family has a merchant empire that spans the globe. A network like that is rich in information, though intel isn't one of their acknowledged products. Most of Naexi's family would rather not engage in spycraft, and she's not the most reliable source. But she's been trying to worm her way into our beds for a hundred and fifty years.

"You're no fun," she mutters and takes the coin from my fingers.

Fae, specifically those tied to the Seelie Court, have developed a strong leaning toward honesty. Once, they couldn't lie. But with all the intermingling of blood-lines that is no longer the case. Fae can lie just like the rest of us, but their ego demands they follow tradition.

With money exchanged, everything we say or ask is sealed by her honor. And no one is more honorable than the Romys family. Even those so-called fae who claim to be building the New Seelie Court, or whatever name they've settled on. Luminous something.

"What is she?" I ask.

Her brows rise. "I would think you'd know by now…"

I stare at her longer.

Naexi sighs. "She looks human to me. What do you mean?"

Belial is silent and pacing again.

"We think she's not fully human."

"And with your extensive records, you don't know?"

"She was born during the plague and both her parents died."

Naexi's face crumbles and she sucks in a breath. The Romys family is also very tight-knit. "Poor thing… Hm. She seems human to me."

"Is there a test? Something you could do to tell for certain?"

"I'm not sure," she says slowly. "This will take time."

"We understand."

She laces her fingers together in front of her. "Also, if she is not yet awakened into what she will become, there's no way to tell."

That is something I'd considered, but that's a nut that can't be cracked until it's ready. There are a handful of beings who, like us, are born mortal and awaken or emerge into their true selves later on. But we are rare.

Belial is wound up, and I don't know why.

"I understand this question might put you in a difficult position... Have you seen any movement of ships around our eastern or western shore?"

"No," she says without hesitation. "Refugees?"

I grimace. "Raiders. The settlement on our southern shore, the ones that don't claim us? It looks as though they've been wiped out or taken."

Her eyes go wide and her brow furrows. "Oh, no. That's terrible. I haven't heard anything, but I have seen some new ships. They never let us get very close. Quick and light, it could be who you speak of. Are the High Lords considering action?"

"Not yet," Belial says as he wheels around. "The settlement didn't belong to us, so officially, what do we have to be upset about?"

"Obviously, we're concerned. That's nearly a whole city wiped away."

"That many?" she whispers.

"Have you seen an influx in the slave trade on the continent?"

She shrugs. "I don't deal in flesh or associate with anyone who does. I wouldn't know, but I can ask around."

We're tallying up quite a debt. I hope we can pay the price when it comes due. Our coin buys her silence and discretion. The answers are another fee entirely.

"Have Ammit's people left?" Belial asks.

"No, most of their vendors are still returning to the ships. If you're looking for honey candy—"

"I'm not." Belial stops, and I hold my breath. I don't know if this is something we should bring up to Naexi. "Someone broke a boundary stone around Privale. I had a little run-in with one of theirs. Curious what your take is on them?"

"Hm, that's an interesting direction. They've changed their branding from god of the underworld to god of candy. I've often wondered what they're after the way they scurry about, but they're a quiet lot. They don't socialize much, even in merchant circles."

A tiny creature barely six inches tall rides in on a typical house cat. The house fairy begins speaking in a high-pitched voice that hurts my ears. Naexi grins and kneels to listen to the creature. Generally speaking, she is kind, generous, and a light taskmistress. The creatures that gravitate toward her are often faithful and industrious to a fault. I know she has numerous brownies who tend her house because this was where Belial brought Teill in the beginning. But fae are odd creatures, and the Brownies under Naexi's roof would not so much as touch Teill.

The lot of them can rot for all I care. Naexi might have pointed us in the direction of a tonic to stop the poison, but she hadn't lifted a finger. She'd have let that tiny child die. For as lovely and kind as Naexi is, she was born to a certain set of rules.

 Lioria

The tiny people have all run off. I'm guessing they call themselves something else, but I couldn't understand anything they said. I'm left standing in a second-floor room wearing nothing but a silken robe. My hair is a mess from having literal people in it.

It's like I've stepped into a fairy tale.

I clutch the fabric around myself and turn in a circle.

There are partially made pieces of clothing, yards of lace, feathers, and strings of beads all laid out in an artful mess.

Who is this woman? Did my demons really bring me here for clothes?

It's hard for me to think that two creatures who care very little about their appearance came all this way for fashion. Once more, I feel as though I'm being left out. I shouldn't. They are the High Lords and I'm...

I'm not even sure what I am anymore.

I wander about the room admiring things and running my fingers over fabrics so fine I worry my work-roughened hands will snag them. I'm going to have to have a serious conversation with them about what is and is not appropriate to do on my behalf. I was willing to ignore the wardrobe changes because that might have been meddling to create the image they wanted. But this isn't about me. It's whatever has them on edge and Belial training so hard.

The scent of sunshine wafts toward me.

"There you are, darling girl. Just look at that hair!"

I freeze as a hand thrusts into my hair. I tense, but don't move. My wavy curls are unruly at the best of times, and they only get worse the more it's touched.

"This is just so thick and luxurious. Oh, you cannot keep braiding it back."

I've had about as much as I can take. I smile and turn to face this merchant fae person.

She's watching me with interest. Those sunburst eyes of hers are unsettling to look at, so I settle on a spot between her brows.

"We're going to be the very best of friends," she says with certainty.

Little suns are all over the place, and when the demons greeted her, they spoke about the sun. I don't know the rules here, but it seems that light imagery is welcomed.

"May the sun never set on our friendship," I say slowly.

She claps her hands and squeals. There's something so very pure about her reactions that makes it hard to maintain my distrust.

"Yes!" She takes my arm. "I need to know *everything*."

"Could I have my clothes back?"

Her nose wrinkles. "That horrid thing? The sun above, no. You have the body of a goddess. Why not show it off a little? Those two demons would surely appreciate it."

I have no idea how to respond to her. "Then what am I going to do about clothes?"

She waves a hand. "They'll be ready soon. Come. Sit with me and talk."

Naexi links her arm with mine and leads me out of the showroom space and deeper into the house.

"You must tell me how you captured them," she says.

"I'm sorry?"

She pulls me to stand on a waxy carpet that looks like a leaf. The moment both my feet are on it, the thing *moves*. It rises and my knees buckle a little. Naexi smiles and grips me tightly, but doesn't seem surprised we are literally rising up through the ceiling. I gape as we pass through what must be the third, fourth, and fifth floors to a sixth. It's a small room, almost entirely enclosed by windows. There's even a little fountain. We're surrounded by flowers and other growing things. Some of what I thought were butterflies at first glance have human-like bodies.

"Go on. Go on, everyone," Naexi says with a wave of her hand.

The little winged people flit down through the hole on either side of the leaf. It's a literal leaf! I just got lifted into the air by a plant.

"Come sit with me, Lioria."

I stare in wonder at my surroundings as we emerge onto the top of the house. There's a tent with a comfortable lounging area set up within its walls that allows us to look out over the harbor and ocean.

"Wow. It looks so... Blue."

"Have you ever seen the ocean before?"

"Yes. I grew up on our north shore."

"Ah, the currents muddy the waters round there. Hm. Shallow ships would move quickly through those waters..."

"I'm sorry?"

She waves her hand. "Nothing. Never mind me. Come sit and tell me everything."

I'm wearing nothing but a robe. She's wearing a few triangles of fabric sewn together. And I'm the only one uncomfortable about this. I take a deep breath and tell myself to not concern myself with what others might see and settle on an armchair that looks as though the legs were chopped off and set on the carpets.

"I must confess two things to you," Naexi says. "I am completely in love with your demons, and I think they hate me," she says.

I blink.

She chuckles. "Oh, your face. I'm not telling you this to threaten you. I think that as friends I should confide my unrequited love, otherwise you might suspect my motives."

"I'm just processing it all," I say slowly.

"I've tried for over a hundred years to tempt them, so it's never going to work out between us." She waves her hand. "But that's not what I really need to confess..."

What does she intend to drop on me now?

"Have you met Teill?"

I'm getting whiplash from her change of topics. "Yes."

"When Belial brought her to me, I didn't offer the full scope of my assistance. I wanted to, but I was warned that some moments would change our future forever, and that the most I could do was refer him to someone else. He doesn't know this. Demons are.... We have multiple reasons not to trust one another. Is she well? Teill?"

I hold up my hands. "I'm sorry."

"It's a lot, isn't it?"

I shift my legs under me while my emotions ebb and flow. "Yes. What do you mean? Helping a poisoned child would change the future?"

She lifts a shoulder and her light seems to dim. "Yes. That was the moment I was born to create. My life's work all to say no to a child. It's not pleasant knowledge, but now that I've met you, it's a little easier to bear."

"That's ridiculous. Who gets to decide that? You want me to believe that the gods paused waging their war to tell you your life's purpose?"

She stares at me for several moments. There are little lines that deepen only to smooth out as a myriad of thoughts and emotions flow through her.

Naexi smiles at me, but it's sad. "You're right. I see why they like you."

Again, there's something I'm not being told.

"Because I say too much and speak my mind? Yes, they seem to find me very amusing."

"You don't accept the normal order. You don't see it, do you? Even now, most humans would not act like you are sitting down with me. But you adapt and you change the people in your orbit."

"I-I'm nothing so remarkable. I'm just a normal girl."

"You've never felt like you belong, have you? You don't want the same things other women your age want, do you? Even now, with all their power, just a kiss away, you want something for yourself, don't you?"

My mouth grows dry as I stare at her. "None of that makes me special."

She tilts her head to the side. "Only because you haven't seen more of the world. I don't think you know any better, or understand what a breath of fresh air you are."

"I don't know what game you're playing—"

"I'm not. For once. Whatever or whoever you are, I think you'll be good for all of us."

"How can you say that?"

She gestures to her eyes. "I have the sun's blessing. All that is under the sun, I can see. To some extent. It's a gift that emerged... After the war began. It's still a great unknown to us, but I know things from time to time."

"What do you know about the war? No one ever speaks of it."

"Those in Eden wouldn't." She smiles and her cheeks sink in as she sucks on the pipe. I watch her blow out a steady stream of smoke. "Anything I say about the war will upset your demons, and I'm resolved to play nice."

"Do you really love them?"

"In my own way. Probably not as they ought to be. I am attracted to unusual things, and the High Demon Lords are unique." Her gaze dips and I resolve to not clutch my robe closed. "As are you."

We study each other openly for several long moments.

Of course, I'm jealous. She's beautiful and obviously wealthy. But as she's said, her feelings for Belial and Eligos are unrequited. I can't fault her for trying.

"If you wanted, could you make them love you?" I ask.

She tilts her head to the side. "It would come at a great personal cost I'm not willing to pay. Maybe I love the idea of them more than I love the demons themselves? See? Changing me already."

"Or you could have lured me up here to throw me off the building."

"I would never do something so vulgar." She grins and I see her second set of pointed canines. "I'd poison a pin, then accidentally stick you with it while measuring you for your wardrobe."

"Wouldn't that be too obvious, though? A pinprick might leave blood."

Her face crumples. "Oh, you're right. Hm. I supposed it would need to look like an accident then..."

I chuckle at the absurd conversation.

"Is Teill well?"

"I'm not sure what to think about that situation..."

She bows her head and the deep creases on her face speak of guilt and pain. "It was a terrible thing to have to do, even knowing she'd survive."

"How do you know? What does the sunburst eye show you?"

She sighs, then pulls on her pipe once more. "Pieces. The pieces are stronger when those of us with the sunburst eye are together. That's when we get clear images of the future, and we do what we can to facilitate the best outcome."

"Best outcome for who? You? Or someone else?"

"Hopefully, the world."

"If the gods aren't guiding you, what or who is?"

She smiles at me. "I hope I can give you an answer. Someday."

Part of me wants to like her. She's eccentric and interesting. It's obvious she's curtailing what she wants to say, but why? I hope she is being honest. Though what she's told me about Teill is disturbing, I can also recognize that my scope of the world is smaller. At heart, I'm a country girl while she is a woman of the world.

"I'm determined to become your very best friend." She tips her pipe at me. "Would you write me?"

"I don't see why not," I say slowly, while trying to think of an objection my demons might have. "You have to know that I'm going to share what you told me with the others."

She lifts her shoulders. "That's your right. The page has turned. A new chapter has begun. I've played my part. Now it's up to you what role I'm cast in."

I stare at her. None of that makes sense, but I don't think I'll get a straight answer out of her. "I don't know if we can be friends, given how much you can't say to me."

"I hope that in time we can say all things to each other. There's time yet. We don't have to rush into our friendship."

That's an answer I can respect.

"Okay," I say and relax back into the chair.

She grins at me, then snaps her fingers. I jump as something falls onto my lap. It's a box.

I lift the beautifully carved box so the sun can glint off the inlay. Unsurprisingly, a blazing sun is displayed on the top. "A letterbox?"

"Of course. How would I write you otherwise?"

"Thank you. I'm sorry I don't have a gift. Belial and Eligos didn't exactly tell me what we were doing today."

She chuckles. "It's freely given. The hope of your friendship is enough."

What does she know that I don't?

BELIAL

E ligos and I leave a shadow version of ourselves lounging in Naexi's parlor. If she's going to make us cool our heels down here alone out of spite, the least we can do is make use of this time. It's harder to traverse the city without being seen during the daylight. We were created to be monsters of darkness, slithering about. This is why Oriax is obsessed with learning all there is to know about magic. We can overcome our design flaws.

Naexi didn't know anything about the movement of forces around our northern shore, but there are others in the city who might.

Eligos becomes a bit of shadow as he folds light around himself to create the invisibility. Then he's streaking off toward the docks.

Alastor's letter this morning, maintaining that nothing was wrong, doesn't sit well with me.

A city doesn't vanish overnight. Boundary stones don't break themselves. My network has either caught or had skirmishes with a dozen very powerful creatures within our borders over the last year. Creatures that shouldn't have been able to get past the barrier. And every time Alastor maintains this was always the way, Eligos and I merely didn't know.

I'd hoped that Naexi would have some information. But our enemies are likely aware of our cordial relationship with her.

I bound over rooftops. I could use my wings, but it's harder to disguise myself in that partially shifted form. It's like magic wants to slide off me instead of holding in place. Handy in a fight, but annoying otherwise.

Coastal cities are a haven for our non-human refugees. They simply don't advertise their presence. They're usually a refugee for a reason other than merely losing a home.

I open my senses and draw in a deep breath. The myriad of smells assault me, but I sort through them. There's one odor I need...

That one.

The scent is oily, but not unpleasant. It brings back memories so long buried I don't have words for all the things in those memories anymore.

I come to a stop atop the pointed roof of a housing building. It's harder to pinpoint the odor because the being moves about the area often enough. I close my eyes and follow my nose, literally. I step off the roof and fall to the ground, landing in a crouch. A woman shrieks and stares at me with wide eyes.

"Sorry," I mutter to her and walk past.

She isn't human, either.

I follow the scent to the apartment building. The trail is strongest around a worn, wooden door. I knock once, then listen, but hear nothing from within.

Dealing with our non-human residents is always tricky. There are rules as well as tradition to follow. And that becomes more complicated if we don't have a working agreement. Eligos and I are content to allow our harbormasters the freedom to admit or reject non-human refugees without interference from us.

I push the door open and stare into the darkness. There's a landing, then an interior door. Otherwise, it's just stairs leading down and the smell of brine.

Figures. He isn't fond of land.

I snort and head inside. The space is too small for my wings, but I let my talons come out. Just because a creature and I have an understanding doesn't mean meetings like this are safe. My claws lengthen into razor-sharp daggers on each fingertip as I descend into the belly of the beast. The stairs eventually turn and let out into an ocean cave. I peer about. The scent is nearly overpowering down here.

A few weak candles sputter and keep enough light to see by. I don't need them, but it's a polite touch.

The cave appears natural to my untrained eye. I can't tell how deep it goes past the coast, but there's a wide chasm between me and the other side. The rock drops a few dozen yards to deep blue water below of indeterminable depth. It must be very deep to allow this resident any comfortable access.

"Cetus," I call out. "I know you're there."

Silence.

I wait and watch the water below.

Cetus has worn many names over time. He is the monster of the ocean. The whale who swallowed Jonah. The creature that idiot Perseus supposedly killed to rescue Andromeda. Cetus has worn many names and played a role in more stories than I can count. He's one of the ancients, creatures as old as I am.

A plume of bubbles and water erupt from the surface right before the great head of what some would call a sea monster. The space between the rocks isn't nearly wide enough for him to fit, and I stagger back. The beast propels itself up, the great body elongating and becoming quite skinny, then snapping together mid-air before he lands in a slosh of wet clothing on the stone in front of me. The resulting form is a man of large stature and girth. He's wearing boots, trousers belted around his waist with a striped sash, and a shirt that's seen a better decade.

Cetus stares at me with one eye, the other squeezed shut. He has a great, bushy black beard and wild hair with bits of seaweed and barnacles sticking to him.

"What do you want, demon scum?"

We might have an agreement, but that doesn't mean Cetus and I like each other.

I snort and pull my offering out of my pocket.

Cetus' other eye pops open and he stares at the fist-sized sphere. At first glance, most would assume it's a pretty crystal that glows blue. But Cetus knows it on sight.

I've never seen this ancient beast more intent on anything in my life. Not even that one time Raum tried to take him on.

"W-what do you want, High Demon Lord?" he whispers.

"This is an offering. It's thanks for all you've done to keep the waters between Eden and the continent hostile." I hold it out. "It's freely given, Cetus."

He snatches the crystal out of my hands and holds it to his chest. "How? Where?"

I shrug. "I can tell you the story I was told, but I don't know if it's true."

He holds it up and stares at the tiny, glowing creatures inside. "Tell me. Is there more?"

"I don't know. When I asked, I was told that someone found a small pool that was drying up. It glowed blue at night. They didn't know where the pool was or who'd first scooped these up. This might be all that is left in the whole world."

There are many things that once inhabited this land that are now gone. The bioluminescent, microscopic creatures in that water used to be rare. I would have assumed they were extinct for hundreds or thousands of years. But life finds a way.

Cetus holds the crystal to his chest.

"Can you care for them?" I ask.

He snorts. "Better than you."

I grin. "Probably. When I saw it, I thought of you. Figured if anyone could bring them back, you'd be the one."

"What else do you want? You didn't come all this way to bring me an offering."

"No." I shove my hands in my pockets. "Have you seen ships with shallow drafts on our southern coast?"

He frowns and his eyes nearly disappear into the creases of his face. "Shallow draft ships?"

"The city on our southern shore was wiped out completely. I've heard whispers of shallow draft ships no one can get close to."

His human nose wiggles back and forth. "I might know something. Let me find out more information than pointless guesses."

"I'd appreciate it, Cetus."

"There have been strange boats on the water. Boats that vanish, then reappear. They're always pointed south."

I grimace. "I fear war is coming to Eden."

"You've escaped it for a long time."

I nod. "Your aid is appreciated, but—"

"I don't like you Demon Lords." His eyes blaze with old wounds and conflicts. We are not strangers. "But no one else is trying to make things better. I'll hold up my end of the bargain."

I open and close my mouth.

As gruff as he is, I would never have imagined Cetus would side with us in a conflict between the content and Eden. His support is a big reason why there's no embargo on us.

"Thank you. For whatever you can do."

"Come back tomorrow. I'll know about your shallow draft ships, then."

He walks off the stony ledge and into the water.

War is coming to Eden.

When we've finally found something worth living for.

LIORIA

I stare at myself in the mirror in utter shock.

"That's... That is *not* me."

Naexi snorts and puffs on her pipe. "Of course it's you. Clothes and product don't change a thing about you, just how people perceive you. And now there isn't a creature on the planet who isn't going to want to fuck you senseless."

"I... I don't know what to say..."

I turn to look at myself at another angle.

Naexi lifts a few locks of my hair, pushing them forward over my shoulder to fall along my breast. "Please don't ever straighten your hair again. It's glorious."

I lift my hand to trail my fingers over the waves. "Growing up, whenever we had to look nice for something, the nannies made me sit for hours straightening my hair by hand. Said it would last longer than if they used magic. They always said my hair was unfortunate and course..."

"That's stupid. Your hair has a distinct texture, yes, but that just means you should style it differently. I think they are wrong. Just look at you. The waves give your hair life. It represents your vibrant personality that isn't flat and boring. Straightening your hair takes away all the luster and makes it lifeless. We're each born with our own kind of beauty. Don't ever try to look like anyone else's standard of attractive ever again."

Despite watching exactly what her little helpers did to my hair, face, and skin, I doubt I could recreate this.

My normally frizzy hair is glossy and falls in waves around my shoulders and down my back. The waves are more pronounced. Whatever cream she had me slick over my skin, makes it gleam. I tap my arm a few times because it almost looks like I'm wet or something.

The make-up is pure art. It's not heavily applied, like the wealthy women in Suncrest preferred. This is just a touch here, a touch there, and a lot of attention paid to my lashes.

"Tell me you love this dress?" Naexi rests her chin on my shoulder and stares at our reflections.

My dark skin next to her paler complexion is like noon and sunset in contrast. She's wrapped me in a color that is such a deep, dark purple it's nearly black, save for around the edges of the garment where the color is more blue. Gold trim accentuates the plunge between my breasts, and little charms dangle at my shoulders as the sleeves split to fall at my sides.

There are other clothes. We've spent the last nearly two hours trying on most of what she's decided I need and having it pinched, pinned, and tailored to perfection, only for her to strip me down to nothing and slip this on me.

"Where do you think I'm ever going to wear this?" I ask her, though my eyes are locked with my reflection.

That does—and doesn't—look like me.

Her smile widens and her sunburst eyes glint.

"That's just the thing," she whispers. "The goal is having it taken off you."

That startles a laugh out of me.

"Have you met Belial and Eligos? Do you honestly think something as beautiful and delicate as this would survive them?"

She arches a brow. "Then give them an ultimatum. Make them do as you please. A goddess can always tell her worshipers how to properly pay tribute."

My cheeks heat at her words. I like my body, but the compliments she's heaped on me make me squirm. I'm not a classical beauty. Upper class wouldn't even call me pretty. But I like my rounded face and the crinkles at my eyes when I smile or laugh. This ample body has gotten me this far in life, and I love it.

A little winged creature zips up to Naexi and speaks in that squeaking voice I can't understand. Her shoulders droop and she pouts.

"It seems they're here to collect you." She sighs and links her arm in mine. "Run away with me? I'll dress you every day in rich fabric."

I laugh at her proposition. "I thought you were in love with Belial and Eligos?"

"I was, but I think you might be the better catch." She squeezes my arm. "I'm teasing. I would not come between you and your demons. That's not the person I want to be, even if I'm jealous. I'll have everything else sent over once it's complete."

Two more tiny flying creatures drift toward us with a cloak clutched between them. It's warm still on the coast, but not as warm as I'm accustomed to.

I wave at myself. "You mean to send me off looking like this?"

She grins back. "It's what girlfriends are for. I hope they ravish you all night."

My face heats, but I'm not opposed to the idea.

I sigh and turn, pulling Naexi into a hug. Her body stiffens, but only for half a second. I've probably done something dreadfully human.

Her thin arms wrap around me and she squeezes far tighter than I'd have expected. I close my eyes and inhale the scent of sunshine and joy that clings to her.

"Thank you, Naexi." I lean back to find tears pooling in her gaze. "What's wrong?"

"I'm just so happy I got to meet you," she whispers. Her eyes go wide and she whirls. "Wait one moment!"

She rushes over to a cabinet with small drawers. One by one she begins yanking them open, only to slam them shut again. Over and over again until she cries out in victory.

Naexi turns to face me, holding out a long, delicate necklace. It looks to be formed from cylindrical, skinny golden tubes linked together, and hanging from it is a pendant of the sun and moon.

"For protection and luck. May the sun always guide you, my new friend." She lays it over my head so that the cool metal falls between my breasts.

I pick it up and can see small sigils on the inside of the gold tubes. They're so tiny I can't make them out, but they're there.

"I can't accept this—"

She lays her finger across my lips, then leans in and kisses her finger. "It's a gift."

"Why do I get the feeling you know more about me than you're letting on?"

"I don't know anything that I haven't already confided in you. I just have a feeling. Here." She presses her hand to her heart. "You're special, Lioria, with no surname or lineage who captures the hearts of Demon Lords."

I'm not convinced, but she isn't going to tell me more.

I depart, swaddled in my cloak with a small bag containing a few gifts, including a tin of spiced tea from Suncrest. Apparently, someone back home has decided to try selling it to merchants and the first samples arrived yesterday. I'm thrilled. Naexi has already vowed to keep me supplied wherever I am.

There's something about her I like. I can't bring myself to fully trust her, but I hope that in time, this is a friendship that grows.

I've been so incredibly lucky since leaving Suncrest. The world has been kind and welcoming to me, and I realize I've been blessed. Me. The girl who couldn't pay attention during services and hasn't said a prayer in two weeks now.

Naexi accompanies me to the doors, which are once more seemingly blown open by air.

I pause and take in the sight of my two demons on the street in their fine clothes, waiting for me. It's surreal and magical. I feel a bit like one of those fabled princesses I used to read about. Only I have two princes, not one.

The only thing that would make this moment better is if Belial or Eligos had even the ghost of a reaction. They're stoic and still like statues.

Nothing whatsoever?

That won't do.

I let the cloak fall open just enough that the cool evening air hits my sternum.

Eligos reacts first with a sharp intake of breath. Belial is almost stone, save for the hint of a growl I can feel more than hear. I grin and glance over my shoulder.

"Thanks again, Naexi."

She wiggles her fingers and cackles.

Eligos grabs my hand and hauls me forward.

I'm trapped between the carriage and my demons.

Eligos leans in, his eyes heavily lidded. "In the carriage."

"Now," Belial says.

I jab them each with a freshly liquored nail. "You will not destroy a single thing I'm wearing. Is that understood?"

Belial fists the split skirt. "I'll buy you another."

I push him back. "No, you will not."

Eligos lifts my hand and presses a kiss on my wrist. "In the carriage now, before someone who isn't us sees you and we have to kill them."

That's a threat I don't want to test.

I turn and climb in. There's a small, magic globe of light embedded in the ceiling that casts a soft glow and catches on the golden threads, making the fleur de lis pattern. I sit back as my two demons squeeze in opposite me.

"Show me," Belial says once the carriage starts moving.

I let the cloak part to reveal the artful scraps of fabric I let Naexi convince me were clothing.

"Holy..." The rest of Eligos' words are lost behind his hand.

The space seems to shrink around Belial. "You walked out of there like that?"

Eligos smacks his shoulder and whatever spatial magic bursts, putting the world right again.

"Stop being an ass," he snaps.

"All this over a dress?"

Eligos barks a laugh while his gaze dips to admire the rest of me. "Damn, Naexi."

Belial reaches over and grasps Eligos' thigh while still looking at me. "Fuck her. Now. I want to watch."

Eligos' grin is swift and there isn't a drop of resistance in him.

"No," I say before either can move. "Either I fuck both of you or neither of you. I'm tired of you holding back, Belial."

His eyes widen in what I might call panic. "Lioria—"

"She has a point," Eligos says and shifts to sit next to me. He slides his hand past the slit in my dress to caress my thigh. "But I don't think the carriage is the best place for that."

I let my legs relax, making room for his hand to slip between my legs. "A compromise then?"

Belial is watching Eligos' arm with interest.

His fingers brush along my bare folds. "What do you say, Bel? She's not wearing anything at all under this handkerchief."

Belial scrubs a hand over his face and sucks in his cheeks. "I don't want to hurt you."

I grasp Eligos' wrist and guide him to apply a little more pressure. "I don't think you will. I trust you."

"Eli?" Belial looks to him for help.

Eligos' fingers plunge into me and I moan. He leans in and kisses my shoulder.

"You better take off what you don't want ripped, my dream," he whispers against my cheek.

My fingers scramble to release the catch holding the cloak together. The plunge down the front is so deep it isn't difficult at all to slip my arms out of the holes and let the material pool at my waist. Eligos runs his knuckles over the curve of my breast and we both watch my nipples tighten.

"Fine," Belial says in a choked voice.

"Show me then." There's something about this dress, or maybe it's a bit of Naexi that's rubbed off on me, but I feel more desirable. Not quite worthy of them, but looking like this? It feels natural. I'm enjoying watching the way lust makes my demons hunger.

Eligos curls his fingers within me and sucks on the skin at the base of my neck while we watch Belial rip the leather belt in half. He takes a little more care with his trousers and only loses a button, which makes me think back to our first ride in this carriage.

Whatever happened to that button?

He shoves his clothes down, revealing his thick cock. He wraps a hand around it and pumps himself roughly.

"I get a taste first," he says.

"Are we negotiating?" I chuckle and shift so that my legs are open a bit wider. "All you ever have to do is say so."

"You are so delightfully naughty," Eligos whispers.

Belial leans forward and pulls Eligos' fingers from my pussy. I whimper at the loss of his touch, but watching Belial suck Eligos' fingers lights a fire in me. I don't know who reaches for whom first, but my demons lock lips in one of those growling, brutal kisses that would destroy me.

I love how free they are with their affection for each other and me. I didn't know my life was missing this until them. They've given me a place to belong and their hearts.

I want so badly to be content.

My demons break apart and turn their gazes on me.

I flutter my ridiculously long eyelashes. "Oh, my. Go easy on me?"

Belial grasps my face and pulls me forward to meet his eager lips. His tongue thrusts into my mouth and I moan while Eligos slides his hands up my skirt to grip my hips. He lifts me, shifting us both so that I'm sitting on his lap with my legs on either side. It lets me rock my ass against his cock while Belial makes love to my mouth.

Eligos cups my breasts, toying with my already stiff nipples. I groan and receive a growl from Belial.

My body aches for them.

I wrap my hands around Belial's impressive cock and begin to stroke him. His fingers tunnel into my hair and pull me closer. I arch my back as my body seems to become alive with sensation rippling through me, and all they're doing is touching my breasts and lavishing me with kisses.

"Suck his cock, Lioria," Eligos says as he pinches my nipples. "I want to watch her make you come, Bel. Let her. Now."

Belial growls slightly but releases his hold on my hair.

I lean forward and wrap my lips around the head of his thick cock. I hear him groan and mutter words that might be curses or praise. I don't know.

"Fuck," he growls to the point the word vibrates in my chest.

I open my mouth as the carriage bumps along and I shift forward, taking him to the very back of my throat.

"Eligos, do something," Belial says in a strained voice, as if he needs saving from my mouth.

I feel something press against me before Eligos pulls my hips back. I stroke my tongue over the pulsing vein along the underside of Belial's cock. And then I feel it. Eligos' hard length at my entrance. He shifts below me, no doubt contorting himself in such confined quarters, but there he is, pressing into me. I moan around Belial's cock at the intrusion.

"Fuck, she's so wet, Bel. I think sucking you turns her on."

"Shut up," Belial growls.

Eligos bends over me, kissing my spine. "You like his cock, my dream?"

I groan as a reply, causing more curses and praise I can't understand to spill from Belial's lips.

Eligos shifts me forward, rocking with the carriage and I constrict my lips so that Belial has to feel me the deeper he goes. His hand presses down on the back of my head and I swallow. Not a moment later, Eligos pulls roughly on my hips, impaling me on his cock. It's a back-and-forth motion with my two demons playing a sensual tug of war with my body.

The carriage rocking adds more sensation as everything seems to vibrate and sway.

"F-fuck," Belial groans.

Eligos rocks up into me, forcing Belial's cock further down my throat. It's a struggle to breathe while my eyes cross and toes curl at the sensations overwhelming my body.

"You will not come yet," Eligos says in a savage voice.

I hold Belial there, lavishing him with my tongue until Eligos pulls me down on him, grinding his cock into me. I whimper as fingers stroke over my clit.

They are mine, and I care about them deeply. I will find a way to thrive in this life and make the most of it. Because their attention is precious.

Belial pants. "I'm going to…"

"Not yet!"

I feel pressure on my anus and suck in a breath.

"Relax," Eligos mutters.

I lift my toes so I'm balanced on my heels and his thighs, as if that will help what's going on, as he slides a digit into me.

"Is it in?" Belial asks.

"Yes. Just one."

"Fuck. Make her come, Eli."

"Fine. Alright. You're both so impatient."

The feel of his fingers on my clit is enough to make me whimper. I grip the bench on either side of Belial's spread thighs and rock myself forward, then backward. The sensation is wholly different with Eligos' finger in my ass and I buck against him, but that only sinks him deeper.

Belial smooths his hands down my back and gathers my hair. He doesn't pull on it, but he doesn't let it go either. And I find a new point to anchor myself to.

"Lioria, Christ... I'm—fuck..."

His body goes tense. I suck in my cheeks and I get my first taste of him.

"That's not right, Bel. That's just not right." Eligos' voice is strained now. "You know she comes first."

Belial pulls me up, his cock falling from my lips. I'm a bit of a mess, but he kisses me anyway. His tongue licks my lips, greedy for more. My thighs are quivering with me bent forward like this, but then Eligos begins to thrust in earnest.

I clutch at Belial, digging my fingers into the fabric of his coat while their fingers tease me higher. I'd beg if I could, but my demon commands my mouth now.

"I'll show him how it's done," Eligos mutters and twists his finger in my ass as he gently tugs on my clit.

I shout, the sound swallowed by Belial as pleasure breaks me apart. It's so intense it feels as though my very soul grows thin before rebounding back together as Eligos plunges deep and holds me there.

My body is spent and I slump back against Eligos.

ELIGOS

I lift the rag to Lioria's face, gently wiping away the make-up Naexi had so artfully applied. I appreciated the delicate touch. Lioria's beauty isn't conventional or anything make-up could accentuate, because what pulled us to her wasn't physical. It was her. The longer she is with us, the more in-tune with it I feel.

"There," I mutter.

She smiles and wrinkles her nose.

Belial pulls her back against his chest, causing ripples in the bath. Her utter delight at the bathing pool was the highlight of this trip. It's a large, rectangular pool that is cleaned, heated, and maintained by a clever magic device.

Lioria shifts so that she can lay her head on Belial's shoulder. He's barely let her feet touch the ground since we arrived at our townhouse in Rosenburg. It's across the city from the fae and warded so well I doubt anyone is aware it exists. It is one of many safe houses across the country.

"Did you two accomplish what you needed to?" she asks.

I glance at Belial. Did he say something to her?

Belial frowns.

Not him then.

"What makes you think we had other motives?" We did, but the idea had been not to tell her.

Lioria lifts her head and stares at me. "Don't act like I can't see you with my own eyes. You were both completely on edge when we left. Didn't speak. Then you were downright rude to Naexi. So, where did you go all afternoon? Did you get what you needed to taken care of?"

Belial chuckles and kisses her cheek. "Don't worry about it."

She sighs, not at all dissuaded.

Neither Belial nor I want to burden Lioria with what we don't know yet. With any luck, we can head off whatever this attack from the continent might be. But if we don't? If those raids breach our borders and threaten the heart of this country? What then?

Then there's the problem of Alastor's message that was waiting for us when we arrived.

He needs to see us tomorrow to deliver something, but he won't say what.

Alastor knows that tomorrow is when we planned to restore those boundary stones. The materials will be ready. It will take us all day to cover the ground necessary with only two of us doing the work. I'd like nothing more than to bring Oriax in on this, but then we run the risk of involving the Mage's Guild and University.

The two organizations might call Eden home and swear to align with us in any conflict, but I don't wholly trust them. Mages are a gossipy lot prone to causing more problems than they fix, but they have their uses. Too bad we can't make use of them.

"Belial and I are doing reconnaissance related to the broken boundary stones," I say.

"Eligos," Belial growls.

"What?" I shrug. "She knows about the stones. What's the harm in telling her we're investigating it? Don't you think she'd like to know she's safe?"

Of course, there's more to it. Namely, that we think an invasion attempt might be on our horizon.

What a fucking great time to find the piece we've been missing.

"What are you getting at?" Belial demands.

So he realizes I have a plan?

Good.

"Alastor needs to deliver something in person. Lioria would be heading back to Privale alone tomorrow. A northern detour wouldn't tack on too much time."

She perks up. "North? Like Oserora?"

I frown. "Yes..."

"Naexi is going there tomorrow. She mentioned needing to sign some documents. We could travel together."

I glance at Belial.

It's always odd business dealing with people who might see snippets of the future. Naexi could be unconsciously aware of this point in history. Is this a sign to move forward? Or turn aside?

"Do you trust me to pick up whatever Alastor needs you to have?" she asks.

"Yes," I say without hesitation.

"It's everything else about this idea I have a problem with," Belial mutters.

"Are you aware Naexi has been in love with you?"

That makes me freeze. Belial has his hand up, completely still.

Lioria chuckles. "I'll take that as a yes. Why don't you like her? Is it because of the business with Teill?"

"Yes," Belial says without hesitation.

"It's more complicated than that. Our relationship with what was the Seelie Court has been contentious. Things have happened between them and us that make it hard to trust."

"What is the Seelie Court?" She draws the unfamiliar word out a touch too long trying to say it.

"Do you want the long explanation or a short one?" Eligos asks.

She curls up against Belial's shoulder and smiles at me. "Something in-between?"

"Very well," I mutter, and tip my head back. Where to start? There isn't a way to completely avoid the war, so I'll say as little of that as I can while sticking to the truth. "There are those among the Vodu who are called fairies, fae, or fair people. Under those labels are other creatures."

"Like Brownies," Belial says.

"It's a point of contention whether you believe they began here, or were created in another world and came here after the fact. For a long time, they were myth and legend, not all that dissimilar to how you might think of them now. They were divided into two courts, the Seelie and Unseelie. The Seelie were fine enough folk, while the Unseelie were often..."

"Violent? Bloodthirsty? Corrupt?" Belial suggests.

"When the war began, the courts were trying to decide how to react and they got caught, half here and half in this other world. That's why we honor Naexi by calling her a shard. She's a descendant of those who were caught here and are waiting to be reunited with the other side. But, in the meantime, those here have attempted to carry on. There was a new Seelie Court for a while, but..."

Lioria's brow creases. "Did you go to war with them?"

I nod.

"They've never really recovered their power since then. Mostly because some from the Unseelie side took advantage. There's a new court now called the Luminous—what? What is it, Belial?"

He shrugs. "Fuck me if I know. Dain fancies himself the new lord of it, though."

Lioria glances between us. "Who is that?"

We're going to have to be careful what we say. "Dain..." What do I say about the horrible fucker? "He is the son of one of our greatest enemies and he hates us. Alone, he holds some power. But the Oni King—a powerful Yokai—has propped Dain up. They give tit for tat to keep each other on top as best they can."

"What divides Vodu and Yokai? I've never understood that."

"History, geography, and a lot of bad blood," Belial says.

I nod. "We'll have to show you a map sometime, but the continent used to be many smaller continents spread out. There was an area in what was referred to as the east where the Yokai were created and gained power. And Vodu is everything else. The people that inhabited the lands with the Vodu spent a lot of time conquering the rest of the world, and Yokai still resent them for that."

She squints at me. "But they don't use those words themselves?"

Belial kisses the top of her head. "Yokai do, but not Vodu. And even among Yokai, they use the word differently."

"I see," she mutters. Lioria stares at the water. "Do you know that Naexi thinks she saw what happened to Teill ahead of time and was told to not help?"

My gaze flies to Belial's face as it turns red with rage.

"I wish you hadn't said that," I mutter.

He wraps his arms around Lioria and buries his face in her hair.

Belial is loyal to a fault, and he's treated Teill like his child for so long I think he forgets she isn't.

"Hey? Hey, look at me?" She cups Belial's face as his nostrils flare and he hugs her tighter. "Teill is okay."

"Suffice to say, we didn't know."

"I knew," Belial growls out.

I gape at him. "You—what?"

He closes his eyes. "I didn't know for certain. I had a feeling. I don't care what their reasoning was, Teill was a child. A fucking child so small I could have crushed her whole body in my hand. I will never forgive Naexi. The future is unwritten. There is no destiny any longer. And I will never forget she was content to let a child suffer. Haven't we learned anything, Eligos? Anything at all?"

Lioria kisses Belial's cheek and whispers soothing words to him. He clutches her closer and I have to marvel at the change in him.

Before we were free, Belial was a brute force. He carved a path of destruction across hell, paving roads with the bones of his enemies. Looking at him, I know we've changed. We've become better. We've evolved. I just hope we've done enough.

LIORIA

Traveling by carriage always sounded so glamorous in stories. That would be because those stories featured normal carriages that bumped along at a normal pace.

Naexi pats my hand. "You'll feel better in a moment. See? The curtains are drawn."

I press a hand to my churning stomach and mutter, "Thanks."

Only part of my discomfort can be blamed on the carriage.

My demons settled down quickly last night. It was nice to fall asleep between them gradually. One moment we were talking about what the stars in different parts of the world looked like and the next I was asleep.

Too bad my anxiety woke me up repeatedly throughout the night.

Had Oriax responded?

Was there a letter waiting for me back at Privale?

My mind keeps going back to this unfinished business.

"Something's bothering you," Naexi says as she settles more comfortably on the bench next to me. She's stunning today in a trumpet shaped dress that's not the least bit tight, but still molds to her body and flares out at her thighs. Unsurprisingly, it's brilliant yellow. That seems to be an ever-present theme with her.

I make a noncommittal sound and smooth the fabric of my traveling dress over my thighs. Naexi practically dragged me out of the carriage and changed me out of my sensible trousers into this lovely thing. The waistline is up under my breasts, and the skirt isn't really a skirt. It's a sort of wrap-around thing and under that, I'm wearing pants. One of the best things about this ensemble is the short corset whose only purpose is holding my breasts higher than my collarbone, it seems.

The boning isn't jabbing into my stomach or soft bits. I want one for every day of the week and I don't care if my clothes will never fit properly again now that I know comfort.

It seems that Naexi has begun to understand me.

She bumps me with her shoulder. "I'm glad you chose to wear my gift today."

I freeze. I keep toying with the sun-and-moon pendant. "It's lovely."

She smiles and her eyes twinkle. "Just happy to do my part. Now, have you met Alastor before?"

"Once, but I don't know that you can say we met..."

"He's not a very friendly gentleman, is he? In his previous lifetime, he would pay me the occasional visit. He's so incredibly controlled. I think I've only seen him once in the last thirty years and he acted like he didn't even know who I was. Can you believe that?"

I lift my brows and nod along. "Quite rude."

But is it? With how long they've all lived, I imagine faces would blur together. That doesn't make her feelings less valid.

"What's the continent like?" I ask and lean back. The discussion last night in the pool has me curious and wanting to know more.

"It's different in every way." She chuckles, but it's a sad sound. "Honestly, I don't understand how anyone chooses to live there and not here."

"What do you mean?"

"Everyone is always at war with everyone else over something. Boundary disputes. Perceived slights. Old rivalries, most don't even know how they began. Prejudice."

"The continent has always sounded like a scary place. It can't all be bad, though, can it?"

"I think it depends on your perspective," she says slowly. "There are negatives about being in Eden."

"Like what?"

She glances at me and her lips twist up. "Like things I am forbidden from discussing. You can ask me all you like, but I've taken vows to keep the peace while my body and mind are here."

"What things would be forbidden?" I ask.

"*They* will have to tell you someday." She reaches over and takes my hand. "When that day comes, don't hold their history against them. Please?"

"The Demon Lords as a whole are powerful creatures. I guess it stands to reason there have been times when they've used that power poorly. And the seven High Demon Lords are more powerful than the rest, so..." I lift my shoulders. "I'm not going to judge what I don't understand. Belial says he was aware that your actions toward Teill were calculated. I can understand why he wouldn't forgive you. I... There's a reason you did what you did, and you believe it was right. For the greater good, maybe. And I can't discount that. I also don't like it. But what I do know is that Teill is in my life because of the choices you made, so..."

Naexi reaches over and takes my hand. "Thank you. I didn't want to turn her away, you see... Either I played my part perfectly or my brother would be killed by the people who raised us."

I stare at her in horror. This tale just gets worse the more I learn.

She smiles at me. "I think about Teill often and I wish her well. That's all I want now."

"Why don't you move to Eden? Get away from all of that?"

"It's not that simple. Loyalty is born into us. And when our sense of loyalty isn't enough, it's carved into us. Without my family, I'd be hunted and killed."

"Why?"

She chuckles without mirth. "For being fae. For having sunburst eyes. For being female. For being free with my lovers. For any number of reasons."

"Why is there so much conflict on the continent?"

"I think it's easier to explain why Eden is so peaceful. When the High Demon Lords brought whoever wanted to live under their rule, they had certain standards. Back then, there was greater variation in human skin tone."

"Like Belial and Eligos?"

"Yes. Belial was born into a holding family that has bucked the Demon Lord's wishes and valued maintaining a darker skin tone."

"Belial wasn't born into a holding family, though."

"No, he was born on the continent, where being fair isn't unheard of. It's uncommon among humans now because of the health risks it poses, but I believe his family's ancestors were kept like pets by some fae because of their fair skin and unusual hair."

"What?"

My mind races to understand what she's saying about my demon.

That poor family.

"The High Demon Lords had a goal to break down the racial barriers between humans and create a homogeneous culture that wasn't fractured by beliefs that one skin color made a person better or worse. That's why you have this lovely, bronzed skin, because their plan worked. The people who came to Eden wanted peace. They were encouraged to marry someone that didn't look like them, and that plan succeeded. You probably don't even know the word racist, do you?"

"No..." I say slowly, not liking the way it rolls off her tongue. "This sounds a bit like selective breeding in livestock," I mutter.

"Oh, goodness, no. No, Lioria." She laughs. "There are those alive who were there for the creation of Eden and they admit, they thought it was an outlandish, horrible idea. And yet, the High Demon Lords have created a peaceful land where there is little to no prejudice."

"As long as you come from a good family," I say.

"No system is perfect, but what they've created here is special."

Given what I know about the continent, I am inclined to agree. Even if I am the very person who slips between the cracks in our so-called perfect society.

"Is this common knowledge? Am I just an ignorant country girl?" I ask.

"I wouldn't say you're ignorant. You just haven't had the chance to learn about the outside world, and at best you only had a few years education. Most other places in the world you wouldn't get that. There are some places where simply being born a woman means you aren't valued as human."

"What? Then who has children? And raises them? And... How is that logical? If women aren't human, then... The stupidity hurts my brain."

"Women aren't as valued as men in my family. Not unless we have a gift." She gestures to her eyes. "Then we're a commodity. I'm still considered young, so my family is humoring me by letting me remain here in Eden."

"What will happen?"

"Eventually the family elders will pick a mate for me that benefits our family in some regard, and then he gets to decide my fate."

"I'll never understand why who you marry is more important than being happy. That alone makes me glad I'm without a pedigree."

Naexi grins. "You might be the only, truly free one among us."

It feels that way. The world seemed ripe for the picking when I was in Suncrest with my plan laid out. Even now, I still have options. I'm not locked onto a path. I'm truly one of the lucky ones.

The carriage lurches suddenly. I'm thrown forward, sliding off the bench onto my knees. Naexi has a hand on my shoulder and her knee on my face.

She grabs my arm as the carriage jostles about and the horses neigh in distress. "Gods, are you alright?"

I grip the opposite bench to steady myself. "What happened?"

The door flies open. It's dark outside and a male figure stands in shadow, save for the shock of pale hair.

Shax.

It's Demon Lord Shax.

But why?

He reaches inside and grabs my arm before I can make my mouth move.

Naexi throws herself forward and over his arm. "No! No, don't hurt her."

Something has to be wrong. There must be an urgent matter and he's acting on some order from Alastor or my demons. That's the only thing I can think of.

"I'll come with you," I shout over Naexi.

Shax's amber gaze flashes as he leans toward Naexi. "Out of my way."

I press my hand to her shoulder. "I'll be okay."

Worst case, I have the ring. But I want him away from the carriage.

"Shax? Lord Shax, I can't move standing on my dress. Please let go of me and I'll get out of the carriage."

Naexi looks from Shax to me.

"I'll be fine," I say to her with confidence I do not feel.

The last time I was alone with Shax, he tried to provoke my demons. He kissed me, and even though deep down it aroused me, that doesn't change the fact that he took liberties with my person out of a desire to provoke a conflict. Whatever his goals are, I don't believe they are peaceful and I will not allow Naexi to be a target because of me.

His grip eases and he slides his palm down my arm to my hand.

I glance at Naexi. "Everything will be fine under the sun, right?"

Her gaze dips to the necklace, and she nods slightly, then picks herself up and sits back on the bench.

The necklace is an odd piece. I can see the sigils. I know it has some magical properties. But I cannot activate it. It's the first item I've never been able to make work. But Naexi believes in it and right now I need to calm her down.

It's like a feast day at the tavern when there's been too much booze and not enough reason when tempers are flaring. This is all about managing rowdy people. If I can separate everyone, there's a chance I can resolve this without a fight. Possibly. I don't actually know, but I'll try.

I pull the skirt out from under my feet, then with Shax's assistance, I step out of the carriage.

The horses and footmen are completely rigid, as if they're statues.

Shax grabs my arm and hauls me past the line of trees bordering the road. There's a horse tied to a low limb that has to be his.

"Is there something I can help you with, my lord? I'm traveling on official business—"

Shax whirls to stare at me. He's tall and muscular. Not wide and built like my lords. Shax strikes me as someone with incredible agility and stamina over strength. His moon-white hair sticks up in all directions while his amber gaze seems to pick me apart. His features are so angular he looks cut from stone, which would explain his perfectly portioned beauty. Sweat beads his brow and his clothes are disheveled, as if he hasn't changed in days.

I close my mouth and fold my hands in front of me, hiding the two rings still on my fingers, and wait.

"What are Alastor and the twins planning?" Shax asks, no, demands.

"Twins?"

"Belial and Eligos," he snaps.

"I-I don't know."

"You're their secretary, and you want me to believe you don't know what they're doing?"

"I only handle household matters and unspelled correspondence. If Alastor communicates with Lord Belial and Lord Eligos, I don't know about it."

His nose wrinkles. "You're a good liar."

"I'm not lying. This is the truth."

Shax's lips peel back in a sneer. "You're fucking them."

I bite the inside of my cheek and stare back at him. What is it my demons have said about Shax? That he balances out some other conflict between the lords? That he isn't pleased with the way things have been?

"If you'd just talk to my lords—"

"No. No. Fucking, no." He scrubs his hands over his face. "You're all so stupid and blind. Alastor has you eating out of his fucking hand. Belial and Eligos, worst of all."

"I..."

I don't know how to respond.

Shax whirls and his hand shoots out. He grabs me by the throat and lifts my feet off the ground. I panic and grasp at his wrist while the heel of his hand presses to my throat, cutting off my ability to breathe.

"You're going to tell me everything," he growls. "I'll drag every fucking detail out of you, so help me..."

Panic fills me.

The Demon Lords are not men and I casually thought I could handle this. All because my demons have allowed me to tame them a little.

I shove my meager magic into the ring. The dome bursts out from my hand, shoving Shax back. I drop to the ground, gasping for breath, and begin crawling backward awkwardly.

Shax bares his teeth and growls before bringing his fists down on the dome so hard I can see the shield tremble.

"Oh, gods. Oh, my gods," I chant and scramble to my feet.

I flinch every time he makes contact with the dome, as if he can pierce it and get to me.

What do I do?

If I rush toward the carriage, he'll follow and then Naexi and the footmen become targets.

If I simply head to the road, there's no telling who else might get caught up in this or what stories about a rogue demon will do.

How long will the dome last? I don't have much magic and I acted too rashly. I poured too much of my magic into the ring to start with.

What do I do?

How far are we from our meeting with Alastor? Could I hold out long enough for him to grow concerned and come searching?

Shax presses his fingers against the dome and pushes. It isn't exactly as if he's pushing me, but the effect is still the same. I stagger back until I'm pressed against a tree.

"Tell me," he growls. "Damn it, tell me before—"

Shax throws his head back and howls in pain.

I side-step around the tree and gape at the bolt sticking through Shax's chest. It's as big as my fist and drips blood.

He staggers to one side and reaches up, snapping the head of the bolt off, then turned.

What the hell? Who would attack a Demon Lord?

A man, well, someone with the body of a man but a scaled, snake-like head and hood stands behind Shax. The creature's eyes are open wide.

Shax whirls and lobs what looks like a sphere of magic at the creature.

Something else darts forward, deflecting the blow.

And behind them, in the bushes, I see a familiar old woman.

The weird honey people.

It wasn't all in my head. That woman really was following me.

I whirl and guilt nips at my heels. I'm abandoning Shax, another Demon Lord. But I'm not safe with him either. My thin slippers slide over the grass as I scramble around the tree while Shax roars his rage and attacks his attackers. My heart pounds as I rush back to the road where the carriage is still locked in immobility.

Naexi is outside, running her hands over the horses. The poor animal's eyes are rolling in their head. They have to be terrified.

"Naexi! We have to go. Run!"

"Where's Demon Lord—"

"Run!"

I let the shield go, grab her hand, and dash across the road into the trees beyond. We can't stay with the carriage and hope everything will be alright. An actual Demon Lord is after us, along with other creatures I don't know.

"What happened?" Naexi asks as we crash through the brush.

"Shax was yelling and then someone shot him in the back. They shot clean through his chest."

"Who?" Naexi digs in her heels until I have to stop. She clutches my hand with both of hers. "Who was it?"

"I saw an old woman who worked for the honey candy company."

Naexi's eyes go wide. "Ammit... Run. Run as fast and far as you can. Don't worry about me."

I don't point out she can probably out-pace me with the length of her legs alone. I pull her after me.

Something crashes down through the canopy. I shriek as a falling branch smacks my shoulder. I fall sideways from the impact and roll.

"Lioria!" Naexi cries out. The next thing I know, my skin is prickling strangely. "Oh, sun above—oof!"

The prickling sensation vanishes and I roll over to see there are two strange creatures that look more animal than human. One is a snake creature with three sets of arms. He has Naexi in his grasp and she's staring at the creature with blank eyes.

The other looks as though its body parts were stitched together. Its body is like a cat's, but its front paws, chest and neck are more like a bird's. The head is broad and the mouth beak-like. Two massive wings sprout from its back. The creature is reared up on hind legs and staring at me.

"Don't hurt her. Please? Don't hurt my friend," I beg. "I-I'll go with you. I'll do whatever you want. Just, please? Don't hurt her."

The stitched-together creature says something in a sibilant language. The snake turns toward its comrade and Naexi's head lolls to the side.

She's out, I hope.

The snake creature slithers toward me with Naexi held in one set of harms close to its body. "Ride the griffin."

"The—what?"

It points at the other creature. "Griffin."

"Is that its name or—"

"Get on, now."

"Okay. Okay!"

Shit.

I look at the griffin — or is it Griffin?

Its bird-like eyes are staring at me and I suddenly feel like I'm a little girl again, about to get chased by the rooster. This is no doubt the universe getting back at me for teasing that damn bird with wooden crickets.

The thing bounds toward me. I ball my hands into fists. I'm not much of a fighter. I think I've thrown exactly three punches my whole life, and each time was to break up a bar fight. Trays and mugs are better tools. Less chance to get hurt.

The creature grabs me in its talons. The nails slice into my clothes and press into my skin. And then the ground rushes away. Branches smack me and I scream as we burst forth from the trees into the sky.

"Oh, my gods. Oh, gods."

I clench at its ankles or legs or whatever they are as it skims the top of the trees for a good distance. A clearing opens up and I see a white tent-top before we plunge downward. My head snaps one direction then the other before I'm unceremoniously dumped on the ground. I cough from the kicked up dust as the griffin, or Griffin, sits back on its haunches and looks at me.

A sharp, feminine voice speaks, and the creature backs away.

I push up and look over my shoulder at a woman wearing an odd headdress and layers of blue tunics and robes. She has a tall staff with a looped top and a short bar. Pouches and things hang from her thick leather belt.

She inclines her head. "I'm sorry if Silverquills was rough. He is young."

I glance back at the griffin. That must be what he is, then.

The woman grabs my hand and I flinch back. She moves faster than I'd expected. Her eyes have a milky blue cast to them from old age, or maybe something else.

"I'm so happy I get to meet you during my lifetime, godling."

"What? No. You must be mistaken. My name is Lioria. I'm a secretary."

The woman stands, pulling me with her. She is no old, crippled woman. In fact, I'm wondering if she's human at all.

"We will reveal all, godling. The scales will fall from your eyes and you will know—"

"What do you want from me? Where is my friend? Why did you attack Shax?"

She pulls at my arm as though I haven't spoken a thing. My options are to be dragged or walk with some dignity. I choose the latter.

The more compliant I am, the more likely they might be to conveniently forget I'm to be watched. It's the same tactic I used with the nannies growing up so that I could slip outside and go on a little adventure.

The woman leads me into a spacious tent. The inside is lined with tapestries, blocking out all the light save for what's produced by a single brazier in the middle. The floor is covered with carpets and cushions. It's like walking on a bed.

"Sit," the woman says and gestures to the area in front of the brazier.

"Where's my friend? What happened to her?" I wish Shax well, but I can't worry about him right now.

"I don't know." The woman waves her hand. "Sit."

"No. Not until I know what you did with Naexi."

The woman's lips thin and she bows her head. "Whatever you desire, godling."

"My name is Lioria, not Godling."

The woman takes a step closer and brushes her knuckles over my cheek. "Your name is a passing thing, but you are a godling."

"What?" I say before I can stop myself.

"I will reveal all," she vows and strides toward the opening of the tent, then back out.

Leaving me alone.

The moment the tent flaps open, I race to peer through them.

I only saw the griffin and woman. Are there others?

I quickly cross to the other side of the tent and begin feeling along the wall, searching for another opening, but the damn thing is solid.

Can I cut through it? Is there time?

But if I escape, what then? Without a plan, there is no point. They'd have Naexi and I can't leave her behind, like I did Shax.

Gods, I hope he was able to get away.

A bolt through the chest.

He could be out there dying, all because of me.

How? Why? And what is this woman talking about? Godling?

I've never heard of such a thing. Belial and Eligos said I'm human. Wouldn't they know?

Whatever or whoever these people think I am, it won't take long for them to realize they've made a mistake. And then what?

That question is haunting me when the woman returns with the many-armed snake man carrying a dazed Naexi.

"Is this the creature you were concerned about?" the woman says in a cold voice.

"Yes. What did you do to her?"

"She's merely in a thrall to keep her quiet and compliant." The woman flicks her hand and the snake-man gently lowers Naexi to the bed of pillows. "Gather the others. The tent needs to move quickly."

I think I hear more of that sibilant language from the snake creature before he leaves.

"Sit, please?" the woman asks again.

"What about Shax? And our footmen?"

"Concern yourself less with the fate of mortals, godling," the woman says in a firm tone.

"No. No, I will not. I don't know why you want me, but these people are blameless."

"Blameless?" The woman's brows rise. "A murdering fae, a Demon Lord, and those two mortals? Blameless?"

"Whatever their crimes might be, I don't want them hurt because of me."

"You're soft," she says, as if caring about people is a bad thing. "The fires will have to temper you into a stronger metal. Come and sit."

This time, invisible hands wrap around my arms and legs, pulling me forward. I sit not under my own power.

The tent flaps open and the man who shot Shax is followed by the familiar old woman, looking like they barely escaped their tussle with Shax.

"He got away," the old woman said.

Some of the tension inside of me eases.

Shax clearly isn't an ally, but he might put aside whatever is going on between us or Alastor in favor of helping us. Or he might not.

The two women stand over the brazier and mutter words. The tent flaps seem to seal themselves while the other creatures find somewhere to lounge on the edges of the space. The floor rolls and my stomach dips, then it feels a bit like I'm on a boat in choppy water.

"Your hand, godling."

"Why?" I ask.

The old woman in blue reaches out and grabs my wrist, then presses my palm to the smoldering coals. I've touched pans fresh out of the oven before. This is a hundred times worse. It's like I can feel the searing pain in my soul. I scream and scream and scream until the world goes dark.

BELIAL

I barrel through trees. Not around them. Not batting them aside. Through them. I feel a thousand splinters and other things, but my entire focus is on the emergency beacon. We've installed these magic devices in many places, and I can count on my two hands the number of times they've been used.

This is the first one that has me truly terrified.

Naexi, damn her, she's powerful. What happened that the damn fae can't handle?

Eligos isn't far behind me. I can sense his bloodlust. They might call me the brawler who paved hell, but there is no vengeance alive that can hold a candle to Eligos' savagery when he's angered.

The bond with Lioria feels strange. It's not right. And she's nowhere near the carriage. While everything in me screams to go to her first, we must answer the beacon. Someone at the carriage needs help, and it is our duty—our promise—to be there for them. It's one of the hardest things I've done in lifetimes, maybe my entire existence, but this is the promise we've made. We can't claim to be better than our past selves if we don't honor these promises.

Suddenly, a dark shape shoots past me.

Eligos.

Fuck.

I pause, clench my fists, and howl my frustration. At the same time, I let go. My demon screams to the forefront.

With a leap, I launch myself into the air.

I haven't done this in a hundred years.

My wings snap out and I feel the breeze catch me. Eligos is drawing ahead of me. He uses his powerful tail to launch him forward like a spring, and in short distances, he's faster. But the wind is on my side today. It takes three sweeps of my wings to build the momentum, but I'm slicing through the sky. We will have to answer for this and this moment will likely change the course of everything. But Lioria is part of us now.

The signal draws closer, much faster now that I'm airborne. The carriage horses whinny and neigh in distress. We might fool humans, but animals know.

I drop to the ground ahead of the carriage by a short distance.

The door has been ripped off and the footmen have been here long enough to secure the horses to a stake in the ground and hobble them. But both footmen are bent over a third form.

A third, familiar form that should not be here.

Any hope I'd had of banishing my demon to the back of my mind disappears. "Shax, what did you do?" I roar.

I've crossed the distance before I know what I'm doing.

A shrub bursts apart as Eligos joins us. He's wearing trousers. The rest of his clothing hangs off him in shreds. His dual rams' horns and violet aura tell me he's got about as much control as I do right now.

Shax is lying limp on the ground with a hole torn through his chest. His blood seeps into the ground. It's a miracle he hasn't bled out already, which probably means he's wearing some object to stem the bleeding and give him a fighting chance.

He expected to be attacked. He'd prepared for it. Otherwise, he'd be dead right now.

The two footmen are jabbering and backing away, but my attention focuses on my brethren. The man who has already subjected Lioria to unwanted advances. The man who has opposed every effort of peace lately. The man who only thinks of himself.

I slam my palm over the hole torn through bone and tissue. My snarl is savage as I shove power into him.

Shax throws his head back and screams as the aimless power shoves itself into every nerve ending, broken bone, and torn flesh. It's an inelegant way of healing. A way that guarantees pain and agony. Shax's face goes red. The veins on either side of his neck and across his brow stand out. His gaze stares up, unseeing, and very human.

There's little to no demon left. He's almost a stranger now.

Is it possible Shax is behind it all?

He's always schemed and plotted against Alastor. Has he finally taken it too far? And why entangle Lioria in this?

"Belial." Eligos grips my shoulder and hauls me back. His tail wraps around the base of one wing, effectively grounding me. "I want to hear what he has to say."

It's restraint I wouldn't have expected from my love.

My whole body trembles and all I want to do is rip Shax limb from limb.

Eligos looks at me. "If he says something you don't like, I'll hold him down while you kill him."

Shax coughs between sucking down air. "Fuck you both."

"What did you do?" My demon and I ask in a discordant voice.

Shax squints at me. "Holy shit."

"Shax," Eligos growls.

Shax closes his eyes and pants. "I just wanted to have a conversation with your little secretary. We were ambushed by some sort of nāga and an old serpopard."

"Ammit," I growl.

"That's a good guess." Shax's face twists into a mask of pain before easing. He pushes up and gives myself then Eligos a hard look. "Is this what you've been hiding with Alastor?"

"You don't get to ask questions right now," Eligos snaps. "What did you do? What are you after? Why, Shax?"

"Did you break the boundary stones?" I ask, cutting straight to the heart of it.

If he has betrayed us that much, then there's nothing else to say.

Shax's eyes widen. "What? No. I would never."

I'm taken aback by the shock in his too-human eyes. Shax can be cunning, but this is him without guile. Honest. I can feel it in my bones, and yet I do not trust him.

He scrambles to his feet slowly and sways. "What the fuck is happening? What are you and Alastor keeping from the rest of us? Open your fucking eyes, mate."

"It's awfully coincidental that you're here exactly when Ammit's people attack our carriage on the way to see Alastor," I point out. "What are you plotting, Shax?"

He laughs without humor. "Are you really this dense, brawler? Can you be this stupid? Alastor is using you. He's seized power for himself and he's pushing all of us out. And you're helping him do it! You idiots."

"You've always been jealous," I snarl.

Eligos' hold on my wings slips away. "You constantly undermine Alastor and want to supplant him."

Shax throws up his hands. "I force him to see the reality of things and not what his pride wants him to see. None of you see what's coming, do you? You're all blinded by—"

Pain so deep and intense it's all I am aware of stabs my soul. My bones begin to burn. I toss my head back and howl. The sound is echoed by Eligos. It's like something has reached into my body and is pulling me apart. Everything twists and turns, all while the pain continues.

Lioria.

We let her slip from our minds for a few precious seconds, but now everything in me is focused on her.

I shake my head and shove down the searing pain.

Eligos roars something and my eyes snap open.

He isn't human any longer. His trousers strain around the thick haunches of his demonic form, fully realized now. His beautiful face is twisted into pure rage I feel echoed in me.

And then I feel the surge within myself and my humanity vanishes...

LIORIA

I don't want to open my eyes again. The pain is so much worse after two and three times doing this. At least that's how many times I think we've done this. There are bits of memory, flashes of moments I don't quite recall. I can't focus on them. I need to survive.

I'm most aware of my hands. They're a bloody, blistered mess. I can smell my own flesh cooking. I don't know what these creatures think I'm capable of, and they won't listen to me.

Naexi sobs. I hear her talking to me, saying soothing words, but the pounding in my head is too great to make her out. They wrapped her in something that's left growing black marks on her skin. The light that always seems to glimmer in her eyes is dying out. But I can't do anything to help her.

This is agony. Dying would be better than this.

The old woman digs her hand into my hair, yanking my head back, and holds the pointed stick up in front of my eyes.

"Denounce the High Demon Lords and embrace your own power, girl," she demands. "Those monsters are lying to you. They're lying to everyone on this gods forsaken continent. You must save us all, girl. Show me what you're made of, godling."

I can't.

I sob, but my throat is raw and I can barely form words. I press my tongue against the bottom of my mouth to avoid biting it again. I think I swallowed part of it earlier.

"She doesn't know what you want her to do. Can't you see that?" Naexi shouts.

"You have the power to save us, godling," the old woman insists.

My limbs are too heavy. All my strength is gone.

I don't know what she's doing to me, but it isn't just burning my flesh. There's magic at work here and it is slowly sucking the life out of me each time she presses my destroyed hands to the coals.

The old woman releases me and I flop back to lie on the carpets. My eyes are grainy and swollen. I hate myself for crying.

I tried using the ring again, but without Naexi in my bubble, my effort was wasted. The woman has the rings now.

What can I do? How do I appease these people and convince them to let Naexi go?

If she is freed, she might be able to get word to my demons. I know they said they could sense my presence, but I don't know if this crone's magic interfered with that.

And what if they don't come? What if they can't? Or won't? What role did Shax play in this?

The old woman straddles me, then sits on my chest, driving all the air out of my lungs. I lift my ruined hands, but stop short of pushing her away for fear of the pain that comes with touching something. She leans over me, her milky white eyes boring into me.

"Don't hold on to your humanity, girl. You can't hide forever. This is what you were born to do, and I will make you realize that if I have to choke the life out of you myself."

Panic fills me and I buck under her, but she's absurdly strong. And heavy.

"What are you doing? Can't you see you're killing her?" Naexi shouts.

"If I have to kill her and bring her back to life in order to break her bonds to this mortal body, I will." The old woman rolls that pointed stick in her hands.

There's no doubt that she means it. Whatever she thinks I am, she thinks this is necessary. She's said it with her own mouth, *for the greater good*. There's so much certainty in her I can't doubt her belief, but her belief does not change what I am.

I'm a serving girl from a small town with no real skill to speak of. My life isn't special. But it is mine to live and I'm not ready to die.

The old woman lifts her hands up, both wrapped around that evil fucking stick. Naexi screams and the old woman scowls.

This is my chance.

I reach out, awkwardly grabbing the ornate, curved dagger at her side. It comes halfway out before catching on the sheath. The woman's eyes go wide and she brings her elbow down on my arm. I scream in pain. It feels as though my bones are brittle and breaking. I do my best to tighten my hold on the dagger, and then it scrapes free of the hilt.

I swing my left hand awkwardly, slapping her and smearing my blood over her face.

She gasps, horror twisting her features as she screams. I scream up at her, because everything in me hurts. It takes all my effort, but I swing the blade, stabbing her in the shoulder. It's not deep, and the blade falls next to me.

The crone drops the stick and scrambles back, hysterically sobbing as her shoulder smolders. And then she begins to burn from the inside out. I smell flesh cooking as she claws at herself. Her human form shudders and she elongates, expanding into a serpent form. She throws herself out of the tent, her screams only becoming louder.

The others in the tent gape at me or the entrance.

The other old woman, the one who followed me back in Privale, shrieks something, then bounds out of the tent.

This might be our only chance. I have to get to Naexi.

I grab the stupid stick and the dagger before rolling over. My hands are on fire and I'm not sure if I'm smelling my own cooked flesh or the crone's. I use my elbows to steady myself on my knees, then push up. My head spins and my stomach clenches. I will myself to vomit so I can get it over with.

Everything in me shudders for a moment and I close my eyes. The crone's screams nearly split my head.

The two snake men seem completely frozen, and I don't know where the griffin got off to.

I force myself to my feet. At least my legs work well enough. It's everything above the waist that's a problem.

"Get away from Naexi right now." My voice comes out in a rough, low voice that isn't at all like my own. It's damaged and raw.

I take three steps toward the snake men and their hooded heads swivel toward me.

The big one with the multiple arms darts through the tent flaps followed by the other, leaving Naexi to lie there, sobbing, and staring at me with wide eyes.

"Naexi?" I'm scared to get close to her. I don't know what that crone did to me, but I'm not right.

Tears streak her face.

"I don't want to hurt you," I croak.

"You have to cut the webbing off her."

I glance around, searching for the faint voice. Where is it coming from?

"Great. Another idiot. Just what I always wanted. Hey. Hypatia-wanna-be? Worry less about where I am and more about your friend. She's dyyyiiinnnnng-gggg."

What am I hearing? I don't even know what *cut the webbing off her* means.

"Gods, you're a dumb one, aren't you? Walk over to the floozy and cut the shit off her. She's only got a few moments left or you'll be down to friend count zero. Sucks for you."

I stagger over to Naexi. Her gaze is roving around, as if she's watching something I can't see.

"What if I cut her?" I whisper.

"You don't want to kill her. She'll be fine. Why do I always get stuck with the slow ones?"

My head is too heavy and everything hurts. I can't reason through the disembodied voice's words, but it's given me answers when there were none.

I reach out and slice at the black fibers that have begun covering her body.

The webbing pops back and something shrill whistles, almost like a scream. But Naexi does not appear to be hurt.

I lean over her, dragging the blade across her skin. It doesn't leave a scratch. Not even a vague white mark.

"Intent," the same voice whispers.

Naexi slumps to the floor, eyes closed.

"No. No. No! Naexi? Naexi, stay with me. Please? I'm sorry. I'm so sorry."

My tears scald my skin and my vision blurs.

This is all because of me, and I don't have the magic to fix this.

Outside, the screaming is cut short, and all is silent. But only for a moment.

ELIGOS

The pain is agony, and it's not even my pain.

The bond with Lioria burns to the point I feel the damage. I want to scream at her to give me more of it, anything that will spare her. If this is what's spilling over, I don't want to think about what she's having to endure.

Torture was once a specialty of my kind. I know the limits of the human body, how to bring it to the brink and keep them there. Unlike the others, my forte was dreaming. The manipulation started long before I had their body, and I was cruel.

I know there's no one out there to hear my prayers, but that doesn't stop me. *God, please, let her live...*

Lioria's location has changed several times. Whoever has her, they've been smart enough to remain on the move. This is one time where Belial's swiftness is working against him. He gets almost to where Lioria is before she changes locations again.

It feels like I'm running in circles, but this time when she might have moved, she doesn't.

Could it be Naexi has intervened?

Hope surges right before a spike of pain so strong my vision hazes and I barrel through a tree like I'm Belial, causing it to shatter into a million pieces from the impact. As the pain rises, so does my rage and my tenuous hold on my humanity.

I am no longer anything remotely human. A small part of my consciousness shrinks in on itself, erecting thick walls as I howl my rage and frustration. The being I have bound myself to is in danger, and I cannot allow anything to harm her. She is my hope. My everything. *My mate.*

The last word strikes a chord in me, vibrating my very being.

I was not created for this. In this state, I don't understand the driving need to protect her, but it is the rule that governs me.

My life for hers.

Nothing is more important.

I howl and surge forward, doing better to avoid trees.

Another howl answers mine. Belial. Even in this form, I recognize him. I will always recognize him.

My talons churn up the earth as I surge forward. And then I'm bursting from the trees into a clearing. There's a massive tent floating almost ten feet off the ground. I dig my haunches into the ground as a massive nāga bursts from the tent flaps. The creature is writhing and screaming.

A snarl tears up through me and I launch myself at the creature that no doubt had a hand in my mate's torture. I sink talons between the scales, into the meat of the beast, and rip. The creature whips around, sending me flying. My tail hooks around an old stump, changing my trajectory, and sends me rolling across the ground.

Overhead, clouds roll and billow behind a single dark shape. I feel his snarl before I hear it. That building rage is echoed in myself. Belial pitches forward into a dive. His wings are a brilliant flash behind him as he hurtles toward the nāga.

Two other, smaller nāga men emerge from the tent. One collides mid-air with Belial and the two tumble to the earth. I snarl as Belial and the creature with many arms tumble body over body. The nāga has the advantage of more arms and a longer, more agile body, but none of that has ever mattered when it comes to Belial's strength. I grin with pride because that demon is *mine*. Mine and my mate's. We will devour these nāga.

I launch myself at the female, hitting her almost-human torso. My tail wraps around her neck, constricting her hood while her snake jaws snap and hiss. But she isn't fighting me off. She's clawing at her chest.

That's when I notice the hole burning from her shoulder. It's a smoldering hole the diameter of my finger, but the flecks are being sucked inward. I watch it grow, expanding to eat more of her chest.

I howl and sink my talons into her. I don't know what this magic is, but I will ensure her death is the same kind of torture my mate felt. The last thing this nāga bitch will feel is loss and torment, because those are my parting gifts. The one thing in my life that was untouched by the evils of this world should not know this kind of pain. I will exact her revenge.

Something hits me. Talons sink into the meaty upper part of my tail and rip.

I twist, driving my elbow into the cool softness of another male nāga, and glance up to find a griffin has entered the fray. I strike upward, raking my claws along the griffin's belly. It screams and digs into my tail harder so I twist my tail the other way, around the creature's leg, and squeeze.

The griffin tosses its beaked head back and screams as I crush and pulverize the bone.

Did my mate scream? Did the griffin take pleasure in the sound?

Something jabs up between my ribs. I press my feet to the nāga's body and push off it. The thing howls as my talons rip long gouges from its body.

Belial has risen into the air with the other male nāga. I catch the first glimmer of magic and look away right before a deafening boom shakes the earth and sends the nāga hurtling toward the ground.

I can't let that one show me up.

Using my tail, I vault up onto the griffin's back. The creature bucks and screams. I press my hand to the creature's shoulder blades and delve into its mind, only to find someone has a hold on the creature already.

I hesitate.

I don't know why.

This creature hurt my mate. It caused her pain and made her afraid.

It should die.

And yet, I hold back.

The griffin dives for the earth, but I have a hold on it now around the body. It could not get rid of me, just as it cannot shake the hand controlling it.

I extend hands onto the astral plane, where dreams and fears are expressed so much easier, and I slice those hands holding the griffin hostage.

The griffin drops to the ground and doesn't move. It might be dead for all I know, but it is free.

The other nāga rushes me and we roll across the ground. I use my tail to maintain the momentum. The creature merely clings to me while I use the controlled roll to position us right where I want. I roll over on top of the thing and grab a branch that must have fallen when I burst onto the scene. I ram the shattered end down, into the creature's soft middle, and force it further, until the nāga is staked to the earth. Its mouth moves, but there's no sound. The single pair of arms flail and it attempts to remove the branch, but the ground is soft and clingy.

I push up to find Belial swooping toward the tent and our mate.

Yes.

I want her. I want her with everything in my being, and I will annihilate anything that keeps us apart. I throw myself into the air, ready to be rejoined with our mate. My momentum takes me deeper into the tent than Belial, who hovers in the entry. As I come to a stop, I stare across at the bloody, blackened creature already cataloging every slice in her skin and burn.

Our mate.

She isn't even recognizable anymore.

A howl of rage sticks in my throat and I want to tear those nāga wretches limb from limb. I want to peel them alive, feed their cooked flesh to them, and take my time bringing them to the brink of death, only to do it all over again. But that doesn't do her any good now.

What can I do?

LIORIA

I clutch Naexi close. I've cut all the black webbing off her, but the voice that knew what to do is gone now. She's lifeless in my arms. She's breathing and her eyes are open, but she isn't responding. I don't know what to do or where the others went. The growling and roars from outside sounded like a war, but they're gone now.

What do I do?

A whooshing sound startles me. One moment I'm alone in the tent with Naexi, the next there's a massive, winged creature looming over us. He's easily seven or more feet tall. The tips of his crown of horns brushes the sloped top of the tent.

"B-Belial?" I choke out.

It has to be.

I know those horns. He practically purred when I touched them. And those wings? They're a work of living art the way light shines through them.

"W-what happened?" I whisper. Hadn't they told me they couldn't take on their demon form?

Belial's demon form is bipedal, but his lower legs aren't human. He looks more like the stone gargoyle statues that sit atop the church back home. His facial features are longer, which makes him seem less human still, but the rest is familiar. Familiar, silver swirls break up his midnight black skin and his eyes glow a lively, bright green that somehow captures the essence of the man I've grown to care about in a single color.

"Belial?" I tentatively reach out a hand toward him.

A streak of darkness leaps into the tent, then scrambles around to the opposite side.

Eligos?

It's harder to make him out. It's like he holds the shadows around him. But the brazier light glints off those ram horns and his tail flicks around, like it's feeling its way.

"Eligos? Belial?" Another wave of tears assaults my eyes. Damn it. None of this is helping. I do my best to make my voice steady. "Please, hear me. Please, help Naexi?"

Both of my demons go unnaturally still. It's as if the world is paused for the span of a few moments.

I glance down at myself. Blood streaks my charred clothing. Most of the skin I can see is blackened or angry red.

Is it possible they don't recognize me?

"I-it's me. Lioria. Your secretary. Don't you know it's me? Didn't you say you'd know me anywhere? That you could find me anywhere?" Desperation makes the tears fall faster.

My vision blurs, but the next thing I know, unyielding fingers are lifting my jaw up. The very touch makes my nerves scream in agony, but it's more proof I'm still alive.

It's Belial's face, and it's not. It's elongated and distorted in a way, but it's still him, with his great big hands and gentle manner. I know it's him.

I reach out and grasp his wrist.

"Please, help her? Please?"

He peers past me at Naexi.

"Belial, please?"

"It will hurt," he says in a rough voice I don't recognize.

"Will she live?"

"Possibly."

Is it my call to make?

I can't let her die like this.

"Please?" I whisper.

He reaches past me and presses his hand to her chest.

Naexi's eyes blaze golden and her spine arches up until her head and heels are all that are on the ground. She screams.

And then she drops back to the ground, body limp and whole. No more markings. Nothing.

I turn toward Belial, shaking and exhausted. He's kneeling so close that I stand between his thighs. His hands hover around me, as if he's afraid to touch me.

"You came," I mutter.

I slump sideways. He catches me, but the press of his hands brings a new wave of torment through my burned and battered body. I cry out, and an answering growl sounds from the opposite side of the tent.

"Eligos," Belial snaps, and the growling stops.

He eases me to the ground and I stare up at Belial.

"How bad is it?" I ask.

His now unfamiliar face is smooth, expressionless. I focus on the deep green of his eyes, like the color of leaves at twilight. "Bad."

"Oh. That's... That's unfortunate."

"Healing will hurt."

"Will I survive?"

He lifts his shoulders.

"What's a little pain, right? Go on. If you can."

"It will hurt," he says again, as if I might not have understood the first time.

"It already hurts."

He touches his fingertips to my chest, and I hiss at the contact. The next thing I know, it's like I've touched lightning. Everything is on fire, constantly. The one thought that revolves in my mind is that I'd be better off dead.

And then it's over.

Belial has me cradled against his chest and I hear Eligos snarling something.

Belial's body ripples and I can only watch as his face shrinks and pales, then his body, as he becomes almost human. His extremities and wings remain that of the demon, but his face and chest are the man I've come to know. He's paler than usual while his eyes blaze.

"What happened?" he whispers.

"Shax waylaid the carriage, hauled her out, and then these creatures showed up. They..." Naexi closes her eyes and shakes her head.

"We found Shax. He said the nāga attacked him. He had a crossbow bolt shot clean through him."

"Yes," I say, finding my voice. "He and I were talking. He was upset about Alastor, then one of those creatures shot him."

Belial's face creases. No matter what, something is going on with Shax. Some deeper plot I'm not sure my demons were aware of.

"Why you?" Belial asks.

Naexi leans closer. "They think she's a god. They called her a godling. That woman, she was going to kill her to try to make her do something."

"She wanted me to do something. But I can't. I'm just human," I say.

Naexi's gaze falls to the necklace she gave me that's still around my neck. Her brow furrows and I wonder what she isn't saying.

"Eligos?" Belial calls over his shoulder.

I peer at the dark form of my other demon. "What's wrong?"

"I'm not sure," Belial mutters. "Could be his demon is still in control. He could be very dangerous, Lioria."

That might be true, but I refuse to fear my demons. I can't. Not after what I just went through. I need them.

I brace my hand on Belial's chest and get to my feet. He steadies me while the tent feels as though it's dipping and swirling around me.

"The nāga, they had a griffin, didn't they?" Naexi asks.

"Yes." Belial grimaces. "It's outside, but..."

"I need to see it. I need to try," she says, as though she's carrying on a conversation I only hear part of.

I take an unsteady step toward Eligos.

"Lioria," Belial says in a warning tone that's human and demon.

I hold up my hand and limp across the tent floor to where Eligos is on all fours. His tail rolls and twists around him. He doesn't have locs in this form and I miss them. I miss how they frame his beautiful face.

They came for me.

They promised they would, and they did.

I think I just fell in love with them.

Eligos growls.

"Get back," Belial snaps.

"Sh," I whisper and ease to my knees. I might be healed, but I still ache.

Eligos shrinks further away, but there's nowhere for him to go. I reach out and take his angular face in my hands.

Is that a tremor I feel?

I lean forward and press my brow to his broad forehead.

"Thank you," I whisper. "Thank you for coming to my rescue."

The somewhat familiar feel of his tail wraps around my thigh. He doesn't reach for me and he won't hold me, but he's here. He came.

I slide my hands up to cup his face, exploring the hard planes of his demonic face. There's nothing soft about him. It's like he's wearing armor, which makes me wonder, what kind of world was he born into that this was necessary?

They're all strength and brute force. It's graceful in the same way that sharks are when they breach the surface. But they were made for death all the same.

What kind of god made them? To what purpose?

"Lioria?"

I glance over my shoulder at Belial. He's wearing nothing but the shreds of his trousers. The lower part of his legs are still very much the demon, as are his hands, wings, and horns. The rest is human.

"I need to take you back to Privale."

"What about Naexi?"

"Fuck Naexi. You are my priority."

I glance behind him, but my friend is gone. "Where'd she go?"

He waves his hand. "The griffin."

Light glints off something on the carpet at Belial's feet.

The dagger, only it is sheathed now. But I didn't have the sheath.

I rise and hobble back to Belial, but kneel and pick up the weapon. "This was that woman's. I... I stabbed her with it..."

He grasps my shoulders. "Lioria."

"Take me and Naexi to Rosenburg. Tomorrow morning, we can return to Privale."

Belial growls low in his throat. "You're infuriating, woman."

"I know. I need this, though."

He scoops me up, then glances back at Eligos. "Townhouse in Rosenburg, man."

"What's going on with him?" I whisper.

"I don't know," Belial mutters.

Belial glides us down to the ground below. The tent now floats above the ground a good ten feet. I've never seen anything like it, but Belial and Eligos act as if it's not significant in the least.

We find Naexi bent over the griffin, Silverwing, working her magic while the creature makes low, distressed sounds.

"Is it dangerous?" Belial calls out.

"No," she snaps, then sobs. "They were using this beautiful creature. They mind-controlled it."

"People will be here soon. You can leave it—"

"No," she yells over her shoulder. "You can leave me."

Belial takes one look at me, then sighs.

Not a moment later, the griffin springs to its feet with a cry, rustling its wings and tossing its head back. Naexi leans against the feathered chest and the griffin bends over her, sweetly preening.

"Will Silverwing carry you home with us?" I ask.

The griffin flutters its wings and Naexi peers up at it. They don't speak and I feel as though I'm intruding on a private moment. I glance away at the rest of the clearing, and my stomach clenches.

There's a massive pile of ash, and I know without asking that's what's left of the crone. I did something to her. I don't know what or how, but she's dead because of me.

The other two smaller snake creatures are still alive, if the tail movements are any sign, but I doubt they'll last long. One is impaled with a branch. The other has a boulder on top of it.

"There was another one. The old woman I saw at the festival..."

"I believe she's dead," Belial says.

Naexi stands and the griffin lowers to his belly. I don't know how I know Silverwing is male, I just do. Naexi awkwardly climbs aboard the creature's back and holds tight.

We're a strange party, but we're alive. We made it.

 LIORIA

We didn't take Naexi home. We delivered her and Silverwing straight to a ship ready to set sail. Between the tents and Rosenburg, which was a surprisingly short trip flying, she looked completely washed out and gray.

The only thing she said is that demonic healing doesn't fix everything.

I don't know what that means or if I made a mistake. But she's gone, and I feel as though I've lost an important part of myself. I barely just met Naexi yesterday. I wasn't even certain if we were friends. Now it feels as though I've known her my whole life. And I might never see her again.

The sadness stays with me as we return to the townhouse in Rosenburg. Eligos has followed us, still in his demon form. He's so fast my eyes can barely make him out, and I know what I'm looking for.

Belial lands on the third-floor balcony and leaves the doors open as he carries me into the spacious bedroom we shared last night. That feels like a lifetime ago.

He pauses and all at once the fireplace blazes to life and the lights begin to glow.

"Better," he mutters and carries me to the carpet in front of the fire where he sits with me cradled in his lap.

"I'm okay," I whisper. Somehow. Because of them.

He ignores my words and presses his fingers to my head, then trails them down my throat to my chest. Deep wrinkles form on his brow.

"Am I dying?" I ask.

"What?" His eyes go wide.

"The way you're looking at me, it makes me think I'm at death's door."

"No. No, you're perfectly healthy, it's just—"

His words are cut off by the heavy thud of Eligos landing on the balcony. He's beautiful with the moon on his dark skin as he leans forward with one hand, bracing himself, and the other poised to strike back at any threat. I feel his gaze on me immediately and while part of me registers his presence as danger, I also don't think he'd hurt me. I don't think he can. Under everything that makes him a demon, we are bound together and I think he knows that.

"What made you change forms?" I ask.

"The footmen signaled us. We met up and made our way to them, then as they were telling us what happened, there was pain. I think it was your pain." He grips my knee and anguish furrows his brow. "Over and over again... I lost myself a little each time."

His mouth opens and closes. The distress on his face moves me to the point that I feel my eyes prickling.

Seeing as how my two demons are attuned to my emotional state and Eligos has almost gone feral on us, I need to redirect this. I need to save them from the despair fear has created. I cup Belial's face and smile.

"You saved me."

He grimaces. "It looked like you saved yourself. W-what happened?"

I shrug. "It doesn't make much sense to me. None of it does."

I recount what I can recall. Once the snake-woman-crone burned me the first time, it was a blur. I did leave out the part about a disembodied voice speaking to me. I'm not certain that was real or all in my head. I was pretty out of it toward the end before they arrived.

Belial glances toward Eligos every so often, but my other demon has crept into the far corner and sits there watching us. I don't like it. His posture makes me think of a dog, and Eligos is practically a king if we had kings here in Eden. He shouldn't be lurking in corners.

"Why don't we get you cleaned up and in bed, hm?" Belial says.

I put my hand on his shoulder. "What about Eligos?"

He bends his head. "I don't know what to do. It's like he's not responding at all."

I wrap my arms around Belial. I don't know why, but I need his nearness. The very idea of leaving to go bathe makes me anxious. I want him with me.

"He isn't hurting anything." I slide my hand up to Belial's horns and run my fingers along the sensitive skin at their base. "Let him watch."

"Lioria." He growls my name. "I am not human."

"I never expected you to be."

He pulls my hand down from his horns. "You should—"

"I'm scared to be alone," I say softly, speaking the truth.

He freezes.

I crumple onto Belial's shoulder. I'm horribly weak. All this bravery is an act. I'm doing everything in my power to be present and not let the memories suck me under.

The events of today seem more real now than they did when I was going through it. Everything that's happened in the last few weeks is so surreal.

"Sh. Sh, I'm not going anywhere," Belial whispers.

He rises with ease, pausing only to glance back at Eligos. "We're going to the bath."

I bury my face against his neck so that I feel his skin on my face and breathe deep in an effort to stem the tears. They're just leaking out and I can't stop them.

"Hold on," Belial whispers.

I turn my head to watch with one eye as the bedroom doors open without a touch from him. He grasps the banister at the top of the stairs and vaults over it. I squeal, but we fall softly to the first floor.

He chuckles. "Sorry."

"You are not," I mutter, but at least I stopped crying.

We pass the main rooms of the house to the very back, down a narrower hall. And then there's a pair of large, ornate doors swinging open. I saw it last night and I still don't quite believe this is real.

Bathing chamber makes me think of the utilitarian room back at the boarding house where us girls would take turns getting the first bath from two wooden tubs a few times a week. I'm still not used to the absolute luxury of my personal bathing chamber in Privale.

This?

This is a level of luxury I can't quite wrap my head around.

It's not a bathing tub.

It's a pool the size of my old room.

Belial must do something, because the surface of the water begins to shift. He doesn't pause to undress, just steps into the water, sinking hip-deep before bending to submerge me in the lukewarm water while his wings twitch a bit restlessly.

There are little stone seats and a floating tray of something swirling around. I think it's soap based on last night's experience.

Belial ignores my question and turns me around, taking care to undo the back of my clothes. I'm still not sure if it's a dress or a top of some kind, but it was beautiful. Now it's singed, burned up one side, and covered in blood.

I hear the clack of nails on the wood and tilt my head so that I can look through the doors at Eligos creeping toward us.

"I hate this," I mutter.

"What?" Belial whispers.

"I hate not knowing why he's being like this."

"I can guess."

I glance up at Belial. "What?"

His face is so open right now. I feel as though I'm seeing past everything to the real man under it all. "Guilt. Self-hate for not protecting you better. Failing you."

"But you saved me."

"We also failed to protect you."

"No—"

He lays his fingers over my lips. "You asked to understand. I'm a simple creature. I want what I want. So long as you're safe with me, I can accept my failure, even if I'm ashamed. Maybe I'm the less honorable of the two of us? Eligos is different."

Belial turns me in his arms so we watch Eligos prowl around the pool to the darkest corner, where he seems to blend seamlessly into the shadows save for his two golden eyes. Shadows will never make me fearful again. Not when they might be hiding my demons.

"Eligos might seem like he does nothing. He'd love for you to believe that he is lazy and good for nothing. But it's all an act. Under that carefully curated façade, he's completely devoted to those he cares about. He's devoted to our duty, to make Eden a place of peace. He's compassionate to a fault. You'd never know it, but all of our refugee programs started because of him. Oriax, Shax, and even

Alastor like to think those are the feather in their caps, but Eligos is where the idea came from. He quietly nudges our brethren to do what's right, all while pretending he doesn't give a damn. But that's his biggest secret. He cares. Deeply. And he is devoted to doing what's best. He can be oversensitive at times, and not all of the laziness is an act. He's the first person who will suggest amusements to escape dull work, but under it all? He might be the best of us. But right now, we both feel as if we've failed you. What's worse? Shax might have been behind this, and that's more difficult to accept. Tomorrow we'll have to face Alastor. We'll have to demand an accounting of what happened today, and that is on us. For not seeing the pitfalls."

I glance up at Belial behind me. "How could you, though?"

Everything he's said about Eligos applies to himself. They're so incredibly alike. *Created from the same spark*, is what he told me.

Two halves of a whole. It makes sense why they would cherish each other so much, and why they would need a third to balance them. This is where I want to be. I want to commit myself to these two and find my peace in their lives while I can have them.

I turn to face Belial and slant my mouth over his. His lips are gentle and yielding. He wants to give me what I need, but I don't just want this part of him. I want everything. His demon, his human, the intensity that drives him.

My top pools in the water. He's already undone the back, so I push it down, kicking out of it. I cling to his shoulders, pulling him down with me.

"Lioria—"

"Are you going to make me beg? Because I will. I have no shame. Belial?"

His eyes go wide and my big demon begins to flush a bright red.

"No! Not no, I mean... Ah, damn you, woman." He groans and tips his head back. "I can't deny you anything you want."

I reach out and wrap my hand around his thick cock. Each time I always think, I must not remember right. And each time I'm reminded, no, that's all him.

Belial makes a whimpering, inhuman sound deep in his throat. I lean in and kiss his neck, then lick the pulsing artery there. He shudders and grips my shoulders, putting distance between us.

"H-hold on."

"Belial—"

"One moment. Please?" His eyes are a little wild. "I can't say no to you. I want to give you everything you desire and I want nothing more than to feel you writhe on my cock. Just give me one moment?"

"Okay." I ease back from him, curious what he needs a moment for.

Belial closes his eyes and draws in a deep breath. He stands to his full height, which is taller than normal, what with his half-transformed legs. The water has grown warm and inviting. I sink down and watch as his wings slowly begin to fold tight behind him. And then his wings and horns are shrinking into his flesh. His form grows shorter. Which is still quite large by normal standards.

He lifts a hand, shoving it back through his messy red hair, and looks at me with a sensual grin. "Now, where were we?"

I ease back into the cool, stone lounge. I'm aware of Eligos' eyes on me, but right now is about Belial and me. The comfort I need is physical, and Elgios can't offer that to me without a measure of acceptance I won't force on him.

This moment is both fraught with tension and perfect. I know I'm drowning a deeper, invisible wound in immediate distraction, and I don't care. I want to remember the things worth living for. I want the pleasure that will chase away the pain, and I know my demons can give it to me.

The soft glow of the magic lanterns and the fireplace glinting off the water lends an intimate air to the room. Droplets trail down Belial's body from his hands. I trace their path down his sculpted chest and abs to the thick erection rising from the water.

He crosses the pool to grasp my knees and pull them apart.

I skim my fingers down his chest, following the trail of the water. "I thought you were wearing pants?"

"The only thing keeping them on were my demon thighs."

"We're calling those tree trunks legs now, are we?"

His fingers press into my flesh, keeping my legs spread wide. "Yes. And? I'm sorry."

I frown at him. "Sorry? For—oh!"

Belial slices straight down the short corset. The shoulder straps had already been burned off at some point, so the garment falls with a splash into the water.

I chuckle and press my hands to his chest. "At this rate, you're going to spend a fortune keeping me in clothes."

His hands skim up my legs to my hips and the waistband of the pants I'd worn under the garment. "Or you could never wear a thing. A body like yours should be admired."

The more Belial and Elgios say things like that, the more I believe them. I've always liked my shape and size. But seeing how they admire me, how their adoration has only grown, it makes me see myself in a new light.

"I'll go as easy as I can," he says as I feel his claws tearing through the fabric at my hips.

"I don't want easy. I want you."

He kneels in the water, pulling the last of my ruined clothing off me so we're both naked. He leans in, kissing my shoulder where the skin is a different texture now than before. I have new scars. My hands don't quite feel like my own. I'm both hyper-sensitive and not.

"In time, this will fade. I'm sorry I'm not a better healer," Belial whispers.

"I'm alive because of you, and that's what matters."

He leans in and kisses me sweetly. I wrap my arms around him and pull him closer, needing him more than the teasing touches.

"I just want you. Now. Please?" I whisper.

Any moment now, this might all go away.

His fingers stroke through my folds. "I don't want to hurt you."

"If you do, this feels more real," I whisper.

His eyes widen.

I grasp his wrist, guiding his fingers into me. "If all of this is a dream, if I'm going to wake back in that awful tent, I want the illusion of my demon to distract me. If it hurts, it's more real than if it's just pleasure."

"This isn't a dream," he says.

"If you're part of my torment, isn't that what you'd say?"

"I'm not the monster of dreams. That's Eligos."

I shake my head and rock against his hand. "Should I beg?"

"No. Damn it, Lioria." He leans in and kisses just over my heart. "I want this to be perfect. I want to do this right."

"If we're together, it's right. That's all that matters. I don't need perfection, just you. It's all I've wanted."

He lifts me out of the water, only to lay me on the stone lounge. I hiss at the coolness of the stone contrasted with the warmth of my body. For once, I don't long for the slow build. I want my demon now. I slide my hands down to his hips while he kisses across my chest. My nipples are aching, but he continues to ignore them, creating a maddening pulsing within me.

"Belial," I groan and pull him toward me.

"You're going to get what you want, but at my pace." Without warning, his fingers thrust into me. I arch up off the stone with a moan, but he presses me back into the water. "Are you ready to take my cock?"

"Yes. Yes, fuck me, Belial. Fuck me now, please?"

The words haven't left my lips before I feel the blunt head of his cock nudging me. This man has done nothing but care for me and shower me with affection. He's nearly come to blows with his other half out of tenderness toward me.

I lift my hips, pressing the tip of him into my channel. His features grow sharper, more like his demon, and I know Belial is fighting with himself. I stare into his green gaze while I rock my hips, fucking just the head of him.

It's a whole new sensation, as he stimulates nerves that are rarely felt together. It's intense and sends a deeper need curling through me.

"You want it?" he says in a low voice.

A shiver rushes through me and I know that I might be asking for more than I can handle. But it's yet more proof that I'm not going back to that tent.

I stare back at my demon and nod. "Yes, I want all of you inside me now."

His hands grip just below my hips as he thrusts. It's not a gentle invasion. I gasp as I'm stretched. My muscles clamp down reflexively and my vision blurs a bit. But it doesn't hurt. I moan as we stay there, my fingers digging into his biceps.

"Don't tell me that's it," I say in a voice gone husky with lust.

My words startle a chuckle out of him.

"Not at all," he says, and a little of the mischievous twinkle I've come to recognize glints in his eyes.

He flexes his hips, drawing out just a little before pressing deeper. I lean my head back and catch a glimpse of Eligos. He's motionless and watching us. I'll figure out how to reach him next, after I know they won't vanish.

It is selfish to put my assurance above their needs. But I can't take losing them. Not now that I've begun to wake up to how much I've come to care about them.

Belial reaches between us, stroking my clit.

"Oh, gods. Don't do that," I beg.

I lift my hips, eager for more of him. At this angle, I can see that maybe half his length is in me, and the thickest part of him is still to come.

Fuck. I already feel stretched tight.

Without warning, Belial draws back, then lifts my hips, impaling me on him to a deeper degree. I toss my head back and cry out.

"Fuck. Fuck. Fuck," he chants.

I writhe on him, embracing the uncomfortable stretching sensation. It grounds me, making this dream I've been living in seem real. Pain with the pleasure.

"Gods, yes. Again."

I feel Belial jolt at my words.

Is that an answering tremor? Does he want to let go as much as I want him to fuck me with abandon?

He leans over me, pressing his brow to mine.

"You precious, precious creature," he growls, and presses a kiss to my cheek.

It's sweet and teases a smile out of me.

He pulls back and thrusts while I'm still basking in his words. I howl as he slides deeper still, the invasion touching all of me.

"My lady," he growls and thrusts without respite. "Mine."

"Fuck, yes." I dig my nails into his shoulders. His hold on me is so strong I can barely move the rest of me, but my hands are mine.

His thick cock spears me down to the hilt. Finally. He pauses and we lock eyes on a long groan. It's uncomfortable, and I couldn't love it more.

"Yes, I'm yours," I whisper. "Show me how much you want me."

He rears back, withdrawing almost completely. My inner muscles quiver, but it's a feint. He plunges in, filling me up with relentless force again and again. The prick of his nails and the unyielding stone are uncomfortable enough. I have no doubt this is reality. I'm not in that awful tent. My demons are my salvation.

"F-fuck. No. No!" Belial clutches me close as his face flames redder than his hair while his eyes roll back in his head.

His cock is so thick I feel it twitching inside of me. I grin and pepper his face with kisses, grinding my hips against him while that same need continues to simmer.

"Fuck, no," he wails softly before burying his face against my neck. "No. No. No. It wasn't supposed to be that way."

I chuckle and wrap myself around him. "It was perfect."

"You didn't come close to coming. It's not perfect."

I kiss his brow and the tip of his nose. My demon has other ways of satisfying me that are nothing but pleasure, and while there's this darkness inside of me that wants to be used roughly still, I can't complain. I'm in the present. Not trapped in the past, repeating the same horrid moments again and again.

"I won't come every time, and that's not what this was about," I whisper and grin at him. I can relax now. Enjoy this. "Besides—"

A low growl almost next to my ear makes me freeze.

Belial and I whip our heads around to find Eligos next to the pool.

My reticent demon wants to play.

I grin and reach out, trailing my fingers along the thicker, lower horn to the base. As I stroke the sensitive skin, Eligos tilts his head ever so slightly toward me, and his gaze narrows.

Belial pulls out of me so suddenly I gasp and my eyes cross.

Gods, I want more.

Belial leans over me, one hand on Eligos' shoulder as if he intends to shove him back. "Eli—*no*."

I sit up and place my other hand on Belial's chest. "It's alright."

Eligos leans into my touch. I feel a low vibration coming from him. Is he...? Could he be purring? Like a kitten? Or is this some other reaction? A low growl?

Belial shoves Eligos back, earning a snarl. Belial whips his head around to gape at me. "No. You don't understand. We haven't told you—"

I wrap my hands around his outstretched arm. "It's fine. I trust my demons."

A dangerous growl emanates from Eligos and though part of me screams to run, I don't. Belial said once to never run from them and I have no intention of doing that.

He lifts me off the bench and backs into the water. "No, you don't understand. We're *physically different* from humans. Eligos isn't thinking right. He *will* hurt you."

Eligos snarls and the aura coming off him now is murderous. My thoughts scream at me to run, to flee, but my heart says stay.

"Belial, I welcome the pain right now."

His chin drops and he gapes at me.

"I love how gentle and attentive you are. No one has ever made me feel more cherished than I have with the two of you. But..." My hands tremble. Seems some of the nightmare sticks with me still. "I want you in whatever form you take whenever you need me."

Belial's eyes are so green, so vibrant, and lovely. His lips move while he struggles to find words. When he fails, he looks to Eligos, who is at the very edge of the water. He's poised to slip in, no doubt trying to sneak up on us.

My sloth demon is tenacious.

"Do you really think Eligos would hurt me?" I ask.

"I don't think he's aware of what he's doing. We aren't always... Tame."

"I think everything you said about him is true, and right now we're all feeling like we failed the other." I think Eligos is hiding in there, but I won't call him on it. Not when ultimately I still crave to be used roughly.

Belial lets me slip off the stone and into the water. My legs are wobbly while I find my footing. All the while, he stares back at his other half.

They're doing it again, even if Belial doesn't realize it. They might not be able to speak with their minds as some Vodu or Yokai are said to, but these two don't need words.

 LIORIA

I turn to lean back against Belial and crook a finger at Eligos. "Come here, you beautiful creature."

His tail slithers into the water first, breaking the tension, then he follows without making so much as a sound. I grin, despite the rapid beat of my heart as he sinks so that just his eyes and horns are visible.

"I'll break your neck if you hurt her," Belial says in a stony voice.

I elbow him gently as the end of Eligos' tail wraps around my ankle. "He won't fuck me with his tail, will he? The hair..."

The concept of being pleasured by his tail is alluring, but there's a surprising amount of hair.

"I wouldn't count on that deterring him if he gets it into his mind to do it," Belial says slowly.

Eligos drifts closer in the water and his tail curls higher on my leg, to my knee, and up my thigh.

Belial growls and splashes the water behind him.

"Not funny," he says in a low voice.

I'm trying not to laugh. The moment is so thick with tension, a little fear, and I'm already aroused.

"What did he do?" I whisper.

"Eli..."

Eligos rises out of the water, his attention on Belial while I'm trapped between two inhuman bodies. I reach out and pull Eligos closer so that there is no getting away from them. I kiss his chest and trace the delicate silver swirls that are more visible in this form.

He leans over me and snaps right in Belial's face, but Belial doesn't flinch. Instead, he captures Eligos' jaw in his massive hand and holds him there. A snarl starts low in Eligos' chest, but Belial merely leans in and presses a chaste kiss to his lover's lips, and the snarl dies.

"Give her what she wants and keep your tail away from my ass," Belial whispers.

I press my face against Eligos' chest in an effort to not laugh.

The tail around my me moves, winding up higher, around my waist with the tip coiling loosely around my neck. I gasp, but the sound turns into a shriek of surprise as Eligos lifts me out of the water using nothing but his tail.

I'm never going to get used to the sheer power of him. I kick my feet and giggle as he turns away from Belial and holds me close. I tip my head up as he crashes his mouth to mine. His lips aren't the same. Everything about this form is hard lines and ridges. But under it all, he's my Eligos. I know it. And I trust he won't hurt me more than I want him to.

He sets me on a pillow at the edge of the pool. A pillow that hadn't been there. It's a small, physical signal that I'm right. My demon is in there, and we both need to heal from this scare.

Belial hovers, watching but not interfering. I want him to relax, to maybe enjoy the show, but I appreciate his concern. I'm still not yet accustomed to having people who care about me at all hours of the day.

I wrap my arms around Eligos' shoulders, then slide one hand up to his horns. They're curved in just the right way that I want to hold on to them. He does that same vibrating, almost purring thing and I feel it on my tongue as he teases my lips and licks into my mouth. I twine my legs around his hips while his heat envelops me.

Eligos is warmer than usual. Is it because of this form? Or does he simply want me that badly?

His tail shifts my right leg to the side, opening me further while he leans over me.

He thrusts his fingers into me and I moan. My pussy is still hyper-sensitive from Belial's attentions. I moan as he roughly fingers me before drawing the digits out. He glances over his shoulder then licks those same fingers, where both Belial and I can watch. That's when I notice two of his nails have been clipped short.

When did he have time for that?

My Eligos is in there. He's merely giving me what we both need right now.

He turns his attention back to me and though I don't know this face, I've stared into those golden eyes enough that I know him in any form he'd take.

Eligos grabs my hips and pulls me forward roughly. I gasp as his cock presses into me. My sensitive muscles seem to ripple around him. I toss my head back and moan. He's even hotter inside me. It's not an unpleasant sensation. In fact, that warmth seems to seep into my muscles, making them more relaxed.

"Gods, that feels good," I mutter.

Eligos leans over me, hands braced on the edge of the pool, and kisses my neck. He begins to move, thrusting in and out in shallow thrusts. It's delicious and frustrating at the same time. I want all of him, not just a little.

I wrap my legs around his hips and drive my heels into the backs of his thighs.

Eligos rocks forward with a growl. His eyes glint with fire and gold right before his hips thrust in earnest. At least!

I moan my appreciation as he thrusts again.

Only, this time there's something not quite familiar feeling. I grasp his shoulders and struggle to orient myself.

I glimpse Belial standing back, one hand covering his mouth while he stares at me with wide eyes.

Eligos presses deeper, and it's like he's swelling, or something. I don't know.

"I tried to tell you," Belial says, but his words are lost amidst the other sounds. "Demon anatomy is *different*."

I clutch Eligos' shoulders. He presses his nose to my cheek and inhales as he grinds the now much larger base of his shaft against me.

"H-how?" I ask over his shoulder.

Eligos shudders and I think he's laughing at me.

Belial smirks at me. "You're about to find out. Just breathe."

I gasp for air as Eligos' tail tightens around me and he thrusts hard. The thicker base of him presses to my opening.

Breathe deep.

I inhale and focus on how warm and good he feels as he grinds deeper.

And then he's in me, and somehow bigger. Bigger than Belial's monstrous member.

At first, it's this uncomfortable sort of sensation as all my jiggly bits bounce upwards, and time seems to slow as this new girth settles inside of me. Eligos rocks his pelvis to mine and that damn piercing at the base of his cock catches my clit just right.

I've been riding this edge since the moment Belial agreed to fuck me. I've hungered for the sweetness of release and now it's got me wrapped up so firmly I feel as though pleasure is all that exists.

My world rotates and I'm vaguely aware that I'm now lying on another of those stone lounges with Eligos over me. He's grinding into me. Whatever it is that makes him different in this form also doesn't allow our bodies to separate. He's locked inside of me, and every time he hits some deep nerve in my channel or my clit grinds on the jewelry, I'm spiraling all over again. My toes curl. I'm digging my nails into his shoulders. I hear myself begging, but I don't know what for.

He seals his lips over mine and I whimper.

This is a new kind of torture, where the only thing I feel is his burning heat and pleasure.

A hand caresses my cheek, but every part of me is so sensitive I flinch back.

"Easy. Easy, you have to bring her down. I know it feels so fucking good buried in her tight pussy, but she can't handle much more."

That's not Eligos.

I pry one gummy eye open to see Belial embracing Eligos. He's got his lips next to his ear and now he's kissing the pointed tip jutting out.

I gasp as another wave of pleasure swells.

"Gods," I groan.

Eligos turns his head enough for Belial to kiss the corner of his mouth. Then Eligos... It's like his very form seems to ripple. Between one blink and the next, his face becomes human. He gasps and peers down at me, almost as if he's not quite ready to see me.

I reach up as far as I can and press my hand to his collar bone. "You've got some explaining to do."

My voice hitches at the end. It's as though his cock pulses inside of me and my eyes cross from the pleasure of it.

"Eli—"

"She wanted pain," he says in a voice that makes me tremble. "I'm giving her pain so good she'll never think about anything else again."

Fuck me.

Belial closes his eyes and presses his brow to Eligos' horn while splaying his hand around Eligos' neck.

My demons. I'm falling in love with them.

"You feel that?" Eligos whispers.

My heart races right before Belial whispers, "Yes."

Do they know? They said once before they could feel me. Can they sense the depth of what I feel?

It's so unfair I can't sense the same from them.

"We aren't done yet." Eligos bends over me, bumping my nose with his, then looks back at Belial. "Get in here."

I freeze, as does Belial, and for a moment we both watch Eligos. Then their gazes turn to me.

It hasn't been a minute since my last orgasm. My brain isn't fully functioning and my body has been abused then fucked to within an inch of my life.

"One more?" Eligos whispers.

Belial groans and that sound alone makes me grin. "Yes."

"This is going to be rough."

I quiver inside. "Promise?"

Belial's arms circle around Eligos' waist and he bites down on Eligos' shoulder. The look of bliss on Eligos' face makes my heart sing. Almost as quickly as the euphoria blossomed, Eligos' face creases right before his hips shoot forward.

"Gods," I moan as he grinds deeper.

"Fuck!"

Belial grabs one of Eligos' horns, bending his head back, and snarls, "You said you wanted it."

Is...?

Eligos grins and he nips the air between him and Belial.

Oh, my gods. We're together at this moment. Eligos in me. Belial in Eligos. They do their best to keep their weight off me, but it's at least four hundred pounds of muscle bearing down on me. Eligos' motions are sharp and rough, driven by the deep plundering of Belial's cock. There are hands all over me. I scream when someone tweaks my too-sensitive nipple and I crash into a cascading orgasm that seems to never end. It is the most exquisite pain.

I might only be human, but in this lifetime I am theirs.

I'm nothing more than a limp doll in their arms afterward. My eyelids are so heavy and I can't move as much as a finger. But that's okay, because Eligos and Belial seem intent on doing everything for me themselves.

Eligos washes my hair while Belial holds me, then they soap up the rest of me using a gentle cloth. I don't even get out of the tub myself. Eligos carries me up to the third-floor bedroom without bothering with a stitch of clothing. Nestled against his warm body, I don't need it either.

We don't say much. On my part, I'm not very capable. My throat has healed from earlier, but like the rest of me, it aches. Only now the ache makes me smile with contentment, which is a first.

"Think you can stand?" Eligos asks.

"Do I have to?"

A puff of breath warms my cheek. "You'll feel better."

I sigh. "Fine."

He stands me on the carpet in front of the fire. One of them thought to close the balcony doors at some point. I wrap my arms around myself as Eligos retrieves something out of a cabinet and comes back to me with a glass jar.

"What now?" I ask eyeing what appears to be some sort of cream.

"It will prepare you for round two."

I groan before I can stop myself as parts of me, especially my pussy, ache with a twinge of pain.

Eligos tosses his head back and laugh.

"I'm kidding." His smile is wider, maybe even lighter than I've ever seen it before. "It will make the ache go away."

"You're terrible. Has anyone ever told you that?"

He meets my gaze. "All the time."

The words of that crone come back to me, but I can't quite grasp them.

Eligos' fingers run along my jaw. "What is it? Where did you go just now?"

I shake my head, banishing the words. "That woman said horrible things about you."

He scoops some of the cream out of the jar then rubs it between his hands. "Like what?"

"I can't quite remember. There are these flashes, almost perfect moments I remember, then it blurs. I thought I remembered more, but..."

"Knocking on death's door like you did messes with memory." Eligos takes my arm and begins rubbing and kneading the cream into my skin.

Gods, that feels good. I want to collapse onto the floor and beg him to keep doing that for eternity.

"Was I really that close?" I finally muster the brain cells to ask.

His eyes seem to trace a meandering line up and down my body as he moves to my other arm. "Yes. Many times. I know Belial didn't want to heal you, but you wouldn't have made it if he hadn't."

"And Naexi?"

"Physically she's alive, but her kind is different. We can heal her body, but... Something was done to her and neither Belial nor I have the power to see or fix that. It makes sense that she would go to her own people."

"And then...?"

He shrugs and steps behind me, applying those talented fingers to my shoulders and neck. "I don't know."

It's increasingly more difficult to hold on to my thoughts. "What aren't you saying?"

"It's complicated." He sighs and massages down my back. "How do I distill a million years of history into something you can understand?"

I glance back at him. "Is that how old you are?"

He pats my bottom. "Never you mind about that. Naexi will be fine. And if not, she's welcome to return here. I'll make sure she knows that."

"I thought you didn't like her?"

Eligos pulls my back to his front and hugs me close. "She tried to protect you. For that alone, from now until the end of time, I will honor that sacrifice."

He says it so simply, but those words seem to stretch out for me, and for the first time I think I'm beginning to understand my demons.

When I met them, I thought this was a passing amusement. That I was the right body type and personality they could both put up with. That's the way they made it seem. But the truth is much different. They've said as much before, but I didn't accept it. I didn't understand how seriously they took those words.

"How can you say something, for all time? Where does that certainty come from?"

"It simply exists."

His hands begin to slick over my skin, spreading the cream.

I don't know if it's working, but just his hands on me like this makes my limbs feel unsteady.

Belial enters with a heavily laden tray balanced on one hand and a steaming teapot in the other with mugs dangling from his fingers. He takes one look at me and says, "She looks ready to fall over. Put her in bed."

The two fuss over me until they've rubbed the cream into every inch of my skin. And I mean every inch. But they make no further move to be intimate. I'm not sure if I'm disappointed or relieved to find myself between them being fed by Belial while Eligos holds a mug of my favorite spiced tea.

The mood has changed. They're somber. I keep catching them staring off into the distance deep in thought. It's not exactly the mood I'd expected after what we shared in the pool. But those moments don't cover up everything else that's transpired since I left this morning.

"What will happen tomorrow?" I finally ask.

They both swing their heads toward me and stare.

I glance from one to the other with no answer. "I don't remember much from earlier, but I do remember that Shax was distressed. He was upset about Alastor blinding you both to some truth."

Eligos and Belial share a look.

I cross my arms over my chest. "You're having a conversation without me."

Belial sighs and holds a piece of cheese and bread to my lips. "This business with Shax is..."

"It's been a long time coming," Eligos finishes. "Don't look at me that way. We both know that sometimes Shax goes to extremes. He's done nothing but cause problems ever since we were fifteen again. I think this time he's gone too far."

"What's too far?" I ask around the food.

"Someone inside our borders had to have broken the boundary stones," Belial says.

"And you think it was Shax?" I frown. "That... No, that doesn't sound right. Shax was frantic. He was worried about something."

Eligos smooths his hand over my knee. "You don't know Shax like we do."

"You're saying you believe he's betrayed not only the six of you, but the very country he helped create? That doesn't sound right."

Belial takes advantage of my open mouth and shoves more food in. "It's the only answer that makes sense. He knows he's revealed himself. We've given him until tomorrow morning before we go to the capital and inform Alastor what he did. After that..."

He doesn't finish his sentence, but it feels final.

After this, there may only be six High Demon Lords.

"Tell her the rest," Eligos says.

My gaze swings back to Belial, who is rubbing his neck.

"We think people from the continent have been planning an invasion. Broken boundary stones. Raids on our southern shore."

"Southern shore?" I take the mug from Eligos and sip quickly. "But no one lives there... It's all wasteland still."

"That's not entirely accurate," Belial says slowly. He sighs and closes his eyes. "When we decided to take this continent, there were other people who already lived here. Most of them were receptive to our plans for taking control of the land. The land here wasn't... It wasn't well, and we had a plan to fix that and make life easier. There was a settlement of a few thousand people who did not, but we'd already started immigrating people. We had a minor conflict, and it was decided that in the interest of peace we would respect their wishes to be independent so long as they kept their distance. They moved to the southern shore and have flourished there. At the height of their population, there were three cities. Famine, weather, and politics shrank them to one city and a few settlements. But two weeks ago when we went by to check on them, we found the city empty, save for the bodies left behind to rot."

I sit in shock, taking all of this in.

"I still can't see Shax trying to tear it all down," I say.

Belial leans in and smacks a kiss on my cheek. "That's because you are wonderful."

Eligos grimaces. "Shax is a greed demon. Sometimes that overrides what we think we know about him."

Nothing they say is changing this certainty I feel.

"I am concerned about what happens when we reach the capital," Eligos says slowly.

Belial nods.

"Will one of you explain?"

"It's hard to explain when we don't have Naexi's knack for seeing the future." Belial tugs the blankets up over my lap.

I'm growing sleepy now that I've eaten a small feast's worth of food.

"What Belial means is that if we have to hunt Shax down, that leaves you unprotected, in a way. Given the nature of our relationship, that makes you our weak spot."

"Then don't tell anyone." I shrug. "I continue on as your secretary you occasionally fuck senseless."

They both let out twin snorts and begin hiding their faces while smothering their laughter.

"What? What's so funny?" I demand.

Eligos' hand slides up my knee to my thigh. "Darling dream, no one is going to see you with us and think, that's their secretary."

I roll my eyes. "Then I wear the glamor of an old man you dote on because he's like your favorite uncle."

Belial lays back, his arm over his face, and mutters, "That is not the visual I want right now."

"Fuck no, which is why it's perfect." Eligos kisses my arm then takes my mug from me.

There's nothing said, but they pull me down to fit between them in a tangle of limbs.

In the quiet of our bed, it's hard to ignore the growing discontent inside me. There are periods like today where everything else drowns it out, but when it's just me, I feel it and I hate myself.

What's wrong with me that I am not content? What more could I want? Am I some selfish, depraved creature that can't be thankful for what she's been given?

I'm growing to love these men, so why is their affection not enough?

PAN

F orerunners, my furry ass.

More like a collection of idiots that can't find their balls.

How pissed was I when I decided this was a good fucking idea?

I've been following this bunch of rabid boot lickers for almost two gods' damned weeks. This is hands down the stupidest thing I've done since playing got your nose with one of those archangel fellows that's all eyes.

Every night, we huddle around the smallest of fires that never warms more than my fingers while the morons talk about the High Court this and the High Court that.

Fools will never see the table scraps from the High Court. They won't ever get a thank you, either. Besides, the whole notion of the High Court is utter pig shit. It's a fanciful dream beings with little to no power have of a peaceful, fair future once the evil Demon Lords have been brought down.

If I've learned anything at all, it's that the grass is never greener than where you shit last.

I've lived longer than I should, thanks to that fucking archangel bastard. In all that time, I've never seen a culture that has enjoyed a peace longer or more complete than those who reside in Eden. It's not perfect. There's a lot about this place that's fucked in the head. But when it comes down to the brass tacks, no one in Eden goes to bed hungry. There are very few types of people or beings that are discriminated against, and by comparison, the snubbing they receive here is a world away from simply being killed in the rest of the world. The medical magic here is unparalleled. There's almost never a child born with a disability anymore. And if they are? The government makes sure they have what they need to live a normal life.

It's a cushy life compared to the rest of the world. So what if history is rewritten a bit? There are conflicts still being waged now that began thousands of years ago. Would it be so bad to simply wipe them away?

This is not the world I was born into, and maybe that gives me a different perspective than these younger fools.

I tug the hood down to block out the early morning sunshine. Out here in the waste, the sun can bake you, then the night freezes you to death. It's cruel. And we've been sitting around with our thumbs up our asses doing jack shit for three gods damned days.

I pace through the growing camp and find another fire to stare into while listening to more idiots talk about the honor of being a forerunner.

Two weeks ago, I thought the forerunners must be highly skilled agents infiltrating the borders of Eden. Now?

I think they're all lambs sent to the slaughter. But why here?

We're in the biggest stretch of wasteland in the Cogruiria province under High Demon Lord Valac's watch, some distance south and east of the capital in the central province. There are mountains between the capital and us, but no major cities.

Were I the type to march an army straight into a conflict, this is a pretty damn good spot. But, these weaklings don't know the first thing about surviving. Most didn't bring enough water with them and have begun asking if it's safe to drink piss.

What's everyone gathering for? What's the greater purpose? They all keep going on about what an honor this is to serve the High Council, blah blah blah. I've never heard so much bullshit in all my life, but something is certainly up.

Suddenly, people start cheering from across the camp. There's probably five hundred creatures here, very few with any real magic. It's like they were all selected because they are the weakest their race has to offer. Is that how they're getting past the boundary? For what purpose?

I squint and make out a figure swathed in dark clothing hovering in the air. He has his arms held out as if he's accepting the crowd's adoration.

There's some jostling as people become aware of this presence and I let the crowd draw me forward. I don't want to get too close. Any creature that's been

around a while might very well know me. I push through the press to the fringes
of the crowd then circle around for a better visual, but he's turned his back toward
me.

Why is he is somewhat familiar?

The figure turns in the air and begins to speak. "Forerunners who have com-
pleted your pilgrimage, I salute you."

No.

There's no way.

My eyes must be deceiving me.

"Your time is now. Let the invasion of Eden begin!"

A magic charge zips through the air. It's so potent I can taste it.

The man next to me leans on my shoulder.

"Back off, mate," I snap and push him off, only for the man to slide to the
ground.

I glance down at the slightly lavender skin of the man with dark, almost black
blood trickling out of his nose.

Around me, others begin to choke, going to their knees while others simply
topple over. And below us, lines etched into the earth begin to flow.

The pieces begin to click together.

I dive to the ground and pull the downed fellow over the top of me. He's already
expired. Whatever ceremony or item they all carry, it isn't affecting me.

It's so obvious now that the pieces are in front of me. There are a few times in
my life I've brushed death. Now is one of them.

The lines begin to glow, then rotate as more life energy is shed. There's something so very potent about the magic that comes from the act of death. Five
hundred or so souls all expiring at once?

The ground rumbles and I force myself to keep still as the death magic washes
over me.

The protections on Eden's borders would never allow an army to come ashore.
And no one has been able to get a magic user of any great skill past the boundary
either. Until now.

I watch through the cooling bodies as an army steps through the portal, yawning in the distance, and keeps coming.

War has come to Eden.

LIORIA

I wake with a start. I'm alone, lying on my stomach. Only this morning, I don't allow my mind to race away from me. I reach out and feel the bed next to me on either side.

The linens are warm, as if they just got up.

Judging by the light streaming in through the windows, it's early to mid-morning. I roll over and stretch my limbs, pleased to find they aren't as sore as I feared they might be.

The desire to lie here and bask in simply existing in this moment is strong. I've recalled bits and pieces of yesterday. Every memory leaves me with another question.

If the rest of the world sees my demons as the offenders in some near-constant conflict, how did it start? What truth is there to what the crone said? And do I want to know? Will it change the growing affection I have for Eligos and Belial?

Naexi had said the words, *ignorance is bliss*, to me at some point. I feel it more acutely now.

"I'm going to wake her," Eligos says from outside the bedroom.

"She's already awake," I say.

Eligos strides through the doors dressed and a haunted look on his handsome face. I sit up and clutch the blanket to my chest.

"What's wrong? What is it?" I ask.

"A lot is happening very quickly right now. We don't have time to explain, but I need you ready to go as soon as possible. Belial will do his best to explain along the way."

"O-okay. You're scaring me."

He comes around to the side of the bed, grabs my face, and drags me toward him for a kiss.

"I'll see you in the capital," he says, then turns around and leaves.

The capital?

We were supposed to return to Privale.

I sit there in shock for a moment longer. I hear a door bang below and that sends me scrambling from bed.

There are clothes in another room that were delivered by Naexi's people yesterday. I tear into a box and put on a sensible enough dress. It has pockets, so it's worlds better than most of the garments my lords had made for me.

What man doesn't think a woman wants pockets in this day and age?

Honestly, what would I do without Naexi?

My breath catches and I pause, getting dressed as a wave of sadness sweeps me.

I hope she's safe. I hope whatever was done can be fixed. I'd like to get to know my friend better.

"Lioria?" Belial calls out.

"In here."

No sooner are the words out of my mouth than he's there. He, too, looks grim.

"I'm almost ready, just, oh, okay then..."

Belial grabs the back of my dress and begins doing up the laces.

Unlike Eligos, Belial wears trousers and boots with an untucked shirt. It's sloppy and what I'd expect from Eligos. Has something happened to make them change roles?

"I've done all I can from here. Do you have a hat? You'll be more comfortable wrapped in something."

"What? Why?"

He turns me in place and takes my left hand. He pulls the rings that were taken from me out of his pocket and slips both onto my fingers. For a moment, he just squeezes my hand. He takes a deep breath and meets my gaze at last. "An hour ago, a large spell was cast from within Eden's borders. Scouts were sent from the capital. Two sent messages back, but none have returned. There's an army marching toward the capital from the wasteland right now. I must return to Privale to muster the troops I've been training, then you and I will fly to the capital where I will... I will have to leave you."

"W-what?"

"Are you ready?" His words are clipped and devoid of emotion while his eyes are in agony.

"Uh, no. My necklace and bag. Then, yes." I pat my chest.

Belial pulls the necklace from his pocket and carefully slips it over my head. "I wasn't going to tell you this, but I think this necklace saved your life. I don't understand the magic or what Naexi intended by gifting it to you, but never remove it. Understand?"

I don't know if he means to frighten me, or if the events of today are simply that scary. I clutch his arm and do my best to not overreact.

"The bag is in the bedroom, yes?"

"Yes. I'm ready," I say.

He reaches back and pulls his shirt over his head.

Fly.

He intends to fly us to Privale.

"Cloak?" he says.

I whirl and grasp madly for the one I left in here yesterday morning.

Belial takes the garment from me and wraps me in it before picking me up like I'm a babe.

"We'd already given orders for everything to be taken to Privale. I've left a note to reroute to the palace." He carries me back through the house to the balcony, pausing only long enough for me to loop the strings of the pretty bag around my wrist twice. One moment he's just a shirtless, attractive man. The next, his nearly transparent wings flutter in his wake. "I sent a note ahead to Teill to tell her to begin packing both your things."

Without warning, he launches into the air. I clutch to his shoulders and squeeze my eyes shut as we swoop low then begin to soar. In a matter of moments, the city is but a memory. It's a gray, dreary day, as if it knew something awful was going to happen.

The wind whistling past us makes it impossible to talk. Or, Belial is preoccupied. Either way, I pull the hood of my cloak around me and do my best to be as still as possible.

How could this have happened?

I get no answers on our journey. I estimate it took us only an hour and a half to make the journey compared to the two hours it took to go there. Belial lands on a great balcony in the wing that contains their bedrooms. It was locked when they were away and I've never glimpsed these rooms.

Teill pops into sight the moment my feet touch the ground. She's practically sheet white and twisting a rag in her hands. She dives at me, embracing me so tight it's hard to breathe.

"Gods, you're safe? You're really safe?" she blubbers.

"Yes, I'm fine," I say, though that's not the total truth. I have scars now. I'm changed in a way I don't fully understand yet.

"Teill, is everything ready for our departure?" Belial asks as he throws a shirt on and hastily tucks it in.

"Yes, everything on the emergency list has been accounted for and packed." She glances at me. "I packed the entirety of your things as well."

"Thanks," I mutter.

"Lioria?" Belial glances at me while doing up the buttons on his vest. "If you need anything from the office, please get it now, then come back here. After I've given the marching orders to the men, I'll be back to collect you and go. Teill, when do you leave?"

"As soon as you leave."

"You may go now," he says.

Teill doesn't move.

He glances from me to her and back. "I won't be long."

Belial strides from the room while Teill and I watch. We both start when the door shuts a little harder than necessary.

"Did he have wings, or are my eyeballs not working properly?" Teill demands.

"Yes, he had wings."

She gapes at me.

I blow out a breath and walk into the room, taking in the worn, dated furniture that seems to be well-loved. It's tidy, but that's all Teill's doing, no doubt.

"This came. I didn't look."

I turn to see her holding a single piece of folded paper.

I grimace and take it from her.

"Were you really taken? What happened?"

I reach out and grasp her hand. "I don't know where to start. It was an eventful trip."

"Do you need anything from the office?"

I lift the letter. "Just this."

"You going to read it now?"

"I'm a little scared to."

"I'll make you a cup of tea and bring you a snack. Then you can catch me up with what you can until you leave. How's that?"

"That sounds lovely."

I'm absolutely starving.

Teill winks out of sight. She might still be there, reading over my shoulder for all I know, but I don't care.

My dearest Lioria,

I'm afraid I don't understand the meaning of your letter. As a close confidant of my brethren and someone who shares a mutual interest in education, I've enjoyed our exchanges. I'm sorry if you've gleaned some meaning from my words that I did not mean. Please, show me where I stepped out of line so that I may clear this up?

Always yours,

Oriax

I frown at the lines.

Does he think I'm stupid?

I suddenly wish I hadn't burned those pages. My conscience got the best of me, and now I can't produce the letters. It's his word against mine, but in my heart I know I was in the wrong.

While I don't believe Shax is behind this invasion plot, he has done something. I don't want to give my demons more reason to vilify Shax, but I need to confess to them the entirety of what I know about Shax and Oriax. Maybe that will appease my conscience?

I sit and wait, which is all it seems I'm good for these days.

BELIAL

I had every intention of concealing my demon's power from the others. An invasion and Shax's betrayal changes everything. I feel as though I caused this. As if me confessing my worst fears in the cave below, Rosenberg somehow made this happen.

I glamour our arrival from any watchers and land on the wide balcony outside my quarters at the palace in the heart of Vlila. I'm not the least bit surprised to find Eligos has beaten us here and is lounging inside.

He isn't idle, though. He stinks of pigeon dung, which means he made a trip to retrieve our communications from our network of spies. I wouldn't say that we are good spy masters, but we are unexpected. Deception has never been something either of us is known for in all our history. We are both cut from a simpler, more straightforward cloth.

In the old days, I didn't wait to gather intel. I just smashed those I didn't like.

"What news?" I ask as I carry Lioria through the wide doors.

"Nothing much." He lounges on the large sofa. "The others are either here or on their way. Apart from what the scouts reported, and we were told earlier, we don't know anything else. I was thinking you or I might should have a look."

"Is that safe?" Lioria asks, then winces. "I guess nothing is really safe now, is it?"

"No, my dream. I'm sorry."

I squeeze her a little tighter to my chest.

Eligos and I, in our demon forms, could do a lot of damage to an army. But at what cost?

"What are you thinking?" Eligos asks.

I glance at him and frown. "Things I would prefer Lioria not hear."

Eligos' face softens. "We cannot save her from the truth."

Lioria smacks my shoulder. "I want to know. What? What is it?"

I sigh and sit with her cradled in my arms. Very soon I won't be able to do this and I'm greedy.

"I was just thinking that Eligos and I, in our demon forms, could probably reduce the army by half."

"But at what cost?" Eligos asks, finishing the thought.

I nod. "Exactly."

"Do we...?" Lioria shifts. "Do we know why this happened? Can we replicate it? Make it happen again? What changed?"

Eligos and I lock eyes.

Her.

She's the only thing that changed.

Something about her calls to our demons. We knew it when we met her, we just never expected this.

"I suppose it's the training we've been doing with the troops," Eligos says slowly.

It's total bullshit and we both know it.

She furrows her brow and taps her chin. "Oriax sent me a book some time ago. It is an index of fairy devices. Maybe I can find something in there that will help?"

That news makes me pause.

Oriax sent her presents. Right under our nose.

"That's a splendid idea," Eligos says in a tone far too cheerful.

He picked up on that, too.

I want nothing more than to tease more information out of Lioria, but an invasion looms. "We should go see Alastor. We need to tell him about Shax and how all this began."

"Yes." Eligos grimaces and gets to his feet.

Lioria stands between my legs and stretches. "What should I do?"

"Stay out of sight for now," I say. "When Teill arrives, study your book, but do nothing to draw attention to yourself. And stay in this suite, understand?"

She frowns at me.

Eligos turns her to face him. "This is serious."

"Even with a glamour?" she asks.

"Yes." He bends and presses a kiss to her brow. "When the others learn we can shift, they might think it's something you did. If there are spies in the castle, you become a target. This wing is spelled so that only the seven of us may come and go. Anyone else must have our seal."

"Still have my ring?" I ask over my shoulder as I pull the rest of my clothes out of the bag. Of course, she does. I put it on her myself this morning.

"Yes." She lifts her hand and frowns at me.

The ring has changed forms. It's no longer the heavy signet ring. Instead, it is a slim, gold band that looks a lot like the wedding rings of old.

"Stay with Teill," Eligos says and pulls his signet off as well. He slides it onto her other hand with no fanfare at all, but I note the action. This is significant. She's under both our protection and all others will know it. "She'll protect you. Until then, stay here."

I'm barely dressed, but this cannot wait any longer.

Lioria will be safe in here.

I repeat that over and over to myself before I gather her close and kiss her.

This war needs to be dealt with quickly because I have so much to get back to. Why, after so many years of peace, has war come to our shores? Why now?

Eligos turns Lioria, then bends her backward for a kiss. She squeals and clutches at him, and I smile at the image they make. I want to hold this moment in my mind forever.

This is worth fighting for. It's worth putting everything on the line for.

They are mine on the deepest of layers. My soul will seek them out for all eternity after this. I just know it.

"Come on," Eligos mutters.

I nod because I no longer trust myself to speak.

We leave my suite and set a fast pace, striding through the Hall of Demons to the more public area. People are bustling about, and there's an undercurrent of fear.

The one thing we haven't done is prepare our people for war.

"We must do whatever is necessary to end this quickly," Eligos says.

"Agreed."

"Where is the line?" he says softer, for my ears alone.

I know exactly what he means. "I don't intend to tell them about her."

"Even if she is the key for us all to shift? We could end this conflict in the blink of an eye."

That statement makes me pause. "Do you think they know? Whoever is behind this?"

"That's the logic that makes sense. Why send an army to slaughter unless you think they have a chance?"

I glance at Eligos. "Or as a distraction..."

"Fuck," he mutters. "I'm not thinking clearly. I'll defer to you."

"Am I making the right decision?"

He doesn't answer and I don't know.

Lioria's influence was immediate. We met her, we knew something was different, and over the course of the last few weeks, our demons have woken up. She didn't do anything. She simply existed and drew us into her orbit.

"We need to talk." Eligos grabs me by the arm and pulls me into a room. It's some sort of scribe room, but the desks are all empty.

"What is it?" I snap. "What now?"

He closes the door and turns to face me. "I meant to pull you aside today and talk about it, but there's no time to..."

"To what?"

Eligos tips his chin up. He's so fucking handsome, but there's an air about him that makes me uneasy. "My demon called Lioria my *mate*."

"What?" I blurt out.

"We don't have mates. That's strange, right?"

"Uh... Yeah..."

"Don't do that." Eligos points at me. "Don't."

I grimace and look away. "I can't help it."

He grabs me by the front of my shirt and drags me closer. "You can be jealous. I'm telling you, because I'm hoping your demon is just a little behind mine. We always said my demon was more awake. It's logical that this would happen to me first."

"What was it like?" I ask.

Eligos glances down and his expression grows dark. "It was back in the tent, I think. I was so angry... I kept thinking, how could they do this to her? How could they do this to my *mate*? I was thinking it before I realized what I was doing."

"Is that why coming back was hard?"

"That..." He grimaces, then sighs. "That was guilt."

I nod. That's what I'd expected. Eligos always did feel deeper than I.

"We won't fail her again." I grab him by the front of his shirt and pull him in for a kiss.

It's brief and crushing and I think I taste a little blood, but it's perfect. We break apart, grinning as two humans enter and stop gaping at us.

I nod and gesture at the door. "Excuse us."

"Lovely writing, lads," Eligos says.

The desire to laugh sends me striding from the room. Oh, the rumors that will be swirling by the end of today...

People move out of our way as we near the central chamber where historically we have deliberated. It's a circular room with a matching table. No doubt Raum's design. Under the muscles and scowls, he's quite the romantic.

I pause just in the door, surprised to find that Eligos and I are the last to arrive.

No one is speaking, and the silence is thick enough I could strangle someone with it.

Shax's seat sits empty.

Alastor sees us first. His eyes go wide, as if he wasn't expecting to see us. Or maybe my face is a mess after that kiss?

Oriax glances up from the book he's leafing through. His long robe is rumpled, as if he rolled out of bed and came straight here. "Look who finally decided to show up."

Raum throws up a hand. "Don't start."

Eligos closes the doors behind us and the air hums for a moment as the spells etched into the walls activate.

"Wait, where's Shax?" Valac asks.

"That's what we need to discuss," I say and look at Alastor.

He doesn't seem surprised. Did he already know?

None of us made it to the meeting with him yesterday, either.

Alastor must be somewhat aware. It's the only thing that makes sense.

"I fear that Shax has betrayed us," I state, ripping the bandage off.

Raum snorts. "Be serious."

Valac's eyes go wide in his delicate face. "Shax? No."

Alastor clears his throat. "Tell us from the beginning?"

Eligos takes over, recounting what we know about Shax's waylaying of Lioria's carriage. The business with Ammit's people, however, we leave out. There's no way to explain that without muddying the waters.

What matters here is that Shax showed intent to harm one of ours and go after Alastor.

"What happened? Valac asks. "Where did he go? How did it end?"

"A huntsman shot Shax with a crossbow bolt and saved our secretary," I say, hating the lie.

"It's just stupid enough to be believable." Oriax thumps his book closed and rests a hand on the back of his seat. "Knowing that idiot, he has some poorly thought out scheme. I don't know that I'd call this a betrayal, but it does explain why he is scarce."

All eyes turn toward Alastor.

It's no secret Shax and Alastor have had issues as of late.

"Let's talk about the pressing matter." Alastor gestures and an illusion of the wasteland with the invading army appears on the table. "What are we going to do about them?"

LIORIA

There is nothing more maddening than inactivity during conflict.

By the time Teill appears almost four hours later, I'm starving and an anxious mess. Thankfully, Teill is literally the best and thought ahead to bring a simple meal of cold meat, cheese, and bread. It's a relief to sit on the floor in front of the fire and eat my feelings.

She sighs and waves the knife at me. "You're going to get sick eating that way."

"I can't help it. What if Shax is here? What happens if they all get into a fight?"

"Then the best thing for you to do is stay out of their way."

I groan and lean back against the sofa.

Her answer is sensible and I know it's for the best. What could I possibly do against a Demon Lord?

I already know the answer to that question.

Nothing.

"You have so little. I did pack up all your personal items and bring them up with me. Did you mean to forget that bag with the box and dagger in it?"

"Box and dagger?" I ask slowly before it dawns on me.

Naexi's letterbox.

And that strange dagger I held on to.

I must have set them down when we arrived at Privale.

I shrug. "I completely forgot about it in the rush. I hadn't realized I'd left it. Thanks. There was a book on my shelf. Do you happen—"

Teill reaches into the massive knapsack she's been hauling around and produces the green, leatherbound volume.

I gasp and reach for it.

Teill snatches it back. "Wipe your hands first, you heathen."

"Sorry. Sorry." I quickly wipe my fingers on the cloth she gave me instead of my skirt, as I'm in a bad habit of doing.

I settle back against the sofa and begin flipping through the book.

"What are you hoping to find?" she asks.

"It's an index of all the known fairy devices. I'm wondering if there's something in here that might stop all this needless violence."

"You're looking for a weapon?"

"Hopefully, not. No. Just something."

"Lioria, your heart's in the right place, but... I'm afraid what needs to happen is to meet violence with violence. It's the only thing people from the continent will respect. Can you do that?"

I think about that for a moment. "Can I do something terrible to protect the people I've come to care about? I think the answer is yes. If I can do something that will save ten lives, isn't it worth it?"

"That's an answer only you can give."

I flip through the pages, skimming words, but my mind is racing through a hundred different topics.

"Teill?"

"Hm?"

"What do you know about Ammit's people? The candy makers?"

"Well... Ammit was a deity of the underworld. The candy has sort of kept his following alive and thriving. That's all I really know."

A loud chime sounds through the suite and I jump.

"That will be a message." Teill rises and leaves me for a moment before returning with a slip of paper. "Meeting is over. Will see you for dinner. Take Teill with you everywhere. What's this?"

I twist to look at her. "Would you mind showing me to the library?"

In a place like this, there must be books about Ammit. Maybe a few about the continent? I don't recall everything that was said in that tent, but I have questions.

"Fine." She plants her hands on her hips. "Now or later?"

"Now, please."

When I asked Teill to take me, I thought it would be a quick stroll. The problem with arriving by air is that the palace in Vlila is practically a city itself. It took us the better part of an hour to simply walk across the whole thing to the main library. Because of course, there is more than one.

It's alarming to see the fear on so many faces. I've watched servant after servant drop something, run into someone else, snap, and a few break out in tears.

War isn't something we know how to deal with. It's something that plagues the continent. The people here are completely unprepared.

That makes my resolve to find a solution even greater. I know my two demons will do what they can, but what if it isn't enough?

The moment we step into the library, the general noise of the rest of the palace subsides. The air of anxiety and fear lessens and I can breathe.

"What exactly are you looking for?" Teill asks as we venture deeper into the library.

For a moment, I stand and stare.

I'd thought that the library at Privale was lavish. That is nothing compared to the floors above us I can see lined with bookshelves.

Most of Vlila is carved from a sparkling white granite. It's a bit cold and sterile looking. But these stone-carved bookcases with the pointed arches above them are glorious.

"H-how do you find anything in a place this grand?" I whisper. "I'm used to one-room libraries where I can browse everything in a day..."

"Can you imagine how much dusting a place like this takes?" Teill mutters. "I hear there aren't any Brownies in Vlila. I bet there's dust everywhere."

I chuckle as she pushes her sleeves up and eyes the first shelves.

"I'm going to have a look around," I say and strike off toward my left.

Teill doesn't follow.

I skim titles that make no sense to me and flip through a few volumes in a language I don't recognize. I don't know how long I wander, finding topics about the stars or marine life, whatever that is. But nothing about Ammit or fairies or the continent.

"What are you lurking about looking for, treat?"

I gasp and whirl around to find Oriax blocking my path. The light from the windows falls over his face, making his golden hair gleam. He's beautiful in a way that takes my breath away and makes me very frightened. I still recall how he froze Kirra in place.

He leans a shoulder against the bookcase and studies me. "I haven't heard from you."

"I was traveling."

"Did you receive my last note?"

I don't know how to respond to that. I want to ignore it all happened.

"Actually, it's perfect timing. I met some lovely people from a candy company. They talked a lot about someone named Ammit? I was hoping to find something to read about them to take my mind off..." I wave my hand, unsure how much I should say. "Is there a guide somewhere about how books are shelved?"

One side of his mouth quirks up. "Yes, there's a system, but you aren't going to find anything about Ammit here. This is the reference library. You'll find all manner of topics relating to science, history, and politics."

"Oh... I wasn't aware there were different kinds of libraries."

He smiles at me and I feel as though I'm the fish who just got caught in a net. "Yes, we outgrew this one a long time ago. There are four. One is for Demon Lords only. I'm afraid what you seek is there."

"That's too bad..." I glance away because I don't want to look at him when I ask this question. Eligos and Belial won't be happy, I've asked. "There is another question."

Oraix takes a step closer. "And what might that be?"

"I've been going through the book you sent me. Are all of those here? In Eden?"

"Most, yes. Some were destroyed."

I nod. "Then are there any weapons among them? Weapons that might end this?"

He closes the distance between us. He smells spicy, with just a touch of the ocean under it all. There's something darkly sensual about Oriax that appeals to me. But I have Belial and Eligos.

What is wrong with me? Don't my demons deserve my loyalty? Why am I drawn to this man?

I need to step away now.

Oriax bumps my chin. That breaks the spell and I step back. But not quickly enough. In one quick move, I should have seen coming, Oriax wraps his arm around my waist, bringing our bodies flush together. He's tall and lithe compared to my demons, but no less strong as he lifts me to press my back to the shelves. He presses his face to my neck, running his nose up to my ear.

"P-put me down," I whisper, and brace my hands on his shoulders.

His lips graze my jaw. "Say it like you mean it, and I'll consider your request."

My body begins to tremble. I should just shout it. Tell him to get the hell away from me. Instead, my voice comes out as weak as I truly am. "This isn't funny, Oriax."

"You're right." His voice deepens into an almost-growl. "It's not funny at all this idea of you taking up arms to protect us. If you were mine, you'd be locked up safe somewhere..."

"I am not yours," I manage to say with some backbone.

"Not yet. You need to fight this, because that's how you convince yourself it's okay. So go ahead, make me the villain here."

He crushes his mouth to mine. I push at his shoulders, but it is a token effort. His lips are soft as he teases mine, only to bite down on my lower lip. I gasp and try to turn away, but he has hold of me and delves into my mouth. My head begins to swim.

"You stopped fighting," he whispers against my lips.

I jerk back in horror and cover my mouth.

I just let that happen.

Again.

What kind of wretched woman am I?

I push at him with my free arm.

He sighs and eases me to my feet, but keeps me trapped between him and the bookshelf.

"This is exactly what I meant, and you pretended I was the fool." I glare up at him. "This is too far."

He lifts my hand to his lips and kisses my knuckles. I shouldn't allow this. The way my body responds to him weakens my resolve and I'm ashamed of myself. I don't know who this person is or why I feel a connection with him.

Oriax smirks at me. "Well, maybe those two idiots will think you've been unfaithful, then I'll be your only choice."

I don't think. I haul back and slap him.

The impact jars up my arm and I feel it on my shoulder. The sound is loud and echoes in this refined space. I gasp as my hand stings and the reality of my actions dawn on me. Oriax blinks, as if he doesn't quite believe someone just struck him.

Fuck.

I've done it now.

"I will never pick you over anyone," I vow, despite my shaking voice.

Oriax takes a step back. His cheek is red, but his eyes twinkle, as if I've played straight into his trap. He bows low and chuckles.

"We'll see, treat. We'll see."

I clench my hands in anger and watch him go.

What I wouldn't give for that pretty jeweled dagger right now. I don't hate Oriax, but I don't understand why this has to be complicated. Why now? When people are so scared? Why create more strife?

Most of all, I hate myself for the deception.

It's time to admit it all.

ELIGOS

How is it a war can necessitate so many meetings?

It's like this no matter the era. Yes, there's some initial action, but so much of war is simply talking about war. I hate it. War makes me wish for hell's constant battle royale. There were never winners or boundaries or anything once we were sealed away. Just the never ending fight to feel alive.

Part of me wants to leave this place and return home for one last night in our bed. Tomorrow we'll go to the front and this war will start for real. Probably with more meetings, since that is how they do it on the continent now.

We've just entered the Hall of Demons when Teill appears out of nowhere. Her face is serious, and she's staring at us as though we might be a threat. I stop and my demon rises to the surface, ready to react. To protect our mate.

Belial presses his hand to my chest. He probably senses my bloodlust. "Teill, what's wrong?"

She inhales and squares her shoulders. If I wasn't concerned, I'd be proud of the little Brownie. Belial has raised her to fear nothing. More people should be like her.

"This isn't my place," she says and glances from Belila to me and back. "Lioria is waiting with dinner. She has some things she feels she needs to say, and maybe she does. My thoughts and feelings about this don't matter. I'm just asking you to listen to her side before you come to any conclusions or decisions or actions."

"Is she okay? Did someone hurt her?" I ask.

She huffs and throws her arms up in the air. "No, she's not okay. That's exactly the point."

"Thanks, Teill," Belial says and brushes past her.

I follow close behind while our adorable Brownie sputters in our wake.

We practically trip over each other, rushing to Belial's chambers. Valac calls out to us, but we ignore him.

Belial charges into his suite. "Lioria?"

There's anxious tension in the air. I have the presence of mind to close the door behind us before I follow Belial into the sitting room where a lovely dinner spread has been set up. But that's not what draws my eyes.

Lioria stands with the round table and a chair between us. Her knuckles are almost white where she's gripping the decorative spindles on the back of her shield. My gaze flickers and I see the traces of demonic energy on her face, hip, and hands.

"I have something to say," Lioria says in a high, thin voice that's so brittle I don't move for fear of breaking her.

"I've... I..." She rapidly, then closes her eyes, gathering herself. "I feel as though I have been unfaithful. And maybe not in the way most people would recognize, but I know what's in my heart and I need to be honest."

The way her voice breaks on the last word has me poised on the balls of my feet, ready to go to her. To tell her I don't give a fuck what she thinks she's done or what she's engaged in, so long as my demon can call her *mine*.

"I have carried on a discourse with Oriax I know you wouldn't approve of. I can't show you the notes because I burned them, knowing what I was doing went against your wishes. At least, in spirit it was wrong."

Belial leans forward and I pull him back, as much to remind myself to stay put as him.

She swallows and breathes deep again, causing her breasts to strain against the neckline of her gown. It's almost the exact shade of green as Belial's eyes. Did she pick it on purpose?

"When I met with Shax, he..." She gestures at her face. "He kissed me out of a desire to provoke one or both of you. I did the best I could to remove it, but... And then today, in the library, Oriax..."

I think we both see her tear at the same time, because we move in unison.

Fucking hell.

We've failed her.

I'm just a tiny bit quicker than Belial, and get to Lioria first. She yelps as I pick her up and bury my face in the crook of her neck. I can almost taste Oriax on her, which I wouldn't mind if it was what she wanted.

"Sh. Sh. Sh." Belial cradles her face in his hands so sweetly as he brushes his lips over her cheeks.

I move toward the sofa and sit with her across my lap. Belial quickly seats himself so that she leans back against his chest. The greedy bastard.

"You did nothing wrong," Belial whispers.

Lioria's eyes are wild as they glance around. As if she doesn't believe us.

I lean in and grasp the back of her neck, pulling her toward me. "Listen."

She clutches the front of my vest while her face crumples.

"Oh, my precious dream. I'm sorry we failed you. I'm so, so sorry."

Lioria chokes a sob. "Why are you sorry? I'm the one..."

I press a kiss to her cheek. "Because we sensed what we guessed was Shax's touch, but we decided to leave it up to you to discuss with us. We should have asked. We should not have allowed you feel this was shameful. He's a rotten bastard when he plays dirty."

"B-but—"

I press my finger across her lips. "No. Shax and Oriax know exactly what they're doing, and we failed you. That's the end of it."

"Eligos, part of me wanted that attention. I don't understand why I can't be happy. Why can't I be content with what we have? Am I so wretched that I have to demand more? What right do I have?"

Her tears flow freely now as she babbles on about all the things she sees as shortcomings.

Belial looks at me from over her shoulder.

We're having the same thoughts, but now isn't the time to speculate.

He nods.

Between us, I'm better with words.

I lean forward and am momentarily taken aback with how content my demon is right now. Whatever is happening, it's not going to break us. If I believed in fate anymore, I'd say she is it. But fate died with the gods. We're all writing our own stories here.

"Lioria? My love? Look at me?"

Her throat flexes and she slowly lifts her gaze to mine. I smile, though most of me wants to punch a hole through Oriax and Shax for toying with her like this.

"There is nothing wrong with you. The failing is on our part. We've drawn you into our world, and you are still trying to apply human rules. What matters right now is that you have nothing to apologize for. I'm not going to tolerate another apology from you, either. The heart wants what it wants, and if you choose to invite more than the two of us to your bed, that is your right. I can't say we will always share nicely, but that's not your problem."

Her face is lined with confusion.

Belial and I are hers to command. I don't know when it happened or why, but it did. The most important thing in my life is no longer the success of Eden.

It's her.

Her troubled brown eyes stare back at me. "I... I don't understand..."

Belial hugs her to him and kisses her temple. "If you wanted someone outside the High Demon Lords, it might be an issue. But if you're saying there are others among us seven you fancy, we wouldn't stand in your way."

"I concealed the truth. I carried on—"

I take her hands in mine and kiss them. "Why? Why did you conceal the truth, as you say?"

She shrinks back against Belial, which I don't hate. She's seeking comfort from one of us, at least. "B-because I thought you'd be angry..."

"We are, but not with you. It's not your fault Shax kissed you. That is a violation of your person, even if you enjoyed it. The same goes for Oriax, though I doubt his intentions were as juvenile. Obviously, we would have concerns about his motives. But what matters right now is that you know you did nothing wrong."

I lean in and press my lips to hers, giving her gentle attention. Her hands cup my face, holding me there.

Nothing would make me happier than if we stayed like this. A perfect triad. That's my selfishness talking. Of course, I want her all to myself. But if I'm genuinely honest? I think I've sensed for some time that Lioria was never meant for the two of us alone. I don't know what she is or how she's changed us, but this is only her beginning.

LIORIA

This is nothing like what I expected. While I haven't seen my demons be violent, I know they hold the power to destroy. There's a reason people call the High Demon Lords our fierce protectors. But it is their tenderness I never expected. I've known people who are so calloused after one lifetime. I'd always expected the High Demon Lords to be similar. Jaded. Cynical. Cold. But against all the odds and horrible realities of our world, my demons are sweet and kind.

Teill never lets an opportunity pass to tell me how much Belial and Eligos have changed since I came to Privale. It's only been a few weeks. How could all of this have happened so fast?

Belial pulls me back against his chest and gently wipes my cheeks with a handkerchief.

"Don't cry," he mutters. "When's the last time you ate? Did you even have lunch?"

Eligos snorts. "Always thinking with your stomach."

"I... I am hungry. I couldn't eat much earlier," I confess.

Belial stands, keeping one hand on my back and the other on my elbow to support me in this odd position. "Let's fix that."

Eligos pinches my bottom. Not hard, just enough that I jump.

I'm still uneasy. They haven't let me fully confess what I believe are my sins. They've kept me so close, I would not have expected this result.

"What?" Eligos asks as he stands, our bodies so close I can feel him from hips to shoulders.

"I thought you two would have been upset or jealous..."

He tugs on a lock of my hair. "Oh, I am jealous, dream. If I had my way, I'm not sure I'd share you with Belial."

A low rumble has us both looking at the dining table where Belial stands with a plate in hand, glaring at Eligos. He wraps his arms around me and blows a kiss at Belial.

Eligos' hand is warm against my neck and chest as he runs his fingers along the border of my dress. "The difference, my love, is that I understand no one person sets the rules for a relationship. We better go over there or Belial might forget that I'm joking."

Belial sets the plate down with a thump. "I'm not in the mood for jokes."

"Clearly."

Eligos gives me a little push, and I join Belial at the table.

We're quiet for a few moments while we portion out the food. It's some kind of roasted meat with long beans and root vegetables. There's fresh bread and sweet butter. I even put out some of the candied nuts from the festival I hadn't yet eaten.

I bite my lip as we settle into our seats.

They're acting as if there's nothing to be upset about. I still don't understand why they are taking ownership of my faults.

"Am I allowed to ask about Shax? What happened?"

Belial and Eligos glance up. Both their eyes have gone demon again.

"Nothing," Belial says in a tone devoid of emotion, which tells me he's not pleased.

"There isn't enough proof he is behind this. We told the others our theories, but they are just that. Theories."

Belial's brows furrow. "Alastor seemed... He was off today."

"I think we're all off right now. We didn't see this invasion coming." Eligos' eyes regain their human appearance. "I would like to talk more about Shax. Maybe there's something we missed?"

"Let her eat a few bites, at least."

"Fine. Okay."

I smile at their banter and tuck in. While my anxiety isn't wiped away, my stomach is no longer in knots. I want nothing more than to devour my food, but I make myself go slowly. This isn't a seaside tavern in a small town no one has heard before. Not that either of my demons care right now. But if I see myself in their lives beyond this season, I'll need to do better. To become more. Worthy of them.

When I'm ready, I begin with the day I met with Shax and all that I remember. It wasn't a long meeting, and it does seem as though his only aim was to sow discord. It's the encounter on the road that's harder to recall.

"He never got time to say anything, really," Eligos remarks while staring out the windows. "What was his goal?"

"Why were Ammit's people waiting for Lioria?" Belial asks.

I blink a few times.

"Fuck," Eligos mutters.

"Lioria, when did you first run across one of Ammit's followers?"

"During the festival. First thing in the morning, Teill wanted to make a handful of stops. She and I both bought their honey candy. I admired this pointed stick that had moon inlay in the, I guess, top part?"

"Could you draw it?" Eligos asks.

"Sure."

"Oriax could pluck that memory from your mind," Belial says in a low, dark voice.

Eligos shakes his head. "Drawing it will suffice. But later. Go on."

So I walk them through my day at the festival, beginning with the strange encounter at the booth, the woman following me, and the odd performers who got chased off. They don't ask questions or remark on any of it.

"That's it, until the road," I say.

"Were they tracking you? Or did they know where you would be?" Belial asks.

Eligos shakes his head. "There's no way they could have known where she'd be. The only people who knew about the meeting are the three of us and Alastor. There must have been some sort of tracking spell."

"A tracking spell neither of us or Teill noticed?" Belial tilts his head and squints at Eligos. "Do you believe that? Really?"

"There's always the chance someone among them is a skilled magic user."

Belial squints across the table, his belief evident in the fine lines around his eyes.

"Which do you think is more likely? Alastor betraying us? Or there being an expert magic user among Ammit's vendors? Hm?"

Belial sighs and shakes his head. "I think there's something else, but I don't know what."

Eligos drops his gaze to the table. "I think, for now, we have bigger problems to worry about."

We're quiet for a moment.

"We still need to talk about Oriax," Eligos says softly. "If you're up to it? It would help us to know what to expect from him in the coming weeks."

This part is painful, because I was actively part of the deception. I recount what I recall from the letters all the way up through earlier today.

Belial drops his fork on the plate. "You slapped Oriax?"

Eligos throws his head back and howls. "That's the best fucking thing I've heard all damn day."

Belial doubles over and pounds his fist on the table. "I wish I could have seen that."

I simultaneously want to crawl under the table and preen.

"What did you say? How did it end?" Eligos asks.

I take a deep breath and close my eyes. "He said something about making you two believe I was unfaithful so I'd have to pick him, and I said I'd take anyone else over him, I think. I'm not sure."

Eligos covers his mouth with his hand and tips his head back.

Belial reaches over and drags my chair so that it is flush with his. He takes my face in his hands and kisses me.

"You are glorious," he mutters against my lips.

"I'm a complete fool. He could have killed me!"

Eligos wipes his face. "He's an arrogant bastard, but he isn't stupid."

Belial plucks one of the candied nuts from the jar then holds it out for me. I feel silly eating the morsel from his fingers, but it's reminiscent of how we met.

Eligos sighs and props his chin on his hand. He always looks ready for a nap, but the weariness is more apparent now.

I lean against Belial's side, needing his comforting touch. "Did you speak to Alastor about me helping?"

Eligos shakes his head. "There wasn't a good time to talk about it."

"I went through the book today and noted a few." I gesture to the green volume sitting on the mantle.

Belial leans in and kisses my temple. "When were you going to tell us that books were the way to your heart?"

I smile up at him. "You did give me access to your library."

He narrows his gaze at me.

"We'll speak with Alastor in the morning." Eligos rises to his feet and stretches. "I demand we retire to bed."

"He demands it," Belial whispers in a mocking tone. "Who are we to deny his majesty?"

Eligos rolls his eyes, but I see a smile curving his lips.

I laugh, while on the inside I'm already fretting about what happens tomorrow. What is war like? Will it drag on? What chance is there that one of them dies? And the people? How much damage will this cause? And now that it's happened once, will it happen again?

I tuck those fears away and let Belial tug me to my feet.

The problem is, I'm not as tired as they are. But I need to be near them.

Eligos holds out his arm and I slide my hand into the crook of his elbow. He leans in and I eye him warily. That glint is trouble.

"Do you want to fuck Oriax?" he asks.

"What? No."

"No as in never? Or, no as in not after today?"

I sputter and glance at Belial who appears to be biting his cheek.

"Why do I put up with you two?" I mutter then sigh. "I can't be with someone who manipulates others like that. You both warned me. I just had to find out for myself."

"He isn't all bad," Belial says. "At his core, Oriax is an idealistic soul who thinks he knows the best way to do and fix everything. I think his vanity is actually his biggest fault. You'd think it would be his anger."

"Hm." Eligos squeezes my hand. "He's too controlled to give into his wrath. You should only do what you think and feel is right."

We enter the bedroom and my two demons begin their nightly routines. For a few moments, I stand there watching them. It's clear that they are comfortable around each other. While Eligos smooths something into the fine hairs along his hairline, Belial pops yet another button off while mindlessly stripping his clothing. I pick it up and set it aside, where Teill will no doubt see it and mend the garment later.

I head toward a narrow wardrobe Teill procured for my things when Eligos stops me. He doesn't say anything, just loosens the laces of my dress, then goes back to wrapping his hair in the familiar cloth. I steal glimpses of them moving about, each time wearing a little less than before.

This is such a normal domestic moment on the eve of something awful. I'm elated, content, and afraid.

Tomorrow everything could change and I might lose all that I've gained.

"What are you doing?" Eligos says.

I tug the nightgown down over my head to find him naked and glaring at me. Belial is already in bed, eyes closed, and breathing heavily.

"What?"

"Take that hideous thing off."

"You expect me to sleep naked? It's freezing."

He grasps the material and hauls it back up my body. I shiver as he strips me and clutch my arms to my chest. He pats my bottom, then tosses the garment on the floor.

Sorry, Teill.

I'm not opposed to sleeping naked, but I worry about every little thing that might happen. A servant. An emergency. A fire. But I'm still bundled into bed between my two demons. And I mean between them. Belial turns in his sleep—I think he's already asleep—and throws an arm over my waist while Eligos' legs follow the bend of mine behind me. It's warm and perfect. Eligos' breath warms my neck while the room slowly dims.

And I'm only marginally tired.

I slide my hand over Belial's side and hold my breath, but he doesn't stir.

Until he does.

His hand slides up and down my bare back. Eligos' palm coasts over me to rest on my stomach and I stay perfectly still.

This is maddening.

Falling asleep after being exhausted by them is one thing. Lying here, casually trying to fall asleep is doing the opposite. I'm wide awake and hyper-aware of every place where my skin touches theirs. And where we aren't touching.

Belial shifts in his sleep, bringing his face closer to mine. He has this intimidating, larger-than-life presence when he's awake. But asleep? He's so gentle and sweet looking. It's hard to merge the violent demon from yesterday with this man, but I don't deny that part of them.

Eligos' hand slides down my hip to my thigh then back up.

These little touches and shifts are going to keep me awake. How can they just lie down and pass out?

"I can practically feel you mind-fucking us," Eligos says into the darkness as his hand dips lower on my stomach.

"I am not," I whisper.

"Too bad," Belial mutters.

Eligos' fingers trail over my mound and my skin tingles. "Wishful thinking?"

"I thought you were both tired?"

Belial leans his body into mine and slides his hand around to grip my ass. "So? That doesn't make me want you any less."

Eligos pushes Belial back. "I think we've had our way enough, don't you? What do you want, Lioria? Command us."

My heart pulses in my throat and for a moment I can't breathe.

What do I want?

Their hands are stroking my body while lust uncurls inside of me.

"I-I don't know," I stammer.

Eligos slides his hand between my legs to cup my sex. "What would feel good right now?"

"It's hard to decide when I feel like I'm having to pick between you."

"We will never make you pick," Belial says in a firm, hard tone.

"Not like that." I sigh.

"Oh." Eligos draws that one word out. "Do you mean, you don't like picking which of our cocks pleasure you first?"

My face heats, but that's the truth.

Belial dips his head to kiss my chest while his hands plump my breasts together. I shiver as he licks across both my nipples.

"Is that what you want?" Eligos says in a deeply sensual voice. "To be filled by the both of us?"

"Y-yes," I squeak out.

"Hm, I don't think your body is ready for that quite yet." I feel his other hand trailing fingers down my spine to the top of my ass. "But, there's always magic..."

"There's magic for that?"

"There's magic for everything if you're creative enough."

I dig my hand into Belial's hair, tilting his head back so I can look at him. "Then, why did you wait? If girth was an issue?"

It's hard to see him clearly, but I think he winces. "I don't like how it feels. I wanted it to be... Us."

His answer is so pure I can't find fault in it.

"The good thing is that I don't mind," Eligos says with pride.

I clench a little as other memories from last night surface.

"Hold on." I wiggle around to sit up. "Someone owes me an explanation about demon anatomy."

Belial has the grace to bury his face in the pillow while Eligos merely rolls to his back, his half-hard cock obvious under the blanket.

"You've seen us as demons," he says and crosses his hands behind his head. "Would you want to get amorous with something that looks like that?"

I consider it. "There's something graceful about them. I wouldn't call either of you ugly, but I understand the point."

Belial clears his throat. "The world used to be a very different place. Shifters call it a knot. We never had a name for it, because that was simply our anatomy. It can be used for pain or pleasure."

"You get to decide?"

Eligos laughs and rolls toward me, throwing his arm over my lap. "It's in how you use it that matters. Isn't she adorable?"

Belial chuckles. "She is."

"You want a taste, don't you?"

"Always."

The globe above us begins to glow and I glance between the two of them. How is it like this every time? The air is fraught with lust to the point it's hard to breathe while my body grows warm and my breasts heavy.

Eligos peers up at me. "What do you want?"

"The same thing I've always wanted. To be between you."

"No," Belial says. "To complete us."

My heart stutters at his words.

He doesn't mean that, does he? This is just some pretty statement, right?

Belial sits up and drags me over his lap until I'm straddling him and we're nose to nose. Eligos moves quickly so that he's behind me. I don't know whose fingers they are sliding between my legs, but I moan all the same.

"Eligos, take it slow."

"You feel how wet she is."

"Fuck. We'll make this feel good."

I lean my head back against Eligos' shoulder. "It already does. Don't make me wait."

"Such a greedy little girl."

Belial leans in until our noses bump. "Fine. But you're my breakfast tomorrow, and I'm going to be very hungry."

"Okay. Yes. Are you doing the knot thing?"

They both still and I know without looking they're doing the silent communication thing without me.

"Not this time," Eligos says.

Belial nods. "One new thing at a time."

I'm only a little disappointed. Honestly, Belial's cock is big enough as it is. The idea of giving him yet more girth is alarming.

Eligos kisses my shoulder. "This is going to tickle a little."

Belial tunnels his fingers through my hair, pulling me to him for a kiss while Eligos strokes his hands over my hips and ass. I don't know what's supposed to tickle because my body pulses with a need so sharp I don't understand it. It's like I crave them. Like being with them sustains me.

I'm acutely aware of Eligos dipping his fingers into my pussy then drawing the moisture back over my other hole.

Do I understand what I've asked for?

Not in the least.

All I know is that I couldn't care for one more than the other. If tomorrow all of this were to end, I want this.

"Ready for the magic?" Eligos says against my ear.

I nod because Belial's tongue is in my mouth.

There's no mistaking the blunt press of Eligos' cock. The feel of him is different. Slippery. I shift my hips only for him to bite down on my shoulder. I gasp, but Belial only pulls me more firmly against him. And then there's a whole new sensation.

I dig my nails into Belial's shoulders and he growls.

Eligos moans into my ear. "Fuck."

Belial strokes my hair off my face while I try to process the sensations. "Breathe."

I gasp as Eligos eases out. That must be what I'm feeling. I was expecting some sort of stretching stimulation. Instead, it feels as though my insides are being stroked.

"W-what...?" I want to understand, because this does not feel like being fucked.

"Do you want him to stop?" Belial asks.

"No."

"Good," Eligos growls out before thrusting.

This time his body rocks against mine. There's no mistaking the intrusion for anything else.

Belial leans in and nips my lower lip. "I cannot wait to share your body."

I pull him closer. I feel wild. "Now."

"Oh, fucking hell," Eligos mutters.

Belial's eyes go wide with surprise for all of half a moment before he grins and pulls me forward, causing Eligos to withdraw. I whimper at the new sensations and shift against Belial's thick cock pressed to my mound. His fingers stroke over and through my folds.

"God, Bel. Fuck," Eligos cries out.

I grin and look back at the way his face is caught in a pleasure filled, soundless shout.

"Eligos likes his balls toyed with," Belial confides.

"I'll remember that."

Eligos bites down on his lower lip and moans.

They're so free with their affection. I've never seen anything like it. And now they are mine.

Then I feel Belial's cock passing through my folds as he guides himself back to my entrance. I swallow and look at him.

"Do what feels good," he murmurs.

I nod and press down on him while Eligos strokes his hands over my sides, stomach, and breasts. Belial grips my hips, keeping me steady while he stares into my eyes. It's as if he wants to see every emotion and reaction play out. And I hold nothing back.

I bite my lip as his girth stretches me.

"Gods," I mutter as my thighs quiver.

Belial lifts me then slowly lets me slide back down. I moan as both cocks ease deeper than before.

"Fuck," Eligos growls. "Do that again?"

"Yes," I say before Belial checks in with me.

They're terribly sweet, but right now that's not what I want.

Eligos cups my breasts and I squirm, pressing down on both of them harder.

"Christ," Belial croaks.

There's a slight uncomfortable twinge to the joining and I love it.

"I was not ready," Eligos says in a strained voice.

"What?" Belial says with an edge of panic.

Eligos chuckles and presses kisses to my neck. "If I'd known you would feel this good, I would never have waited."

I no longer care about words or witty banter. I want to fuck and be fucked. Belial must sense this because he lifts me, only to drop me. Gravity sends them so deep I swear I can feel where we all fit together.

Belial rocks forward and Eligos clutches me to him. I suck down air as their lips meet. I lean my head against them, part of this.

I rock my hips and they both groan. I can't help but grin at how easily my all-powerful demons are toppled.

Belial tweaks a nipple and I gasp. "Feeling proud of yourself?"

"Yes."

Eligos kisses my shoulder. "She should."

Belial's eyes twinkle and he lifts me with one arm. Eligos and I moan in unison.

My muscles feel liquefied while my body is full. It's mostly Belial moving me. I wasn't prepared for the delicious sensation of my demons in me at the same time. I'd thought before it was like having all my pleasure points rubbed at the same time. This is that, but stronger.

I turn my head, kissing Eligos' cheek. He tilts his head and tugs on my hair, slanting his lips across mine. Belial's warm breath fans across my neck as he kisses a path to my shoulder and bites gently. His grip around me slips and I take both of them in deep.

"F-f-fuck," Eligos says on a moan.

I gasp for breath, my vision blurring from the pleasure of it.

"I... Fuck, I need," he mutters.

"I think we've almost broken him," taunts Belial.

I'm feeling a little fractured myself, in the best way possible.

"I don't know..." I shift my hips back against Eligos and my breath catches. "What did you say about his balls?"

He groans and I feel Belial chuckle. He leans in and kisses me, but his hands aren't on me.

"Fuck you both," Eligos growls.

Then he's moving.

My gasp turns into a whimper as Eligos' hips smack against me. Belial hungrily takes my mouth, deepening the kiss until it feels as if they're in me in all the ways possible.

A hand wiggles between Belial and I. Elgios. He's intent on a path as he fucks my ass. I know the touch is coming, and I still whimper as he catches my clit between his fingers and gently squeezes it.

Belial rips his mouth from mine, tipping his head back. "God, you're so tight still."

Eligos has one hand on my breast, the other stroking my clit while his hips move in short thrusts that rock me forward against Belial. I dig my nails in and whimper.

"Fuck," he groans. "You're going to make me blow my load doing that."

I'm so close.

Eligos gasps and his body tenses behind mine, then his hips are working frantically. His moans are all I hear. Belial grips my hips and does his best to match Eligos' pace.

"Gods," I cry as I tip over the edge.

Belial roars something and shifts so that Eligos is holding me while Belial drives into me. The hard thrusts stroke my orgasm higher until I'm certain the pleasure of it has ruined me. My limbs are heavy and my mind spins from the euphoria of what we just shared. We're an even more complicated knot of limbs and bodies than ever before, and I love this.

I love them.

Maybe it's too soon to say something like that, but we fit together. As if I were made for this.

Eligos speaks first. "I think the two of you depraved souls just ruined all other sex for me for the rest of my existence."

His words send me into a fit of laughter. Belial groans and does his best to cover my mouth, as if that will stop me.

Eligos untangles himself first, then pulls me from the bed and carries me into the bathroom where Belial joins us in cleaning up. These are tender, normal moments, and they're my favorite. When I forget they're all powerful and just the men who hold my heart.

I wish we could stay like this. I wish that tomorrow we didn't have to face this war. And I wish I had more than one lifetime with them, but I am merely human.

Belial hooks his fingers in mine. "Come to bed, my lady."

"Actually, I'm hungry. I'll be there in a little bit."

Eligos smacks the firm curve of Belial's ass. "You're rubbing off on her."

I laugh and take one of three robes hanging on the hooks. It's smaller than the other two, but still swallows me. I leave my two demons to banter as they make their way slowly back to bed and the rest they need.

I'm restless despite the beautiful moments we've shared. And, I'm hungry. I have two kinds of stress. The kind of stress where I eat everything I can. And the stress that won't let me eat at all.

I pick a few things from the remnants of our dinner table and wander about the room until I come to the side table where I left Naexi's box and that strange dagger. I flip open the lid, but nothing is inside. I sent her a note earlier today, just in case she might get it out on the ocean. But no such luck.

Why did I pick up the dagger? Why did I bring it with me?

I haven't touched it. Earlier I used the bag to place it on the table.

At no point do I recall either Belial or Eligos retrieving the sheath. I don't even remember why I took the thing with me. Only that I clutched it tight.

I set my plate down and pick up the blade, turning it this way and that.

The artistry is beautiful. It's silver with squares of pearl and other buffed stones that shine even in the low light.

Did I imagine something talking to me when I held the dagger?

I pull the blade from the sheath and look at the wickedly curved edge.

"Fucking hello to you, too. Done getting railed?"

I gasp and drop the blade, dancing back as it falls to the ground. I glance around, looking for the source of the voice, but hear nothing.

"Why is it always the idiots?"

"Show yourself or my demons—"

"Your demons won't do anything to me."

I turn, searching for the voice. I hear it. Belial and Eligos are in the other room. Are they not alarmed by a male voice in the suite?

"They can't hear me. Only you can, you busty bimbo."

"Why are you so rude? Where are you? Why can only I hear you?"

"Down here. Remember me? The helpful dagger that saved your ass and your friend?"

I peer down at the blade. Something ripples across the surface.

"Why don't you sit down? We have a lot to talk about..."

ELIGOS

The morning comes far too soon, and it's not a good one.

Our plan of talking to Alastor is a failure. He's already headed to the front with the first troops taking to the battlefield. The army from the continent has positioned themselves on a flat stretch of the waste. I'm no tactician, but I think going to their chosen ground to meet them is an idiotic idea. Judging by the way Belial is grinding his teeth, so does he.

I want to leave Lioria at the palace. I want her far from the nasty business that is war. But she sticks to our side and is doing her best to be a fierce warrior on our account. I can't deny that my demon wants her close at all time.

No part of me likes the plan we've arrived at, but it is the best one possible. Which is why I am here, outside the Hall of Mages where those sworn to Eden are preparing themselves for a day we'd never thought would come.

The entire army from the continent can use magic. Most humans in Eden haven't nursed that ability. Our numbers will overwhelm the continent, but their magic makes one of theirs equal to a hundred of ours. It's not good odds.

I stride through the crowd, people jumping out of my path. I can sense Oriax. None of us are shielding our power. We need to be able to find each other when necessary.

Oriax is such a pompous asshole.

He knows I'm here, yet he keeps his back to me until the very last moment. He turns, a book in one hand, and gives me a bored stare.

"What?" he demands.

I hold up a slip of folded paper.

His brows lift and he reaches for it, but I pull it back.

"No more games, Oriax," I say.

He shrugs and takes the paper from me. I watch his eyes widen and his chin snap up as his gaze returns to my face.

"Do you have it?" I ask.

"Yes. Yes, of course."

"Do you believe she can use it safely?"

He pauses and tilts his head. "With guidance, yes. I take it you want me to stick by her side?"

I tap the paper. I don't like this plan, but it could work. And it could keep our side from losing lives needlessly. "Do you think this changes our odds?"

"Possibly..."

"Then we're decided." I reach out and grab the front of Oriax's robe, yanking him until we're nose to nose. "Know one thing, you arrogant bastard. She makes the rules. Not you. Not us. I will kill you if you cross her or harm her. Are we understood?"

Oriax's lips twitch. I think he wants to grimace, but he manages a sardonic smile. "Perfectly."

I let him go and take a step back.

He would never confess it, but Oriax is almost as vain as Valac. In a way, it makes Oriax predictable where Valac is chaos.

If Oriax wants Lioria, he'll have to work to earn her trust, and I intend to enjoy the show. It's past time someone reminded Oriax that he doesn't know everything.

LIORIA

I don't like war.

I don't think anyone is supposed to.

And blood hasn't been shed yet. At least, not that I'm aware of.

I want to be excited about traveling through portals, not anxious about what I'm about to commit to.

All of this feels wrong.

Why are we fighting to begin with? Why is a conflict thousands of years old not over with yet? Are immortal beings really this childish? Or is there something else going on?

It's almost noon by the time Belial, Eligos, and myself are scheduled to go through with one of the last groups of soldiers. The training yard where students from the mage's university are maintaining the portal is littered with cots. For now, they serve the worn-out students who exhausted themselves and their magic. Later, they'll be for the wounded.

I fear there aren't enough of them.

Belial speaks to a steady stream of military types either seeking his counsel or looking for orders. He's a completely different creature in this element. From his armor right down to how he's standing. The Belial I've come to care for is easy-going, quick to smile, and understanding. This man is none of that. He's firm, commanding, and doesn't hesitate to bite someone's head off figuratively. He exudes confidence and though many men walk away from him stinging from a rebuke, that same confidence seeps out into the men under him.

Eligos and I are, for the most part, left alone. I'm playing the secretary and wearing the guise of a middle-aged man. What's worse, my demons thought it would be a great idea for me to wear a men's protective tunic. It's a long, quilted caftan with some sort of knife material between the external fabrics. There are protective wards literally sewn into it. While the garment won't necessarily save me, it makes it much less likely I'll die. Between that and Naexi's gift, I'm as protected as I can get.

My demon tips his head toward me. "Ready?"

"Not really."

He chuckles. "Eyes straight ahead and keep going, okay?"

I nod and stare at the blue, shimmering archway as the people just ahead of us disappear through it. Their forms on the other side are shrunk to a few, tan-looking blobs no more than knee high.

"Eligos," Belial barks, but he looks at me. "Let's go."

"Waiting on you," Eligos drawls.

What Belial has called the rear guard is all that's left. They watch the three of us cross the open ground. I want to stop, to marvel at this sight, but Eligos' words have me putting one foot in front of the other.

I thought it might feel like water given the shimmering, blue surface, but it's more like mist. For a moment it seems as though the portal is touching every cell in my body at once, then I'm through. I stumble as up stops being up. Up is now somewhere behind me.

"Damn it, couldn't they have picked a better spot?" Eligos grumbles and lends me a steadying hand.

I want to cling to him, but what middle aged man would do that?

Today I'm the secret weapon. At least, that's the plan.

Belial marches around, bellowing orders others jump to obey.

"Are you turned on watching him like this?" Eligos whispers.

"No. Sorry."

He grimaces and glances at me. "Don't apologize. I keep forgetting this is new to you. Come. Let's go join the others. Belial can catch up."

I lick my lips and glance around as I follow Eligos between the ranks of soldiers.

We're on the very edge of the wasteland. Behind us, green growing things are doing their best to encroach on the dead waste. I've only ever seen the wasteland from a boat before. It's so flat and barren save for the occasional rocky hill dotting the large expanse. A teacher once explained that the reason the wasteland is so dead is because of the range of mountains that extends, cutting north into south. The mountains hold the rain on our side, leaving none for the south. But I struggle to believe that as I watch clouds pass freely over the mountains at our back in the distance.

It's all so strange.

"W-where are they? The invading army?" I ask.

Eligos nods ahead of us. "They're there. You just can't see them."

My elbow catches on the hilt of my dagger. I'm not accustomed to carrying it yet. Neither Eligos nor Belial said anything when I mentioned wearing it today. I asked Teill for gloves specifically so I don't touch it. I know last night happened, I'm just not ready to believe anything an inanimate object says to me. It's too much to deal with right now, so I've chosen to not deal.

Whatever is possessing the dagger is not happy about it, but fuck what it thinks. I didn't ask for this.

Guards snap to attention as we pass ring after ring of heavily armored soldiers surrounding a single tent. I'm peering around, trying to understand why, when Belial steps through the flaps and I stupidly follow him without asking questions.

"About damn time."

I've heard that voice before.

Eligos moves deeper into the tent and clasps hands with a petite....person. I can't tell if they're male, female, or simply not human, but they are lovely. They're maybe my height with a lithe body. Just the way they sway back and forth while speaking with Belial is graceful. Their face is angular and achingly perfect, but it's the combination of pale purple eyes and silver hair that is the crowning glory.

"Valac, I'd like you to officially meet Lioria."

I watch this beautiful creature turn toward me and tilt its perfect face.

"Oh!" Belatedly I curtsy, but forget I'm wearing a caftan and end up popping my hands out to my sides like some floundering bird that can't fly.

"No need to be so formal," Valac says.

"Sorry," I mutter and move to stand a little behind Eligos.

He frowns at me. "Take the glamor off. I don't like looking at you like this."

"Please, let me do whatever makes you happy," I mutter and let the glamor fade.

Valac grins and his eyes widen. "You! I was wondering what happened to you."

He takes a step back, regarding the two of us with a wide grin.

I'm painfully aware of Oriax bending over a table with another man I recognize. Alastor, supposedly the mightiest among them.

"How is this working out?" Valac asks.

"It's none of your business," Eligos retorts. He gestures at Valac. "Remind me, is this a they-them life, or a...?"

Valac shrugs. "It's a what-do-I-feel-like-today, life. You know what? We're High Demon Lords today and that's a lot of masculine energy, so he."

The conversation has just moved faster than I understand.

"Lioria, if you get separated, find Valac." Eligos glances at the other demon. "He? He will be here."

Valac pats Eligos' shoulder. "You're doing great."

"Fuck off."

Valac reaches out and grabs my hand. I find myself staring into his beautiful eyes. "When this is over, I'd love to have you all as my guests."

Eligos shoves Valac back. "Hands to yourself."

Valac sticks out his lower lip. "I wasn't doing anything."

Eligos thrusts his finger under the other demon's nose. "Do you really want to play this game, you little imp?"

Valac grins and it might be my imagination, but his teeth seem sharper briefly. As lovely and delicate as this demon is, he has fangs.

Eligos leans toward me and nods at the table. "That's Alastor."

"We spoke briefly in Suncrest. He probably doesn't remember me, but I recognize him."

"He's a hard presence to ignore, isn't he?" Eligos' voice is reverent. And who wouldn't be? Alastor is supposed to be the most powerful creature on the planet.

I nod, because what do I say to that? The answer is obvious.

Oriax glances up at Belial and Valac hums something.

I'm still not happy with Oriax. Eligos spoke with him, but refused to tell me anything about the exchange.

The Oriax today is more like the first version I met of him. He's wearing sturdy boots, as if he expects to move around a lot, and dark trousers. The vest or jacket he's wearing under his mage's robe is worn, as if it isn't the first battle it's seen.

The gold thread amidst the deep green is worn and broken in places. Compared to the snowy white perfection of his robes, it's a stark difference. The points of some sort of star or sigil fall over his chest, shoulders and back in more green and gold. He's pulled his long, golden hair back into a loose ponytail that seems about to fall apart. It somehow makes this perfect image he's created real.

Oriax glances back to Alastor and says something, then turns toward us. My stomach does an uncomfortable flip and I glance around the tent.

Unlike my last experience with a tent, this one is plain. The walls glow with the sun trying to shine through the material. The floor is a few carpets thrown over the hardpacked earth. There's no decoration, just some chairs, a few folding tables, and the main map table.

"Oriax," Belial says in a cool tone.

I glance at the other man who stands a polite distance from us while Valac looks on, like this is some entertaining drama for his amusement.

Oriax inclines his head the slightest bit. "Eligos."

Both their gazes slide to me.

"Lioria, will you come with me, please?" There's no emotion on Oriax's face, which I don't like for some reason. I've grown to know him. I've shared things with him. I called him a cow once. But we are now strangers.

I nod and though I don't want to, I turn to leave the tent with Oriax.

I knew this was going to happen. We discussed it. I'm still uneasy about being alone with him.

My hand rests on the hilt of my dagger. I grip it for a moment before the words return to me.

I can even kill demons. Permanently.

I jerk my hands up to smooth back my hair, but Oriax stops in front of me.

He glances over his shoulder. "Forgetting something...?"

I stare at him, waiting for the word treat to fall from his lips, but it doesn't.

What am I forgetting?

Right.

The glamor.

With a single drop of magic, I'm a middle-aged man.

Oriax wrinkles his nose.

I can imagine his voice saying something like, couldn't they have picked a more pleasing appearance?

Instead, he says nothing and we exit the tent in silence.

The High Demon Lord's tent is on a slight rise that allows for the tiniest glimpse of the invading army. From this distance, it looks like a dark blob on the horizon, but soon that shape will become people and creatures. Beings I will do my best to kill.

We proceed forward, toward a large tent bustling with activity. Here, almost everyone wears a white robe with smaller stars on their shoulders.

The mages.

As I understand, people come the world over to train in Eden under Oriax. He's brilliantly gifted and has mastered many different forms of magic. Students are only allowed to train to a certain point, at which they must agree to come to Eden's aid should she ever call. It's why most of the students are humans. Because other creatures and beings cannot make a promise of that nature.

Is being segregated like this a good thing?

Why do we have to be locked in this conflict? What does it gain anyone?

The mage's tent is completely different. The sides are rolled up and canvas walls partition the space a bit. I don't know what the groups clustered together are doing or preparing for, but they are intent.

"In here," Oriax says at last.

There's a central square in the tent that's separated from the rest with long, white walls. Oriax pulls a flap aside and I step into what looks like a field office. There's a desk, a chair, and some things I don't recognize along with a trunk.

"Belial conveyed your plan. It's a good one, but I insist you understand what you're proposing before we do this." He turns to look at me. The indifference is gone and I see maybe a spark of warmth from him.

I don't hate Oriax. I'm angry with him. And I can't trust him. Not after the ultimatum, he tried to push on me. But I'm also mourning the loss of someone I thought was a friend. I don't know what we are, but for now, we are student and teacher. At least these roles are familiar.

Oriax grabs the trunk and sets it precariously on the other chair in the space. The trunk is old, the wood stained red with worn, brass fittings. He presses his fingers to the top and fixes his stare on me.

"This is the Muki. The book I gave you says this is a device created with the purpose of mining, but when it was created, the destruction potential was so great it was locked away and never used. That's only part of the story. So many years ago I can't begin to count, some fae—a type of Vodu—wanted an easier way to obtain a valuable, rare mineral called limthenite. It's had many names, so for simplicity's sake I'll only mention what we call it. Now, the fae—"

"What's so special about it?" I wince. "Sorry, go—"

Oriax's gaze bores into mine. "Don't apologize for wanting to understand something. Limthenite is incredibly strong. I've only heard of a handful of items made out of it breaking. It's also beautiful. Out of the ground, it has this tarnished, red hue from the rock around it. But once it's purified, it's like... Moonlight. It is also an excellent conductor of magic, which is rare in the natural world. If you want to know why that is, I'm afraid you'll have to enroll. That is a year's long course."

I chuckle and though he doesn't smile, the mood seems lighter.

"Fae don't like going underground. There's a long history of creatures trying to subjugate them, so while they wanted the limthenite, they couldn't or wouldn't go deep enough to get it themselves. Instead, they enlisted an ancient race of creatures called the Nāga. They resemble a mix of serpent and human."

My stomach clenches.

I know all too well what they look like.

"The nāga used to live exclusively underground. Their burrows go deep into the planet's core, where the limthenite is found. So the fae struck a deal. They would create a tool to mine the limthenite and give it to the Nāga in exchange for a steady supply of the ore. But when the fae smelters finished their creation, they realized that the power needed to mine the limthenite was so great it could be used as a weapon. So they locked it away."

I wait for him to say more, but that seems to be the end of that lesson.

"They never used it?" I ask.

"If the oral history is to be believed, no."

"You haven't tried it just to test it out?"

"I did try, but it wouldn't work for me. Some of these fae creations are..."

"Particular?"

He nods.

I'm curious to look at it. Is it really all that bad?

"What else should I know?" I ask.

He lifts his shoulders and opens the trunk. "You tell me. We're into your area of expertise now."

I peer into the trunk.

Most of the devices I've seen are small objects. Jewlery, something that fits in your hand, maybe attached to clothing. This is none of that.

It's as long as my leg. I don't know much of mining equipment. I know it's mostly done with the aid of magic, and that's it. The device has a central shaft with four smaller shafts around that, then smaller shafts between those forming a ring around the biggest one. Two sets of mug-like handles are attached stacked on top of oeach other on either side.

"The Nāga often have multiple arms." Oriax reaches down and grips one of the handles. "My guess is that these are the hand holds."

I nod. "You're right. Look here? Isn't this a rotten, leather grip?"

"My thoughts exactly."

"How would you hold the thing?" I stand behind it, at least what I think is the back side of it, then lean forward to hold my hands over the handles. "This would be awkward with only two arms. The hands on the back of the device hold it, while the ones at the front aim."

"What if you turned it on its side?"

I nod. "I think that would work."

"Are you going to touch it? Or look at it?"

"You just said this device has never been used, and it's theorized to be strong enough to cut a swath through an army. I'm going to be careful."

My answer seems to amuse him because he smiles and steps back.

But he is right.

In order for this to work, I have to put my hands on it.

I take a deep breath then reach down, taking hold of the handles closer to the middle of the device. It's not as heavy as I'd feared, but carrying it will be difficult. I frown as I try to imagine holding it out in front of me.

"No, tuck it against your side," Oriax says.

"Oh..."

I tuck the first handle under my arm. It fits up into my armpit perfectly, allowing me to grip it with my elbow to an extent. I hold on to the grips and find it isn't a terrible way to carry it.

"This should do," I mutter.

Oriax crosses his arms over his chest. "And?"

I ignore him and extend my mental fingers over the device, searching for the seam. Only, the moment I caress it I feel a surge. It's like everything goes white-hot in my mind. I yelp and jump back, letting the device fall to the ground while every hair on my arms and legs seems to stand on end.

"What the hell?" I snap.

Oriax has his hands up and a dome over the Muki. "Are you alright?"

"Yes. Fine." I'm trembling, because now I understand what those people of old meant by, too powerful. "It will work. Maybe too well?"

"Nothing ever works too well during war, I'm afraid." He bends and presses a hand through the dome to grip the weapon. "It's dormant again."

"Well, it works."

Can I do this? I don't want to, but I also don't want my peaceful home to be thrown into the kind of war that sends boatfuls of people into a dangerous ocean to die for a dream of peace.

He places the Muki back in the trunk while I twist my fingers together.

"That's an interesting dagger you have there," Oriax says.

I don't answer.

More like I can't.

They'll all think I'm crazy if I try to explain.

"I'm sorry to hear about Shax's poor behavior," Oriax says slowly. "I did not know there was tension there, and... I'm sorry on his behalf. For all of us."

"Us, who? Men who kiss unwilling women?"

Oriax regards me for a moment, and I can't tell what that serene face of his is hiding.

"High Lord? My lord?" someone calls out.

Oriax turns from me and sweeps the tent flap open. "Yes?"

A young boy wearing armor fit for a man is on the other side. "My lord, the other lords are calling for you."

"Thank you," Oriax says with a gentle tone. He glances at me. "Shall we join them?"

He waves his hand, and the Muki floats into the trunk, the lid shuts, and the whole thing lifts off the ground. I shake my head and choose to walk beside the thing.

If anyone is going to be responsible for this, it shouldn't be them. This was my idea, and it terrifies me.

I wrestle with my decision on the walk back to the tent with the other Demon Lords.

I'm making the right call. I just don't like it.

The others have arrived while we were gone. Out of the six present demons, it's easy to pick out the one I haven't officially met yet. Raum.

He's the one with flowing brown hair. It's pulled back, revealing the sides of his shaved head and the tattoos inked into his skin. He's a big man with an imposing presence and pale blue eyes that seem inhuman. Alastor is across the table from him decked out in black armor with a cape that looks like Oriax's mage robes. It's as if Alastor is trying to appear as imposing and intimidating as possible. Reminding our enemies what he is under his humanity?

Alastor glances up, looking to each demon in turn, but never me. "In an hour, the parley begins."

Raum lifts his head, and it feels as though the whole tent is holding its breath.

"Do you really mean to negotiate with them?" Raum asks.

Alastor doesn't look at Raum, but his gaze finds the man's face. It's odd, actually. "This is how war is done on the continent. If we want to negotiate a peaceful way out of this, we do it their way."

Belial steps up to the table directly across from Alastor, giving him no option but to look directly at him. "If someone breaks into your house, do you serve them dinner and ask them to leave? No."

I jump a little at the force behind that one word.

Raum nods. "We hit them with force. We drive them back. We make them wish they'd never attempted this."

Alastor sighs, as if he's dealing with children. "We outnumber them, but they have the magic advantage."

"Actually," Oriax says and clears his throat.

Belial glances back at me then Oriax before nodding. Belatedly, I remember to banish my glamor.

"I think we have the advantage," Oriax says.

Alastor's brows rise. "Oh? Are you hiding a legion of mages I don't know about, brother?"

Oriax gestures to me. "No. Just the legendary weapon, Muki, and someone who can wield it."

"That's not all." Eligos comes to stand beside me. "I'll fight in my demon form."

Alastor snorts. "You can't be serious…"

"He's serious," Belial says. "We both are."

The tent becomes eerily silent.

Oriax's eyes are wide as he looks from Belial to Eligos then me. I don't look at any of them.

"It seems we've resorted to keeping secrets from one another," Alastor says with a bitter bite. "Regardless, we are not animals. We parley. We—"

"No," Raum snaps.

Belial speaks over them with a, "Hell no."

Valac steps up beside the High Demon Lord. "Alastor, I know you mean well, but the only way this force will take us seriously is if we meet them with violence. If they wanted to meet us in the middle, they'd put an embargo on our ports. Don't allow anyone to trade with us. Cut us off from the mainland until we have to agree to negotiate terms. This? This is an act of all-out war. How we decide to begin it matters."

Alastor looks around the tent. "You are all decided then? You would have the rest of the world think us monsters?"

"Shax isn't here to point it out, but we stopped giving a shit about the rest of it when peace was not welcomed. They can do what they want on the continent, but here, we keep the peace. At whatever cost," Eligos says.

What price have they had to pay?

I don't think I want to know.

"We attack at noon," Raum says.

Alastor taps the table. "This is a mistake."

With those words, he turns and stalks out of the tent.

Everyone seems to breathe at the same time.

Valac sighs and lifts the tent flap to watch after Alastor. "He means well..."

Raum turns, looking at each demon. "Will someone tell me why Shax is not here? Where is he?"

"He's hidden himself," Valac says slowly.

"Why?" Raum asks.

Belial and Eligos stay quiet.

Oriax appeared to have known something of my history with Shax. But not the others. Did Eligos tell him? Or possibly Shax?

"Shax should be here," Raum says again.

"But he isn't," Eligos snaps. "We'll do the best we can without him."

Raum turns toward me. "What of her? You were in Suncrest."

"She is ours and we are hers, it's that simple," Belial says.

Valac grins and glances at me again.

Raum blinks a few times, tilts his head to the side, and seems to accept that.

"Can you two really shift?" Valac asks.

"Yes," Eligos says.

Raum throws his hands up. "When were you going to share that?"

Eligos shrugs back at him. "We weren't."

"Oh my," Valac mutters with glee. It's like he's enjoying this drama playing out despite its seriousness.

"We'll have time to talk about it later, after we've beaten these bastards back to the land they came from," Belial says over them.

Oriax takes a step forward. "Immediately after."

"Fine. Yes."

Raum folds his arms over his chest. "Show us."

Eligos sighs. "Seriously?"

Belial shrugs out of his coat. Honestly, it's like he's been waiting for this.

Without ceremony, both Belial and Eligos strip out of everything except their trousers, which now that I look at them, seem baggier than normal.

This was their plan all along. They'd mentioned it when I proposed my idea. But I'd been so caught up in what I was doing I hadn't considered what they were about to do.

And then their forms are shifting, elongating, their skin giving way to the harder hide of their demons. Belial's horns press up against the tent roof before he remembers to duck while Eligos is crouched.

"Fuck me," Valac says.

Eligos shakes his head. "I thought you weren't into sex this lifetime?"

Valac ignores the question and crosses to practically press his nose to Eligos'. "That's amazing. You're still hideous."

Belial lowers to crouch in the tent, his gaze seeking mine. I'm hyper-aware of the other demons, but I don't hesitate in crossing to mine. He holds out his hand, and I put my palm against his. It's comical how drastic the difference in our forms are now.

He bends his head. "This will be over soon."

I nod and lift up on tiptoes to press a quick kiss to his lips.

There's no way for him to know how today will end, but I'll let him lie to me because I want to hear it.

I start when Eligos' tail curls around my waist. I shouldn't, but I'm on edge. He lifts me off my feet and pulls me to him.

Belial glares at his love. "Was that necessary?"

Eligos wraps his arms around me in a tight embrace. "Yes."

"How sweet," Valac coos.

Raum clears his throat. "I need to shuffle troops around and warn the archers. Wouldn't want you to become a pincushion, thanks to our side."

Eligos buries his face against my neck. "Oriax behave himself?"

"Yes."

"Good." He kisses just below my ear. "He'll protect you."

I nod, because that much I believe. It's after this war business that worries me. How did my life get this complicated?

"You two should hang back," Oriax says. "Your appearance will cause a stir and the longer the other side questions whether or not we'll appear in our demon forms, the better. Lioria? We need to make our move."

Valac steps into my path. He's serious now, which seems out of place. "Try to come back in one piece, okay? It would be a shame to lose someone as interesting and lovely as yourself."

"Valac? Move," Oriax says as he lifts the trunk into the air.

"I'll do my best," I say, because what else can I?

This time I remember the glamor before I'm reminded. I glance back at my demons and smile.

I have to believe this will be over soon.

I understand the theory behind what will happen. I recognize that war is a terrible, horrible thing and what we do today will be more of the same. And I am resolved to do my part, no matter the sins this heaps on me.

We have to walk quite a ways from the tent, past ranks of soldiers who have never seen battle before besides the yearly mock combats.

No soldier of Eden has ever died in battle. Not one.

I'd like to keep it that way.

I'm aware of people's eyes on us. Oriax makes no effort to hide his identity, and so people stare. Part of me hopes that what I'm about to do is credited to him. Because no human should wield a power as great as what I just touched.

We make our way past archers and the forward ranks of mages who will do their best to shield our side. There's a small platform, and he guides the trunk there before letting it come to rest.

Oriax glances at me. "Sit and rest. It won't be long. How are your nerves?"

I perch on the edge of the platform and bounce my knees. "I'm trying not to think about it."

"War is terrible business."

"What are they hoping to accomplish?"

Oriax tilts his head. "They want to weaken us. Or at least make us look weak. Best-case scenario? This force makes it to the capital and we have a drawn-out siege battle our side eventually wins. But not before heavy losses. We go from being the sleeping force in the south to the cowards behind their invisible wall. This might look like a physical battle, but what we're really fighting for is the moral of our people."

"Oh..."

"Once our people no longer believe we can keep them safe, it's only a matter of time until we're deposed and this country becomes fair game to anyone strong enough to take it."

"You see it all so easily..."

"Not so. I've spent a long time devising ways to topple what we've built and doing what I can to prevent exactly that scenario."

"So, what happened this time?" I ask.

His gaze meets mine. "I never knew there was a threat until it was at our door."

I don't know what that means.

In the distance, I hear a horn, and my stomach knots.

"It's time," Oriax says softly and opens the trunk.

I swallow and get to my feet.

Muki sits on the bed of velvet, looking deceptively harmless. There isn't time to think and ponder. I grab the device and tuck it under my arm like before. Oriax takes my elbow and guides me onto the wooden platform.

The opposing army is visible from here. I can see the lines of them in the distance, and a small entourage on horseback heading through the ranks toward us.

Oriax stands just behind me, his hand on my shoulder. "If you're rethinking this plan, our intelligence tells us that they sent around five hundred of their own people here. Mostly people who had little magic and eeked out a pitiful existence in the slums. They were promised that if they successfully made it to this spot, today, they would be taken care of. Instead, five hundred beings were slaughtered to provide the magic necessary to create a portal. That will be just the beginning if we don't stop them."

I lick my lips and stare at the group of people that would be the parley delegation. The people who have broken into our home, killed our people, and now feel entitled to demand more from us. I don't believe violence is the way, but they've left us with no choice.

"When?" I ask.

"When you are ready."

A month ago, my heart wanted simple things. Good tea, time with my friends, and someday a family that might come to love me. I don't hate the idea of that life, but I can't imagine going back to it. Not now that I've glimpsed what the world has to offer.

I nod. "Let's do this then. For Eden?"

Oriax grasps my shoulders and I'm glad for his support. "For Eden."

Aming Muki is difficult at best. I point it toward the enemy, blow out my breath then inhale deeply. My body feels strange, not quite right, but it's probably the nerves.

My demons would do anything to protect me. I need to be willing to do the same.

With that thought, I reach out and touch Muki with my mind.

That same white, hot, nebulous thing grasps back at me, like it wants to meld with my being. I feel the jolt of the device and see the barrel of spokes glow white with power. My heart hammers and Oriax is pressed to my back now with an arm around my waist. He's supporting me, but my gaze tracks the delegation that's stopped in the midst of their army.

Muki jerks in my hands as a white beam shoots out. Where it touches the earth, it churns the ground. I push down on the end under my arm, and the beam slices up, through the center of the invading army in a wide swath. Where there were people is nothing now save broken, battered earth.

My body begins to shake. My arms seize, locking into place. Muki falls with a loud bang to the platform and my legs give way.

"Lioria!"

Oriax has me. He lowers me to the platform while my body feels as though it's on fire. I can't move. I can't breathe. My stomach clenches, but I can't vomit.

"Breathe. You have to breathe through it. This is magic depletion. It's your body reacting to your magic being used up." Oriax turns his head. "Bring a draught. Now!"

Did I do it? Or did I imagine a third of that army simply vanishing into thin air?

A cheer roars around me. Or is that the pain in my head? It's hard to tell. I squeeze my eyes shut and rock over on my side, unable to curl up into a ball.

"No. Lie back." Oriax's touch is gentle as he cradles me. "Try to swallow. If you can't, don't breathe and let it trickle down."

It's hard to control my body in this state. All I want is to die.

He presses something to my lips and I don't resist. Slowly, he trickles a warm liquid down my throat. I try swallowing, but all I manage to do is spit some on him.

"Doing great. You did fucking fantastic. God. Okay. Let's see if I can ease you?"

Oriax keeps muttering to me, but I can't hardly listen. He presses his fingers on my face, and I gasp. It's not relief, but my muscles relax and most of the pain subsides.

"There she is," he mutters and smiles down at me.

I'm lying on the platform, cradled in the arms of a man I don't trust. I dearly hope this isn't how I die.

"Do you want to look?" he asks.

No, but I owe it to those whose lives I just took to acknowledge what I've done.

"Yes," I croak.

He helps me sit up.

The invading army has pulled together under a purple dome. Where the waste stretched away from us in almost pristine condition, it's rubble now.

I did that.

I cover my face with my still shaking hands and pull my knees up.

Oriax snaps something at one of the nearby mages. I'm too busy staring at the destruction I caused to pay any attention until Oriax scoops me up. I squeak but he merely glares at me when I try to wiggle away.

"I don't know what is so remarkable about you, but I begin to think you'll change all of us," he says softly.

"I'm nothing special," I get out with a little slurring.

He snorts.

I have no more strength for conversation.

This is nothing like when I tried using the device at the inn. It's like something tried to liquefy my insides and suck them out of my ears.

Will this be enough? Could our first volley scare the army back through their shameful portal? Or is this just the beginning?

I think I lose consciousness, because the next thing I know I'm lying on a cot in the tent. Belial and Eligos are human again and clutching my hands.

"W-what happened?" I ask looking up at them.

Eligos kisses my knuckles. "We're just anxious to see your smiling face."

They're concerned. It's etched into the lines of their face.

My glamor.

I look down and see my hair. "I messed up..."

Belial leans in. "What?"

"My glamor..."

Eligos shakes his head. "Nevermind about that."

"Are they gone?" I ask.

"No. Alastor sent a delegation over. We're waiting on word from them."

"Will they be okay?" I ask. It feels like it takes forever for the words to come out of me.

"You mean, will they retaliate?" Belial shrugs. "Maybe."

Alastor paces the tent on the far side. I don't see Raum or Valac, but Oriax is sitting on a folding stool watching me and my lords intently.

What happened out there? What did he see or sense?

"How are you feeling?" Belial asks.

"Not good."

My tongue is too big for my mouth. I'm hungry and nauseated. The muscles in all parts of my body burn.

No wonder Muki was never used before today.

A chime sounds in the tent and all the demons turn as one to look at the box on the table.

"The delegation," Eligos whispers.

I nod and wait, watching Alastor open the box and pull out a rolled-up parchment.

We watch him read the page for several long moments. A furrow develops between his brow, as if he's not pleased with what he's reading.

"What is it? What do they want?" Belial demands.

Alastor looks not at the demons, but me. "They want what they're calling the godling. If we give up the godling, they'll withdraw."

Fuck.

Oriax's face scrunches up. "The—what?"

Me.

I'm human.

It's what I want to believe.

No part of me ever asked to be special. I never wanted to be born above my station. I've never tried to reach for greatness. I've always been content where I was and with what I am. But this world is not content to allow me that privilege.

"I-I'm going to be sick," I whisper.

Oriax stands and takes the scroll from Alastor. "What is a godling? What are those idiots going on about?"

"I've got you." Belial scoops me up and strides out of the suddenly stuffy tent, and around the corner.

I pitch forward in his arms, barely managing to miss the soldier outside as I heave up whatever Oriax gave me earlier.

Eligos pulls my hair back and leans in. "We need to get her somewhere safe."

"Agreed," Belial says.

"Lets take her to the healers. She'll be safe enough there until we can gauge what the others will do. If things go poorly—"

"I'll take them out, you get to her."

"Agreed."

They're talking over me like I'm not there. I want to tell them to slow down. I want to talk about this. Because I still don't understand why a so-called godling is so important. What is it? Some mediator to the gods? A way to talk to them?

Anyone who knows me is aware of the fact that I am the least spiritual person on this planet.

Neither of my demons consult me, and I am so tired and aching I can't stop them. Which is how I find myself given into the care of a pair of older women who set about treating me for magic withdrawal. I hear Belial and Eligos say something about how they'll be back, that I'm safe here, but whatever the women pour down my throat makes the world go topsy-turvy around me.

When I open my eyes again, I'm blissfully alone. It's not quiet, but it's peaceful. Except that now my bladder needs attention.

That's the last thing I want help with, so I hobble to my feet and around the partition that offers me privacy—and walk straight into the last person I want to see.

Shax.

SHAX

I hate myself.

I hate myself for what I'm going to do.

I hate myself for not stopping this madness sooner.

I hate that I'm the only one who sees what's so glaringly obvious.

"Please? Please, no." Lioria tugs on my hand, but she has all the strength of a newborn kitten in this state.

It was blind, dumb luck I ran into her with no one around. I wasn't counting on her being able to see through my glamor. I wasn't aware she could do something like that, but thanks to Belial and Eligos telling the healer staff to make her comfortable, there wasn't anyone around.

With luck, no one will know she's gone until this is done.

I'm sorry.

"What are you doing?" she asks.

I don't answer.

I can't.

There's something undeniable about her. I sensed it during our meeting. There was so much to cover, that was my chance to finally open the other's eyes. And the whole time, I was aware of her like a pebble in my boot. I don't think Belial and Eligos have any idea what's going on. They aren't sensitive to the pull of things the way I am.

No. Don't think about it.

My resolve is set.

This must happen.

I drag Lioria forward, using a spell to fold the ground under us so one moment we're in the Eden camp, and the next we're standing just outside the protective dome.

I fish out the medallion from my pocket and press it to the hard, magic surface. "I've come to bargain," I say loudly.

Figures move on the other side. It's distorted and I can't make out their forms. Lioria tries to twist her arms out of my grasp, but I don't let her go.

I know what my brethren think of me and I do not care. I've never concerned myself with that. They won't forgive me, and I can live with that.

An archway appears in the dome and an assortment of magic-wielding mages of varying races exit, their focus on me. And then comes the person behind it all.

He wants the world to call him Oberon, after his predecessor. But that creature has been dead for ages.

Dain Grevyre.

He who sits on the Lucient Throne.

He's tried to imitate the Seelie Court in an effort to gather the fae who still believe in the courts under his banner. And he has always been our enemy.

"High Demon Lord." Dain smirks at me, but his gaze quickly slides toward Lioria. "What have you brought me?"

"I propose a trade." I have no way of knowing what he asked the others, but I know what I want.

"Oh?"

"I want the real Alastor returned to us and your withdrawal from Eden."

Dain's eyes go wide. He's mocking me with this false disbelief. "The real Alastor? Oh my, what state are the High Demon Lords in, hm?"

I don't say anything.

I know beyond a shadow of a doubt that the man currently masquerading around as Alastor is no demon. He is not my brethren. He is not one of us. He is a sham, and I intend to prove it.

Dain sighs. "Let's say you're right. What could you possibly offer me?"

"The godling, as your people call her." I pull Lioria to stand in front of me. She wavers on her feet, so unsteady I don't think she can support herself.

The shock on Dain's face isn't fabricated. This is real. He stares at Lioria as though she's the world's greatest prize. And she might be. Within her could very well be the power to reinvent the gods. Create new ones. Something that will knock this world out of the cycle we've been stuck in for almost a million years. Ever since our gods were consumed, and we were left to rot on this dying planet.

Dain waves at someone and takes a step forward.

"No." I hold out my hand and they stop.

I might not be as powerful as I once was, but I am strong enough. Ever since I realized Alastor was not who he pretended to be, I've been preparing for combat while the others have grown soft.

"S-Shax?"

I jerk my head around and stop breathing.

Alastor—the real Alastor—staggers toward me. He has a metal ring around his neck. Blood trickles down his chin. His clothes are dirty and torn.

My demon reaches toward him, but nothing reaches back.

Something hard smacks against the back of my head and I am flung forward against a bar. No, a collar. It clicks around my throat. I grab hold of the band and pull, but it burns my flesh.

No.

The one thing that nullifies my magic.

Enochian runes.

"No. No, please! No," Lioria wails.

Shit.

God, what have I walked into?

A fist drives into my jaw and I stagger and watch everything crumble around me.

I stare up at the fake Alastor in horror as he sneers at me and wipes the blood away.

He sneers at me. "You just handed everything to us."

"Alastor?" Dain glances at him. "Return to the capital and wait for instruction."

Fake-Alastor whirls. "What? But—I'm supposed to return with you. This is the end. Right?"

"Plans have changed." Dain crosses to stand in front of Lioria, who is shrinking back from him. "Hello, godling."

Fake-Alastor points at Lioria. "She just slaughtered our people."

"How many gods have bathed in blood? This is merely the cost of her ascension. Bring her. And the demon. Alastor, wait for my orders."

Rough hands grasp me by the arms. I can fight back, but without magic, what good is a hard jab?

What have I done?

What does war mean for Eden? Where has Lioria gone? What was Shax thinking? Find out in Demon in My Cell, releasing October 2022.

What about Teill? Or Kirra? Or Naexi? Don't worry! Their stories are not over. The first part of Teill's story will be coming to Syd's newsletter in an exclusive short story called Teill's Tryst. Join the newsletter now! If you want to find out about Kirra and the mystery behind the Silver Roo, preorder the Dissent charity anthology releasing this fall. That story will be exclusive through the end of 2022, after which it will be re-released.

Make sure to check out the paranormal serial, Warblade Online: Four to Party, currently releasing on Radish and Kindle Vella. Bri gets stuck in a magical video game with her worst enemies. Will they survive together, or fail? (If serials aren't your thing, don't worry! The "seasons" will release as novel bundles.)

If you have a moment, please consider leaving a review! Your opinion—good, neutral, or bad—is valuable for other readers. More reviews and "social proof" also help authors book promo, which in turn means more readers and inevitably more books. My Demon Lords is intended to be a five-book series, but there are so many other stories to tell. Who do you want to read about next? What aspects of the world are you curious about?

Thank you for coming on this journey with me. Lioria's story has been knocking around in my head for ages and has taken on so many different forms. I'm excited about writing the final evolution of who she becomes and sharing that journey with you. I can't wait to see where we go from here!

Sydney St James is the more-the-marrier pen name of NYT & USA Today Best-selling author Sidney Bristol. She is a recovering roller derby queen, bookaholic, and tattoo addict. She grew up in a motor home on the US highways (with an occasional jaunt into Canada and Mexico), traveling the rodeo circuit with her parents. Sidney has lived abroad in both Russia and Thailand, working with children and teenagers. She now lives in Texas where she splits her time between writing, reading, and binging TV with her husband.

You can contact Sidney at MissSidneyBristol@gmail.com or Syd@SydneyStJames.com

Visit www.SidneyBristol.com for all the latest news. Join the mailing list to stay up to date today!